TAINTED

DAVID EVANS

ABOUT THE AUTHOR

Born and brought up in and around Edinburgh, David Evans graduated from Manchester University and had a successful career as a professional in the construction industry before turning to crime ... fiction that is and writing thereof.

TAINTED is the fourth in his Internationally Best Selling Wakefield Series.

THE WAKEFIELD SERIES:
TROPHIES is the first in the series
TORMENT, the second, was shortlisted in 2013 for the CWA Debut Dagger Award.
TALISMAN is the third
All are available in ebook and paperback formats.

His other novel currently available is *DISPOSAL,* the first of a planned series set in the Tendring area of North Essex.

Find out more by visiting David's website at
www.davidevanswriter.co.uk
or follow him on Facebook at
www.facebook.com/davidevanswriter
and Twitter @DavidEwriter

ACKNOWLEDGMENTS

I have been privileged to meet some amazing people, without whose help, encouragement, support and above all friendship got me through some occasions when it would have been easier to walk away and do something else with my time.

First and foremost, I have to say a huge thank-you to Sally Spedding who was the first in the publishing industry to take my writing seriously. I owe her a great debt for all her continued support and encouragement.

I am also fortunate to have a great little band of writing friends and I would like to thank Sarah Wagstaff, Jan Beresford, Julie-Ann Corrigan, Manda Hughes, Lorraine Cannell, Glynis Smy and Peter Best, all of whom are talented writers in their own right and have made some significant contributions.

I am also fortunate to have the input of Colin Steele, ex-Detective Superintendent of the Essex Murder Squad and Tom Harper, ex-Principal Crime Scene Coordinator for the Kent & Essex Serious Crime Directorate. Both have given their time and guidance generously. Any residual errors here, are all mine.

Thanks to Bernie Steadman, author of the successful DI Dan Hellier books set in the West Country, who agreed to her cameo role within these pages, following a competition in 2017.

Finally, a huge thank-you to the various bloggers and readers who have supported this series over the past few years, especially Caroline Vincent who organised various tours for me.

For all the readers, without whom,
none of this would be worthwhile.

TAINTED

David Evans

DAVID EVANS

1

Wednesday 13th February 2002

The heady mix of sexual excitement, anticipation and tension along with percolating fear hung around her like the thickening fog. She pulled the Ford Ka to a halt alongside the familiar Mercedes. Looking over, she saw his outline sitting in the driver's seat. She unclipped her seat belt and opened the door. Her black stilettos sank into the damp grass as cold air swirled around her legs, her short black dress offering little protection. He liked hold-ups, so she was wearing the black lacy ones.

Opening the passenger door of the Merc, she quickly climbed in, shivering.

"God it's cold out there tonight," she said, rubbing her hands together before leaning over and kissing him.

"I thought you were going to stand me up," he said.

She gave him a broad smile and placed her hand on his crotch. "As if."

"How long have we got?"

"Plenty of time." She grinned. "He's gone to the game, so as long as I'm home for ten, I'll be fine."

He turned and kissed her, running a hand up her leg. When he reached the top of her thigh he stopped and pulled his head back a couple of inches. "Ooh my favourites." His hand moved again. "But have you forgotten something else?" He was like a small boy who'd just found his hidden Christmas present.

"I thought it would save time taking them off."

He began to play and she began to moan.

Without warning, she tensed.

"What's up?" He drew back and looked at her.

"There's someone out there." She indicated towards the windscreen into the darkness.

"Don't be daft. No one comes here at this time of night."

"I tell you Marcus, I saw a light. A torch." She pulled her dress down and sat on her hands, suddenly cold. "I'm not into this dogging lark, so if you've brought me here to ..."

"No way."

She gave a shudder then focussed on the toilet block about fifty yards away. "Must be over there," she said.

"Look, there's no one ..." He stopped abruptly as two silhouetted figures appeared against the white rendered wall of the building.

"This is making me feel nervous."

He turned to her and smiled. "I thought you liked that edge; the risk of discovery?"

"This is freaking me out."

"I'll check." He placed a hand on the door handle.

"Wait!" She grabbed his other wrist. "Let's find somewhere else."

He turned back towards her. "But there is nowhere else. Not without driving around for ages, and that's just wasting time. No, it'll be fine. I just want to see what's going on." He opened the door and climbed out, then leant back in. "Won't be long."

"No, wait ..."

The door closed and she watched him disappear into the dark blanket of a moonless night. Now alone, she hugged herself, trying to become as small as possible.

Inside the car, ticking sounds from the cooling engine; it had been switched off for at least ten minutes. She checked her watch; four minutes since Marcus had left. She looked for any movement outside but saw nothing.

Her body began to shiver involuntarily. What was she doing here? Thirty-two years old, no kids, married to a husband who never gives her any attention. And then *he* came into her life. It was the office Christmas lunch when she first noticed Marcus. There again, she didn't have much choice in the matter as she'd been placed next to him in the restaurant. Those sideways glances, the warm feel of his thigh against hers, the flutter in her stomach. She was sure he felt the same, his face told her that. He admitted it afterwards too. Then that first time, in the cleaner's cupboard of all places. After so long, someone who really wanted her. But now, was this all she had to look forward to? Stolen evenings freezing your tits off in a remote car park?

There!

Suddenly, she was sure she saw it. Yes! A torch beam scanned the building, fuzzy through the mist then swung around towards the trees. Instinctively she ducked down just before a weak beam of light swept through the car. A minute passed with no sign of any further activity. She risked peeking out through the windscreen. All seemed quiet. What was he up to? Where had Marcus gone?

Another check of her watch; almost ten minutes since he'd left. She couldn't stop the shivering. And then she heard it; the vibration of her mobile phone from her handbag. Rummaging inside, she grabbed it. The display told her it was her husband. Shit.

"Hello," she answered quietly.

"It's me," he said, as if she didn't know.

"What's up?"

"It's this fog. The referee's only called the bloody game off, hasn't he?" In the background she could hear the murmur of voices then an indistinguishable tannoy announcement.

Her heart rate quickened. "So what does that mean?"

He gave a snort. *"It means they're emptying the ground, so I should be home in an hour."* There was a pause. *"Why don't we go out for a drink? I was thinking we don't seem to do much together these days. What do you think?"*

She looked towards the building once again. "Yeah, okay," she said, after a moment's hesitation.

"Is everything alright?"

"Of course." Trying desperately to stop the shaking from affecting her words, she took a breath. "I'll see you when you get home," she said, ending the call abruptly.

Sod this, she thought and, as quietly as she could, opened the door. The interior light came on. Instantly, she raised a hand to switch it off. Sitting still for a few seconds, she peered through the fog that seemed to be thickening, listening intently. The only sound was the incessant dripping of moisture from the trees.

She fumbled in her bag for her car key. Toying with the fob, she braced herself in readiness for her next move. At last she scurried from the Mercedes and jumped into her Ka. Firing up the engine, she put the car into gear and drove off the grassed parking area. Accelerating away along the tarmac lane, she had to brake sharply as a dog raced across in front of her. Her nerves already jangling, she drove on towards the exit then finally made her escape onto the main road. Whatever Marcus was playing at, she'd had enough. She had to get home within the next forty-five minutes if she wasn't to be caught out. Was it worth it, she was thinking; was it really worth it?

2

George Brannigan parked his BMW by the north gate of the park. As he stepped out, a taller younger man did the same from the passenger side.

Brannigan glanced at his watch. "Time to go, Andy," he said.

The two made their way into the park as they'd been directed. Andy's head was swivelling, afraid they might be ambushed in the darkness as they made their way to the rendezvous. It was obvious Brannigan didn't share his concern, striding out confidently. He'd spent twelve years in the army. One of the fittest bastards Andy had ever come across. He might be getting on a bit, well over fifty anyway, but he was solid muscle. He also indulged in his love of martial arts. But one thing did concern Andy about Brannigan; tonight he was wound up like a coiled spring.

The mist swirled around them as they walked through the park. At various points, Andy switched on the torch and swept the beam all around. When they reached the building, he did the same again.

"Put that fucking torch out," Brannigan said, obvious irritation in his tone.

A lone male figure in a hooded top emerged from the gloom. He looked at the two of them and smiled.

"Fuck off weirdo," Brannigan snapped.

The smile evaporated from the man's face and he scurried off.

Inside the toilet block, in the dim fluorescent light, Brannigan led the way past the urinals to the cubicles. One of the fittings flickered, the tube beginning to fail. "Here," Brannigan instructed Andy, holding out the sealed plastic bag he'd brought with him. "End cubicle. Get up on the pan and place this in the cistern."

As Andy did so, he heard another set of footsteps enter.

"You come for it then," he heard Brannigan say. "So where is she?"

There was a mumbled reply before the sounds of a scuffle then a thud.

Andy stepped back down off the pan, still with the bag of money in his hands, to see a well-dressed man crumpled in a heap on the floor. "What the …?" he started.

Brannigan was bent over the man feeling for a pulse before looking up at him, a surprised expression on his face. "I thought he'd come to collect."

Andy glanced at his watch. "Not yet; eight o'clock they said. He's probably only some poof come for a meet."

"In that case, let's not disappoint," Brannigan's face hardened. "Give me that spare plastic bag you brought," he ordered.

A minute later the man had been placed on his knees, face down over the pan, plastic bag placed loosely over his head and trousers and underpants at his ankles.

"Let's get out of here," Brannigan said.

"But what about …?"

"They'll have to get back in touch."

"No, I mean …"

Brannigan cast a backward glance. "He'll be fine. Come on."

3

The mist that formed earlier had become dense. In the park, flashing blue lights reflected back on themselves, bouncing off the other emergency vehicles parked around the building. A uniformed constable stepped forward and held up his hand to the approaching car.

Detective Inspector Colin Strong produced his warrant card and stated his name and rank for the benefit of the young lad.

"Sorry, sir," the PC said, "I'm new on the team."

"And you are?"

"PC Gary Monk, sir."

Strong smiled as the constable lifted the plastic police tape to allow him to pull forward inside the cordon. The white Scenes of Crime vans were already there and a couple of their team were walking towards the building in white coveralls, boots and masks, carrying cases with their equipment.

As Strong got out of his vehicle, the familiar short stocky figure of Detective Constable Luke Ormerod approached. Hunched in an overcoat, hands thrust deep in the pockets he looked serious.

"Salubrious surroundings," Strong commented, indicating the white rendered public toilet block. "Do we know who the victim is?"

"Not as yet, guv. We're waiting for the SOCO boys to finish their first sweep before we search his pockets. The only thing to go on so far is the solitary parked car over there." Ormerod waved a hand into the gloom and Strong could just about make out a shape standing on the edge of the car park below the trees about fifty yards away.

As they talked, Strong nodded to a couple of officers he knew and crossed to one of the white vans to get himself kitted up in a protective suit. Ormerod followed.

"So, any clue there?" Strong asked.

"It's unlocked and the keys are in the ignition."

"It's a wonder it's still here then."

"Registered to a Marcus Weaver." Ormerod referred to his notebook. "Address on the outskirts of Leeds."

Strong led the way to the Gents' toilet entrance. He paused at the doorway, looked to his DC and pulled a disgusted face.

Ormerod merely nodded in response, no words necessary.

Inside, arc lights had been set up. Even through the mask, Strong's nose was attacked by the pungent odour of stale urine. "Delightful," he commented.

Dr Symonds, the duty doctor turned away from the second cubicle and greeted him. "Colin, another top rate venue you've brought me to."

"I try my best, Andrew," Strong greeted as he peered past the medic to catch his first view of the body. A pair of trouser-clad legs with decent shoes poked out. He took a step forward and saw that the trousers and underpants had been pulled down around the lower legs. The body was facing the wall, slumped over the pan with a plastic bag over the head.

He recognised the familiar form of the Senior Scenes of Crime Officer, Doug Norris, who was squeezed into the cubicle, carefully placing a plastic bag around the victim's right hand. A flash of light from the photographer's camera made Strong blink.

He turned to the doctor and asked, "How did he die?"

"We'll know for sure once we get him back to the mortuary but possibly suffocation?"

Strong looked bleak. "Some form of sex game gone wrong, do you think?"

"It has been known," Symonds said. "There was that MP a few years ago, but ..." Symonds paused, glancing down at the victim's rear. "On first inspection, it doesn't look like he was involved in any sexual practices but, like I say, you'll know more when the pathologist can examine him properly."

"Bloody Hell," Strong said quietly. "How long before we can do a search? We'll need to check identity."

"I can do that for you now, Colin," Norris said through his mask. He stood up and shuffled his way out of the confined space before bending down and searching the victim's right-hand trouser pocket. He pulled out a brown leather wallet which he popped open.

"Well it wasn't robbery," Norris said, flicking through one section and holding it towards Strong so he could see. "There's ... eighty-five pounds in here." From another section he drew out a driving licence and turned it over so the name and address were visible.

Strong nodded, the name tallied with what Ormerod had told him; Marcus Weaver, with an address in Horsforth. He noted it down. "Thanks Doug." Turning to Dr Symonds he asked, "Time of death Andrew?"

The doctor chuckled. "How long have we known each other, Colin? Ten years at least, I'd say. And you always ask me that."

"Best guess?"

"And what do I always tell you – somewhere between when he was last seen alive and when the body was discovered."

Strong shook his head, knowing the answer would probably surface later and in any event, would only be a rough estimate.

"But," Dr Symonds went on, "the body is still warm and as you well know, that could be misleading. If he'd been killed some time ago and the body kept warm before being dumped here, but ..." He held up a hand. "if you asked me to put money on it, I'd say that if the dog had bounded in here a bit sooner, he'd have found the perpetrator on scene."

"So fairly recent then?" Strong persisted.

"That's as much as I'd speculate, you'll have to check your other sources first."

Strong glanced at his watch. "So between eight and eight-thirty. Thanks Andrew."

Dr Symonds shook his head and gave a wry smile. He clicked his pen, indicating he'd completed his paperwork. "Once the photos are taken, I'm assuming he can be moved tonight so the pathologist will schedule the PM for tomorrow morning, probably. Will that be you?" he asked.

"Very likely."

The doctor closed up his medical bag. "I can confirm life extinct." His sharp eyes looked at Strong over his mask. "Goodnight, Colin."

"Goodnight, Doc." Strong watched the man raise a hand and make his way outside.

Ormerod was at Strong's shoulder. "First thoughts, guv?"

"I think we need to keep an open mind." Strong led the way back out into the gloomy night and sucked in a deep breath of fresh air. "The doc mentioned a dog. Who found him, by the way?"

"A dog walker, Samuel Pemberton." Ormerod indicated one of the marked patrol cars. "He's sitting in the warm up there."

Strong walked towards the vehicle. "Let's hear what he has to tell us and get a statement."

Pemberton was sitting on the back seats of a Ford Escort, his black and white mongrel dog in the footwell. Strong and Ormerod opened the doors and sat in the front. The man looked to be in his seventies, wrapped up in a coat, scarf and flat cap. Ormerod introduced his DI then asked the man to relate what had happened.

"Well I were giving Trixie her evening walk. I only live two streets away over there." The man indicated the park entrance.

"Is this a regular walk for you?" Strong asked.

"Aye, but I tend to steer clear of here." His face was a picture of disgust. "You wouldn't believe what they get up to in there, not that I've ever been in mind."

"Until tonight, of course," Ormerod added.

"Well, that weren't my doing," the man responded quickly. "It were Trixie here. She ran off and wouldn't come back. She obviously knew something were wrong because she ran straight in. I shouted and shouted her but she wouldn't come out. So in the end, I had to go in and ... Jesus, I've never seen 'owt like it."

Ormerod was jotting down notes as Strong probed. "Did you see any activity here tonight, Mr Pemberton?"

"I think there was some bloke round the other side of the building when we came into the park and another two I spotted walking towards the toilets on my way up past."

"Did you recognise any of them? Could you describe them?"

"Not really, it were dark and foggy. Just three blokes in dark clothing, shoulders hunched and hands in their pockets."

"And nothing unusual about any of them?" Strong persisted. "I mean fat, thin, tall, short? Anything at all."

Pemberton shook his head. "Not really, just average. But then ..." The old man screwed up his face in thought.

"Go on," Strong encouraged.

"As we were coming back round to head home, there was a car, not that big un that's still there, this were smaller."

"What about it?" Ormerod asked.

"It was driving off. In a bit of a hurry like. And that's when Trixie went running off down to the toilets. It nearly bloody ran her over."

"Do you know what kind of car, Mr Pemberton, colour maybe?"

"It were small, like a Fiesta or summat like that. And it were dark, that's about all I could tell."

"And when you chased after your dog, there was no one else around here then?" Strong asked.

"Quiet as the grave. Oh, perhaps I shouldn't say that."

"The other car, the Mercedes, that was there the whole time?"

"Aye."

"And have you ever noticed that car here before when you've been walking Trixie?"

Again another shake of the head. "No, can't say as I have."

"Well thanks Mr Pemberton you've been a great help," Strong said. "If you give your contact details to DC Ormerod here, someone will be round to see you, probably tomorrow for a statement."

"So can I go 'ome now? Mavis'll be wondering where we've gotten to."

"Of course."

Once Ormerod had jotted down the man's address, Strong stepped out of the car, pulled the collar up on his coat and opened the rear door for Mr Pemberton to leave. When the old man had gone, he turned to Ormerod. "Let's have a look at the Merc then," he said.

Strong approached the front and felt the grille, then the bonnet. "Still a bit warm," he said. Then, with a latex-gloved hand, he opened the driver's door. The interior light didn't come on so he pulled a torch from his pocket to look inside. As Ormerod had told him, the keys were still in the ignition. He leaned across the seat towards the passenger side and sniffed.

"Anything, guv?" Ormerod asked.

The DI manoeuvred himself back out of the car.

"A scent, Luke. A female perfume rather than male aftershave. And it's not clap cold in there either, so I reckon if he drove here, our first estimate of between eight and eight-thirty is about right."

Closing the door, he walked round to the front of the car and looked down at the ground by the passenger door. About four or five feet away were a clear set of tyre marks. Shining the torch closer to the gap in between, he knelt down having spotted something else. After a few seconds, he straightened up.

"Let's, get this area taped off. And get Forensics over here. I think our friend Mr Weaver had company earlier. A woman, if I'm not mistaken. Either that or a bloke in high heels."

4

In the semi-darkness of the bedroom, Andy lay awake; the dim glow through the curtains from the streetlamp outside the only illumination. He hadn't been able to sleep; how could he? In between sessions of rocking back and forth on the bed, he paced the room. He felt sick. How could Brannigan have done that? Despite what he'd been told, he didn't believe the man in the toilets would be okay. What sort of man was he - to leave him like that? But more importantly, what did all this mean for Felicity?

The man himself was downstairs; this was his house, the house attached to the business; George Brannigan, Scrap Metal Merchant. Well it made sense for Andy to stay here whilst all this was going on. Almost two days now. Two days since he'd last seen Felicity. Over thirty hours since the first phone call. *'Thirty grand,'* the voice had said. *'Used twenties.'* That was just the start of the nightmare.

Brannigan had quizzed him over every detail. The problem was he *had* no details. When he left home on Tuesday morning, Felicity was still in bed. That wasn't unusual; she only had to be at work by eleven. It wasn't until the phone call at six o'clock on Tuesday evening when his world tumbled upside down.

Brannigan had taken the second phone call yesterday morning. The demand was repeated, same voice, heavily disguised but definitely male. He took a note of place and time. Then came the hard bit; getting the cash together. That's where Brannigan came into his own. They'd only got twelve hours, but in his line of business, cash was a ready commodity. Eight o'clock the previous night had been the time for the drop, in that God-forsaken shit-hole; literally.

The phone began to ring downstairs. Andy glanced at the red figures of the clock on the bedside table; two-seventeen. He darted to the door. The living room door opened and he heard Brannigan make his way to answer the call. Andy dived down the stairs two at a time but the man held up a hand. "Calm down," he instructed. "I'll deal with this."

Brannigan lifted the receiver and waited for someone to speak. After a moment's hesitation, the voice on the other end did; Andy could also hear it clearly.

"Well George," they said. *"You well and truly fucked things up last night, didn't you?"*

"Listen you piece of shit …" Brannigan began.

"I don't think you're in any position to give me any agro," the voice interrupted. *"I think your arse is on the line now. I hear that temper of yours came to the surface again."*

Brannigan looked shocked. "I don't …," he stuttered.

The voice cut in again, *"So … let's be sensible about this. You have one last opportunity, or you'll never see her again."*

"Just a minute …"

"We'll be in touch." The line went dead.

Andy looked at Brannigan and for the first time he saw fear take over from anger.

"That bloke … What do we do now?" Andy asked, tears leaking down his cheeks.

"I'll sort it."

"Like you did last night," Andy responded, not quite able to hold his tongue.

Brannigan lunged at him and grabbed his shirt lapels. "Last night was an accident. You got that? I thought the bastard was coming to collect."

Andy couldn't hold his stare.

"I'll not let Felicity down, Andy. Now you just remember that." He tapped Andy's face then let go of him, walked back into the sitting room and closed the door.

5
Thursday 14th February 2002

For many, 11th September 2001 changed lives forever. Colin Strong was no exception. On that day, he almost lost a close colleague in a near fatal shooting for which he blamed himself. It had been a difficult decision for him to continue as DI in Wakefield's Wood Street CID team, he'd been sorely tempted to pack it all in. After the traumatic events of last September, it seemed as if he was drifting through life until Detective Chief Superintendent Flynn suggested, although it was more like an instruction, that he take some time off. For three weeks before Christmas, he'd holidayed on Gran Canaria and given serious consideration to a complete change of lifestyle, even looking at buying property there. But a combination of support from his wife Laura, son Graham and daughter, Amanda and encouragement from the members of his team, especially the victim of the shooting, DS Kelly Stainmore, had persuaded him to continue.

At eight that morning, the team assembled in the CID room to be briefed by DCI Rupert Hemingford on the events of the previous night. Hemingford was a tall, slim, thirty-seven-year-old; a graduate entry fast track high-flyer who had joined West Yorkshire from the Cambridgeshire Constabulary back in August last year. He was another reason Strong had thought long and hard over his future. After twelve months in an acting-DCI capacity, Strong was passed over for the permanent role.

As Hemingford began to give an overview of where the investigation into the murder of Marcus Weaver stood, Strong was sitting at a spare desk next to Luke Ormerod and Kelly Stainmore. After a minute or two, Strong was invited to go through the details and mark up a whiteboard with what they now knew.

Strong stood up and pointed to the name of the victim written on the board. "Marcus Weaver," he began, "thirty-nine years old, married and living at this address in Horsforth." He wrote the additional details next to the name. "At eight thirty-nine last night, Luke and I attended the male public toilets in the park where the body had been discovered in one of the cubicles."

A few groans and muttered comments greeted this information.

Strong held up both hands. "I know, I know," he said. "This location has a certain reputation but for now, we're keeping an open mind on this one. We'll know more following the PM which is scheduled for ten o'clock at Pinderfields. Luke and I will attend."

"Does the widow know?" DC John Darby asked.

"Leeds sent a couple of uniforms for the 'agony visit' last night but I'd like Kelly and yourself, John, to call there after we've finished," Hemingford responded. "You know the score," he continued, addressing Stainmore. "Get a statement; when did she last see him, anything worrying him, that sort of thing. And we will need a formal ID."

"I'll let you know when that can be done, Kelly," Strong added. "Hopefully this afternoon."

"Anything else we should know, Colin?" Hemingford seemed to be in a rush to conclude the meeting.

"There are a couple of things," Strong said, "First, our dog walker told us on his outward journey he saw three characters in the vicinity of the toilet block before his dog discovered the body on his return; one by the toilets and another two approaching. Nothing to distinguish them, so I'd suggest we do the usual pull of all the local nonces."

Another round of mutterings.

"And second ..." Strong put a finger up to his chin as if in thought. "I think, contrary to what first impressions we may have ... I think our friend here was with a woman last night." He tapped Weaver's name on the board then moved back to the desk he'd been sitting at and picked up a brown envelope. "I've just got these in from SOCO." He began to remove some photographs. "I asked them to study an area near Weaver's Mercedes. It looks like there was another car parked next to it. Our dog walker spoke of a small dark car, possibly a Fiesta or similar, driving away from the scene just before his dog found the body." He stuck the pictures on the board as he spoke. "Also, between the cars there were some shoe prints; female with stiletto heel marks, size six our forensics boys think. They're also looking at what type of car may have left those tracks."

"What about Weaver's car itself?" Hemingford asked.

Strong walked back to the desk and leaned against it. "SOCO are doing the full monty on it. It would be interesting to see what they get from the front passenger area. That's where I detected a slight smell of perfume."

"Could have been Mrs Weaver's?" Ormerod pondered.

"It could, but it's early days yet."

"I agree," Hemingford said before proceeding to allocate various tasks to the team. "... and then Colin and Luke will attend the PM later this morning," he concluded. "Right, let's go to it. Back here at four for an update." With that, the DCI strode from the room.

"Couldn't get out of here quick enough, could he?" Ormerod commented to Strong in a quiet voice, stroking his black bushy moustache which resembled a huge hairy caterpillar. He was one of Strong's most trusted colleagues, having turned forty late last year. He wasn't particularly tall but powerfully built; definitely someone you'd want covering your back.

"Hmm," was all Strong said in response. He glanced at his watch. "I'll check through a few things for now then see you in about an hour before we head off for the PM."

Back in his office, Strong allowed his thoughts to drift. Whenever he saw Stainmore, he couldn't help being reminded of how close she had come to death. As well as himself, he'd also partially blamed his best friend since primary school, journalist Bob Souter, for the build-up to those fateful events. Finally, last month, Strong had put his feelings behind him to stand as Souter's best man at his wedding to Alison. This returned the favour of Strong's own wedding back in 1980.

6

In the offices of the Yorkshire Post on Wellington Street in Leeds, some ten miles from Wood Street Police Station, Bob Souter opened the door to the Archive Room. Situated behind Reception, this was the domain of Phyllis. She seemed as old as the newspaper itself but still took the same pride in her appearance as she did when she worked as a receptionist. She'd retired a few years ago but had come back two days a week to update the paper's archive. Hair back-combed and lacquered, she sat at a desk, busily transferring sheets to microfiche.

She glanced up as he entered. "Ah, Mr Souter, I haven't seen you in a while."

"What's all this 'Mr Souter' nonsense?" He smiled at her. "I'm Bob, remember. But I have been busy, Phyllis."

"With that nice young lady of yours, I'm told." She looked at him over horn-rimmed glasses. "Glad to see you made an honest woman of her."

Phyllis referred to Souter's recent wedding to Alison Hewitt. They'd met during the course of an investigation he'd carried out two years ago. After the events of last September, Souter thought he might have to work hard to persuade his friend, Colin Strong, to be his best man but in the end, he couldn't let him down.

"I'd always have done that," Souter said.

"I know. So when is the baby due?"

"21st March is what they've told us, but that's just a guide."

"Well I hope you're taking good care of her. That must have been dreadful for you last year; both of you."

He struggled to respond. "It was, Phyllis." His body shuddered as he took a breath. "It was the not knowing. Those five days before she could make contact. Those were ..." his words trailed off as he was reminded of his state of mind last year. He'd thought Alison, the love of his life, was lost, perished in the collapse of the South Tower of the World Trade Centre. Only later had he discovered she had been confined to her hotel room six blocks away, throwing up; the effects of her pregnancy. Souter was totally unaware of her condition until their friend, Sammy, told him as he watched events unfold on TV. That doubled his agony as he initially thought he'd lost his unborn child as well as his lover.

Phyllis stood and came towards him to place a protective hand on his shoulder. "I'm sorry, Bob, I didn't mean to open up old ..."

He stopped her. "It's okay. I know." He nipped his nose between thumb and forefinger.

She removed her hand, studied him for a second then continued, "So what brings you in here?"

"Twenty years ago," he began," we ran a story about the murder of a fourteen-year-old schoolgirl from Wakefield, found in Horbury."

"Oh, God, yes I remember," she said. "Was it Claire someone?"

"Very good. Claire Hobson."

Phyllis's gaze drifted as she tried to remember some details. "Did they ever find out who did it?"

"No they haven't."

She snapped back to the present. "Right. Well let's start with this one." She approached the shelves containing the microfiche records and pulled a couple out. "These are from 1982. You check this one and I'll do the other. We should find what you're looking for quicker that way."

Souter took the offered file. "Look, I don't want to distract you from what you're supposed to be doing," he said.

"I'm bored with that. I'd rather do something interesting." Her face lit up with a big smile as she clipped her file into one of the readers.

Earlier that morning John Chandler, the newspaper's Deputy Editor, had called Souter up to his office. "I've got something of interest for you, Bob," was his opening line.

Souter had been intrigued.

"I know you're bored regurgitating stories about Princess Margaret," he'd gone on, referring to the death of the Queen's sister the previous week.

"Just a bit, John," Souter had responded.

"Well, I've been contacted by Louise Hobson and I think this would be a great campaign story. The boss has agreed."

Souter had looked blank, so Chandler outlined his thoughts to bring the story of murdered schoolgirl, Claire Hobson, back to the public's notice, refresh memories, see if any new evidence would come to light and prod the police into some sort of reaction. The twentieth anniversary of the crime was looming.

"So research the case, go and talk to Mr and Mrs Hobson then do a piece on them, their ongoing anguish, all that sort of stuff."

"'All that sort of stuff'?" Souter had quoted back incredulously.

"You know what I mean, Bob. Now off you go but keep me informed."

Suitably dismissed, Souter had made his way down to the Archives.

Twenty minutes later, Phyllis gave a shout. "Here! It's here."

Souter stopped his search and walked over to the other machine. She stood up to let him sit down and study the edition.

Monday 8th March 1982.

MISSING GIRL
BODY FOUND ON RAILWAY WASTELAND

He scanned through the article, opened his notebook and began scribbling down a summary of what was known at that time.

The body of a young girl had been found on land that had some old railway sidings at Horbury, just outside of Wakefield. Two boys aged ten and nine had been exploring some of the still extant sidings, which stored old coaches and wagons, when they'd made the grim discovery. Described as trainspotters, they were shocked to make their discovery just after 10:30 on Sunday morning. Police had yet to confirm identity but it was speculated that it was fourteen-year-old Claire Hobson who had been reported missing from her home on Friday night after failing to return from her friend's house on Wakefield's Lupset Estate.

Souter flipped through the pages to the updated reports in the next day's paper. By then the girl's identity had been confirmed and photos of Claire and her distraught parents accompanied an appeal for information from the Detective Superintendent in charge of the murder enquiry.

Phyllis had been looking over Souter's shoulder and tutted. "Shocking," she said. "Such a young girl. And her parents were in an awful state." She looked down at him. "You just can't imagine losing a child, can you? I mean, it's not supposed to happen that way round, is it?"

Souter's guts turned upside down. Phyllis didn't know it but he really did know how that felt. The anguish and grief he experienced for Adam, the seven-year-old son he lost, rushed through his system. Taken by his first wife to Canada, he had drowned in August 1999. That had screwed his emotions inside out during those hours when he thought he'd lost not only Alison but his unborn baby in New York.

"No," Souter struggled to say. "It isn't supposed to happen."

He stood up and walked to the door. "Sorry, Phyllis, I just need to …" And he was gone, pulling his handkerchief from his pocket.

7

Detective Chief Superintendent Flynn slipped quietly and unnoticed into Strong's office. It was only when he closed the door behind him that Strong looked up from the paperwork on his desk.

"Ah, sir. Sorry I didn't …"

Flynn held up a hand. "No, don't worry. I wanted a quiet word, Colin." A tall, slim man with a rim of black hair around a bald pate, he walked over to sit in the chair opposite the DI.

That was when Strong saw the file Flynn had brought with him. He sat back in his seat. "Something wrong?"

Flynn looked down at the file then across to Strong. "This is a little delicate," he said. "Have you come across a new recruit constable by the name of Monk, Gary Monk?"

Strong screwed up his face in thought. "Oddly enough, I think he was on the cordon last night when I attended the body in the toilets. Took my name; didn't know who I was. Why? What's up?"

Flynn took a breath before continuing, "You're aware of the new regulations for recruits these days; the systematic taking of fingerprints …"

Strong nodded.

"… and now DNA."

Strong leaned forward, arms on his desk. "Something strange?"

"You could say that. Do you remember the Claire Hobson case?"

Strong felt his heart rate rise. "Fourteen years old, raped and strangled, found on old railway land in Horbury."

"That's right. Spring of 1982. The bastard's never been caught."

Strong was ahead of Flynn. "But PC Monk would only have been about two or three ..."

"Not an exact match, a familial one."

"Familial?"

"Yes. Apparently it's a new technique the scientific bods at the DNA Lab are developing, looking at certain aspects of matching. If we get a result from this and it gets to court this will be the first time this type of science will have led to a conviction."

Strong puffed out his cheeks. "Christ," he said quietly. "But how come his DNA has been compared to ... what exactly? I mean two things here, sir. Firstly, I thought all police personnel profiles were held on a separate section of the National DNA Database. What do they call it, the Police Elimination Database. I didn't think any comparisons could be run without the authority of a management board police request."

"Normally, you're quite right."

"Don't tell me someone had grounds to get that request?"

"No, Colin. It would seem this happened due to a complete cock up on our part – and by our part I mean some pillock in Huddersfield Police Station mixed up his sample. When they were supposed to take Monk's sample with the rest of his cohorts, the technician was called away, so he had to make separate arrangements later. Huddersfield was more convenient for him, so that's where he went. And his sample was included with a batch of detainees and hence found its way onto the main database.

"But then, in 1982, they wouldn't have identified any DNA profiles from the crime scene. That didn't come in until a year or two later with, who was it now, the Colin Pitchfork case in Leicestershire."

Flynn nodded. "A landmark case, yes. But thankfully the Claire Hobson enquiry is one they decided to keep the evidence from. It was last reviewed ten years ago in

1992 under some cold case initiative. No new evidence came to light then but they did manage to obtain full profiles from the material they have."

"So you say it's proven to be a familial match?"

"Yes. He doesn't have any older brothers and the lab think it's most likely to be his father."

"So why me? Why not DCI Hemingford?" he asked.

Finally, Flynn placed the file on the desk. "Local knowledge, Colin. Plus, I think you'd be the right man for the job. Discretion is paramount. If the media get hold of this, it could be disastrous; and not just for the West Yorkshire Force. We need to investigate but we need to do it with tact and diplomacy." He tapped the file. "This is a copy of PC Monk's personnel file. I don't need to tell you to keep this secure, away from any prying eyes."

Strong spun the file round and opened it. "I'll keep this somewhere safe." He scanned down the first page. "But ...hold on." Strong frowned then looked up at Flynn. "It says here his father died two years ago."

"That's right. And before you say it, that doesn't mean we don't investigate. The Hobson family still need answers."

"That wasn't what I was going to say," Strong closed the file. "And I'm with you on the family being entitled to know what happened to Claire. But am I to do this single-handedly?"

"What are you thinking?"

"Well it means I'll have to interview Mrs Monk for a start ... without alerting her. I'm just thinking that might benefit from a female touch."

"Kelly?" Flynn said.

Strong nodded.

"How's she coping, by the way? After ... you know."

"She seems okay."

Flynn pursed his lips. "Good," he considered. "But no one else. Not without my express permission. We need to keep a firewall round this."

"Understood."

Before Flynn could leave, Strong spoke again. "The DCI," he said, "Is there something I should know?"

Flynn looked slightly on edge. "No, why do you ask?"

"Well I heard what you said about me having local knowledge and being discreet when it comes to Gary Monk's situation but ..." Strong paused, trying to gauge Flynn's reaction. "I couldn't help but get the feeling DCI Hemingford didn't really want to be in the briefing this morning."

Flynn walked to the door. "No, everything's fine, Colin," he said and closed the door behind him.

Strong suspected there was something more but shook it from his head and opened Monk's file. For the next few minutes, he studied the contents. How the Hell could he probe this without alerting the family?

A knock on the door interrupted his thoughts. Looking up, he could see Luke Ormerod through the glass panel standing outside, coat on looking at his watch. Closing the file, he casually slipped it into his top desk drawer and beckoned him in.

"We need to get going, guv," he said.

"Do you think you can handle the PM on your own Luke? It's just something's come up I need to deal with."

Ormerod looked surprised. "Sure. Everything okay? Only I saw the Chief Super come in a bit earlier."

"No, everything's fine. He just wants me to have a look at something for him."

"I'll be alright. I'm a big boy now." Ormerod smiled at his boss.

"Let me know what's found."

"Sure." Ormerod turned to leave

Strong stopped him. "Oh Luke, is Kelly still around?"

"No, guv. She's gone off with John to see Mrs Weaver."

"Okay, not to worry, I'll catch up with her when she gets back."

8

Souter called Alison to check she was okay. She was at home in the stone-built terraced house she had owned for the past ten years. Bob had moved in with her just before they married and was renting out his one-bedroomed apartment near Wakefield's Westgate railway station. Alison's house was more homely, plus the flat in town was a better bet for rental, so the decision had been made.

"What's up, Bob?" she asked. "You don't normally call me in the day."

"Oh nothing," he responded. "I just wanted to hear your voice and know you were alright." He certainly wasn't going to mention his upset at what Phyllis had said. It wasn't the old girl's fault; she wasn't aware of the sad events in his past.

Alison told him that Sammy and Susan were calling round that evening. That cheered him up. He'd grown to love those two, like younger sisters, or possibly daughters. He rescued a badly injured Susan from a derelict farmhouse basement in September 2000. She was twenty-four at the time. At that same point, a nineteen-year-old Sammy walked into the Yorkshire Post offices and entered his life when she sought his help. Over the course of Susan's hospital stay, Sammy and Susan became firm friends. They now shared a flat in Leeds. Susan was in her second year of a degree course in Broadcast Journalism at Leeds University. Sammy meanwhile had been helped to sort her life out by Bob. Alison had also assisted Sammy in securing a job in the office where she worked. With the baby due in about five weeks, Alison had dropped her hours to three days a week but would still be keen to hear what was happening in her place of work from Sammy.

"That's great," he responded. "I'll look forward to seeing those two tonight." With that, he ended the call.

About to start re-reading the notes he'd made from the newspaper reports at the time of Claire Hobson's murder, Janey Clarke bobbed her head over the screen dividing his workstation from hers. Janey was a smart young reporter of twenty-seven who had been at the Post for five years. He was impressed by some of the stories she'd written since he'd been back in Yorkshire.

"Heard about what happened in the park in Wakefield last night?" she asked.

He looked up. "No. What's gone on?"

"One up on you then." She said, then sunk behind the screen again.

He was about to stand up and continue the conversation when his desk phone rang. A few minutes later, he did stand and walked round to Janey's desk.

"Pretty nasty by the sounds of it," he remarked, giving the impression it was to no one in particular.

Janey smiled but concentrated on the piece she was writing. "Finally found out then?" she asked.

"The local murder?"

Eventually, she turned from her computer screen. "A bit more than that."

"So what've you heard?"

Janey leaned back and tapped her teeth with a pencil. "You first."

Souter considered for a second. "Okay, I've just spoken to someone who reckons they found the body."

Janey raised her eyebrows. "Impressive. Did he say who the victim was?"

Souter leaned against her desk. "No, only the description of what he found and where. A well-known cottaging haunt, apparently."

"I'll bow to your superior knowledge." She made a face. "Well, I have an idea who the victim might be."

"And how do you know that?"

"A witness told me they'd taken a car away from the scene, under wraps and on a low loader."

"So how does that help you if it was covered up?"

"Ah, well, you see, before they did that, he saw what vehicle it was and the registration number." Janey grinned. "A call to my friendly contact with access to the DVLA database and ..."

Souter pushed himself back upright. "I am impressed. So what's our next move?"

She laughed. "*Our* next move? I don't know about you but I know what I'm going to do next."

"Come on Janey, we can work this together."

She was on her feet shrugging into her coat, all good humour vanished. "Like you kept me in the loop with that Lofthouse Development scandal *we* were supposed to be working together last year, you mean?"

Souter held both arms out in an apologetic gesture. He'd got no counter-argument. He had kept information from her.

"I don't think so," she said and headed out through the door.

Souter smiled to himself. The girl's learning, he thought.

Back at his desk, he dialled a mobile number and let it ring until the answer message kicked in. No surprise that his old friend Colin Strong wouldn't speak to him at the moment; probably up to his ears on this murder enquiry. A second call to Wood Street Police Station and he found out that there would be a press conference about the case later this afternoon. Until then, the police would be making no statement.

Only one thing for it, Souter decided, he'd have to pay a visit to Samuel Pemberton before the press conference to see if he could wrong foot the team.

9

In a flat in a street not far from Wakefield's Kirkgate railway station, Felicity Barrett stood in front of a milky mirror and applied mascara. She was an attractive, confident, shapely twenty-six-year old with long dark hair. Normally she would be dressed to impress but today, she wore a loose-fitting top and tracksuit bottoms. She wasn't going out. The room was tatty, like the rest of the flat but it was serving a purpose. The curtains were closed. It was daylight outside but there was nothing of interest to see anyway. Besides, the damp grey weather did nothing to encourage her to open them and so the room was lit by a bare sixty-watt bulb.

"What are you doing?" Mark Thompson sounded annoyed as he walked into the room. "You're supposed to be being held against your will, you can hardly be seen out all dolled up."

"Chill out, will you. If I'm going to be here in this dump, I may as well make myself feel good. Plenty of time to create the right impression later."

He relaxed a bit. "Here, tea for you," he said, holding out a Millennium mug to her. "And I got a copy of this morning's Post." He sat down on a matching easy chair and opened out the newspaper.

She put the mug on the floor and slumped into the comfortable old sofa. "So it's true then," she remarked, spotting the headlines.

BODY FOUND IN PARK TOILETS

"So it would seem. Fits with what that bloke told me last night at the gates and all the police activity." His head was down reading the report.

"That's him," she said angrily. "All he had to do was follow instructions. I'll bet he lost his temper with someone. He was always doing that with Mum."

He looked up from the newspaper and across to his cousin. "We don't know the details but it doesn't help the situation."

"Well get back onto the bastard and fix up Plan B." She took a large gulp of her tea then pulled a face. "Christ, Mark! How long have you known me?" She stood up. "You know I have two sugars."

"Sorry."

When she came back from the kitchen, Mark folded up the paper. "Plan B means little Danny," he said.

"Danny'll be fine." She took a sip of tea. "He knows what to do. All you need to tell him is the time."

"I'll call him in a bit." Mark pulled a cigarette from the packet on the chair arm.

"We need to get this sorted tonight. Christ I only wanted to be out of circulation for a couple of days. I hadn't planned on this for any longer. The sooner we get things back to normal, the better."

He lit up, took a deep drag and exhaled. "It wasn't me who cocked things up."

She calmed down. "I know. I'm sorry to drag you into this."

"Oh it's okay. If it helps you two I'm fine with it." He flicked ash into a tray on the chair arm. "Have the salon tried to contact? They would have expected you on Tuesday."

She picked up the mug from the floor and wrapped her hands around it. "I don't know. I've kept my phone off, if you remember." She sipped some more. "What about you? Have you heard from Andy?"

"Me? No. Why should he try to call me?"

"Looking for me, of course. I'd have thought he'd try some of my contacts."

"I did tell him not to speak to anyone about this, apart from your step-dad, of course."

She nodded and drained her mug. "And this time, make sure he goes on his own. I don't want the bastard sending Andy and keeping a lookout himself."

"Don't worry," he said, tapping the ash from his cigarette. "I'll make sure Andy has to stay at the house. He'll have to wait there for the message telling him the drop has been made and where to pick you up."

"Well go on then," she said, agitation in her tone. "Make the calls."

Mark stubbed out the cigarette and retrieved his mobile phone from his shirt pocket.

10

Ormerod had surprised Strong when he reported back from the post-mortem. The actual cause of death was a myocardial infarction. But he'd suffered an intra cranial bleed shortly before death, where he'd been struck on the left temple. The bone was thinner than expected at that point. That would probably have proved fatal in any event.

"What did the pathologist reckon to that?" Strong asked.

"His take was that our victim was struck once to the side of the head and was rendered unconscious," Ormerod responded. "He suffered the heart attack and would have died minutes later. The plastic bag over the head was just a prop to make us think he'd suffocated; plus it wasn't airtight anyway. In actual fact, he was already dead."

"Christ, so what are we dealing with here? A lucky punch? Someone with some kind of martial arts training … or army?"

Ormerod shrugged. "Not sure. But as Dr Symonds thought last night, there were no signs of any sexual activity despite how he was found."

"You mean the trousers and underpants pulled down?"

"Yes, guv. So either the perpetrator was disturbed or …"

"Or some form of humiliation," Strong continued.

They were both left wondering what sort of creature was capable of that. And more puzzling, why?

Later that afternoon, Strong spotted Kelly Stainmore taking off her coat in the CID room. She looked healthier than she had last year. She'd lost most of the weight she'd put on then. Her skin and hair looked far better and there was no evidence of the lethargy she'd been suffering from. Only just before the shooting had she told him that tests had revealed the problem was down to an underactive thyroid. Medication would put things back on an even keel. She certainly looked a whole lot better now, despite her traumatic experience; more like a healthy thirty-four-year old. Short blonde hair framed a face that positively glowed. He stood at the door, caught her eye and beckoned her towards his office. She made a mime of a drink and nodded towards him. He shook his head and returned to his desk.

A few minutes later she appeared at the doorway, polystyrene cup in hand. Strong asked her to close the door behind her.

"How did you get on?" he asked.

"Mrs Weaver was in a desperate state, as you can imagine." She sat down opposite her boss and placed her drink on a mat on his desk. "No idea why her husband would be in a Wakefield park last night. She thought he was meeting clients in Leeds. That's what he'd told her anyway."

"What does he do, this Marcus Weaver?"

She bent down and pulled a notebook from her bag. "He's a senior manager in an insurance office." She flicked over a few pages. "Been there nearly fifteen years."

"And the home situation?"

"How do you mean?"

"Well, family, what does she do?"

"Oh, they've got two kids, a girl who's ten and a boy, eight." She paused to take a drink. "Her mother collected them from school and brought them back while John and I were there. Mrs Weaver works part-time in the accounts office of a small building firm nearby."

"And what sort of feel did you get from Mrs Weaver, about their marriage, that sort of thing?"

"Hard to gauge much, guv. She was distraught." Stainmore closed her notebook and dropped it back into her bag. "The Family Liaison Officer Leeds have allocated, was there. She explained that at some point an official identification would be necessary. I think she's trying to organise that for later this afternoon but that's only if she thinks Mrs Weaver's up to it."

Strong proceeded to tell Stainmore what Ormerod had reported following the post-mortem.

"So the way the body was left was just to put us off?" she asked, taking a sip of her drink.

"Possibly, or some message of humiliation," Strong considered. "I still think Mr Weaver was meeting a woman."

The conversation stalled as Stainmore drained her coffee before Strong leaned forward onto his desk and looked at her earnestly. "Listen Kelly," he began, "I haven't had the opportunity to talk to you much about … well, what happened last year …"

She put up a hand to stop him. "It's okay, guv. There's no need to treat it like an elephant in the room. Honest."

"Is that how you see it?"

She shook her head. "No, but I think you might."

He leaned back again and sighed. "But if I'd known the full picture, I'd never have let you come with me." He grimaced as the events of that rain-soaked night the previous September at the abandoned offices of the Lofthouse Colliery flashed through his mind.

It was her turn to lean forward. "But you didn't. And I insisted on going. I wasn't going to let you go on your own either. It's fine." They were silent for a moment before she continued, "Look, if it wasn't for what you did for me after it happened, I wouldn't be here."

"But if I hadn't …"

"No, guv." She was insistent. "You can't say that. Now, it's fine. Let's move on."

"Okay," Strong said, with a grim smile. "So how is everything … with the wound and your thyroid?"

"Yeah. It's all good."

"You certainly look great."

She flushed a little. "Thanks."

"Anyway," he continued quickly, "There's something else I need to speak to you about. It's confidential and a bit delicate."

"I'm intrigued."

Strong spent the next few minutes explaining what DCS Flynn had asked him to investigate. "I thought it would be prudent to have a female perspective on this too," he concluded. "And Flynn agreed, provided we ... and he, are the only ones who know about this."

He brought the copy of Gary Monk's file from his drawer and let Stainmore read it through. When she'd finished she looked up.

"So how do we approach Mrs Monk without alerting her or Gary that something isn't right?" Strong wondered.

Stainmore thought for a moment. "What about a home visit?"

"Well, obviously, but we can't just go ..."

"No, I mean the home visit that he should have had as part of the vetting process before he joined. I know, there was one but, as we all know, the HR department aren't always that efficient. I mean, let's say the report has been misplaced and we need to repeat it. A mere formality, of course, but something that has to be done."

Strong slowly smiled. "A box-ticking exercise, you mean. Brilliant, Kelly. I knew you'd be the right person for the job. If you set it up, I can come along with you on the pretext that we've both been out to look at something nearby and rather than drop me back off at the station first, I'm just sitting in. How does that sound?"

She leaned down to her bag and retrieved her notebook. "I'll give her a call," she said, noting down a telephone number from the file before closing it and handing it back to her boss.

"You can make that call from in here, if you want. We need to be discreet."

"Of course."

"And then," Strong continued, "I think we need to visit Weaver's place of work and see what we can find out."

11

Strong drew his car to a halt by the barrier to the car park of the building where Weaver spent his days and dropped the window to speak into the box on the post. Stainmore was sitting alongside. After a brief exchange with a remote male voice, the barrier lifted and Strong found a spare space in a group of four marked 'visitors'.

On the run to Leeds, Luke Ormerod had called to inform them that the briefing scheduled for four had been cancelled. DCS Flynn had arranged a press conference for five and the next team briefing would be held at eight tomorrow morning.

After signing in at reception, the detectives had only a minute or so to wait before a man, introducing himself as Duncan McKenzie, Marcus Weaver's director, arrived to escort them to an upper floor. McKenzie, around six feet tall, spoke with a cultured slight Scottish accent and appeared to be in his mid-forties with well-groomed salt and pepper hair and dressed in an expensive suit.

"This is dreadful news," he said as they rode in the lift. "His wife must be devastated."

"Do his work colleagues know?" Strong asked, annoyed that word had leaked out of Weaver's demise before his arrival. His identity had not yet been made public.

"You know how these rumours spread," McKenzie said. "They know he hasn't turned up for work today." He stopped talking as a ping announced their arrival on the fifth floor.

As the doors opened, a young blonde-haired woman holding some files stood to the side to let them walk out. A flash of recognition crossed her face before she dropped her head, keen to avoid the visitors. She quickly stepped into the lift as McKenzie, Strong and Stainmore passed through the fire doors and onto the main floor.

McKenzie's office was situated at the far end of an open plan area. Strong could feel the eyes of a dozen people on his back as he was led towards it. Once inside, door closed, with the detectives sitting on comfortable chairs, the director offered them coffee from the percolator sitting on a long cabinet. He handed cups to Strong and Stainmore before taking his own to sit in the leather chair behind his desk.

"So how can I help you, Inspector?" he asked.

"Mr Weaver, Marcus," Strong began, "was found dead yesterday evening In Wakefield, as you've heard."

McKenzie nodded his head.

"We understand he was supposed to be meeting clients here in Leeds last night?"

A brief smile flashed across McKenzie's face before a sombre expression returned. "It's not something I'm aware of." He opened an A4 book on his desk and scanned the page. "This is Marcus's desk diary, and I've checked his online diary too and there's no mention of any meeting yesterday, let alone last night. I wouldn't expect him to meet clients after office hours anyway."

Strong turned to Stainmore who was taking notes. They exchanged looks.

"If we could have a look at that, Mr McKenzie." Strong leaned forward. "We can let you have it back in due course."

The director handed the diary to Strong as he spoke. "If there was any evening entertaining, and it doesn't happen very often, that would be conducted by myself or my fellow directors."

"I gathered from your expression just now that you were ..." Strong searched for the correct word. "...amused by what Mr Weaver was supposed to be doing? It didn't seem a surprise that he might have used this as an excuse at home, although he was somewhere else?"

McKenzie frowned and clasped his hands on his desk. "You're right, it didn't surprise me to hear you say that. Is that what his wife told you?"

"I'd like you to explain," Strong said without responding to the question or giving any clue as to who had given him that impression.

McKenzie sipped his coffee and considered his answer. "I've suspected for a little while now that Marcus was having an affair."

"Do you know who?"

"No. We weren't that close. It was strictly professional," McKenzie answered. "But it wouldn't have surprised me. I picked up on a few things in recent weeks." He drained his coffee, looking from one detective to the other. "This is in strictest confidence?"

Strong was becoming irritated. "This is a murder enquiry, Mr McKenzie."

"What I meant was ... Of course. I suppose having been there myself, and I'm not proud of it," the man added quickly. "I can spot the signs."

"Such as?"

McKenzie took a deep breath. "Taking more pride in his appearance, overdoing the aftershave and generally in a better mood on certain days. More attention to his mobile phone."

"Who would be closest to him here in the work place?"

"Well, Bill and Dan were his close work colleagues; they may well know more than I do."

"Was it likely to be someone from these offices?" Stainmore asked.

The director's eyes widened. "I wouldn't like to say. As I said, I've not heard any rumours as such, much less any names, it's just an impression I'd formed ... that he was possibly involved in a ... liaison."

"So, these work mates, Bill and Dan, would it be possible to speak to them?" Strong came back.

"Well Bill Crossley's on a day's leave today but Dan Sykes is in. Would you like me to fetch him?"

"Please Mr McKenzie. And if it would be possible to use your office here so we can speak to him in private, if that's okay?"

McKenzie stood up. "Sure. I'll just go and find Dan."

When the director left the room, Strong got to his feet and strolled over to the window to look out. "Impressions, Kelly?" he asked over his shoulder.

"Fits with your spot of the female shoe prints at the scene."

Strong turned and leaned against the sill. "But do you think he wouldn't know who Weaver might have been messing around with?" Strong nodded in the direction of the office door where McKenzie had disappeared.

"Would you, guv?" she responded.

"Hmm," was all he said, as he gave that some thought.

"What about his phone?" Stainmore added.

"SOCO have that and we'll no doubt get a full report on it fairly quickly. That might give us a lead as to who he was meeting last night."

"And then ..." Stainmore stopped as McKenzie returned accompanied by a rotund man of around forty with thinning brown hair and black framed glasses.

"This is Dan Sykes," McKenzie said. "I'll leave you to talk." With that, he left his office and closed the door.

Strong introduced himself and Stainmore then asked Sykes to take a seat.

"I understand you are a close working colleague of Marcus Weaver," Strong said, once the man was comfortable in his chair.

"Well, we've worked together in the same team; myself and Bill, Bill Crossley, for something like three years."

"So you'd know Mr Weaver reasonably well?"

"Do we ever know any of our workmates, though," Sykes responded.

"Perhaps we could leave the philosophical discussion for another time, Mr Sykes," Strong said, trying to hide his annoyance. "What we're trying to establish is some background information on Mr Weaver."

"Sorry. Of course. It's just that the news … it's been a Hell of a shock. I mean, we were only sitting next to one another this time yesterday."

"Did he say anything about what he would be doing after work? Did he plan to go out anywhere?"

Sykes pushed his glasses up the bridge of his nose. "No. I think we even talked about what was going to be on the telly. As far as I was aware, it was just another Wednesday."

"So he was talking about what would be on TV last night?"

"We all were."

"And he didn't mention doing anything after work? Going for a drink with anyone, meeting someone?"

Sykes looked puzzled. "No. Why? Did he?"

"That's what we're trying to find out."

The man held out both hands. "I'm sorry, I can't throw any more light on this."

"Okay, thanks, Mr Sykes. And if you think of anything else, something Mr Weaver said in passing, no matter how insignificant you think, give me a call." Strong handed Sykes his card.

"Didn't exactly get us very far, did it, guv?" Stainmore pondered as Strong drove them back to Wakefield.

"Oh I don't know. It was interesting that McKenzie suspected Weaver of having an affair."

"He's a smarmy sod," she offered. "But Sykes was a waste of space. Let's hope his other colleague is a bit more switched on."

"Or at least open to confiding what he might know." Strong glanced over his shoulder as well as checking his mirror before taking the Mondeo out into the third lane of the M1. "If he was having an affair, my money would still be on someone who works in that office."

Stainmore was quiet for a minute.

"While we're driving, why don't you try that number for Mrs Monk."

By the time they returned to Wood Street, the press conference arranged for five o'clock was over and Hemingford was in Flynn's office. Darby had left a post-it note on Strong's computer screen to say that the FLO had accompanied Mrs Weaver to Pinderfields that afternoon and she'd confirmed identity of her husband's body.

With a briefing arranged for eight the following morning and an appointment for Stainmore and Strong to visit Gary Monk's mother at ten, Strong left the station.

12

"Something smells good!" Souter shouted out as he stepped through the front door of the house he shared with Alison.

"Hey!" she responded from the kitchen through the back.

He put his briefcase down by the side of the settee, looked up to the mantelpiece and saw the Valentine's cards they'd given one another this morning. He took in the sounds of a Joe Cocker album playing on the CD then saw the bouquet of flowers arranged in a vase on the dresser.

Alison emerged, wiping her hands on a towel.

Souter smiled and nodded towards the flowers. "Do you like them?"

She followed his gaze. "They're lovely, thank you."

"Specially for my special girl." He approached her, holding out both hands to gently feel her stomach. "How's our bump?" he asked, kissing her.

Arms around his neck she pulled her head away to look at him. "Our bump?" She grinned. "At the moment it's solely mine and it's been pretty lively. I wish you could take over for me now and again."

He ran his hands down her back and gently squeezed her bum. "I can't wait to meet him or her," he said.

She pulled away and playfully slapped his arm. "And you can stop that sort of behaviour Mr Souter. That's what got us into this situation in the first place."

"I know." He gave her a cheeky look. "It was great though, wasn't it?"

"Well calm down, Sammy and Susan will be here anytime."

"So what delights have you got for tea?"

"I've done a meat and potato pie."

His eyes widened.

"I suddenly had this urge for pastry," she explained. "Now go and get freshened up. I'm just going to check on the veg."

Ten minutes later, Souter and Alison were relaxing on the settee when the front door burst open and Sammy and Susan tumbled in, chattering away like they'd not seen one another for months.

"What's all the excitement, you two?" Souter asked.

"Take your coats off first and have a drink." Alison got to her feet, moved forward and gave the pair a hug.

"How are you?" Susan asked.

"We've brought you some grape juice." Sammy held out a bottle. "You can pretend it's red wine."

"Thanks," Alison said in a mock disappointed tone. She took hold of the present. "I'm looking forward to my first glass of Chianti once this is all over," she quipped.

Susan and Sammy shrugged out of their coats, Sammy hanging them up in the cupboard by the side of the front door. "You'll never guess," she said, running both hands through her blonde hair.

"Just listen to this," Susan joined in.

Souter laughed. "Slow down you two and just tell me."

"Well Alison, have you heard?" Sammy called through to the kitchen where Alison had disappeared with the bottle.

Alison re-appeared in the doorway. "What?" she said, a broad smile on her face.

"You know the victim of the murder in the park last night? You know the one that's been all over the news?"

"Yes," Alison responded slowly.

"You'll never guess who it is."

"Go on then."

"Only Marcus Weaver. You know him, don't you? Quite a good-looking bloke works in that department under McKenzie on the next floor up from us."

Alison put a hand to her mouth. "No."

"It's true, we had your mate in this afternoon," Sammy said, turning to Souter.

"Who? Colin?"

"Yeah, and that detective who was shot last year, Kelly Stainmore."

Souter's thoughts immediately shifted to the news conference he'd just attended at Wood Street. Colin and Kelly hadn't appeared. DCI Hemingford and DCS Flynn were put up alongside the Force's media relations person, some thirty-something stern-faced dark-haired woman he'd not seen before. He didn't learn much more than he already knew. It seemed they were keeping a lot of cards close to their chest. All that was stated initially was that a thirty-nine-year old married man from the Leeds area had been found dead in the park the night before and police were treating his death as murder. They were appealing for help from anyone who was in the vicinity between the hours of seven-thirty and eight-thirty to get in touch. One hack Souter knew pressed them on the exact location which then prompted some speculation as to whether the murder had been sexually motivated. A bland response of looking at all possibilities was all that was forthcoming. Souter irritated the officers when he asked if there were any unusual circumstances in which the victim had been found. Again, the answer was non-committal, although the expression on Flynn's face was one of concern that perhaps Souter knew far more than they would have wished.

"Would he have been thirty-nine and living in Leeds?" Souter asked.

Alison looked across at him. "I'd think he'd be around forty, yes," she said. "And I think he comes in from Horsforth. Always seemed a nice guy. God, I can't believe it. What do you know, Bob?"

"Only what I've been told at the press conference just before I came here."

"Come on then, spill," Sammy said excitedly.

Souter gave a brief summary of what he knew, omitting any details that old man Pemberton had given him.

"That place has a right reputation," Susan joined in, once he'd finished. "Do you think he was ... you know, batting for the other side?"

"He was married, Susan," Alison said. "I think he's got a couple of kids too."

"That doesn't mean anything," Sammy said. "Sometimes married men like to try something different."

"Look, can we just stop this conversation right now." Alison put her hands on her hips. "I want to enjoy my meal."

"So what are you working on at the moment, Bob?" Susan asked. "Not including our friend in the public toilets."

Alison left for the kitchen and could be heard opening and closing cupboards and moving plates around. Sammy joined her. "Can I give you a hand with anything?" she asked.

"No, I'm fine," she replied. "Everything's under control."

After a second or two in thought, Sammy spoke. "With Mr Weaver," she began, "have you heard any rumours?"

Alison stopped dishing up the pie. "What sort of rumours?"

"You know, having it about with someone in the office."

"Well it's certainly not me," Alison laughed. "Not in this condition." She looked down at her stomach then resumed her task. "Why? Have you?"

"I'm just thinking back over the past couple of months ... since Christmas ... I think I've seen him with a woman who works in another section."

"With a woman? How do you mean? What woman?" Alison said. "And give them a shout." She gestured towards the doorway.

"Oh, it doesn't matter. It's probably completely innocent." Sammy walked away to the living room.

"You probably won't remember but you might have heard talk of it," Souter responded to Susan's question. "The murder of fourteen-year-old Claire Hobson back in 1982."

"I think I have heard of that," Susan said. "Is that still unsolved?"

Souter nodded. "Coming up for twenty years now so Chandler's asked me to do a report on what's happened in between; a sort of anniversary piece, focus on the family, new appeal for information maybe, that sort of thing."

"Sounds interesting." Susan was thoughtful. "Listen, I've got a project to do this term ... I don't suppose I could help you on this one, could I?"

"Oh I don't know, Susan ..."

"I'm sure Mr Chandler wouldn't mind. After all, he took me on last summer."

It was true, she had somehow charmed her way around his boss, especially when she'd asked for a week's holiday part way through her temporary job. But then, there did appear to be some sort of unspoken bond between all four of them, Susan, Sammy, Chandler and Bob, when they'd watched events unfold on the television in the deputy editor's office on that fateful day last September.

Souter hesitated. "I'm not sure ..."

"At least ask him," she persisted. "Think about it, I could bring a female perspective to any meets you might have with her family."

Souter felt as though he'd been ambushed and was being slowly worn down. "I'll speak to him, that's all I can do."

She clapped her hands, a broad smile on her face. "Thanks."

"But I can't promise anything."

"What are you two so animated about?" Sammy wondered as she appeared in the doorway. "Anyway, the food's ready, so come and get it."

13

Brannigan drew the black BMW to a halt under the streetlamp. He was following the directions given by the caller earlier that afternoon. He checked his watch; five to eight. The wipers swept across the windscreen and he could see the phone box on the corner on the other side of the street. He looked all round but the street was deserted. Not surprising considering the rain lashing down and the temperature only a few degrees above freezing. This was the Lupset estate just to the west of the city. Another check of the watch then he felt for the package under his jacket. Stepping out into the rain, he lifted the hood over his head.

He pulled on the door to the phone box and was immediately assaulted by the stench of stale urine. He checked the phone was working and held the door open with his foot. At exactly eight o'clock the phone rang. Brannigan lifted the receiver and waited for the other person to speak.

"I'm glad you're following orders, George," the familiar distorted voice said. *"I will know if you're not on your own."*

"I'm on my tod," Brannigan responded.

"Look down the street towards the next road on your right."

"What about it?"

"Walk towards it and after fifty yards you'll see a green BT junction box. There's a garage tight up to the pavement and to the left-hand side a gap in the fence. Place the bag through that gap and walk away. You have three minutes."

Brannigan repeated the instructions.

"And make sure you do. Because I will know."

"But what about ..." Brannigan stopped. The line was dead. "Bastard!" he said and slammed the handset down.

He walked down the street towards the junction box. At this point, the distance between the streetlamps was at its greatest; combined with the rain, it was pitch dark. He saw the garage. Either side was bounded by a thick privet hedge and a mesh fence. He spotted the gap, large enough only to fit the bag and his hand through. He hesitated. A glance up and down the street told him it was as empty as when he'd first parked up. He bent down and pushed the bag through. Lingering for a few seconds, he stepped back and scanned all round.

He was about to walk away when he heard something scrambling about behind the fence. Bending down again, he put his hands back through the gap. Nothing. And then the sound of someone running a few paces then the squeak of a bike. Peering through the hedge, he managed to spot a small figure pedalling away down the service road.

"Hey!" he shouted then ran back to his car.

Brannigan drove round the streets of Lupset for half an hour before giving up. Apart from some teenage girls walking away from the chip shop and an elderly couple waiting at a bus stop there was nobody out and about. No kids on bikes, which is what he was searching for. He only hoped that this wasn't a total con. But whatever else happened, he resolved to find out who was behind this. And when he did ...

*　*　*

"Let's have it then, Danny," Mark said.

The little kid with the baseball cap turned back to front, dressed in an anorak and jeans looked up at him. "Where's my money?" he asked.

Eleven years old and an attitude, Danny had known Mark all his life, living next door to him and his parents on a street not far away until Mark had moved to a flat of his own in town.

Mark produced a twenty-pound note. "Here," he said. "Did he spot you?"

Danny passed over the plastic bag. "Nah. He tried to get it back though; when he heard me pick it up like."

The two of them were standing on a service road at the back of a row of shops on Dewsbury Road. Mark put the bag inside his coat and zipped it up. "And all he might have seen is some lad in dark clothing pedalling away on a bike," he suggested.

"I did see him drive around for a bit after." Danny wiped his nose with his sleeve. "I think he might have been looking for me."

"But you stayed hidden?"

The kid grinned. "Nobody knows this estate like me."

Mark put a hand on Danny's shoulder. "Good lad. That's why I knew you'd be the best for the job."

"Listen Mark, this isn't drugs is it?" His face was screwed up with concern. "I don't get involved in that."

"No Danny, I can assure you it's nothing like that. This is just about teaching someone a lesson."

"That bloke?"

"Best you don't know. And listen ..." Mark continued, "If anyone asks ..."

"I don't know anything," Danny said as he prepared to pedal away.

"You take care now."

14

In a narrow street in a decaying part of Huddersfield, hemmed in between the railway line from Leeds to Manchester and the old canal, the gates to Brannigan's scrap yard remained closed and locked, as they had done all day. A few old streetlamps gave little light as steady rain poured down.

In the adjacent house, Andy nervously paced, waiting for the phone call. He only hoped Brannigan had followed instructions this time. If anything happened to Felicity, it would be his fault. Felicity said he was impulsive and a bully. He'd seen that for himself these past few days. But in the end, he had come good with the money.

Walking into the downstairs bathroom, he ran the tap then splashed his face. In the mirror, a gaunt young man stared back, hair unkempt and patchy stubble apparent. He couldn't grow a beard, even if he wanted to. The strain and worry of these past few days was etched in his features.

Drying his face on the towel, he wandered around the ground floor of the house. It should be better than it was. Brannigan was a hoarder. The sitting room had various boxes spread over the floor. He looked inside one; magazines from the 1950s; a lot bought at a recent auction. Another contained a china tea set carefully wrapped in paper. Newspapers were scattered over the sofas and armchairs in the big room.

Out in the hallway, more clutter. Various ornaments adorned every flat surface, window sill and occasional table. He'd picked one up to look on the bottom for any well-known maker's mark when the phone rang. Startled, he ended up juggling it in both hands before securing it in his grasp and putting it back in its place, relieved.

"Hello?" he answered.

"Andy?"

He recognised the distorted voice from the overheard conversation with Brannigan. "Yes."

"The back lane with some garages by the side of the Flanshaw Hotel. Half an hour."

"But wait …"

Andy stood stock still for a second, holding on to the handset, hearing the dialling tone before he sparked to life. Slamming down the phone, he grabbed his jacket and dashed out through the front door, banging it behind him. Jumping into his car he started the engine and sped off towards Wakefield.

The Flanshaw Hotel was easy to find, Andy knew it well. As he drove slowly past, he spotted a back lane to the left hand side of the pub. The lane was unlit. He pulled in. As the headlights swung round into the darkness, a bedraggled figure appeared from between two of the garage blocks. He skidded to a halt and dashed from the car to embrace Felicity.

"You took your time," she said "I'm soaked and bloody freezing."

Her grim smile cheered him. "What happened? Who did this?"

"Let me get in the car," she said.

"Of course." He led her round to the passenger side and helped her in.

He began to drive, heading for the M1.

"Where are we going?" she asked.

"George will want to see you safe and well and there's hot water for a bath."

"Sod that, I'm not going there. Take me home."

He glanced across, a surprised look on his face. "Are you sure?"

"Yes, now get a move on."

*　　*　　*

His house was in darkness when George Brannigan returned home. After a fruitless attempt to find the kid on the bike, he'd tried to contact Andy on the landline. When that wasn't picked up, he tried his mobile. His calls ignored, he was growing angry. Had he been stitched up? Thirty grand he'd just parted with for the supposed safe return of Felicity. Felicity, his step-daughter. And where was her husband now?

"Andy! Andy!" he shouted as he opened the front door.

He listened. The only sound was the grandfather clock's loud slow tick in the hallway.

Up the stairs, he threw open the door to the bedroom where Andy had been staying. A rumpled, slept-on bed but nothing else to show anyone had been there. Brannigan pulled the mobile from his pocket and speed dialled Andy's number once more. It rang twice then went to answer message. Redialling to Felicity's number, the message kicked in immediately that her phone was switched off.

"Shit," he muttered. This was more than suspicious.

Back down stairs, he walked along the hall to the kitchen, checked the dining room then into the lounge. All was as he'd left things a few hours ago. There was only one thing to do. He stormed from the house, climbed back into his car and drove off.

*   *   *

Home for Felicity and Andy was a one-bedroomed rented flat in a two storey Victorian house off College Grove. They'd lived there since they married three years ago, just before her mother died. On the ten-minute journey, Andy tried to probe his wife for details of what had happened to her.

She gave no meaningful responses, only that she needed to have a good wash and get rid of the residue of duct tape that had bound her wrists and ankles and covered her mouth.

Andy's phone rang while he was driving. He gave it a quick glance and showed it to Felicity. "It's George," he said.

She snatched it from him and pressed the red button to cancel the call.

"He'll be worried too," Andy said.

"Not just yet," she countered.

They reached their street and parked up.

Andy waited patiently in the living room of their first floor flat whilst Felicity sorted herself out, beginning in the bathroom, then the bedroom. Finally, in a change of clothes she walked into the room and sat down next to him. She went to kiss him but he pulled away.

"Are you going to tell me what happened? I was so worried," he said.

She took a deep breath then related her story of how she was walking to work on Tuesday when she became aware of someone approaching her from behind. Just as she began to turn round, a hood was placed over her head and she was bundled into the boot of a car.

"So where was this?"

"O ... on Pinderfields Road," she stammered.

"But where exactly? I mean we could get CCTV, find out who was behind this."

"No! No, we can't. He said he knows where I live and if I told the police and started investigating, he'd come back."

"He? So it was only one person."

"What? Well I suppose so, there was only the one voice I ever heard."

"So was there anything distinctive about this voice?"

"No, look, just leave it be. I'm back now, aren't I?"

"But where did he keep you?"

She leaned back on the sofa and closed her eyes. "Please, I'm tired."

"We're all tired."

Felicity opened her eyes again. "And anyway, what happened on the first ransom drop?" She sat up straight. "Things got a bit fraught when that failed."

Andy coloured. For an instant he'd actually forgotten the events in the park toilets, had blotted them out of his memory. "We got disturbed," he finally said, head down.

She leaned closer, looking straight at him. "Andy? What happened?" She put her hand under his chin and saw tears run down his cheeks. "Andy? Was it that bad?"

"He ..." The sounds of a car drawing to a halt interrupted him.

She ran to the window and peeked through the curtain. "It's him," she said.

Seconds later, with the sound of feet on the stairs, Andy stood and composed himself. The door rattled and he opened it.

"Why the Hell haven't you answered your phone?" Brannigan asked. "Is she safe?" He bundled past Andy and walked into the room. "Felicity, are you okay?"

She was on her feet as he rushed forward and put his arms around her.

"I'm fine," she said, stiffening slightly.

He turned to Andy. "Why didn't you bring her back to mine?"

"I just wanted to come home," Felicity answered for him. "I needed to wash and get a change of clothes."

"So what happened?" Brannigan looked intently at his step-daughter.

"It was ..." she covered her face and began to cry.

"She just told me she was abducted on Pinderfields Road walking to work on Tuesday," Andy said.

Brannigan looked to him. "Right. There must be CCTV around there. We need to see it."

"But that would mean the police," Andy argued. "And ..."

"Not necessarily. I could have some private investigator probe."

"No," Felicity said. "We can't risk police or anyone else. He said he'd come back if we did."

"He? The same bastard who called us?" Brannigan fumed.

"Please," she pleaded. "Let's just leave it. I'm back now. I just want to get on with my life."

"But I'm thirty grand down. Someone's turned me over and I won't have that."

She straightened up. "Is that all that matters to you? Money? Your pride? No one's going to know about this. Not from us anyway."

"I'll want to know everything you can remember," Brannigan said. "I'll get the bastards who did this, mark my words."

Felicity threw herself onto the sofa, covered her face and sobbed.

"Please George," Andy said. "She needs time to rest and recover."

Brannigan looked from one to the other, face set hard. Finally, he relaxed slightly. "Okay. But I will want to know details."

"We'll talk later," Andy said.

"We will." Brannigan spun around and quickly left the flat.

The tension eased from Andy's shoulders as he heard Brannigan's footsteps on the stairs. He turned and looked at Felicity, not completely convinced by her act. The sounds of a car door slamming before it sped away drifted up from the street.

15
Friday 15th February 2002

Next morning, the newspapers were full of the Marcus Weaver story. Strong felt sympathy for his widow. Just forty-eight hours previously, she'd kissed him goodbye as she had done hundreds of times before and he'd set off for work in the office. Only this time, he wouldn't return. This time, her whole world was about to explode. From feeling secure in a marriage with two young children and a husband who provided for them to finding out that their relationship was based on a lie would compound her grief. Not only that, the unsavoury rumours being expounded in the press, mention of the place he'd been discovered, a well-known meeting point for homosexual men, and all the speculation that it brought, might be enough to push anyone over the edge.

Still, as he drove to work that morning, Strong reckoned that aspect of things didn't add up. His thoughts returned to the shoe prints and that second car. He also felt that McKenzie hadn't told him everything he could have done.

"Morning, guv," Ormerod greeted, as he walked into the CID room for the eight o'clock briefing. "Have you seen Kelly this morning? She was looking for you earlier."

"Not seen her, Luke."

A few more bodies began to gather; John Darby came in talking to DC Trevor Newell followed by another couple of officers in the team.

Just before eight o'clock, Hemingford appeared, followed closely by Kelly Stainmore. Finally, Doug Norris the SOCO entered.

"Morning everyone," Hemingford said, walking to the whiteboard displaying photos of the victim and the crime scene. "Marcus Weaver," he began, "what have we been able to find out?"

Darby reported that Mrs Weaver had now made the formal identification. Stainmore then spoke of her visit, along with Darby, to Mrs Weaver yesterday morning before giving an account of the afternoon's call along with Strong to Weaver's workplace.

"So the feeling is that our happily married victim was conducting an affair of some sort?" Hemingford suggested. "Possibly something a little unsavoury, bearing in mind the location?"

"I don't think so," Strong responded. "I still suspect he met a woman in the car park on Wednesday night."

"Ah yes, the footprints … and the tyre tracks." Hemingford turned to Norris. "What can you tell us about those, Doug?"

"We did find footprints next to the passenger door of Weaver's Mercedes; women's, size six. Matching soil from outside was found in the passenger footwell too. And having taken measurements and spoken to some motor manufacturers, we think the tyre marks are from a Ford Ka."

"That would tie in with the dog walker's mention of a small vehicle driving off in a hurry." Strong commented. "He said small, like a Fiesta – well that might not be dissimilar to a Ka when he saw it drive off from a distance. He is in his seventies and it was foggy. Dark coloured, he said."

"No other witnesses come forward?" Hemingford asked, almost in desperation.

Mumbles were the only responses.

"Not surprising," Strong said, "seeing as the location has a notorious reputation. Why don't we offer a more sympathetic ear to any of the usual suspects? You know, absolute discretion."

"You were trawling through all the local nonces?" Hemingford addressed one of the detectives.

"So far nobody admitting they were there last night, but we're still working on it," the officer replied.

"I also checked out the victim's phone," Norris said. "Apart from a call to his home number at 17:49 on Wednesday evening, there were no other calls in or out until 23:17 when his home number called him. The phone was in our lab then and his wife ... I assume it was her, left a message asking when he was likely to get home."

"That checks out," Stainmore added. "Mrs Weaver said she'd called him last night to find out what he was doing."

"And no other numbers of interest on his phone records?" Strong asked.

Norris shook his head.

Strong contemplated this for a second.

"There is one other thing," Doug Norris continued, "In the adjacent cubicle to where we found the body, the top to the high-level cistern had been moved." He pinned a couple of photos to the board to reinforce the news. "Might not be anything to do with last night, but we lifted some prints from the cover. No matches as yet."

"What about Weaver's car, Doug? Any news on the forensics sweep?" Strong asked.

"Still on with it," Norris replied. "We got some prints from the passenger side as well as the interior light switch which were smaller than that of the deceased. Now they could be Mrs Weaver's but we'll need hers to compare."

"John, Kelly, could one of you organise that?" Hemingford instructed.

Darby nodded.

"I'll speak to the FLO to arrange something," Stainmore said.

"Make sure she treads carefully, Kelly," Strong warned. "We don't want to compound Mrs Weaver's grief."

"We can also try and get DNA from some of the surfaces on that side of the car," Norris went on. "But what we did get was some material from under the finger nails of the deceased's right hand – nothing on the left – and we're analysing that now too."

"How long before we can get some comparisons off the database?" Strong asked.

"Middle of next week, I'd hope."

"That's got to be a priority." Hemingford said. "In the meantime, anything from any work colleagues as to what he might have been up to?"

Strong voiced his opinion that he thought there was more to glean from that avenue and that he intended to speak to another of Weaver's team later in the day.

Hemingford brought the briefing to a close by quickly summarising duties for the various officers.

Ormerod leaned over to Strong as Hemingford left the room. "That displaced cistern cover, guv," he said. "I'm wondering if Weaver stumbled across something he shouldn't have."

Strong shrugged. "Somebody placing something in the cistern? But what? Drugs?"

Stainmore joined them. "Not heard of drugs being distributed from there, but it might be worth checking with the Drugs Squad in Leeds, Luke," she suggested.

"I'll get on it." Ormerod walked back to his desk.

Stainmore waited until he was out of earshot before addressing Strong. "Don't forget we're off to see Mrs Monk at ten."

16

Souter came back down the stairs from Chandler's office with a smile on his face. He'd been up to see the Deputy Editor to persuade him that Susan Brown could become involved to help him in the task of speaking to Claire Hobson's parents and producing some appropriate articles. The only concession Chandler insisted on was having Susan's university exercise run by him first.

"Good pieces you and Janey have put together on the Wakefield park murder, by the way," Chandler said as Souter was set to leave his office. "Anything interesting to follow up?"

Souter nodded. "There are a few avenues to explore," he said.

Back in the newsroom, Souter sat down at his workstation. On the other side of the half-height partition he could hear Janey Clarke busily tapping away on her keyboard.

"Chandler liked our stories," he said over the top. He heard her stop.

"I suppose you claimed total responsibility?" Janey was on her feet looking over at him.

"As if I would," he said with his best innocent look. "No, seriously, he made some positive noises. It was a good source finding out the victim's identity ahead of the pack."

"Hmm," she said, clearly not impressed. "So why didn't you use some of the details your old dog-walker told you?"

"Thinking ahead. I didn't want to piss West Yorkshire off too much." He thought of Colin. "I've also got some other angle I want to check out first."

"I don't suppose there's any chance of you sharing that then?" she asked.

"Correct," he said, turning back to his computer screen.

"Arsehole," he heard her say under her breath as she sat back down. That brought a broad smile to his face.

After dealing with a few emails, Souter made his way to the Archive Room.

As soon as his head appeared round the door, Phyllis pounced. "Ah, Mr Souter ... I mean Bob," she said.

He was amused that although he insisted she call him by his first name, old habits die hard. Phyllis was a different generation who wasn't used to informality.

"Yes Phyllis," he said.

She stood up and picked a pile of sheets from her desk. "I thought you might appreciate these." She held them out to him. "After your last visit, I thought you might be doing something to mark the twentieth anniversary in a few weeks."

Souter looked at the top sheet; a print-out of the front page of the Yorkshire Post from Monday 8th March 1982. Flicking through some more, he saw that they appeared to be subsequent reports on the progress of the murder enquiry as it unfolded back then. He looked up and smiled. "This is great. I was just coming in to look all this out." He took a step towards her, leaned forward and kissed her forehead. "You're a star. Thanks."

"Oh, well ..." she flustered, coloured up then walked back to her desk.

Souter sat down and began to study the sheets, making notes as he went.

After half an hour, he tidied everything up and walked out to the car park. He needed to make a couple of calls.

17

Stainmore knocked on Strong's office door just after ten past nine.

He beckoned her in.

"I've spoken to the Leeds FLO and she's arranging for Mrs Weaver's prints to be taken. Just routine to eliminate hers from his car, I told her."

Strong raised his eyebrows. "This FLO, she doesn't know we think there was someone else in the car with him on Wednesday night, does she?"

"I only said we were looking at the possibility of others trying the door handles when it was parked."

"You know the more I think about it, the more I think he was having an affair with someone he worked with."

"I know that's a possibility," Stainmore responded, "but what makes you more certain?"

"The phone records. If he was arranging to meet there would have been a call, either received or made, to confirm or arrange the meet. But if he worked with them, then he would have fixed it up at the office."

"Fair point, guv."

Strong was thoughtful for a second, before focusing on the Monk enquiry. "So whereabouts are we actually going?"

"Denby Dale. Just off the main A636."

He glanced at his watch. "I suppose we better head off." Closing the file he'd been studying, he opened a desk drawer, placed it inside then locked it. "Don't want anyone to start wondering what I'm doing with a copy of a personnel file," he said.

At that time of the day, despite the rain, it was a pleasant drive to Denby Dale. The town itself was famous for baking pies at various points in history since 1788.

"Did you know," Strong was saying, "They hold the record for the largest meat and potato pie in the world."

"Amazing," Stainmore said, feigning boredom.

"Yep, and the last one was baked in 2000 to celebrate the Millennium. The first slice cut by Barnsley cricket umpire Dickie Bird."

"Who?"

He smiled as he glanced over to Stainmore. "You'll be glad of that one day if you're ever asked in a pub quiz."

"Yeah, right," she said, but he could see the grin form on her face.

Traffic was light as they passed through Clayton West then Scissett before turning off the main road to the right as they entered Denby Dale itself. By the time they got there, the drizzle that had been steadily falling all morning had stopped and a couple of breaks had appeared in the clouds.

Annabel Monk's house turned out to be a neat semi-detached bungalow in a quiet street on a small estate of similar properties. The front garden had small manicured lawns either side of the path separated by borders containing pruned rose bushes, all clear of weeds.

The knock on the door was answered by a woman they knew to be forty-eight.

"Mrs Monk?" Stainmore enquired. "I'm DS Kelly Stainmore. We spoke on the phone yesterday."

"Yes, come in," the woman said.

"And can I introduce my superior, Detective Inspector Strong." Stainmore smiled at the woman. "Normally I'd conduct these visits on my own but, as I said yesterday, we were planning to be nearby on other business, so it made sense."

"That's okay," she said, standing to one side to allow the officers to enter, "Gary's just putting the kettle on."

"Mrs Monk," Strong greeted.

As they passed, he noticed that she was a couple of inches shorter than Stainmore.

Annabel Monk showed them into a neat comfortable living room with a lit gas fire on a low setting.

A moment later the tall dark-haired figure of the young man Strong recognised as the constable he'd spoken to on Wednesday night appeared.

"Hello Gary," Strong said, holding out a hand,

Monk shook it. "Sir," he said. "I didn't expect to see you again so soon."

"I've just been with DS Stainmore on some other business over Holmfirth way and she'd organised to call in on the way back to Wood Street."

"Would you like some tea?" Monk offered. "I've just boiled the kettle."

Strong and Stainmore accepted the offer. "Actually Gary," Stainmore said, "we could probably conduct the interview in the kitchen, if that's okay."

"Well, about that ..." Gary looked puzzled. "I don't quite understand. I had some DS from Dewsbury come and speak to me back in August."

"So I believe but the paperwork isn't on file and they want me to conduct the home interview again, just to complete the process." Stainmore rolled her eyes. "I tell you, the HR department are useless."

Strong chuckled. "You'll find that out for yourself soon enough Gary, once you've had a few years in. I'll stay here with your mum, if that's okay."

A few minutes later, with Gary and Stainmore in the kitchen, Strong was seated on the settee in the living room with Mrs Monk on one of the armchairs, mugs of tea in front of them.

"How do you feel about Gary being in the police, Mrs Monk?" he asked.

"Please, call me Annabel," she said. "I worry, of course but it's what he really wants to do, so ..." She sipped her tea and looked to some framed photographs on a unit by the side of the fireplace. "I suppose after Richard died, it sort of focussed his mind on what he wanted out of life."

Strong followed her gaze. "Richard was your husband? Gary's dad?"

"Yes. He was only fifty."

Strong stood up and walked over to the unit. "May I?"

She nodded and got to her feet. "That was one of the last photos of us together," she said as Strong picked up one of the frames. "Christmas 1999; in this room. We'd decorated it like we always did. Gary loves Christmas, always has done."

Strong studied the image of Annabel leaning in towards a fair-haired man with a chubby face, both wearing paper hats, no doubt pulled from a Christmas cracker. "What happened?" Strong asked. "Sorry," he added quickly, "I quite understand if you don't want to ..."

"That's okay," she replied. "Sometimes I find it quite cathartic you know, talking about him. I miss him every day."

Strong looked at her and placed a hand on her arm. "I can understand that," he said.

"It was his heart," she went on. "He had an undiagnosed weakness. He liked his food, as you can probably tell." She smiled at the photo. "He was carrying a bit of excess weight." She looked off into nowhere, seemingly drifting into an unseen distance before returning to the living room. "He'd just got back into his car at work to leave for home and collapsed. The paramedics reckoned he was dead instantly." She looked up at Strong. "I suppose the only good thing was that he hadn't set off driving. He might have taken some other poor innocent souls with him."

"I'm sorry to hear that, Annabel. Fifty's no age."

"No, it wasn't. But that's the hand I've been dealt," she said philosophically, resuming her seat.

Strong put the photograph back where he'd found it. "You keep a very tidy garden, I've got to say," he said glancing to the front window.

"Actually, that was Richard's pride and joy. I try to keep it as he would have liked. The back was our little oasis. Would you like to see?"

Strong thought for a second. "Yes. Yes I would," he replied. "My Dad is big into gardening and he does a bit for me, but I'm always interested in other people's ideas. What grows well for them."

"It's not at its best at the moment but there again, it is only February. I'll be getting back out there and preparing for the season next month." She led the way out into the hallway and past the door to the kitchen before unlocking the back door and stepping out into the garden.

The plot was long. Another neatly trimmed lawn with a pathway down one side led to two large empty vegetable plots, a greenhouse, a cold frame and a large potting shed at the far end.

Strong followed her down the path.

In the kitchen, Gary sat at the small table opposite Stainmore with his back to the window, Stainmore had run through a few of the standard questions when she paused, catching sight of Mrs Monk and Strong walking down the garden path.

Gary turned, following her gaze. "That'll be Mum showing Mr Strong her pride and joy. She loves the garden, although Dad was the prime mover, she always got involved." He turned back. "Since he's gone, she's sort of thrown herself into it. Almost as if she'd be letting him down."

"I was sorry to hear about your father, Gary," Stainmore said. She watched as Mrs Monk opened the door to a shed at the bottom of the garden and led Strong inside.

"Thanks," was all he said.

"So, as I was saying, we normally run through a few scenarios and check that your responses are appropriate for a police officer, but seeing as how you're now, what, two weeks into the job, it seems a bit irrelevant."

"Beginning of the month, yes," he confirmed.

"So what are your first impressions of the real thing?" Stainmore's attention was caught by Strong's re-emergence from the shed, clutching what looked like an old shirt.

"Well, a bit of excitement the other night, of course," Gary responded. "I was at the park murder in Wakefield then helped with some door-to-door enquiries."

Stainmore smiled at the man. "It's not all as high-profile as that." She began to tidy up her paperwork.

"No, I realise that. But I like my mentor and I think I'll enjoy the job."

"Any longer term ambitions?" Stainmore asked as she noted Gary's mother and Strong arriving at the back door.

"CID, I suppose, or Traffic."

"Best of luck then, Gary. No doubt we'll come across each other from time to time." She held out her hand and he shook it.

As Strong pulled away from the kerb heading back towards the main road, Stainmore looked at him. "Go on then, what's the story with the old shirt?"

Strong gave a short laugh. "I couldn't believe it myself, Kelly," he said, pausing to check for a gap in the traffic on the main road. A car flashed its lights to let him in and he held up a hand in acknowledgement before accelerating away. "She insisted I view the garden, which was a labour of love, I must say." He glanced at Stainmore. "And when she showed me the potting shed and said how her late husband Robert used to keep everything in neat order and that she hadn't been able throw anything out or even remove his favourite shirt he used for gardening, well... The thought just came to me."

She looked over to the back seat where the plaid shirt had been placed in a plastic evidence bag on the rear seats. "What did?" she asked.

"I heard myself make up some tale about how our senior SOCO is conducting research into how long, in practical terms, DNA can be obtained from clothing after the wearer has discarded it." Strong couldn't help smiling to himself.

"But if she was so attached to her husband's possessions, how come she let you take that away?"

"I suppose she trusts me. I told her it would only take a day or two and she would have it back unharmed. The fact that we can pinpoint that it was almost two years to the day since he last wore it means that it would provide a very useful fixed measure for our forensics team," he said. "In this research project they're working on," he added quickly. "It may help in some small way on future cases."

Stainmore raised her eyebrows. "And she believed that guff?"

Strong moved his head towards the back. "It's there, isn't it?"

"And what if it does prove that Richard Monk was responsible for the rape and murder of Claire Hobson?"

Strong drew a deep breath before answering. "Well then I'll have to cross that bridge when I come to it."

"Gary won't be fooled by that load of old bollocks though, will he?"

"Maybe not, but the important thing is we'll know for sure." He looked across at Stainmore briefly. "What happens then can be for Flynn to decide."

"So where to now?"

He glanced at his watch. "I think we should return to Weaver's office and hear what Bill Crossley has to say."

18

"You didn't have to come back just to give me a lift in to work, you know." Felicity checked her teeth and lipstick in the vanity mirror on the car's sun visor.

"Look, it was the last time you walked in to town when you were grabbed, so there's no way I'm letting you go on your own today." Andy was driving them in his VW Golf towards the centre of Wakefield.

Felicity looked across at him. "What about your work?"

"It's lunch time." Andy appeared stressed. "As long as I'm back for half one, it'll be fine."

He drew to a halt outside the salon. A few heads under dryers were visible and he recognised a couple of Felicity's fellow stylists.

She leaned over and kissed him. "Love you," she said then wriggled in the seat and undid her seatbelt.

"Love you too." He hoped he sounded sincere; still far from satisfied with her sketchy account of what had occurred. "I'll pick you up at seven."

She stepped out of the car and he watched her walk to the salon. She turned and waved before disappearing inside.

On the other side of the street, George Brannigan looked in the window of a shop. Reflected in the glass, he watched the touching scene play out; the final turn and wave before Andy pulled away from the kerb. She seemed calm, he thought, too calm for someone who'd just been freed from a recent kidnap situation. He needed to talk to her – on her own without Andy interrupting. She definitely knew more than she was letting on, he was sure of that. He'd let her settle in then call into the salon and confront her there.

As Brannigan watched, another vaguely familiar figure approached the hairdresser's. He racked his brains to remember who it was. A young lad, younger than Andy but taller and with darker hair. He was carrying a small holdall. He glanced around before entering the shop.

Felicity had taken off her coat in the staff room at the rear of the shop and was making a coffee before bracing herself for the perm Mrs Crowther would want when she turned up for her appointment in about fifteen minutes. It wasn't carrying out the hairstyle that she was dreading, more the endless chatter telling her how successful her eldest daughter was.

She came out from the back and glanced up as the salon door opened. Mark appeared, furtively looking around. He spotted her and she beckoned him over.

"It's my cousin," she said by way of explanation to Sharon, the owner. "Just bringing something in for me."

Sharon continued combing and cutting the hair of her client, paying no further attention.

Mark followed Felicity through to the staff room at the rear.

"I thought you were coming later," she hissed. "After dark to avoid being seen as much as possible."

"I just want to get rid. I'm getting worried about this."

She checked no one was within earshot then continued in hushed tones. "Look, everything's fine."

"Yeah but you're not the one walking round with a load of cash."

"I didn't want to leave it in here for too long either." She held his gaze for a second. "Okay, let's sort it now." She took the holdall from him and unzipped it. Her face lit up in a broad smile when she saw the banknotes inside. "Have you checked it?" she asked him.

"Of course."

"And it's all there?"

He nodded.

"Have you separated your share?"

Mark pointed inside. "That's it there in the plastic bag."

She pulled the bag out from the holdall. "Thanks Mark," she said and passed it over to him. "Put that out of sight and we keep a low profile for a while." She zipped the holdall back up then placed it in one of six lockers against the rear wall of the staff room. She locked it and put the key in her pocket.

Mark tucked the plastic bag into an inside pocket of his jacket. "You know he'll be round to speak to you?" he said.

"It'll be fine. Anyway, he doesn't know you were involved."

Mark's head was down, talking to his shoes. "He's one unstable bastard though, from what you've said in the past. Then there's what happened on Wednesday night." He looked up at Felicity. "Has Andy told you what happened?"

"No, I haven't pressed him." She gave a brief smile. "But there again, he hasn't really pushed me for what happened either." She sighed. "I suppose we'll have to talk soon. But I just want to finalise some plans first."

"I hope you know what you're doing." Concern was etched on Mark's face.

"Trust me, it'll be fine. Now ..." she put an arm on his to guide him out. "You need to go. You can't be seen here. Just stay out of sight. I'll contact you when things have calmed down."

He paused and looked her in the eye. "You take care of yourself now, won't you?"

"I'll be fine. Now go."

19

Souter had called Susan and told her that Chandler had agreed to her involvement in his project. Then he'd called the number Chandler had given him for Claire Hobson's mother. It turned out to be a work number. She was a receptionist for a doctors' surgery near the town centre. After a brief introduction, telling her he was following up on what he'd been asked to do by his Deputy Editor, Louise Hobson suggested he call round tomorrow afternoon when both she and her husband, Michael, would be around to talk about the article.

The rest of the morning he spent working through some leads for more information on the Weaver murder and a few other stories he was working on. About to get up and make himself a coffee, his mobile rang. He recognised the number. "Hi Sammy, how's everything?"

Sammy told him she was meeting Susan for lunch, a celebration of the end of the week and did he want to join them?

He glanced at the clock on the wall; a quarter to twelve, and gave it careful consideration for all of a nanosecond. "Okay, I'll see you then," he said, deciding a pint was more inviting than a coffee.

Tucked away on Swan Street, a narrow thoroughfare running parallel to The Headrow, was The White Swan pub, one of Souter's favourite areas of Leeds. In close proximity was another venue he loved, the delightful Horse and Trumpet; and between the two, the world-famous City Varieties Music Hall.

At just after half past twelve, he strolled in through the doors and spotted Sammy and Susan sitting at a table. The place was buzzing, people standing around, dozens of conversations going on and the odd outbreak of raucous laughter. He caught their eye and mimed the offer of drinks. They both shook their heads, Sammy holding up her glass of white wine and Susan her half of lager.

At the long narrow bar he selected a pint of Leeds Brewery bitter and ordered himself a steak pie chips and peas. Indicating where he'd be sitting, the barmaid said someone would bring his food over.

He made his way through the throng to join the girls at their table and sat down.

"Susan tells me you've managed to get her involved in the interview of Claire Hobson's parents," Sammy said, once he'd placed his pint on a mat.

"I managed with a bit of persuasion," Souter said, a wry smile on his face.

Susan leaned forward. "So what do we know?"

Souter summarised what he'd been able to ascertain from the archives. Nobody now on the Post team had been around when the murder occurred in 1982.

"So we're focusing on the effect that the unsolved crime has had on the family," Susan said, more of a statement than a question.

"That'll be one of the aims, yes. The other, of course will be to appeal for new information."

"After all this time?" Sammy was disbelieving.

The conversation was interrupted by food being brought to the girls. "Yours is just coming," the waitress said to Souter.

He waited until the waitress had retreated. "You'd be surprised," he said. "Situations change. Wives and girlfriends who aren't close to boyfriends or husbands any more perhaps remember something that didn't add up around that time. They no longer feel they have loyalties they once had or the need to give them the benefit of any doubts."

"Yes I can see that," Susan said.

Another interruption as Souter's plate was delivered. "Thanks, love," he said.

"And what about the lads who found her," Sammy wondered. "Are you planning on speaking to them?"

"They were only nine and ten. We didn't identify them and Chandler hasn't said anything about them, only to concentrate on the Hobson family."

"I'll bet Colin will know who they are," Susan added.

"I'm not speaking to him about that," Souter snapped. "He's still a bit pissed off with me with that business last year. Besides, I'm not sure he could go digging around an old case like that, not without drawing attention to himself. No, we'll just do what Chandler has asked." He took a swig of his pint.

Susan looked at Sammy who gave a small shrug.

"Sorry," Souter said. "I didn't mean to bite your head off."

"That's okay," Susan said. "I understand if things are still a bit raw."

Souter chose to ignore her comment and tucked into his meal. After a few minutes of silence, he spoke again. "Any further gossip from your office, Sammy? Alison said you thought Weaver might have been having an affair with a woman who works there."

Sammy lined up her knife and fork having finished her meal and took a sip of wine before answering. "There are a couple of possibilities, thinking about it."

"Busy man," Susan remarked.

"No, I'm not saying both of them. But I'll do a bit more detective work; see what I can pick up."

The rest of the lunchtime break was spent chatting about what Susan had to do to complete her coursework for the second year of her Broadcast Journalism course and what Alison had to look forward to with the birth of the baby.

20

Brannigan watched as the young man left the hairdressing salon; this time, no holdall. He still couldn't shake the feeling that he'd seen him before. He might not even have been calling on Felicity but his suspicions were aroused.

He waited for another five minutes before crossing the road and entering the shop. Sharon approached him as he came in. "Have you an appointment, sir?" she enquired.

He could see Felicity looking at him in the mirror in front of her chair as she wrapped her client's head in a towel.

Conscious of his bald head, he resisted the temptation to ask if she was taking the piss. Instead, he took a breath and said, "I've just come in for a word with my step-daughter." He nodded towards her.

"Felicity's a bit tied up at the moment, could you come back later?" Sharon replied.

"If you have a seat for ten minutes, George," Felicity said from the other side of the floor, "I can spare a few minutes when Mrs Crowther is under the drier,"

Sharon turned to Felicity and glowered. "Only if you're sure, Felicity. You're first priority is your client."

Brannigan sat watching his step-daughter perform her skills on the middle-aged woman in the chair. Now and again he'd catch a nervous glance from her in his direction, in between the endless chatter from the woman. He could tell she wasn't paying much attention to what the woman was saying.

Eventually, with Mrs Crowther under the drier obscuring any further talk from her, Felicity led Brannigan into the staff room.

As soon as the door was closed, she turned to face him. "Look, what do you want? You shouldn't be coming here," she said.

"What do I want? What do I want?" He was incensed but kept his voice low. "I just shelled out thirty grand yesterday because someone kidnapped you. What do you think I want? I want some bloody answers."

Felicity began to pace the small room. "Well I've none to give. I have no idea who was responsible. I was kept somewhere with a blindfold and my arms and legs were taped up the whole time."

"You know more than that and I want to find out who was behind this."

She was up close to him now. "I'll tell you what I know, shall I? I know you nearly cocked things up on Wednesday night. I heard how angry and annoyed they were. I heard them on the phone to you."

"They? So there was more than one?"

She shook her head. "No. I mean I don't know, it's just a figure of speech. Anyway, what I want to know is what happened in those toilets? Apart from the fact that some bloke is dead. Andy showed me the paper. I hope you didn't drag him into any of that. Was that you and your temper again."

He raised his hands.

"That's right, thump me like you used to thump Mum."

He stopped, arms in mid-air then slowly turned his hands to his forehead then rubbed his eyes. A grin began to appear on his face. "Always could wind me up," he said. "The pair of you."

"What's going on in here?" Sharon burst in to the staff room. "I can hear all these raised voices. Just as well the ladies are all under the driers now."

"It's okay, Sharon," Felicity said. "My step-dad is under a bit of pressure at the moment. He's a bit upset."

Sharon looked from Felicity to Brannigan and back again. "Well this really isn't the time or the place."

"Sorry, Sharon."

The owner seemed to calm down. "Well, I don't know what's been going on with you Felicity," she said. "But something's not right. I saw Andy drop you off then your cousin visits you and now your step-dad. This isn't good for business."

"It's okay," Felicity said, "George is just going."

Brannigan nodded slowly. Of course, the young lad – he was sure he recognised him; her cousin, what was his name now? "We'll need to talk some more," he said. "But you're right." He addressed Sharon, "I apologise. This is the wrong place to talk." He turned to Felicity. "I'll catch you later."

Brannigan walked calmly from the salon, confident that all was not as it had seemed just a few days before. He'd have to track down Felicity's cousin. His thoughts travelled to Veronica, his late wife, Felicity's mum. Three years he'd been on his own now. Despite all Felicity said, he missed her mother dreadfully.

A car tooted its horn as he took a step into the road. He was about to gesture then thought better of it, raising a hand in apology. He crossed behind it and turned up a side street to collect his car. That cousin, he must be Veronica's sister's lad. That would be his next priority, he needed to track him down.

He was about to climb into his BMW when his mobile rang. He looked and recognised a customer's number. Shit, he thought, he'd an appointment in Huddersfield in half an hour. Despite all that had been going on, he still had a business to run. The lad would have to wait, for now.

Early evening and George Brannigan took a sip of one of his favourite single malt whiskies. He replaced the glass alongside the Talisker bottle on the table beside his chair. Classical music was playing softly from his stereo system as he turned over the events of the past few days in his mind. He regretted what happened to that bloke who walked in on them in the public toilets on Wednesday evening. But it wasn't really his fault. Who goes to a place like that at that time of night without some dodgy purpose? It was a natural mistake, thinking he was the one come to collect. How was he to know that the one blow he struck would be fatal? He blamed his army training for that. Twelve years in the Green Howards; happy days.

But things didn't add up. Felicity wasn't telling him everything. He didn't go for all that upset she was keen to display and not remembering; she was stronger than that. God, she and her mother lived with him for over ten years, of course he knew her character. Always was a tough little sod, and then she grew up. Precocious little madam when he first met her mother. Felicity didn't make it easy for his relationship. Slowly, Veronica won her round, but she was always apt to put in the odd word of criticism that made him angry.

He'd need to speak to her again. And then there was that younger lad he saw visit the salon today, her cousin. He remembered his name now – Mark. He'd been at Felicity and Andy's wedding. And what did Andy know? She must have told him what happened to her? He could try him on his own too. Now Mark, he was sure he was Veronica's sister's lad. He'd never mixed much with Veronica's family. They lived in Wakefield but he wasn't sure where. Of course they came to the funeral. But hold on, Lupset rang a bell. Was that where Mark lived? Bloody coincidence that that's where he had to make the drop on Thursday. And that little shit on a bike; he'd only be doing a job for whoever was behind this. Thirty grand. Thirty big ones he'd been taken for.

Veronica kept an address book. Now where was it? He rose, walked to the bureau and opened the second drawer. After rummaging towards the back for a few seconds, he drew out a book decorated in flowered paper. Back in his chair, he began to flick through the pages. Bingo!

He glanced at his watch then looked to the whisky bottle. Half past seven and he'd only had the one glass.

No time like the present, he thought, stood up switched off the stereo and grabbed his car keys.

21
Saturday 16th February 2002

Susan drove to Alison's house in Ossett at lunchtime. Sammy came with her too, wanting to spend some time with Alison.

"Have a quick look through these," Souter said to Susan, handing her the copies of the news reports Phyllis had organised for him. "The family moved from the house where they lived on the Lupset Estate a year or so after Claire died. They're now in a council house just off Flanshaw Lane."

At ten past two, Souter set off from Alison's with Susan alongside. The rain grew heavy again and lashed the windscreen as he drove down Dewsbury Road towards town. He turned right onto Townley Road.

"Where are we going?" Susan asked.

"I thought we'd have a look at their old house," he said. "Just to absorb."

Bare trees lined the street. It would be a month or two before leaves would sprout. A few turns and they came to a road where the pebble-dash rendered houses changed to red brick-built ones, giving a warmer feel. Finally, he drew his Ford Escort to a halt outside number twenty-seven.

"Is this it?" Susan asked looking to her left.

"No, it's over there," Souter replied, indicating the right hand one of a pair of semi-detached houses opposite. "Number Thirty."

They looked at the house with net curtains at the windows, half-glazed timber front door and neatly cut privet hedge.

"Looks well-cared for," Susan said.

After a few seconds, Souter set off again; a few more left and right turns

"Where are we going now?" Susan asked.

A minute later, Souter had stopped again, this time outside a pebble-dash rendered property. "Number seventeen," he said, "Home of Claire's friend, Sally Green."

Susan turned to look at him. "So are we talking to her?"

"Could be a bit difficult, she's married and living in Australia now. But I thought it important to see how close, or far apart the two girls lived. On the Friday night, Claire left Sally's at five to ten to be back home as her parents had insisted by ten o'clock."

"Only she never arrived," Susan said, wistfully.

Souter set off again and ten minutes later drew to a halt outside another red brick council house, this time about a mile away on the Flanshaw estate.

"Ready?" Souter asked.

Susan gave a slight nod and reached for the door handle.

Souter opened one of the gates to the driveway and walked to the front door past a blue Vauxhall Astra parked on the hardstanding. Fortunately, the rain had eased to a light drizzle. Before they reached the door, it was opened by a woman in her late fifties, around five feet four inches tall with short grey hair and glasses. She pulled a cardigan around herself as she spoke.

"Mr Souter?" she asked.

"Bob Souter, yes," he replied. "Mrs Hobson, this is my colleague Susan Brown."

"Come in," she said and stood to one side.

Souter and Susan waited for the woman to close the front door then show them in to a comfortably furnished front room. A man of around sixty years of age stood up from an easy chair he'd been sitting in, TV remote in hand. He switched off the set in the corner and introduced himself. "Michael Hobson," he said. "I'm not sure what you can achieve after all this time. This was my wife's idea."

"Mike, don't be so negative," the woman said. "Please sit down." She indicated the settee. "Can I get you something to drink? Tea? Coffee?"

"No thanks, Mrs Hobson, we're fine." Souter and Susan sat down.

"Please, call me Louise," she said.

Michael resumed his seat and Souter couldn't help but think he looked dead behind the eyes. When he'd stood up, he guessed he was around six feet tall but he had a large beer belly and a buzzed head.

"Thanks for agreeing to see us, Louise ... Michael." He looked to the man in an effort to include him in the conversation. "I think it's a good idea to bring your situation back to the public's attention. Twenty years is a significant anniversary."

Michael snorted. "After all this time, I don't see what can possibly be gained by raking all this up." He sat further back in his chair. "It's only going to satisfy all these weirdos who get off on reliving other people's hurt."

"I do understand your concerns, Michael, if I can call you Michael?" An imperceptible nod from the man. "But like I was discussing with my colleague here, things can change in twenty years. Someone who has some vital piece of information might now realise its significance or might not now have reason to withhold that." Souter could see Mr Hobson was unconvinced, so he moved on. "Could we start with some background information on Claire," he said, looking from Michael to Louise.

"She was just your typical teenager," Louise began, "Into her pop music. She had a thing about Paul Weller and The Jam; posters on her bedroom wall. But she was a young fourteen-year old."

Souter was taking notes.

"She was doing okay at school," Louise went on, "and she had a couple of friends she seemed close to; Sally, of course, Sally Green where she went that night." She broke off, pulling a piece of paper tissue from her cardigan sleeve and dabbing her eyes.

"This is what I mean," Michael jumped in. "All this is going to do is bring upset back to the surface."

That comment seemed to upset Louise more than talking about Claire.

Souter stopped writing.

She looked across at her husband earnestly. "But I need to find out what happened. I can't just live my life not knowing who was responsible."

"I'm going to the garage," Michael said, standing up and leaving the room.

Louise waited until he'd gone. "He's taken it hard. They were close, Claire and her dad." She turned to Souter. "He told me once how he felt he'd let her down, how he wasn't able to protect her like a father should. I told him that was nonsense but that's his logic, anyway."

"I do understand," Souter said, pausing for a second. "So on that Friday, Claire went to her friend, Sally's house?"

"That's right. She left home just after her tea, around seven. She was looking forward to listening to some new records Sally had bought, up in her room. We told her to be back by ten. It was something she'd done quite a few times before, or Sally or one of her other friends would come round to ours. It was only about a five-minute walk."

"She obviously got to Sally's alright," Souter prompted.

"Yes, Sally's parents were distraught when they heard Claire had never reached home. They'd seen her set off about five to ten."

"And they would be the last people to see Claire?" Souter deliberately left off the word 'alive'.

Another dab of the tissue to her eyes as Louise nodded.

"So when did you suspect something wasn't right?"

"As I said, she was pretty good in getting back when she said she would. We left it until the ten o'clock news had finished at half past. When she hadn't turned up by then, we rang Sally's. That's when alarm bells started ringing. Mike went out to look for her. He was out for over an hour. He'd asked a few people he saw if they'd seen her but he drew a blank."

"When did you call the police?"

"Must have been around midnight. They sent an officer round about one. She took a photo and description of Claire and said she'd get the patrols to look out for her. But it wasn't until the following lunchtime and she still hadn't shown up when we got the visit from the plain clothes people."

"Do you remember who attended?"

"I do, it was a DI Hartley and a female detective, DC Woods."

Souter screwed up his face. "Not names I'm familiar with," he said.

"After that," Louise went on, "things just seemed to happen in a blur. My Mum came round, I remember. Poor soul, she's passed on now. And when it got to Saturday night with no news, I was in pieces. Mike was out with a load of his mates scouring the streets, asking anyone they came across if they'd seen her. It must have been some time in the early hours before he came home. I was still awake. I couldn't sleep. And then ... Oh God." This time Louise broke down in floods of tears.

Souter saw that Susan was struggling to keep her emotions in check too.

"Look, Louise, if you'd prefer we left it for now – come back another time?"

The woman shook her head. "No." She recovered, reached for a fresh tissue from the box on a nearby unit and blew her nose. "I'd like to carry on."

For the first time Susan spoke. "Could I make you a cup of tea, Mrs Hobson?"

Louise got to her feet. "You know what, I'll do it and I'll make you two one as well. What would you like?"

Susan was about to get to her feet, insistent on making the drinks but Souter gave her arm a restraining touch. He felt Louise would benefit from the break as well as doing something she wanted to do. Susan settled for a coffee and Souter a tea. Whilst Louise was out of the room, he took the opportunity to study some of the photographs that were on display. In hushed tones, he said to Susan, "You can see how they're both coping."

"Except Mr Hobson isn't," Susan remarked.

"Grief handled in different ways."

22

Mavis Skinner had worked part-time at the 24/7 store on the corner of Dewsbury Road and Townley Road for the past five years. She'd had her fair share of drama with awkward customers, young thugs after some cigarettes or cash from the till, but overall, she'd enjoyed the experience. At over sixty years old she felt she was giving her life some purpose after her husband had died eight years ago. She liked to engage with the customers.

By ten past three, she had quite a collection of flattened cardboard boxes ready to be put in the waste bin at the back of the store. The rain that had lashed down for most of the day had eased.

"Just going to take these out," she said to her colleague behind the till.

Scooping up the cardboard, she paused at the doors as two uniformed police officers appeared. They stopped to let her out first.

"Thanks, Dennis," she said to the older of the two, a regular visitor to the shop.

"Here, let me help you with that, Mavis." Dennis stepped forward to take the load from her.

"I'm alright thanks. You need to get your fags and sweet supplies before you get a shout." She grinned at him.

As the two PCs went into the shop, Mavis walked down the side and turned again into the small service yard. Putting the cardboard on the tarmac, she raised the lid of the large blue bin then bent down to pick up the flattened boxes. As she threw them in, something inside caught her attention.

She leaned over and shuffled some of the cardboard out of the way. That's when she was sure.

She ran back into the shop. "Dennis!" she shouted. "Quickly, out here."

Flustered, she scurried back outside, PC Dennis Tate in quick pursuit.

Ten minutes later, the service yard was a flurry of activity, three marked cars with blue flashing lights.

They were quickly followed by a dark grey Mondeo. DI Colin Strong stepped out from the driver's side; the short stocky figure of DC Luke Ormerod appeared from the other.

Dennis Tate raised the blue plastic Police tape he'd just strung across the entrance. "Over here, sir," he said and led the way to the big bin with the lid open.

Strong peered inside. Lying on a bed of cardboard was the prone figure of a male, dressed in dark trousers, trainers and a puffa jacket. The left arm was stretched out with a watch exposed. The head was turned so that the left side was visible. Discolouration of the cheek and eye was clear, some blood traces from the nose and side of the mouth.

"Who found him, Dennis?" Strong asked.

"Mavis the older woman who works here came out to put some old boxes in the bin," the officer responded. "She's in the back office with my colleague."

Strong turned to Ormerod. "Is SOCO on their way?"

"Yes, guv. And the doc."

"Right, let's have a word with Mavis."

The store had been closed and an officer was guarding the door. In the office at the rear, Mavis Skinner nursed a mug of coffee alongside her workmate. The uniformed officer in attendance left the room when Strong appeared. He introduced himself and sat down opposite the women.

"I know this was a terrible shock for you Mavis, but I need to ask you a few questions."

Mavis appeared calm and nodded when Strong spoke.

"When you took out the waste, was that the first time today you'd been to the bins?"

"Yes." She looked to her colleague. "You didn't go out earlier, did you?"

"Not me, love."

"So, nobody has been in that area since yesterday?" Strong phrased it as a question.

Both women looked at each other and shook their heads.

"Is there CCTV for the rear yard?"

"For the shop, yes," Mavis answered, "but I'm not sure if the outside camera has been working for the past week. I think I heard Joe, he's the manager, saying he was waiting for someone to come and have a look at it. He'll tell you himself, he's on his way down. We thought it best to call him in."

"Good," Strong said. Before he could say any more, a knock on the door interrupted.

Luke Ormerod poked his head in. "Sorry, guv," he said. "Doc Symonds is here and Scenes of Crime too."

"Thanks, Luke. I'll be out in a minute." Strong turned back to the older woman. "We'll need to get a statement from you Mavis, if that's okay."

"Sure."

"And one last thing, did you see the man's face?" Mavis nodded briefly and looked away. "You didn't recognise him, did you? I mean, he's not been in the shop before?"

For the first time, Mavis looked visibly upset. "I'm sorry, Inspector. Whoever it is looked in a bad way. I couldn't say."

"That's fine." Strong stood up. "I'll get someone to take your statement and then you can go."

As he was about to leave, the other woman asked, "Can we open up the shop again, or is that not on?"

"I'm afraid you'll need to stay closed for a while longer. We'll let you know."

23

The living room door opened and Louise Hobson reappeared with a tray of steaming drinks.

Once Souter and Susan were settled back in their seats, he was keen to push on. "So how did you learn of the dreadful news on the Sunday, Louise?"

She took a sip of her tea before answering. "I saw a car pull up outside and watched as DI Hartley came up the path. DC Woods was with him. We had a policewoman staying with us and she opened the door to them." Louise paused and looked over at the framed photographs for a second then took a deep breath. "Mr Hartley and the woman asked me to sit down. Mike remained standing but soon crumbled when they told us they'd found a body." Tears filled her eyes and she looked directly at Souter. "I never want to feel like that ever again. And I don't want any other parent to experience that." She broke off and took another drink.

Souter and Susan said nothing, allowing the woman time to compose herself and resume her account when she was ready.

"Later, I also realised how horrible it must have been for those two boys, the ones who found her. Little Kenny Green was only nine and his friend Paul Nichols was ten. When I think how that must have affected them in later life." She looked distant for a second before focusing on Souter. "It was the Monday morning before they took us to Pinderfields to identify her. She looked so peaceful. It was as if she'd just fallen asleep. Only she'd never wake up again."

"Did the police have any suspects at the time?" Souter asked.

"No one they ever mentioned to us by name. I think there were one or two ... you know ..." She made a face. "Horrible men they questioned. But no, nobody serious."

"You moved from the house on Lupset," Souter stated.

"Yes. We didn't feel comfortable there anymore. It must have been about fourteen months after Claire ..." She left the sentence unfinished. "We talked about it as a family, Mike, Martin, Charlotte and myself. You know Claire had an older brother and a younger sister?"

Souter nodded.

"Martin works down south now, London. Doing well for himself. He was eighteen when it happened." She smiled. "He's married now, two children, Katy and Alison. And Charlotte, she was only twelve. I think it affected her more than Martin. As I said, Claire was a young fourteen and she and Charlotte were quite close, similar tastes in music and both quite sporty."

Souter jotted down a few more notes then looked up. "Do you think they'd talk to me? Martin and Charlotte, I mean. It would give another dimension to any article."

"I think they might. I'll ask them and get them to give you a call, if that's okay?"

"Sure. We've got some time to put this together and Mr Chandler ... I believe you spoke to him initially at the Post?"

Louise nodded.

"I'm sure he'll want to keep the timing of any publication fluid for best effect."

"Of course," she said.

So we've got some following up to do on this now," Susan remarked as Souter pulled the car away from the kerb.

"Martin will be a telephone call. She didn't say where Charlotte is now. I'll follow that up with a call to Louise next week."

Susan shuffled through the photocopies Phyllis had produced. She'd left them in the car whilst they were talking to the Hobsons. "Strange," she said. "The story seemed to drop out of the news fairly quickly afterwards."

"I think the investigation stalled. And then don't forget the events that swamped it, "Souter said as they drew to a halt at a set of traffic lights.

Susan looked puzzled. "How d'you mean?"

"South Georgia was invaded by the Argies a couple of weeks later; and then The Falklands. After that, the war was in full swing; the news was dominated by it."

The lights changed and he swung right onto Dewsbury Road to head back out to Ossett. As he drove, activity ahead on the left-hand side of the road caught his attention. "'ello, 'ello, 'ello," he said, mimicking Dixon of Dock Green. "What's going on here?"

An array of police vehicles, all with flashing blue lights were parked up outside the convenience store. Souter slowed then spotted a car he recognised. He indicated left then turned onto the side street. He managed to find a space about thirty yards up. "Stay here a minute, Susan," he said.

Her hand was on the door handle in a flash. "No way," she responded. "I'm just as nosey as you."

He approached one of the constables, Susan at his shoulder. "Something serious, Officer?"

"Just move on please, sir."

Souter spotted a familiar figure emerging from the shop doorway. Leaving the constable, he walked towards his friend. "Colin, what's going on?"

"Christ, are you tuned in to the police radios?" Strong responded.

"Would you believe, just passing."

"Right." A look of disbelief passed over Strong's face then altered to one of annoyance. "Well there's nothing I can tell you at the moment."

A black private ambulance pulled up as they spoke.

"So who's been killed?" Souter persisted.

Strong took his friend by the elbow and led him away from the shop. "Look Bob, I've only just got here. Do me a favour and just disappear for now. I'll give you a call when I can."

Susan had watched the conversation between Souter and Strong then caught sight of a young woman, leaving the shop and putting her arms into the sleeves of her jacket. She could see her company overall beneath. Taking her chance, she slipped unnoticed past the two men.

"Hi," she said to the woman. "What's going on? Is the shop closed?"

"Oh, drama this afternoon," the shop girl replied. "I don't think we'll be open until tomorrow at the earliest."

"So what's happened?"

"Mavis, one of the women who works here, she found a body in one of the bins."

Susan put her hand to her mouth in a gesture of exaggerated shock. "Oh no, that's dreadful. Do they know who he is?"

The woman shook her head. "Whoever he was has been given a good hiding Mavis said but she didn't recognise him." She fiddled with the zip on her jacket.

"Is Mavis still around?"

"She's still in the shop giving a statement."

"Have the police said anything about how he died or how he ended up in the bin?" Susan asked.

The woman stopped what she was doing and screwed up her eyes as if looking at Susan for the first time. "You seem to ask a lot of questions," she said.

Susan gave a shrug. "Sorry, don't mind me, I'm just always interested in what's going on."

The woman held Susan's gaze for a second before turning away without another word.

Susan watched her flip up the hood on her jacket and hurry away.

Just then, Souter approached her. "Find out anything?" he asked.

"A body in the bin apparently," Susan said. "Given a pasting but they don't know who the victim is."

"Colin said he'd call me later. Sounds like a murder case though." Souter grinned. "And here we are, first on the scene. I'll jot down a few notes and call the newsroom. Come on, let's go." He began to walk back to his car.

"Hold on," Susan said. "Don't need to be too hasty."

Walking back, he looked at her, intrigued. "What are you thinking?"

"I think we should hang about a bit longer." She looked around at the growing number of onlookers. "We might get a bit more."

No one paid any attention to the little lad who looked about twelve, riding a bike that seemed too small for him, baseball cap turned back to front. He rode around at the back of the crowd, watching what was going on but saying nothing to anyone.

Just as a serious looking man in his forties with a bald pate pulled up in an Audi and walked to the shop, the young lad moved nearer to Souter and Susan, stared at them for a second or two then rode off into the estate.

Five minutes later, Mavis emerged. Susan took her chance and approached her. "Mavis, is it?" she asked.

The woman looked at Susan and then to Souter standing alongside. "Who wants to know?"

Before Susan could answer, Souter jumped in. "My name's Bob Souter, we're from the Yorkshire Post," he said.

At least he said 'we', Susan thought.

"Press?"

"Could you spare us a few minutes?" Souter asked.

"I'm not sure," Mavis responded. "I need to get home."

"We could give you a lift?" Souter offered.

She considered for a moment then nodded. "Okay, it's not far."

24

A quarter to five, just as the football results would be coming through on the televisions and radios of the nation, Colin Strong stood in front of the group of detectives called in to the CID Incident room. DCI Hemingford was in Manchester and DCS Flynn in London. Those were the results of his phone calls and so it fell to him to start organising the latest murder enquiry. Two in the same week piled the pressure on the team. 'Keep things calm until I get back on Monday morning,' Hemingford had said.

The photos from Wednesday's incident in the park were prominent on the two display boards at one end of the room. Now, along one side, another board was being set up with pictures from this afternoon's find in the bin behind the shop on Dewsbury Road.

"First priority," Strong began, "we need to identify our victim. Initial feeling is he is in his twenties. Severe head injuries consistent with a prolonged beating."

"No identification on him, guv?" one detective asked.

"Initial search of his pockets provided some loose change and some keys. No wallet," Strong responded. "The other thing we need to establish, well two really, is time of death and when he was deposited in the waste bin."

"According to Mavis Skinner, the shop worker who found him, nobody had been round to that bin all day, so he must have been dumped some time between eleven last night and six this morning," Luke Ormerod added. "I spoke to the shop manager and he tells me the CCTV camera for the yard had stopped functioning last Thursday and he's waiting for the security company to come out to it on Monday."

"Shit, so we've got nothing from that." Strong was frustrated. "Who's on door to door?"

"Uniform have a team conducting that," Ormerod replied.

"Get them to see if there are any cameras in the area," Strong said. "A long shot I know but I think we might need everything on this one."

Ormerod jotted a note.

"We've also got a team of uniforms doing a fingertip search of the yard," one of the team said.

"And the PM is scheduled for tomorrow morning," Strong informed them. "So Luke, you and I will cover that."

"What about Kelly, guv?" Ormerod wondered.

"I thought we'd leave her to enjoy her weekend off for now. She'll come in fresh on Monday."

"Might be pissed off she's missing the action."

"Hardly action," Strong said. "In the meantime, let's check any missing persons reports; see if any could tally with our victim." He looked at the board before turning back to his team. "And taxi drivers. Check with all the local firms. Did any of their drivers see anything suspicious last night in the vicinity of the shop or on the Lupset estate itself? There's usually a fair taxi trade there. Okay, that's it for now. Anything comes up, let me know straight away."

He left the room, fetched himself a coffee and returned to his office. He stood for a minute looking out the window to the Town Hall opposite, the rain driving into the windows. Plenty to think about. He sat down and took a sip of his drink, surprising himself that he still persisted with the drinks machine.

His thoughts drifted to the previous afternoon when he and Kelly returned to Weaver's office to speak to his other work colleague. They'd waited again in the smart reception area for a few minutes before a short, overweight man in his late thirties appeared and introduced himself as Bill Crossley. No fancy upper floor office this time, merely a functional meeting room behind the photocopiers.

When it came down to it, Crossley had his suspicions but couldn't throw any light on who Weaver had been seeing. According to him, it wasn't anyone in the department but that wasn't to say it couldn't have been someone else in the office. After all, he told them, the company was spread over four floors and seven different departments.

And so Strong was no further forward on Weaver's clandestine meeting partner.

He was rubbing his face with both hands, trying to bring his eyes back into focus when Ormerod knocked on his door. Strong beckoned him in.

"Guv, we have an identity," he said.

"Who?"

Ormerod consulted the sheet of paper he had in his hands. "Mark Thompson, twenty-three years of age and an address in town, near Kirkgate station."

"Anything known?"

"Previous for shoplifting, but that was as a juvenile. Lived on the Lupset estate then. Identified by his fingerprints."

25

"You'll never guess," Susan blurted out, as soon as she stepped over the threshold of Alison's house.

"What are you so excited about?" Alison asked. She was laid out on the settee nursing a mug of tea that Sammy had made for her.

Sammy walked in from the kitchen. "Go on then, spill," she said.

Souter ignored the women's enthusiasm and made his way to the kitchen. After time standing out in the cold and on his phone in the car to the newsroom, he needed the comfort of a hot drink. Whilst Susan related events on Dewsbury Road, he turned over in his mind thoughts of his conversation with Claire Hobson's mother. There wasn't really much of an intercourse with her father. He wondered about trying to speak to him again. Would that be welcomed? Possibly not, but he'd like to make at least one further attempt to get him to open up. Perhaps that was the difference between men and women; men struggled to talk about things that had such a devastating effect on their lives. Women were more open. Or was that just a stereotype? If it was, he certainly wouldn't like to be accused of biasing any article on that narrow-minded thinking.

The kettle clicked off and he poured water onto the tea bag in his mug. The chatter from the living room continued.

And then there were the two boys who'd found Claire's body. Were they still in the area? He'd start looking into that on Monday.

When he walked back into the front room, Susan was concluding her account of the afternoon's events. "I tell you," she said, "talk about right place, right time."

"And you've no idea who the victim is?" Sammy asked.

Susan shook her head. "Not yet. Bob will no doubt be on to Colin for more information. Mavis, who found him, didn't recognise him. We gave her a lift home but there wasn't anything else she could add."

"Look, I know this is all so interesting for you," Alison said, "but can we drop this gory subject."

"So what's for tea?" Souter asked.

Alison threw a cushion at him then closed her eyes.

Whilst Souter thumbed through the collection of take away menus that had been accumulated, pinned to the cork board in the kitchen, Susan spoke quietly to Sammy.

"You know you've got a certain reputation," she said.

Sammy's eyes opened wide.

"Your internet skills in finding people," Susan added quickly.

"These two lads?" Sammy responded, "The ones who found Claire's body?"

Susan nodded.

"You've got names?"

Susan handed her friend a piece of paper.

"No problem, leave that with me."

"How about a pizza?" Souter said, emerging from the kitchen with a menu in his hand. "Segundo's?"

26

By the time Strong got home, it was gone eight o'clock. He'd spent a difficult hour, along with Luke Ormerod, at Mark Thompson's mother's house to break the bad news and gather some initial information. He hated these visits. Leaving an experienced Family Liaison Officer with them, they would be back the following day.

Laura had kept a meal warm for him in the oven. He'd been ravenous. Now replete, he was lying on the settee in the living room, eyes closed, thinking.

"Dad, do you want a cup of tea?" Amanda shouted from the kitchen. She then appeared in the doorway. "Mum's asking."

He opened his eyes. "Great. Thanks, love," he replied, then before she could disappear again, "Hey! How's the course going?"

Home for the weekend from Manchester where she'd started her course last October, she stood for a second, studying him. "It's okay, but you look tired, Dad."

"Do I?"

"Everything alright?"

"Just things to think through, that's all."

She put her hands on her hips, but her look was soft. "You made the right decision, you know; to carry on."

"I know."

She turned and left.

He knew she was right. But he also knew he couldn't have carried on without the family's support. He realised he was being selfish by even considering moving abroad, but he did like Gran Canaria, and the villas they'd been shown last December were outstanding. But he also realised his was a knee-jerk reaction to all that had happened in September. And then there was Laura, his rock. She loved her job and she was now in line for the headship at the school where she'd been deputy for the past five years. Also it would have been intolerable to have disrupted Amanda's studies. She was obviously enjoying the experience of student life. Then there was Graham, in his final year at Hull on a History course

A few minutes later, Laura walked in with two mugs. "Here, she's right you know, you do look exhausted."

He sat up and made space for her on the settee while she handed him his drink. "It's just these cases," he said. "It's been a while since we had two murder investigations running at the same time."

She sat beside him and cupped her mug in both hands. "And the other two, Flynn and Hemingford they're nowhere to be seen?"

"Well the DCS is down in London. That's a long-standing arrangement I knew about but Rupert is in Manchester, apparently. I only found out today. 'Every confidence in you,' he says, 'just keep things on an even keel until Monday.'" Strong's tone implied exactly what he thought of those remarks.

Laura raised her eyebrows and sipped her drink. "Do you think he's up to something?"

"Like what?"

"I don't know, but you mentioned something the other day about him not being interested."

"Did I? Well, yes I suppose I did … I mean do."

"And that's what's testing you?"

"Amongst other things, yes." He took a drink, placed the mug on a mat on the table beside him and rubbed his eyes. "Anyway, are you prepared for Tuesday?" he asked, referring to her interview for the headship.

"As well as I can be."

"You'll walk it. They'd be daft not to give it to you. You know the place inside out; you've acted up when the head was away."

"I can't approach it that way," she replied. "I thought they should have made your acting DCI role permanent but they didn't. And I wasn't the only one to share that opinion."

"Oh … well," was about all he could say. He leaned back again and thought how bitterly disappointed he'd been last year when, after acting up as DCI for almost a year, the powers that be had brought Rupert Hemingford in as DCI from outside. That was another factor that had caused him to consider his future in the job.

He stood and picked up his drink. "Look, I'm going up. I'll need to be up and about early tomorrow with all that's happening."

"Go on," she said, "I'll not be long."

Laura watched her husband leave and heard his slow footsteps on the stairs.

27
Sunday 17th February 2002

"Why don't we go out for a drive, Andy?" Felicity was lounging on the settee in the flat on Sunday morning. She'd avoided giving him any further details surrounding her ordeal.

Andy wandered in from the kitchen, still in pyjamas, scooping some cornflakes into his mouth from the bowl he was carrying. He sat down at the small dining table by the window. "Is that so we're not in when George comes calling?"

"No," she said indignantly.

"Because he will. He's still looking for answers." Another mouthful of cereal. "And so am I."

"I just thought it would be good to get away from this place for a while. I mean look," she pointed to a corner by the side of the window. "That wallpaper has been peeling off for the best part of a year at least. And I'll bet it's damp. She sat up straight, looking alert. "Have you never thought how good it would be to get our own place. I don't mean one we rent but actually buy?"

Another mouthful of cornflakes. "Of course, that's why we're saving up isn't it?"

"But have you never wondered how it might be to leave all this behind? Move right away where nobody knows us and start again. Somewhere new. A fresh start."

He gave a disparaging laugh. "Oh yeah, great. We just walk out with no job, no place to stay, no friends."

"We haven't got that many friends here. Besides, you can get a job anywhere in construction. They'll always need someone like you. And I can style hair anywhere." She snapped her fingers. "London. There's always plenty going on down there."

"And how much do you think we'd need to be able to make that move? We'll end up in a shit hole down there that'll make this place look five star and paying double what we do here." He put another spoonful in his mouth. "Anyway, as I said before you tried to divert me, I still want some answers for what happened to you."

"Oh Andy ..." She laid back and closed her eyes. "I've told you all I know. I can't remember any more details."

He scraped the bottom of the bowl. "Not even where you were held; a warehouse, a garage, a flat? You must have some idea."

"I think it was a flat. He sat me on a chair for most of the time."

He looked over to her. "What about going to the toilet."

"I was allowed ..." She stopped as her mobile phone rang. She looked at the screen and pressed a button. "Aunty June, how are you?" she said.

Andy watched her expression change from one of delight to one of concern then one of fright. He stood and took a pace towards her. 'What's up?' he mouthed.

She held up a hand. "When was this?" then, "Oh God, have they said what happened?"

Andy could hear the indistinguishable voice talking through the phone. Finally, it stopped.

Felicity moved her mouth to speak but no sound came out. A tear ran down her cheek. Eventually, she said, "Thanks for letting me know." She pressed another button then buried her face in her hands and began to sob uncontrollably.

Andy moved forward and wrapped her in his arms. "Felicity ... love ... what's happened?"

Her body rocked and loud gasps emerged between large howls.

"Come on, you can tell me," Andy persisted.

"It's ... it's Mark."

"Your cousin? What about him?"

"He's dead." More sobs. "They found him ... in a waste bin at the back of the convenience shop ... on Dewsbury Road."

"God, Felicity. In a waste bin? Does that mean …?"

"Someone murdered him." She wiped her eyes on her sleeve and sniffed. "And I've a good idea who."

28

"Mrs Thompson ... June," Strong addressed the distressed woman in front of him. "Can you tell me the last time you saw Mark?"

He and Luke Ormerod had returned to the neat semi-detached house on the Lupset estate where Mark Thompson's mother still lived with her other son and daughter. They'd arrived directly from Pinderfields where they'd both attended Mark Thompson's post mortem. Strong only hoped the aroma from the chemicals of the mortuary hadn't lingered on their clothes.

With her daughter and younger son sitting on the arms of the chair on either side of their mother, protective arms around her, June Thompson struggled with her emotions. "Like I told you last night," she said, in between sobs, "he called in to see me on Friday tea time."

"That's right," Becky put in. "He turned up about half five and was gone by seven." Rebecca – Becky, Mark's younger sister, was an attractive girl of nineteen. She appeared to be holding things together for the three of them. Edward, Mark's brother, was fourteen and struggling with the news.

Mrs Thompson put her arm around her son and drew his head close to hers and the pair cried uncontrollably.

Becky stood up and suggested they leave her mother and brother for a while and continue the conversation in the kitchen.

Strong and Ormerod followed her, leaving the female FLO with June and Edward.

Refusing Becky's offer of a drink, they sat at the small kitchen table. "I'm sorry to have to ask these questions Becky," Strong said.

The girl nodded. "It's fine. Anything that'll help catch who did this to Mark."

Strong leaned forward, hands on the table. "So you were here when Mark visited on Friday?"

"Yes." Becky swept her long blonde hair behind both ears with her hands. "He'd spoken to Mum on the phone earlier and brought fish and chips for us. We sat and ate them on our laps watching TV."

"And everything seemed as normal?"

The girl hesitated. "I think so ... although ..."

"Something?"

"He was in here with Mum for a while – before they came in with the food – and, thinking about it now, Mum seemed a bit, I don't know, uncomfortable, I suppose."

"And Mark?"

She screwed up her face. "I suppose a bit pre-occupied I think I'd describe it as."

"You haven't spoken to your mother about it?"

"No, it's only just struck me now."

Strong leaned back, thoughtful. "Mark left home a few months ago, I understand?"

"Just after Christmas. He thought it best to get himself somewhere in town, a bit of independence, he said."

"Was that a surprise?"

"Not really. I mean he is twenty-three ..." Becky cracked. "I mean was ..." She stood and turned away from the table, pulled a piece of kitchen roll from the holder on the wall and sobbed.

Strong and Ormerod said nothing, just waited.

Finally, she wiped her eyes and faced them. "I'm sorry," she said. "I think he wanted to be closer to his work and have somewhere with a bit of privacy. He was a healthy boy. It isn't easy to ... to have a private life with all of us living here."

"I understand." Strong gave a brief smile. "Did Mark have a girlfriend, do you know?"

She shook her head. "I don't think so, not at the moment."

From outside in the hallway, noisy footsteps could be heard ascending the stairs. A second later, the door opened and June Thompson entered, the FLO close behind.

"He's taken it hard," she said. "Since their dad walked out, Mark sort of stepped into his shoes. Edward looked up to him."

"Do we know where Mr Thompson is now?" Strong asked. "Someone will need ..."

"He died. Six months ago now."

Ormerod stood up. "Please, Mrs Thompson," he said, indicating his chair.

She gave a swift smile then sat down.

"Becky here was just telling us about Friday evening," Strong said. "How was Mark when you spoke then?"

June Thompson looked sharply at her daughter then down at her hands.

"Mrs Thompson?" Strong persisted. "Was everything alright?"

She looked across once again at Becky before standing and walking to one of the cupboards above the worktop over the fridge. She opened a door and reached inside, drawing out a tin box. Opening it, she pulled a wad of banknotes from it. "He gave me this," she said. "Five hundred pounds."

"Mum," Becky cried out, "Where did he get that?"

"He said he'd done a favour for a mate," June said.

"What sort of favour would be worth five hundred pounds?"

"I don't know, Becky. I just hope to God this wasn't the cause of his death."

The girl looked at the cash before thinking of something else. "But don't forget Uncle George turned up later too." She looked to Strong and explained, "Well, he's not my real uncle. He was looking for Mark, you said."

June made a face. "I told him nothing, horrible man." She looked at Strong. "He was married to my sister Veronica. God knows what she ever saw in him." She shook her head. "Veronica died nearly three years ago now. She was only fifty. A brain tumour, but he made her life hell for the last few years."

"I'm sorry to hear that, Mrs Thompson," Strong said.

"It's Felicity I felt sorry for. But she did well and got out of there before her mother passed on. Married a nice lad, Andy."

"So Felicity is George's daughter?"

"Oh no, Felicity was Veronica's by Dave, but he died when she was seven. Tragic really, Dave was a good man but he was killed in a road accident. No, Veronica took up with George and then married him about ten years before she died."

Strong had flipped open his notebook. "And this George ..."

"Brannigan. George Brannigan," June Thompson answered.

"... George Brannigan, he turned up here on Friday evening looking for Mark?"

"That's right."

"And what time was that?"

Mrs Thompson looked to her daughter. "It must have been about ... ooh, just gone eight?"

"I think so," Becky affirmed. "Maybe about ten past."

"Did he say why he wanted Mark?"

"Only something about having a bit of work for him," Mrs Thompson said. "He said he might be able to do him a favour."

"Someone else who wanted Mark to do a favour for," Strong remarked. "Becky said he'd moved into a flat in town earlier this year. Did you tell Mr Brannigan that?"

"No, I wasn't going to tell him anything. I just said he wasn't in and was staying with mates. I didn't want Mark to get involved with the likes of Brannigan."

"This George Brannigan, what does he do? Do you have an address?"

"I don't but he has his own scrap metal business over in Huddersfield. Should be easy to find."

29
Monday 18th February 2002

"Mark Thompson," DCI Hemingford began, "Discovered on Saturday afternoon in a re-cycling bin behind a convenience store on Dewsbury Road." He waved a hand past several photos pinned to the action board. "Twenty-three years old, lived in a flat on South Street near Kirkgate railway station. Moved out from the family home he shared with mother, June who's divorced and still living in the house on Lupset, not far from where the body was found." Hemingford looked round the assembled team. "So, let's start with the PM."

Strong gave a slight shift of the head in Ormerod's direction.

Ormerod took his cue. "DI Strong and myself attended yesterday morning, sir," he said, producing his notebook. "Cause of death was due to a massive haematoma on the brain produced by a blunt force trauma. Samples of man-made fibres and particles of brick dust found in the wounds to the back of the head, so possibly smacked with a brick and man-handled by someone wearing gloves afterwards."

"Or thrust against a wall?" Hemingford pondered aloud.

"Plenty of them nearby," Ormerod murmured.

Before Hemingford could respond, Strong jumped in. "And no material under the fingernails I'm afraid," he said.

Hemingford stared at Ormerod for a second before turning his attention to Strong. "So what other enquires have been carried out?"

Strong listed off the tasks that had been organised since the victim had been discovered – fingertip search of the service yard, a search for any CCTV footage, house-to-house enquiries, a search for potential witnesses and background enquiries. Various members of the team outlined what stage those enquiries were at.

It was reported that the search of the yard had produced nothing useful and John Darby chipped in that the uniformed team had come up with nothing significant from their door-to-door enquiries. Sam Kirkland had trawled the area for CCTV footage and was working through that with Trevor Newell. He repeated what the shop manager had already told them, that the camera to the rear yard was defective. They'd located several cameras nearby but none from any of the nearby houses, which wasn't surprising given their council-owned status. So far, nothing of any significance had revealed itself but the process was ongoing.

"So basically, we've got Jack Shit." Hemingford sounded exasperated.

Strong and Ormerod exchanged glances. To Strong, Hemingford was wound up about something. This wasn't the usual frustrations of the early days on a case. "Well, Luke and myself visited his mother on Saturday evening, and again yesterday," he said. "Obviously a huge shock. We didn't get too much from her then – she'd last seen him on Friday evening when he'd called to see her at tea time. Two things she and her daughter, Becky, told us were interesting. Firstly, Mark gave his mother five hundred pounds when he called on Friday; said something about having done a favour for a mate. And secondly, Mrs Thompson had a visit from a George Brannigan who was looking for Mark."

"Who is this Brannigan character?"

"Apparently Mrs Thompson's sister, Veronica was married to him for ten years before she died three years ago. There seems to be no love lost between Mrs Thompson and Brannigan. Anyway, yesterday afternoon Luke and I called in to the scrapyard in Huddersfield where Brannigan is based but no one was around. Looks like he lives in a big house adjoining the yard. We plan to try again later today.

"In the meantime, we have a FLO with Mrs Thompson and I'll be speaking to her later today." He looked over to Kelly Stainmore. "I'll go with DS Stainmore and see what else we can tease from her. And, of course, we have forensics looking at his flat."

"Do we know where he was attacked? If the fingertip search of the yard has come up with nothing then it wasn't where he was found," Hemingford said.

Ormerod took up that one. "Nothing obvious. There again, it has pissed it down for most of the time since Friday night."

Hemingford let out a big sigh and turned to the other boards. "So where are we on the Marcus Weaver murder?"

Strong outlined what they knew and what was suspected – not much further on from Friday's briefing. He still felt that Weaver was conducting an affair with a female from his workplace but his colleagues either didn't know who, or weren't saying.

"Could he be having it off with another man from work?" Hemingford asked. "It has been known."

Strong puffed his cheeks. "I honestly don't think so. We have the footprints and tyre tracks plus the female scent in Weaver's car. But we're in that limbo period waiting for results from various forensics tests."

"Right, I'll speak to the DCS and see if he can apply pressure to hurry things along there." Hemingford began to walk to the door.

"And I had results in from the fingerprints we took from Mrs Weaver," Stainmore added. "They don't match the ones on the passenger door handles, either inside or out."

"One other thing, sir," Ormerod said.

The DCI paused. "What's that, Luke?"

"I spoke to the Drugs Squad and, as far as they know, those toilets are not on their radar for trafficking."

Hemingford turned and continued on his way, head bobbing in a nod.

Ormerod watched him go then walked over to join Strong. "He doesn't seem to be that interested, does he?"

Stainmore joined them. "He's got something else on his mind," she said.

"You might be right, Kelly," Strong agreed.

"Anyway," Stainmore continued, "thanks for bringing me on board on Saturday. I missed all the action."

"That's just what *I* said, Kelly." Luke held out his hands. "I told him you'd be pissed off not being involved,"

"I just thought you'd appreciate a weekend off with your folks," Strong responded.

Stainmore's face broke into a broad grin. "Too bloody right. It was pissing down on Saturday and my mum's roasties are to die for."

30

Alison slumped into her chair and moved it as close as she could to her desk. That was the third time this morning she'd been to the toilet. The bump was decidedly uncomfortable now. Thank God she only had two more days after this. Her maternity leave began on Wednesday.

Four emails had arrived in her inbox since she'd been gone and she opened the first message. Before she could read it, she was interrupted.

"Hi." Sammy approached her desk, a batch of manila folders in her hand. "I called up before but they said you'd gone to the Ladies'."

"I see more of that place than I do my computer screen," Alison quipped.

Sammy looked her friend up and down then smiled. "You don't look too comfortable sitting there. Do you need a cushion?"

"I've already got one," she said, patting the bump.

The two of them burst out laughing, prompting a couple of Alison's work colleagues to look up from their desks and smile.

Regaining her composure, Sammy leaned forward towards her friend. "Have you been able to pick anything up?" Her voice was just above a whisper. "Regarding Mr Weaver's bit of …"

Alison looked round at the rest of her colleagues, all now pre-occupied, heads focused on their computer screens. "No," she answered. "Have you?"

"Oddly enough …" Sammy gestured towards the stairs then walked off, the folders still in her hands.

"Oh God," Alison exclaimed, "I'll have to go back to the loo again." She stood up and waddled out, following Sammy.

They walked into the small kitchen off the stair lobby. Sammy had already made sure nobody else was there.

"Go on then, what do you know," Alison asked, closing the door.

"Well, you know I said on Thursday that I thought I'd seen him with a woman … well, you know, not 'with a woman' as such but …"

Alison grew impatient. "Sammy, just tell."

"Okay, you know the New Claims department one floor down?" Sammy paused to glance through the vision panel in the door. The last thing she'd want would be to be caught spreading rumours.

Alison filled the kettle and switched it on. "Yes. Is she one of them?" she asked, dropping a tea bag in a mug.

"I think so. I heard a couple of other women chatting about Mr Weaver earlier on in the toilets. Then they dropped their voices but I heard a name. And then they went all concerned, you know, with an exaggerated shocked expression on their faces."

"Do they know you heard?"

"No, I'm positive they didn't. I was at the far end and I got the impression they were completely wrapped up in their conversation."

"So who is it?"

"You know as you go in to their section, there's a woman on the left-hand side with medium length dark hair, curly?" Alison was nodding. "Probably early thirties, usually wears a beige cardigan. Her name's Charlotte."

"Oh, I know, Charlotte …" Alison screwed up her face trying to remember then snapped her fingers and pointed at Sammy. "… Watkins, Charlotte Watkins."

The door opened and a middle-aged woman with a mug proclaiming she was the best mother in the world entered.

"Hi Alison. How long have you got to go now?" the woman asked.

"Another month. But this'll be my last week." Alison moved towards the door. "Kettle's just boiled."

"Hope all goes well for you."

"Thanks." Alison opened the door.

"Is this yours?" The woman picked up the empty mug with a tea bag in.

"Oh, I'll come back for it later. We just need to do something first," Alison said. "Come on then, Sammy, let's crack on."

Once outside, Sammy pushed the button to call the lift.

"Where are we going now?" Alison wondered.

Sammy tapped the folders she had tucked under her arm. "Well I thought we'd go and see Charlotte and discuss one of these new claims."

"You crafty sod."

Charlotte Watkins was at her desk when Sammy and Alison walked in to the department.

"Hi, it's Charlotte, isn't it?" Alison said.

She looked up from the paperwork she was studying. "Yes, it's ... Alison from upstairs."

"That's right," Alison replied. "And this is my colleague Sammy Grainger."

"Hello Sammy."

"Hi."

"What can I do for you?" Charlotte asked.

Sammy passed one of the manila folders to Alison. "It's this claim," she said. "I think it needs to be dealt with by this department down here."

Alison opened the folder and placed it on Charlotte's desk so she could see it.

Charlotte began to read through the paperwork. "I think it does," she said.

"That was shocking news last week, wasn't it?" Sammy said to Alison in a conversational tone.

"What was that?" she asked.

"Mr Weaver. From upstairs," Sammy explained.

"Oh God, yes. I was off on Thursday and Friday," Alison replied. "Only on three days." She patted her stomach. "In fact this is my last week until ..." She stopped, aware of Charlotte's reaction to what she and Sammy were saying.

Tears were streaming down Charlotte's cheeks. She snatched open a drawer on her desk and pulled a handful of tissues free from a box that was there.

"Sorry," she said, stood up and dashed from the room.

Alison looked across at Charlotte's work colleagues. They just shrugged and carried on with what they were doing.

Alison and Sammy walked in to the female toilets on Charlotte's floor. Sobbing could be heard from behind the one cubicle door that was closed.

Sammy quickly checked the other toilets were unoccupied, then nodded to Alison.

"Charlotte," Alison said softly. "We didn't mean to upset you."

More sobs.

"Please Charlotte, come out. We think we know," Sammy said. "But this is between us. We won't tell a soul."

Sounds of sniffing and nose-blowing. After a few seconds, the toilet flushed and the bolt slid across. Slowly the door opened and a puffed face with bloodshot eyes peered round. "I need to tell someone," Charlotte said, looking from Alison to Sammy and back. "Can I trust you?"

31

Strong and Ormerod stepped from the Mondeo onto puddles that were still frozen from the overnight sharp frost. They cracked like broken windows as the pair walked to the open gates of George Brannigan Scrap Metal Merchant Ltd's yard. A diesel train rumbled across the viaduct at the side of the premises, its throaty sound announcing its imminent arrival at Huddersfield railway station.

They made their way to the green portakabin office at the side of the yard nearest the house. Fluorescent light could be seen inside. The yard was quiet with no obvious activity taking place. Piles of scrapped cars and vans were lined up opposite along with a couple of skips. At the far end, a mechanical crusher stood silent, threatening; a crane with its grab arms hanging over it.

Strong opened the office door and a bald thick-set man wearing glasses looked up from the desk where he was busy filling in forms.

"Can I help you ... officers?" the man said pointedly.

"Mr Brannigan, George Brannigan?" The DI asked.

"Yes, gentlemen," Brannigan said, removing his glasses, putting down his pen and rising from behind the desk. "What can I do for you?"

Strong and Ormerod flashed their warrant cards and introduced themselves, an unnecessary action given Brannigan's instinctive reaction to them.

"I understand you were in Wakefield on Friday evening?" Strong began.

The man looked puzzled. "Was I?"

"According to a witness you were. Are you denying that? Have they got it wrong, or can't you remember?"

Strong was trying to hide his instant dislike of the man. He was aware of Ormerod tensing too.

"Look, what's this about?" Brannigan asked.

"Do you deny being in Wakefield on Friday evening?"

"No, I don't but I'm just curious as to your interest. Have I done something wrong?"

Deciding it was probably best to reduce the tension that was building, Strong asked if they could all sit down.

Brannigan agreed then said, "Can you just tell me what this is about and maybe I can help you?"

"Do you know a Mark Thompson, Mr Brannigan?" Strong asked.

A definite reaction. "Well, yes. He's my late wife's sister's boy."

"I understand you were looking for him on Friday. Can you tell me why?"

"I ... er ... I wondered if he was looking for a bit of extra work. I thought I could do him a bit of a favour."

Ormerod turned round, looking out of the window. "You don't seem too busy to me, Mr Brannigan," he said.

"It can be deceptive," Brannigan answered.

"Did you speak to Mark on Friday?" Strong asked.

"No. No, I didn't. I called at his house but his mother said he was out and staying over with friends, I think."

"So, just to be clear, you never saw Mark on Friday, or spoke to him?"

"No. I said, didn't I? He wasn't in."

Strong flipped open his notebook. "So you were in Wakefield at Mark's house at about eight ten, I understand. What time did you get back here?"

"I dunno, maybe about nine."

"And can anyone confirm that?"

Brannigan was becoming irritated. "No. I live alone. Look what's all this about?"

Strong stood up, Ormerod following suit.

"Mark Thompson was found dead on Saturday," Strong said as he studied Brannigan's face. "We may need to talk to you again."

As the detectives walked to the door, all Brannigan could manage was, "But ... how?"

"He was murdered Mr Brannigan," Strong said, closing the door behind him.

They waited until they were back in the car before either spoke.

"Do you believe him, guv?" Ormerod asked.

Strong blew air from his cheeks. "Judging by his reaction, and I think that was genuine, I don't think he knew Mark Thompson was dead. But I don't buy this bollocks as to why he was looking for him in the first place, Luke."

"That's exactly my feeling too."

* * *

Brannigan stared at the closed door for several seconds after the detectives had left. What the Hell was going on? He could see how it looked. He turns up trying to find the guy then later that night someone does him in. He needed to speak to Felicity. Did she know about Mark?

He pulled out his mobile and rang her number. Straight to answer message. Andy, he must pick up, surely. Three rings then answer message too. Bastards are avoiding him.

He walked to the office window, mobile in hand and looked out. No sign of the coppers. But they'd be back, he was sure of it. And when they did, he had to have his story straight.

He studied his phone and scrolled through his contacts before choosing one. After three rings, a voice answered.

"Patrick," Brannigan said. "I think I've got a job for you."

* * *

"Ah, Colin," the desk sergeant greeted as Strong walked through the main entrance doors to Wood Street Police station, Ormerod close behind.

"Yes, Bill," Strong said.

"There's someone to see you. Said it's important. Something about the Weaver case. I've put him in the front interview room for now." He pointed his thumb to the ceiling. "I've just rung upstairs and they said you were out. I was going to get someone else down but, seeing as you're here ..."

"To see me specifically?"

"Asked to speak to the officer in charge of the case." The sergeant squinted at a note by the phone. "Name of Pearson, Timothy Pearson."

"You may as well join me, Luke," Strong said, making his way to the interview room.

Seated at the table was a man of around thirty, slim, clean shaven with dark brown hair, dressed in a suit, shirt and tie.

"Mr Pearson?" Strong enquired. "I'm Detective Inspector Strong, and this is my colleague DC Ormerod. I understand you wanted to speak to me?"

"You're in charge of the enquiry into the murder in the park on Wednesday night?" the man asked.

The detectives sat down on the two spare chairs opposite. "That's correct. I believe you have some information?"

"Well ..." the man paused and gave a nervous cough. "This is in strictest confidence, right?"

Strong leaned forward onto the table between them. "Mr Pearson, we're not interested in why you may have been in the vicinity of the park toilets on Wednesday evening, we're dealing with murder here. And we'd like to catch whoever was responsible for that. Now, if you have something to tell us that may help our investigation, that would be very much appreciated."

The man looked down onto his lap for a second then up to hold Strong's gaze. "I was there," he said. "Not in the toilets at the time but outside earlier."

"So what time was that?" Strong asked as Ormerod opened his notebook.

"About a quarter to eight."

"So what have you got to tell us?"

"There were two men who approached the building. I thought ..." Pearson hesitated, a concerned look on his face. "I thought they were, you know ... interested."

"I get the picture," Strong said.

"Well I smiled at them. Then one of them said ..." Pearson broke off and looked to the ceiling.

"Go on, Mr Pearson," Strong encouraged.

"He said, 'Fuck off, weirdo,' to me." The man looked visibly upset.

"Can you describe these two men?"

"It was dark and foggy but the one who spoke, he was older, maybe around fifty? He was short and stocky. The other one was taller, much younger; in his twenties maybe, quite good looking."

"Do you think you'd recognise them again?"

"I'm not sure. I only got a brief glance."

Strong turned to Ormerod. "Luke, do you reckon you could flesh out Mr Pearson's descriptions here and see if it would be worth trying to create some sort of artistic impression?"

Pearson grew nervous again. "Look, I'm only on my lunch break. I wouldn't want to ..."

"We understand. We'll be as quick as possible," Ormerod said.

"There is one other thing," Pearson added, "The younger man seemed quite nervous. As he approached, he kept switching on a torch and sweeping it round and about."

"And after the shorter man spoke to you, what did you do?" Strong asked.

"I left. I wasn't hanging around when he seemed so aggressive."

"And did you see anyone else?"

Pearson thought for a moment. "Only some old bloke with a dog."

"Okay, Mr Pearson, thanks for coming in." Strong stood and indicated Ormerod. "My colleague here will be as quick as possible."

Strong left Ormerod to it and bounded up the stairs to the CID room. He could see a handful of detectives on the phone or head down on their computers. Kelly Stainmore looked up from her desk as he walked in. She stood and approached him as he studied the board for the Weaver murder.

"How did you get on, guv?" she asked.

"Oh, Brannigan?" He looked over to the other whiteboard with the photographs, lines and names relating to the Thompson murder. "Yes, reluctant at first but admitted to 'looking for Mark Thompson' because he 'wanted to do him a favour', whatever that meant. However ..." He turned back to the board in front of him and tapped the comments below Pemberton, the dog walker's name. "Downstairs, Luke is taking a statement and some descriptions from a witness who saw two men approach the toilet block on Wednesday night shortly before Weaver was murdered. I think he was the solitary individual Mr Pemberton saw."

"Sounds promising," she said.

He turned away from the board. "So what have you been up to this morning?"

"I've been down to Thompson's flat on South Street." She thumbed towards the other whiteboard. "First floor in the block. A bit scruffy, second-hand furniture, threadbare carpets and not a lot of personal belongings. SOCO are down there seeing what they can find. Looks like he had female company recently though. A nice lipstick stain on a mug that hadn't been washed up and some make-up wipes in the bathroom."

"No sign of violence there?" Strong asked.

"No, nothing. We found bank and credit card statements, so I've been in contact and they'll call if there's any activity on the accounts."

"What about nosy neighbours? Anything useful there?"

"I've left Trevor down there seeing if anyone's around," Stainmore answered. "Anyway, when do you want to head out to speak to Mrs Thompson again?"

He studied his watch. "Give me fifteen minutes and I'll come and get you."

"Fine," she said and made her way back to her desk.

Strong meanwhile studied the board for a few seconds longer then walked back to his office and closed the door. As he sat down, his desk phone rang.

"Strong," he announced.

"Colin, it's Bob. How are you?" the unmistakable voice of his old friend sounded through the earpiece.

"Up to my armpits in it, mate," Strong said. "Anyway, how's that woman of yours?"

"Last week at work this week. She'll be putting her feet up for a bit now."

"I don't think she'll see it that way. No problems though?"

"So far so good. But I just thought before we get too close to the delivery date, I wondered if you fancied a pint tonight?"

"Oh I don't know, we've got a lot on at the moment," Strong responded.

"Including the body in the bin I stumbled across on Saturday afternoon?"

"Yep, that too." Strong glanced at his watch. "Listen, I'll ring you a bit later, I've just got to go out but ..." He considered for a moment. "We could have one in the Black Horse maybe. Catch you later."

32

Andy stared at the unzipped holdall then looked to Felicity. For the past half an hour, they'd told each other everything. Felicity spoke of her idea to make George Brannigan pay, literally, for the way he treated her mother; the plan she hatched to fake her abduction and, most regretted of all, the involvement of her cousin Mark with such tragic consequences. Andy had paced the room, anger rising and subsiding as she expanded on the details.   Andy, for his part, related the events of Wednesday night in the public toilets in the park; the interruption by the man now known to be Marcus Weaver and Brannigan's actions. Felicity had become incensed at this. Now, they were both calm, Felicity sitting on the bed, Andy standing by the dressing table.

"We can't use that money, Felicity," he said.

"But this is our chance," she pleaded. "He owes me for how he treated Mum."

Andy shook his head. "This money … it's tainted. How can we use it knowing what had been lost to get it? Your mother wouldn't want us to."

"My mother suffered at his hands."

"And now two more people have suffered." He turned away, hands on his head and stared out of the window. After a few seconds, he turned back to face her. "Jesus, Felicity, if you can't see that."

"So what do you suggest we do? I'm not giving it back."

"You have to. It's not yours."

Felicity had persuaded Andy they needed a break, so here they were in a guest house bedroom in Whitby finally talking. Andy's boss wasn't best pleased to get the phone call that morning saying he had a family emergency to deal with. Andy had put a lot in to his job over the past year and so his boss had reluctantly accepted the situation.

"Have you spoken to your Aunty June since she called to tell you?" Andy asked.

"No," Felicity said. "I suppose I should really." She took her mobile phone from her handbag. "Christ," she said.

"What is it?"

"Three missed calls from him; Brannigan."

Andy checked his phone. "Me too. He'll be round to the flat soon, if he hasn't been already."

Felicity dialled a number and waited.

Andy listened to one side of the conversation between Felicity and June Thompson. A few surprised and shocked expressions passed over her face during it.

'What? What is it?' Andy mouthed several times only to be waved away.

Eventually, the conversation ended. Felicity, leant back on the bed, put the phone down and sighed.

Andy, standing in front of her, was growing impatient. "What did she say?"

"He'd been round."

"Who?"

"Brannigan, who do you think?"

"What, looking for us?"

"No, you idiot. On Friday night looking for Mark."

Andy sat down on the bed next to her. "Christ," he said quietly. "That's who you meant when you said you thought you knew who had done it."

"Well who else can it be? Within hours of him turning up trying to find Mark, Mark ends up dead." She looked across at Andy. "Shit, we can't go back now. He'll be after us. He must know."

"But let's be sensible, Felicity, we're not going to get far on thirty grand now, are we?"

"Twenty-nine."

"How do you mean?"

"I gave a thousand to Mark."

33

The Black Horse pub on Westgate was pretty full. Strong and Souter were standing in the middle of the main room, pints in hand. Normally they'd prefer to sit down. They'd already decided to move on somewhere quieter for the next one.

"So you must be up to your eyeballs then, Col," Souter said. "Two murders on the go."

"It's a bit hectic, I must admit."

"Have you made any progress?"

Strong grinned at his friend. "Only what you read in the papers."

"Still not found the woman then?" Souter threw in before taking a mouthful of his pint.

"What woman?"

"The one with ... oh, what's his name now?" Souter made a point of appearing to trawl his memory. "Weaver. On Wednesday night."

"How did you know ..." Strong should have guessed by now that nothing ever surprised him at what his friend could find out. "I don't suppose you have?" he asked.

"Not exactly but I do know who might."

Strong shook his head and took a sip of his beer. "I don't suppose you'd like to tell me?" He gazed over his friend's shoulder to the bar.

Souter rocked his head from side to side. "Mmm, might do," he said. "Depends what you've got for me."

Strong looked back to Souter and gave a wry smile. "So what are you working on?"

"Apart from your same two murder cases ..." Souter paused. "Well, actually ... I don't know if I should tell you."

."Come on, Bob, don't be a prat all your life."

"Okay," he said, took a gulp of beer then continued, "Do you remember Claire Hobson?"

Strong felt his heart rate quicken and the colour flush his cheeks. "I do actually," he said. "What about her?"

"Is there something going on I should know about, Col?" Souter had probably worked out he'd hit a nerve.

Strong drifted off, his attention focused towards the bar. He'd noticed the short blonde woman frequently looking over at them. He was puzzled; he knew her from somewhere but couldn't think where.

Souter followed his friend's gaze. "You pulled?" he said.

After another glance and a word with the man she was standing with, the woman walked over to them. She gave a quick glance to Souter. "Nice stilettos, Bob," she said before locking onto Colin, "but Colin, Lurex is so last year."

A huge grin broke out over Strong's face. "Bernice, isn't it?"

She nodded, laughing. "Bernice Fowler, as was but I prefer Bernie now, Bernie Steadman."

"I thought you looked familiar."

Bob's expression told her he'd remembered her too. He looked her up and down then leaned in closer. "Listen Bernie, don't take this the wrong way but, if I were you, I'd get my money back for the sex-change operation."

She slapped his arm. "You always were a cheeky beggar, Bob Souter. Anyway, I see you doing well; name in print regularly."

"Can't complain."

"And you, Colin. You're in CID now, they tell me."

"And they'd be right. But what about you? Where have you been for the past twenty-odd years?"

"It's a long story but ..."

"Are you with that bloke over there," Souter interrupted, indicating the man standing at the bar. "He seems to be a bit agitated."

The man in a smart jacket she'd been speaking to earlier was looking over and pointing at his watch.

"That's my husband," Bernie said. "Sorry boys but I've got to go. We've got tickets for the Theatre Royal over the road. Been great to see you both. You're looking well." With that, she turned and walked back towards the bar. Linking arms with her husband, she left the pub without a backward glance.

Souter looked at Strong. "Well that was a surprise," he said. "Little Bernice Fowler. She was a nice little looker at school; too short for us though." Strong didn't react. "I said too short ..."

Strong was deep in thought. "Didn't she have an older brother?" he finally pondered.

"I think so, but I didn't fancy him."

"What?" Strong glanced at his friend, slightly annoyed. "No I mean, she had an older brother. Now he looked nothing like her or her parents." He was thinking back to a different time. "I seemed to remember rumours ..."

"I don't know what the hell you're on about, Col."

Strong stared at his friend. "Like Mr Fowler wasn't her brother's real dad."

Souter drained his glass and shrugged. "I don't really remember. Another?"

"Go on, then," Strong responded. "There's a table over there, people have thinned out to go to the theatre. I thought it was unusually busy."

When Souter came back with the drinks, Strong carried on the conversation. "Why did you ask about Claire Hobson just now?"

Souter carefully centred his glass on the mat then proceeded to tell Strong about the commission he'd been asked to carry out for the paper.

"So you're basically doing a, what do they call it now, a human interest perspective on how the murder affected the family?"

"Exactly that. Plus, of course, the usual appeal for new information."

Strong took a sip. "So when is this likely to hit the streets?"

"I think Chandler's looking for it to coincide with the twentieth anniversary at the beginning of March."

"I'd best mention it to the DCS then," Strong said. "Are you going to be talking to him?"

"I hadn't thought about it. I mean, he wasn't here twenty years ago. But I suppose if I'm making a request for new information, it would make sense to speak to him."

Strong folded his arms and studied his friend. "So who knows who this mystery woman is then, Bob?"

"Ah well, this Marcus Weaver character worked at the same place as Alison ... and Sammy, of course."

"Ah ..."

"Sammy saw you and Kelly Stainmore come in the other day. But you didn't notice her. I thought you were detectives?"

"Piss off." Strong sipped his beer. "So Alison – or Sammy – has told you who it is."

"Well no, not exactly. I heard them talking about it the other day and how Sammy thinks she knows who it might be. She's not sure, but you know what she's like, she will find out."

"So I'd best interview Sammy then?" Strong said, a smile breaking on his face.

*   *   *

Sammy sat down at the small table that doubled as a work station in the flat she and Susan rented in Leeds. Susan had made the meal that they'd eaten earlier that evening and they were now keen to do something productive.

Sammy produced the piece of paper Susan had given her on Saturday. "So, these names you want me to find, Suz?"

"Oh, yeah, hold on." Susan rummaged in her handbag for a notebook then flipped it open. "I've got a couple more on here for you," she said and pointed to a list.

"Right," Sammy said, firing up the laptop they shared. "I can't really do this on the computers at work anymore." She sipped a coffee Susan had fetched from the kitchen. "They've clamped down on what sites we can visit and they've got some new virus and spyware software, so they'd know."

Susan walked over to the settee and flopped down, feet up. "Be interesting to see what you come up with. Bob and I will need to talk to them about Claire Hobson." Susan picked up a book, found her place and began to read.

After a few minutes, Sammy looked over at her friend. "Well, here's the last address for Kenneth Green," she said, jotting down the details next to his name in Susan's notebook.

"We worked out he must be twenty-nine now," she threw over her shoulder.

"Spot on." Sammy continued writing. "Looks like he's married and, this could be handy, he lives in Ossett."

"Sounds good."

Sometime later, Sammy spoke again. "This is weird," she said.

"What is?" Susan asked.

"I can find no record of Paul Nichols since 1990."

Susan placed her book open and face down on the floor to keep her place. "He would have been eighteen then," she said thoughtfully, rising to her feet.

"Last known address back then in Horbury." Sammy made a note.

Susan studied the list with the updates written on. "I think you'll find that one is London somewhere," she said, pointing to one name. "But she should be local."

"Okay, onwards and upwards," Sammy sighed. She looked up at her friend and grinned. "Another coffee might help."

Halfway through her drink, Sammy had indeed confirmed a London address for the name she had. But not long after that, she stopped and leaned back in the chair. "Oh, bloody hell," she said softly.

Susan put her book down and sat up. "What do you mean, 'Oh, bloody hell'?"

"Come and have a look at this."

Susan swung her legs off the sofa and walked over to where Sammy sat in front of the computer screen. She pointed to a name and address.

"What about it?" Susan asked.

Sammy then explained.

34
Tuesday 19th February 2002

"George will be looking for us you know?" Andy lay on the bed and stared at the cracks in the ceiling. He'd also been following the progress of a spider in the corner above the wardrobe.

Felicity sat on an old chair in front of the 1950s dressing table mirror, applying her make up. "Let him. He won't find us."

He sat up. "Please Felicity, you have to give it back."

She glanced at him in the mirror and continued with her mascara. "I didn't go through all that for nothing."

"Go through what?" Andy's raised his voice slightly. "You haven't been through anything. While you were with Mark, I was worrying myself sick with your odd-ball step-dad." He stood up. "And you didn't see what he did to that bloke," he added in a quieter voice.

"And neither did you from what you told me earlier."

"No, but I saw the results. And don't forget, he roped me in afterwards."

She spun round. "He's a shit. And that's why I'm keeping this." She tapped the bag at her feet below the dressing table.

He looked at his wife as if he didn't recognise her. "I'm going out." He picked up his coat from the back of a chair and put it on. "I need some air," he said, opening the door.

"Where are you going? I'll come with you, if you give me a minute."

"I need to clear my head. I'll see you later."

The door closed and Felicity could only sit and stare at it. After a few seconds, she went to the window and looked out. Andy appeared down the path and turned left, heading into town. Before he disappeared from view, she saw him take his mobile phone from his pocket, check the screen and put it away again.

She took in the room where they were staying. God, it was no better than the grotty flat they were renting in Wakefield. Surely she could do better than this. She smiled to herself at that thought; not the subject particularly but the fact that she had only included herself in it. She saw the bag on the floor and unzipped it. The notes were all there, used and untraceable. Maybe that could describe her too. Certainly she felt used. And now, could she be untraceable?

*   *   *

It was ten to one when Strong caught sight of the woman he'd suspected of having been in the park with Marcus Weaver. He was sure Weaver had been liaising with a woman that night, despite the site's reputation. And now, walking into the café on Commercial Street in central Leeds, an attractive woman in her early thirties with dark curly hair framing an oval face, was the one he hoped could provide some answers.

He stood, recognising Alison who had just walked in with her. It was Alison who had called him that morning with the news that she worked with someone who had some information regarding the murder enquiry he was conducting. And that had followed on from his conversation the previous night with Souter.

"Colin," Alison greeted. "Not seen you since the wedding. It's good to see you."

They kissed each other on the cheek.

"You too, Alison," he said. "Everything alright with you and, what does Bob call it, 'the bump'?"

She gave a laugh. "All good, but I'll be glad when it's all over. Anyway," she turned to the woman who had walked in with her. "This is my colleague, Charlotte Watkins. I think she needs to talk to you."

Strong held out his hand which Charlotte shook before sitting down at the table.

"Can I get you ladies a drink?" Strong offered.

Five minutes later, Strong was seated opposite Charlotte, with Alison sitting uncomfortably alongside her.

"Thanks for coming." He looked from one woman to the other and back again. "I understand you have some information relevant to the case I'm investigating." Charlotte was about to speak but Strong held up a hand. "I'm also aware that your situation, shall we say, may be a bit difficult for you. However, I can assure you that anything you say to me will be treated in the strictest confidence."

Charlotte looked tense. "You're right," she said, glancing towards Alison for a second. "This has been difficult."

"So in your own words, if you can tell me what happened on Wednesday?"

In a quiet voice, and regularly pausing to look around to make sure no one could overhear her, Charlotte began to recount what had happened on that fateful night nearly a week ago in the car park near the toilet block.

When she thought she'd completed her tale, she looked across at Strong and asked, "Will all this come out?"

"As I've said, I'll treat this as strictly confidential, Charlotte. But I will need a formal statement from you. Then it would depend on whatever happens with any potential court case."

The woman sighed and dropped her head. "He's going to find out, isn't he?" She looked up at Strong. "Steven, my husband, Steve, he'll know."

"Like I said, I will try and keep this confidential," he reassured. "From what you've told me, you can't provide any identification of whoever was there that night anyway." He looked down at the notes he'd taken. "Two silhouetted figures, one taller and slimmer than the other and you think one of them had a torch. No indication of age, build, or anything like that?"

She shook her head. "It was foggy and there was no real light to speak of, just two shadowy figures. Oh, but I think there was someone walking their dog, it shot in front of me as I was leaving the park. I had to brake sharply."

Strong nodded. "Yes, we know about the dog walker. It was him who found Mr Weaver." Strong began to notice a concerned expression on Alison's face but continued the conversation with Charlotte. "So how long were you and Mr Weaver seeing each other?"

Alison shifted in her seat, physical discomfort obvious.

"It began just before Christmas," Charlotte answered, "At a Christmas lunch."

"Was that the office one?" Alison joined in. "Sorry, didn't mean to interrupt."

"Are you sure you're alright?" Strong asked as he watched Alison twisting her wedding ring on her finger. That like the rest of her hands appeared swollen.

"I'm fine, honestly," she insisted.

Strong didn't believe her but resumed his conversation with Charlotte. "Have you met in the park before?"

"Twice, yes."

"And did you see anyone else hanging around on any previous occasion?"

"No, but we'd parked further away."

"Okay, Charlotte, thanks for coming forward. It was important you did that. I don't see there's much you've been able to tell us that wasn't already known but I will need a formal statement, just to keep things in order. Can you give me a mobile number I can contact you on?"

Charlotte picked up a paper napkin and wrote a number on a corner. She nervously passed it across.

Strong looked at it and folded it away in his pocket. "I'll get someone to call you and arrange to sign something off. We'll be discreet, and provided there's nothing else that you've omitted to tell us, then that could be the end of the matter."

Charlotte looked alarmed. "No. I've told you everything."

Alison took hold of her hand. "It's all right, Charlotte. Colin is only covering everything; it's his job."

Strong got to his feet. "Thanks for talking to me," he said, "You've done the right thing." He offered his hand once again, which Charlotte shook, lightly. Then, after kissing Alison on the cheek, he left the café and disappeared into the lunchtime crowd.

Alison turned to Charlotte. "Well done. You had to speak up."

"I'm just so worried Steve will find out." She covered her face with her hands. "Oh God, what a mess." She looked to Alison. "Why did I do it?"

"Listen, don't worry about it. We all do things we regret. Look on this as a narrow escape. I'm sure Colin will do all he can to keep your situation quiet."

"Thanks, Alison. I don't know how I'd have coped without you, and Sammy."

"Right, that reminds me, we'll need to get back." Alison looked at her watch and smiled. "It'll take me a bit longer than normal."

35

Strong made it back to Wood Street for half past two. The first person he saw as he walked up the stairs was Kelly Stainmore heading downwards. "Ah, Kelly," he said. "I'll want you to do something for me."

She turned round and followed her boss back to his office. On the way she told him that Sam Kirkland had something interesting for him. "And the DCI has been like the Scarlet Pimpernel," she quipped as a final shot.

Back in his office, door closed, he recounted his meeting with Charlotte Watkins. "So some time in the next day or so, I'd like you to get a formal statement from her. This is her mobile." He produced the folded napkin with the number written on it. "And I promised we'd be discreet."

"So nothing of any use for us then?"

"Basically confirmed what we already know and not able to provide any helpful descriptions – certainly nothing to improve on the sketchy ones we've got from Mr Pearson, our toilet visitor."

Stainmore screwed up her nose. "How can anyone ..."

"Don't go there, Kelly. Anyway, you said Sam has something. And where is Hemingford?"

"Good question, guv. Not seen him all day." Stainmore turned and opened the door.

Strong stood up and followed her out into the CID office. They walked over to Kirkland's desk where he was sitting studying his computer screen.

"I hear you've got something, Sam?" Strong asked.

Kirkland looked up from the screen. "Not sure, guv." He tapped a few keys and turned his screen towards the DI. "This is Friday night and I've picked up this car, a BMW, travelling down Townley Road. As you can see ..."

He indicated the clock timer in the corner of the screen. "It's timed at 20:07. It appears again travelling in the opposite direction at 20:24."

"So what's raised your hackles on that?"

More tapping and fresh images appear. "Well this was the day before, on the Thursday. You can see it appears at 19:48; and then is seen again in the opposite direction at 20:29."

"Is it someone who lives on Lupset?"

"Not sure. The quality isn't good enough to get a number plate. But it's this that got my interest ..." Again, Kirkland called up different footage. "This is on Waterton Road which cuts across the estate. Look here." He pointed to a dark BMW driving slowly past. "This is timed at 20:04 one way; in the opposite direction ..." He ran fast forward. "20:12. Then again one way ... 20:16 and the other ... 20:20."

"Hold on, Sam." Strong said. "Run that back again." Kirkland did. "What's that?" Strong pointed to the screen. An image of a young lad on a bike passed across.

"Oh, he appears several times that night," Kirkland said.

Strong looked over to where Luke Ormerod normally sat. "Is Luke around?" Several of the detectives sitting at their desks looked over and shrugged.

"Gone for a piss, guv," DC John Darby offered.

"Thanks for that, John," Strong responded in ironic tones.

"By the way, that's your phone, Kelly," Derby said to Stainmore.

"Excuse me, guv," she said and walked over to her desk.

"Anyway, there's something else," Kirkland went on. This time he called up another camera. "This is from Wednesday night. On Horbury Road, look." He pointed to a similar dark coloured BMW driving slowly past the camera. "Timed at 19:44. Then again, it appears in the opposite direction at 20:21. There also seems to be two people in it this time."

"And what are you thinking?"

"Well, this is around the right time for Weaver's attack and it's near to the other entrance to the park."

"Seems a bit of a leap, Sam. Can we get a number from this footage?"

Kirkland made a face. "They're not that good."

"So we can't be sure it's the same vehicle."

Luke Ormerod approached the group. "Looking for me, guv?" he asked.

"Yes, Luke. When we attended the Thompson murder scene on Saturday, there was some kid on a bike riding around, do you remember?"

Ormerod thought for a moment then shook his head. "Can't say as I do. There were a lot of people milling around. Why? Something up?"

"It might not even be the same character. It's just I'm sure I remembered seeing this kid about twelve nosing around, baseball cap back to front. And on Sam's CCTV footage from Thursday night, a similar figure appears."

"Thursday night?" A puzzled expression appeared on Ormerod's face. "Why are we looking at Thursday night?"

"I'm not really sure, Luke." He turned to Kirkland again. "So why are you looking at Thursday night, Sam?"

"Just covering all bases."

Strong snapped his fingers. "Luke, can you check and see what vehicles are registered to George Brannigan?"

"On it."

Stainmore walked over as Ormerod sat down at his desk and picked up the phone. "That was the bank," she said. "Someone used Mark Thompson's card on Sunday."

"Where?"

Stainmore handed the post-it note she'd written the details on to Strong. "An off-licence on Agbrigg Road."

"Right," Strong said. "I'll come with you."

"I just need to wait for a copy of the transaction slip. The bank said they'd fax it through within the next ten minutes."

*   *   *

Andy felt he had to do something. He couldn't stand all this hiding away; his logical mind couldn't handle that. Sooner or later Brannigan would find them. They'd have to return. Felicity couldn't see that, or didn't want to. No, it was down to him to do something.

Before he knew it, he found himself by the swing bridge over the River Esk in the centre of Whitby. Crossing onto the bridge, he looked over towards the North Sea. A gale was blowing in and rain had started. In the distance, he could see waves crashing over the breakwater. What the Hell was he doing here on a freezing cold day in February? If Felicity couldn't see sense, it would fall to him to sort it.

On the other side of the river, an inviting pub called to him. He walked on, went inside, ordered a pint and sat down at a table in the corner. It was quiet, only an old man sitting at another table on his own near the log fire. That was giving off a warm glow. After a sip of his beer, he pulled out his mobile phone and dialled a number.

"I was wondering what had happened to you," Brannigan answered.

"I think we need to talk." Andy turned his beer glass on its mat.

"So talk. Where are you?"

"That's not important. But I'm trying to persuade Felicity to see reason."

*"So she **was** involved. I thought so. And she has my money?"*

Andy's eyes took in the room; the old man had his head down and the barman had disappeared. "She sees it as part payback for how you treated her mother."

"What!" Brannigan snapped.

"Look, I'm not voicing an opinion one way or another, George." Andy spoke in a calm voice. "I'm just trying to sort this."

"You can sort it by returning my money. And for the record, I loved Veronica. I never hurt her." There was a pause. *"Did she tell you how her mother died?"*

"She said she suffered from a brain tumour."

"That was only half the story. Her tumour caused her to react in all sorts of odd ways. Veronica told me that would happen when she was first diagnosed." Brannigan sighed. *"Five years she had it before ... Well, some of the things Felicity saw weren't quite what she thought."*

"She says you raised your hands."

"Like I say, she saw what she wanted to see." Another pause. *"I gave that girl everything when she came with her mother to live with me, and this is what she thinks ... how she repays me."*

Andy took a swig of his pint and glanced over as the door opened and two elderly men walked in, coats buttoned up tight and scarves wrapped around their necks. The wind whistled in behind them as they closed the door. Before they got to the bar, the barman was pulling the first pint for them. The old man at the other table looked over to them and held up his empty glass.

"She knows about Mark," he said.

"Not surprised, it's been all over the papers."

"She thinks you had something to do with it."

Brannigan gave a snort.

"Well did you?"

"What do you take me for? Of course I didn't."

Andy took a breath before he said, "I saw what you were capable of on Wednesday night."

*"You didn't **see** anything."*

The two newcomers walked over to their friend and sat down with three fresh pints before mumbling something about the state of the weather.

"I need to have something to persuade her to come back," Andy said.

"Well try this, I might just tell the police that it was you who did for that bloke in the toilets. After all, the evidence will be there to prove you were at the scene."

"What are you on about?"

"Think about it – I was wearing gloves. Who lifted the cistern cover? Hmm?"

"You can't ..."

"Obviously, I wouldn't want to but I just thought you might want to consider that."

Andy was quiet for a second. "If I did persuade her, there would be no repercussions would there?"

"Just bring back my thirty grand."

Andy thought it best not to mention that the total had already been depleted. "I can only try," he said before ending the call.

36

Agbrigg Road was a multi-cultural area of Wakefield. On one corner, a mosque; on another a Chinese take-away; yet another a European food store. At the far end stood the Duke of York pub. The off-licence they sought was about half way along the street.

Strong pulled the Mondeo to a halt kerbside and he and Stainmore got out. As they entered the shop, a couple of youths who looked no more than sixteen dashed out, one carrying a plastic carrier bag with bottles, the other unwrapping a packet of twenty cigarettes. Stainmore gave Strong a knowing look.

Behind the counter a skinny man in his early twenties sat on a stool reading the sports page of a newspaper. He glanced up, his expression registering the fact that two police officers had entered.

At the far end, a male dressed in jeans and a tracksuit top put a six pack of lager back on the shelf and walked out.

Strong approached the assistant. "Something I said," he quipped, indicating the door swing shut behind the departed customer.

"How can I help?" the man asked, folding up his paper.

Strong introduced himself and Stainmore, unnecessarily showing the man his warrant card. "Were you working here on Sunday?"

"Yeah. Something wrong?"

Stainmore unfolded the fax sheet she'd brought with her. "Do you remember a transaction at two seventeen on Sunday afternoon in the sum of thirty-two pounds and eighteen pence, Brian?" she asked, making a point of studying his name badge.

"Not a bloody clue," Brian responded.

"You should do. This was by credit card," Stainmore responded. "And I can't imagine you'd have many of these in here. Mostly cash, I'd have said."

"We'd like to see your records of transactions for Sunday, Brian," Strong added.

"Won't you need a warrant for that?" Brian folded his arms.

Strong afforded himself a smile before leaning forward, both hands on the counter top. "We could easily do that." The smile had evaporated. "We could also bring Trading Standards back with us too. They'd be very interested in you selling alcohol and cigarettes to minors."

"I don't ..."

"Just like those lads who were leaving when we arrived," Strong interrupted. "Now ..."

"Look, I was only joking," Brian said, nervously.

"Your transaction records then," Strong said. He nodded to the ceiling mounted fixture. "And your CCTV tape for Sunday too. As soon as you can."

Brian opened his mouth to reply but said nothing, hurrying off into a back room. Two minutes later he returned with a box file of till receipts. He thumbed through a few. "Here." He pulled one out. "Thirty-two quid, wasn't it?"

"And eighteen pence." Stainmore said.

"Yep, that was two bottles of Bells whisky and twenty Benson and Hedges."

Stainmore took the till receipt and studied it. "The time ties in too so, let's have a look at the tape. Unless, of course you can save us the trouble and tell us who bought this?"

"I can't remember, it's quite busy on Sundays."

"Well let's see if we can help you remember, Brian," Strong said.

A worried expression came over the young man's face. "But ... how ...?"

"You have a player in the back office, don't you?"

"Well, yes, but I'd have to shut the shop, and the boss, he'll ..."

"It shouldn't take long. We can narrow down the time after all."

Five minutes later, the shop locked, Strong, Stainmore and Brian were huddled in the office around a TV screen. Brian found the time period they were looking for. Two youths in jeans, dark jackets with hoodies underneath approached the counter with the two bottles that Brian had identified. The camera position was on the ceiling facing the counter. Up to that point, the youths' faces couldn't be seen. The detectives watched as one youth produced a card. Brian placed it in the machine and swiped the receipt note back and forth before handing it to the youth to sign it. Transaction complete, the two turned away from the counter but kept their heads down as they walked to the exit.

"Shit," Strong muttered in disappointment.

"They bloody knew," Stainmore said. "They were aware of the camera position."

"But you must have seen their faces, Brian," Strong said.

"I can't really remember, I wasn't paying that much attention."

"Obviously, or you would have noticed the signature didn't really match the card." Stainmore tried to hide her annoyance."

Strong kept up the pressure. "And you didn't think it suspicious that these two kept their hoods up the whole time?"

"No, not really," Brian responded. "It's the fashion. Besides, it was pissing down all day on Sunday." He looked frightened as he went on, "They're not regular customers though. I would have recognised them if they had been."

"So you did see their faces?"

"No. No, I didn't mean ...I just meant I knew I hadn't seen them before."

Strong studied the man for a moment before deciding he believed him. After all, if they were using a stolen credit card, it would make sense not to do so in one of your regular haunts. All the same, the pair were camera aware.

"I'll need to take this," Strong said, ejecting the tape from the player. "Our forensics people might be able to get something from it. That is okay with you Brian?"

The shop assistant nodded. "Sure," he said.

Once outside, Stainmore looked to her boss. "You think we got everything from him?" she asked.

"As much as we can for now, Kelly. In the meantime, ask Trevor to come down here and get hold of whatever CCTV he can. Our two might have known where the camera was in the shop, but I'm not convinced they're that smart that they won't have been caught out somewhere nearby."

* * *

On his way back to the B & B, Andy hardly noticed the rain, heavier than ever. Brannigan hadn't made an idle threat, he was sure of that. Every detail of that night in the toilet block passed through his mind on his walk. It was true, Brannigan was wearing gloves. And he never gave it a second thought when he was asked to take off the cistern cover to place the money inside. His prints would be on that.

He opened the front door of the guest house and walked up the stairs to the first-floor room where they were staying. As soon as he opened the door, he knew there was something wrong. The room was empty; no Felicity. The wardrobe door was ajar. Looking inside, the small suitcase they'd packed quickly on Sunday afternoon had gone, along with all her clothes. There was no sign of the holdall with the money either. The only clothes left were his.

Pulling out his mobile, he sat on the end of the bed and dialled Felicity's number. Instantly, he was informed that the mobile he was trying was switched off. He looked up at the dressing table and that's when he saw the note. Picking it up, he sat on the bed and read:

> *Sorry.*
> *Have to do this for Mum.*
> *Don't worry about me, I'll be fine.*
> *And don't try to find me, just get on*
> *with your own life.*
> *Felicity x*

She can't be right in the head, he thought. And then anger slowly overcame him. The selfish cow. She'd pissed off with her little bit of tainted money, justifying her actions through some twisted logic leaving him to sort out the mess. Well he wasn't having that.

Jumping up off the bed, he looked out of the window. He hadn't paid any attention when he arrived back but he was pleased to see his car was still there. Gathering up his clothes, he rolled them into a ball as best he could and took them downstairs and out to the car. When he came back in to settle up and leave the room key, the landlady was waiting for him.

"I hoped you weren't just going to disappear," she said.

Somehow, Andy managed to contain his anger at that remark and merely said, "I'm not like that. Now, I'd like to check out."

"Had a falling out have you?"

"Felicity's had to go back to work. Now the bill, if you please."

"Just with her going off in a taxi ... That's sixty pounds in total."

"Sixty? But we've only been here one night."

"But it's after 12 – time for check out."

Andy finally snapped. "Yeah, and they're battering your door down to stay here. Now here's thirty, and even that's overcharged for this dump." He slammed the notes down on the hall table, put the room key alongside and quickly left as the landlady shouted insults after him.

First, he tried the railway station. The only train to have left that afternoon was the slow to Middlesbrough. He couldn't see her taking that option. Next door was the bus station. There had been a few of the longer distance coaches setting off that day, one to Leeds, one to York and another to Scarborough.

He sat down on a bench under the canopy of the bus station and took her note from his coat pocket. Reading it again, he decided it wasn't worth it. Why should he go chasing after someone who had set him up and acted so selfishly? Other incidents crossed his mind. Had he really been so gullible? Putting the note back in his pocket, he left the bus station and got back into his car. Nothing for it, he'd have to face Brannigan himself, threats or no threats.

* * *

Strong was on his way back to Wood Street when his mobile rang. Stainmore was still at Agbrigg Road briefing Trevor Newell on what they were looking for. She'd get a lift back with him.

He pulled over into a bus stop. Laura's name was on the screen.

"Hey, how did it go?"

"Ooh, not so sure," she said. *"You can never tell. I think I said all the right things."*

"I'm sure it'll be fine," Strong reassured. "You know you're the best person for the job."

"We'll see."

"So when will you know?"

"They'll phone tonight, apparently."

"That's good, they don't keep you hanging around."

"Will you be home in good time?"

"Yeah … should be."

She picked up the hesitancy in his voice. *"Everything okay?"*

"I saw Alison at lunchtime. She arranged for me to speak to one of her colleagues where she works. You know she and Sammy work in the same office as the park murder victim."

"Something wrong?"

"I'm not sure. She seemed to be in a bit of discomfort. Tried to hide things but I'm wondering with her condition and all. Her hands looked swollen."

"Not unusual when you're pregnant. I'm sure Bob will keep an eye on her. Look, got to go."

"Me too."

"See you tonight."

With the call ended, Strong sat for a moment before a bus came up from behind flashing its lights and sounding its horn bringing him out of his thoughts.

With an acknowledging hand, he put the car in gear and pulled away.

37

Andy turned the key in the lock of the door to the flat. He half expected Felicity to bounce out towards him but all was quiet. He'd had plenty of time on the two-and-a-half-hour drive from Whitby to mull over his thoughts. It should only have taken just under two hours but an accident on the A64 put paid to that. It was dark outside and the gloomy interior depressed him even more. He would have to move out; no way could he stay here now.

Picking up some mail from behind the front door, he walked down the hallway to the sitting room. He threw the envelopes down on the small dining table in front of the window. The only light came from the dim glow of a streetlamp on the opposite side of the road. Leaving the lights off, he sat down on the sofa, leaned back and closed his eyes.

He must have nodded off because the next sound he heard was frantic knocking on the front door.

When he opened it, George Brannigan pushed his way in. "Where the hell is she?" he demanded.

Before Andy could reply, the visitor had stomped into the sitting room and switched on the light. Andy closed the front door and followed him up the hallway.

"She's gone," Andy said.

Brannigan met him at the sitting room door. "What do you mean 'gone'? She was with you this afternoon, wasn't she?"

He was up close and Andy could smell his stale breath. "Here," he said, pulling Felicity's note from his jacket pocket. "When I went back to the guest house after talking to you, this was all that was there. She'd packed and left in a taxi."

Brannigan read the letter then pushed it back in Andy's chest. "You didn't ask?"

"Who? Where?" Andy took the crumpled piece of paper and stuffed it back into his pocket.

"The landlady? The cab company?"

"I drove down to the train station and the bus station but there was no sign. She could have gone anywhere. Middlesbrough, Scarborough, York, Leeds or even further afield."

Brannigan paced the sitting room. "She'll not get away with this." He turned and faced Andy. "Did you tell her? What I said about her mother's condition? How it would affect her?"

"I didn't get the chance. Like I said, she was gone when I got back to the room."

"Spoilt bitch," he spat.

Andy drew his head back, holding Brannigan's stare. "So her cousin, Mark – did you have anything to do with what's happened to him?"

"I told you already, I never went near him."

"But you did go looking for him the night he was murdered."

Brannigan snorted and turned away. "I saw him, at the salon, just after you dropped her off on Friday morning."

Andy's face was screwed up in disbelief. "You followed us?"

"I thought there was something funny about all this kidnapping bollocks. And I was right, wasn't I?"

"And then what? You searched him out too? He wouldn't tell you anything, so you killed him?"

Brannigan pushed his face into Andy's and grabbed him by the lapels. "I'm going to say this once more for the final time – I did not find Mark on Friday night and I did NOT attack him. You got that?"

Andy flinched. He knew he'd pushed as much as he could. And to be honest, he'd started to believe him. But at the back of his mind was what had happened in the toilets that night just a week ago. And then there was his threat.

"And you just remember whose DNA and prints would have been found in that toilet block." Brannigan slowly released his grip. "Now when you hear from Felicity, you be sure to call me. Okay?" He tapped Andy's cheek, a bit harder than he needed to. He stared at him for a second, the smile he had on his face false, walked past him and out into the hallway.

Andy heard the front door close then let out the breath he'd been holding.

38
Wednesday 20th February 2002

The knock on his office door made Strong look up from the file he was studying at his desk. Through the glass panel he could see Doug Norris, the SOCO standing, holding some folders in his hand. He waved him in. "Hello, Doug, how's things?" he greeted.

"That shirt you sent me …"

"Yeah, what news?"

"Well, I concentrated on the collar and cuffs. If you remember that's where I said the usual wearer would leave the most trace."

"And?"

"They don't match."

"What do you mean, they don't match?"

"The DNA from the shirt doesn't match the sample from the Claire Hobson evidence. So it's not a match for the rookie PC you thought. You can see here …" Norris pulled out three sheets of paper from one of the files he'd brought with him. "This is the DNA profile of the perpetrator." He pointed to the first sheet. "And this is PC Gary Monk's. You can see the matches. But this …" he said, pointing to the third sheet, "is from the shirt. No similarity at all."

Strong studied what Norris had presented then looked up at him, nodding. "So what's in the other file?" he asked, knowing full well he'd made another discovery.

"Ah. That's where things get really interesting." A self-satisfied smile appeared on Norris' face as he pulled two sheets from the second file he'd brought. "This," he said, pointing to the first, "is the DNA profile obtained from material we recovered from under the finger nails of Weaver's hand. The right, if you recall?"

Strong nodded.

Referring to the second sheet, he went on, "And here is the profile we have on file for Claire Hobson."

Strong looked surprised and leaned forward to look closely at what had been presented. "You mean *actually* Claire Hobson? Not the perpetrator?"

"That's right." Norris stood back. "Thought that would interest you. We have a number of similarities, as you can see."

"Hells bells, Doug, does that mean a sister?" Strong asked, already suspecting the answer.

"Whoever Weaver touched before he died was directly related to Claire Hobson."

"And I know who that is," he said, standing up. "I interviewed her yesterday."

Once Norris had left, Strong walked into the CID office and spotted Stainmore sitting at her desk. "Kelly," he called. "Can I have a word?"

She stood and approached him. "Trevor's come back with something interesting from talking to some of Mark Thompson's neighbours, guv. A description of a young woman seen leaving with him on Thursday night."

"That's good," he said before lowering his voice. "Doug's just brought Mr Monk's shirt back."

"And?"

"He's not Gary's dad, or our perpetrator. So I'd like you to come with me when I take it back. In the meantime, this is all confidential."

"Of course," she said, indignantly.

"Sorry, Kelly. I didn't mean … anyway, Charlotte Watkins … have you taken her statement yet?"

"Seeing her at one today," she answered.

"Hmm." He looked to the ceiling for a moment.

"Something wrong?"

"No that's fine." He saw no gain in telling her what he knew about her true identity. Well, not yet anyway. "I'd best see Flynn," he concluded.

"Oh, meant to ask," she said, as he began to walk away. "It was Laura's interview yesterday, wasn't it?"

His face broke into a big smile. "She got it."

*   *   *

Sammy walked into the kitchen area on her floor of the office building where she worked. Alison was already there pouring herself a glass of water, tablets in a bubble pack lying on the work surface.

"Everything okay, Alison?" She approached her friend.

"Oh, hi Sammy," she answered. "I'm alright. Just a bit of a headache that's all."

Alison popped a couple of pills from the pack, put them in her mouth and took a gulp of some water. She screwed up her face as she swallowed them.

Sammy studied her closely. "But you're not, though, are you?"

Tears began to well in Alison's eyes. "Not really," she said. "I've had a hell of a headache since I woke up. And ..." Two tears ran down her cheeks. "I've not felt the baby move today."

"Here, sit down." Sammy guided her to a chair. "If you're worried, we can go to the LGI and get checked out." It was true, the Leeds General Infirmary was a short walk away and they had a Maternity Unit on site.

"I don't know, Sammy. I don't want to fuss." Twisting her wedding ring, she looked down at her feet. "But look at this ... my hands have swollen up and my feet ...I've got cankles now."

Sammy followed her gaze then cracked into a smile. "I love that word," she said. "Look, I'll get your coat and we can take a steady walk down there."

When they arrived at the Maternity Unit, they were met by a midwife at the Nurse Station who was filling in forms and engaged in conversation with an Indian man whose badge announced he was an obstetrician.

The doctor walked away and finally, the midwife turned her attention to the new arrivals. "Can I help you, love?" she asked.

Alison explained her symptoms.

"If you want to come with me, we can have a look at you," the midwife said, leading her into an examination room.

Alison insisted Sammy came with them.

After taking Alison's blood pressure and some personal details, the midwife walked to the door. "I'll just get a colleague to examine you, Alison," she said.

"Is everything okay?" Sammy asked.

"Just want to have our senior midwife have a look at you."

An older midwife in a different coloured uniform and a badge with the name of *Debbie* came in. She asked Sammy to leave them for a minute whilst she examined Alison. After a few minutes, Sammy was asked to re-join them.

"I've just been explaining to your friend that she's suffering from a condition known as pre-eclampsia. It's quite common in mothers to be," the midwife said.

"Will she be able to come home?" Sammy asked.

"Oh no, sweetheart," she said. "We'd like to keep Mrs Souter in." She glanced down at Alison who was lying fully clothed on the bed. "Because of her age, and she's a primip, we need to monitor her blood pressure and start medication." She caught Sammy's puzzled expression. "Sorry, primip just means this is her first baby." Turning back to Alison, she patted her hand. "Now don't worry sweetheart, I'll arrange for a bed for you."

When she'd gone, Sammy sat on the chair by the side of the bed, concern etched on her face. "I've heard of that pre-eclampsia thing," she said.

Alison had her head back on the pillows. "High blood pressure, ha!" She began to chuckle. "Her calling me 'sweetheart' every few seconds isn't helping."

*   *   *

Souter had tried to speak to Michael Hobson, Claire's father, but he was given short shrift. The man didn't see the point of all this media activity; he just wanted to be left with his own thoughts. But Souter had spoken to Louise Hobson the day before and been given Claire's brother, Martin's telephone number. He'd just made that call and spoken to him in London and was reading through the notes he'd made. Martin was surprisingly open in his thoughts about how the murder of his younger sister had affected the family and how he still thought of her every day. He was pleased that Souter was planning to bring the unsolved murder back into the public eye and hoped that it would tease that one vital piece of information to the surface to unlock the mystery of who was responsible for what had happened to Claire. The next call he planned to make was to his sister, Charlotte.

About to pick up the phone again to call Charlotte's number, his mobile rang.

"Bob, I'm with Alison," Sammy's voice announced. *"Where are you?"*

"In the office. Why? Is everything okay?"

"We're at the hospital. The LGI. Nothing to worry about but you might want to come over. We're in Maternity."

"She's not … It's not coming is it?"

"Not as far as I know but she wants to see you."

"She hasn't lost the baby? Surely not."

"No, Bob. Stop panicking. Just get your backside over here."

He ended the call and jumped from his chair.

"Where are you off to in such a hurry," Janey Clarke shouted at him. "Something breaking?"

"I hope not, Janey," he said, shuffling into his coat. "Alison's in the hospital."

"That's early, isn't it?"

"Got to go." Souter strode to the stairs. "Tell Chandler." And was gone.

39

Detective Chief Superintendent Flynn listened intently as Strong brought him up to speed with what he'd learned regarding Gary Monk's DNA familial match.

"Christ," he said. "This isn't going to be easy. Did Mrs Monk give you any clue as to whether she was aware of this?"

"No sir. From what I could tell, she adored her husband."

Flynn sighed, stood up and looked out of the window for a second.

"This is going to be worse than an agony visit," he said quietly, referring to the occasions when officers must visit relatives of the deceased to break the bad news.

He turned back to face Strong, thrusting his hands in his pockets. "I'm assuming you'll take Kelly with you again?"

"Of course. She's ideal."

"How's she fairing after all she's been through?"

"She's fine, sir. We had a chat about what happened and she seems to have moved on quite well."

"She certainly looks healthier," Flynn said, resuming his seat. He studied his desk and Strong had the distinct impression he wanted to talk about something else.

"Is everything okay?" Strong asked.

Flynn rubbed the bridge of his nose between thumb and forefinger. "This is a bit delicate, Colin," he said.

Strong smiled ironically. "Last time you said that, you landed me with the Gary Monk situation."

The DCS paused a beat. "It's about Rupert," he finally said. DCI Hemingford; Strong knew something wasn't quite right but he offered no response, only let the silence hang in the air between them.

"He'll be moving on," Flynn declared. "But this is strictly confidential. I'm telling you because I think you deserve to hear it from me first."

Strong sat back in the chair. "I did wonder … He hasn't been fully … focused, if I can say that."

Flynn nodded. "It'll be announced at the end of the month officially. He'll be joining a new unit being set up in Greater Manchester."

"Explains a lot, including the trips over there."

Flynn looked at Strong, a grave expression on his face. "What I'd like to do, Colin, is talk about what happens next."

"No," Strong said instantly. "I'm not going through all that again."

"It'll be different this time."

"How?" Strong's hands gripped the arms of the chair but he took a breath before going on, "You'll have me do the job then bring someone else in, just like you did with Hemingford."

"I can't say just yet, but trust me." Flynn responded. "You have some friends in higher places this time."

Strong gave a snort. "Yeah, right."

Flynn held out both hands. "Look, don't say anything for now. Nothing will happen for a week or so. Just think about your situation."

"I am."

"I understand your reaction, Colin. But …" Flynn paused, shook his head and decided to move on. "So when do you plan to speak to Mrs Monk?"

Strong got to his feet, sensing the meeting was drawing to a close. "I'll check young Gary's duty rota. We need to go when he's not around. Tomorrow, hopefully."

"Okay, thanks." Flynn held out a hand. "And we'll talk again."

Strong looked at the offered hand then shook it. "Sir," he said then made his way out.

Strong finished reading through the statement Stainmore had obtained from Charlotte Watkins. There was nothing new from what he'd been told the day before. She was sitting opposite him in his office, door closed.

"Nothing much to help us there, guv, as you said," Stainmore reported.

"What did you make of her?"

"Nervous, as you'd expect. She was desperate that her husband didn't find out."

"Was that all it was?"

She frowned. "Is there something else I don't know about?"

Strong looked back down at the statement, avoiding Stainmore's gaze.

"You were a bit obtuse when we spoke about it earlier," she said. "There is something, isn't there?"

"In strictest confidence, Kelly ..."

She leaned forward. "I'm listening."

"Charlotte is Claire Hobson's younger sister."

"Bloody Hell," Stainmore said softly. "So now she's had two major traumas in her life. And she could do with the third, like her husband finding out, like a hole in the head."

"Exactly."

A knock on the door broke into their conversation. Strong saw DC Newell standing outside.

"That's just between you and me for now, Kelly," Strong said, then raised his voice. "Come!"

The door opened. "Sorry to interrupt guv, sarge," Newell said, looking from Strong to Stainmore and back. "I've got a couple of things that you might want to hear."

"Sit down, Trevor," Strong said, indicating the seat next to Stainmore.

He did as asked and began to speak. "When I was trying to get some information from Mark Thompson's neighbours, I spoke to an old girl in the next door flat. She'd told me that she'd seen Thompson and an attractive looking girl get out of his car on Tuesday afternoon, that's Tuesday 12th. She next saw them leaving at around half past eight on the Thursday night, the 14th. At the time I first spoke to her, she said she thought this girl, well young woman really, was familiar to her but she couldn't remember where."

"Did she give you a description?" Strong asked.

"Yes. But she's just rung me this afternoon. She told her daughter this story and when she began to describe the woman, the daughter prompted her. Apparently, this woman works as a hairdresser in a salon in the Bullring. The daughter gets her hair done there regularly, not with this woman, with somebody else and sometimes, her mother goes with her and that's why she'd seemed familiar."

"And?" Strong prompted, grateful for the detail but hoping the young lad would get to the point.

"That's all I know at the moment but I was planning on paying the salon a visit."

Strong nodded. "Good idea. Let me know how you go on."

Trevor moved to stand up.

"Was there something else?" Strong asked. "You said there were a couple of things."

He sat back down. "Oh yes." He looked to Stainmore. "You asked me to go down to Agbrigg Road and see what CCTV was available."

"Got something?" Stainmore said.

"Sam's running through it now but I think so. A couple of likely suspects further along the road from the off-licence at around the time Thompson's card was used."

"Good lad," Strong said.

40

"Bob must be worried sick," Susan said.

The women were sitting on the sofa of the flat they shared, eating meals from trays on their laps.

"He's with her now. She's been admitted. They want to keep a close eye on her." Sammy said, shovelling a forkful of risotto into her mouth. She had texted Susan earlier in the afternoon to tell her about Alison being kept in hospital.

Susan put her fork down, a concerned expression on her face. "You know his history? With his son, Adam?"

"Tragic. But this will be okay, won't it?" Sammy was looking for some sign from her friend. Susan had experienced feelings before; not premonitions as such but something she couldn't really explain. She remembered when she had reassured them that Alison was safe last year when Bob had thought all was lost.

"I haven't had any dark thoughts, Sammy, if that's what you're asking?"

"Good." Sammy resumed eating.

"But I don't think he'll be too interested in this Claire Hobson story we're working on," Susan said. "You didn't mention anything to Alison about what we found out about Charlotte, did you?"

"No, of course not." Sammy looked closely at her friend. "But you want to push on with this story on your own, don't you?"

Susan grinned. "Well, you managed to get contact information on Kenny Green. All I did was call him and arrange a meet for me and Bob, so it would be a shame to waste it."

Sammy placed her knife and fork together on her plate and sat back. "What are you thinking?"

"You could come along instead? I wouldn't want to see him on my own, just in case ... well, you know."

"When are you meeting?"

"Tomorrow night. Half seven in some pub called The Shepherds Arms on Cluntergate in Horbury."

Sammy chuckled. "Careful how you say that address."

Susan punched her friend's arm. "Cheeky mare," she said.

Sammy's expression grew serious. "Have you mentioned to Bob the connection with Charlotte?"

Susan leaned back on the settee. "No, I haven't had a chance."

"And you're in no rush to."

"As I said, I think he's got other priorities at the moment."

Sammy picked up Susan's tray, along with her own, and carried them through to the small kitchen the flat offered. "Are we going in to see Alison?" she asked over her shoulder.

"I think we should, don't you?" Susan stood up and walked to the kitchen door. "Leave them for now. Do you know if visiting's the same time as it was on Orthopaedics?" Susan referred to the time she spent in LGI some eighteen months ago.

"I think so."

Half an hour later, Sammy and Susan were walking down the corridor towards the Maternity Unit, a bunch of flowers and a box of chocolates between them, when Souter emerged.

"How is she, Bob?" Susan asked.

"Can we see her?" Sammy added.

He smiled. "Hello, you two. She's fine, just resting. I've only come out for a bit of air while they examine her again." He looked at the flowers. "She'll love those. Shall we get a coffee or something, then we can go back in?"

They settled on a nearby pub, the hospital cafeteria already closed. Souter returned to the table with three soft drinks – he didn't fancy a pint and the girls thought it best not to see Alison with alcohol on their breaths. Souter involuntarily patted his coat pockets before sipping his Diet Coke.

Sammy noticed. "How long now, Bob?"

He laughed. "The one time I need a cigarette and I can't. Nearly five months," he said. "I promised myself after I found out Alison was safe, I'd give up. Colin's done it as well, you know."

"I don't ever remember Colin smoking," Sammy said.

"I think he'd given up just before you met. He still has a packet of cigars in his inside jacket pocket. If he feels he needs one, he just gives it a reassuring pat."

"So what's our next move on the Claire Hobson story?" Susan asked.

"*Our* next move? I thought you'd have some Uni work to be getting on with."

"It is part of it." Susan was aware of Sammy's eyes on her.

"Well, for the moment, I'm putting it on the back burner. I've got more important things to worry about."

"What about the Thompson murder? Any developments on that?"

"Look, Susan, I'm not being funny, but I'm not bothered about any of that. I just want to see that little bundle delivered safely and Alison back to full health."

Sammy nudged Susan's leg under the table in a sign that meant enough was enough. "So shall we go back and see the mum-to-be then?" she said, draining her glass.

The friends got up and made their way from the pub to the Maternity Unit.

41
Thursday 21st February 2002

Hemingford had conducted the briefing that morning. Strong felt he looked ill at ease. Flynn had probably told him that he'd broken the news of his impending departure to Strong. Again, the team felt it was a rushed affair, so Strong picked up a few of the main points once Hemingford had left.

The two youths suspected of using Mark Thompson's card in the Agbrigg Road off-licence had been picked up by CCTV further down the road both before and after the time the card was used. The images weren't clear enough to identify faces. They'd even appeared to have turned their jackets inside out in an attempt to confuse identity, the jackets light coloured as opposed to the dark ones worn in the shop. But the team was sure they were the same two who had committed the fraud.

"I think they're local to that area," Strong said. "Let's see if uniform have an idea who they are."

Luke Ormerod reported that, according to a DVLA check, Brannigan owned a BMW 5 series saloon, Mediterranean Blue.

"Interesting," Strong thought aloud. "I think we'll pay our scrap dealer another visit, Luke. But first I need to check something else."

With that comment, the meeting drew to a close and Strong sought out Gary Monk's sergeant, who confirmed that he was on a late shift starting at two that afternoon.

"Perfect, "Strong said to himself and went back upstairs to the CID room to speak to Ormerod.

Brannigan's scrap yard was quiet when Strong drew to a halt outside.

"Does he ever do any business?" Ormerod wondered as they stepped from the car.

"Where there's muck there's brass," Strong quoted.

This time, the frost had gone and they stepped around the puddles and mud toward the green office. They opened the door and caught the swift movement of a youth sitting behind a desk. He relaxed when he saw them and pulled an electronic gaming device from under the pile of paper on the desk. It beeped.

Strong smiled at the young lad. "Think it was the boss?"

He looked to be around sixteen with a sullen expression. "I'm only keeping an eye on things for him," he said.

"Is Mr Brannigan around?" Ormerod asked.

"I think he said he was going to an auction in Halifax." The lad relaxed and resumed his game. "Don't know when he'll be back."

Strong glanced at his watch. An auction would most likely start around ten o'clock and it was nearly half past now. He wouldn't imagine Brannigan would return before mid-afternoon. "He'll have gone off in the Beamer, then?" Strong said.

The youth looked up from the screen. "Yeah. It's lovely. Have you seen it?"

A chord struck, Strong thought. "Five series, yes?"

"540i, yeah." Enthusiasm spread all over the boy's face. "4.4 litre V8 engine and goes like sh... well, goes like the clappers. He showed me the engine once."

"You like cars then?" Ormerod asked.

"Who doesn't."

Ormerod took a photograph from inside his coat. "Is this Mr Brannigan's car, do you think?" He placed a still image from the CCTV footage from the Friday night in front of the youth.

A split second of recognition spread over his face before he became suspicious. "What's this about?" he asked. "You're police, right?"

"We're just trying to help Mr Brannigan in an insurance matter," Strong joined in. "Now, do you think this is his BMW?"

The youth studied the photograph. "It could be his. But can't you enhance this, or whatever you do and get the number plate? That's what they do on the telly."

Strong looked to Ormerod. "He's a bright lad, Luke." Turning back to him he said, "No, you see mate, not all cameras are that good – cost savings and all that."

The lad sat back from the desk. "Like I say, it could be. It's definitely a 5 series."

As Strong and Ormerod came into the station through the door from the car park, Trevor Newell spotted them.

"Ah, guv," he said. "I've just been back to the hairdressing salon where this Felicity woman works. You know the one identified by Thompson's neighbour as having been seen with him the day before he died."

"Yes Trevor," Strong said, leading the group up the stairs to the CID room.

"Well, according to her boss, Sharon, Felicity Barrett, as she's called, has suddenly left. No notice, just rung in yesterday to say she wouldn't be coming back."

Strong paused at the door to the Incident Room. "Felicity?"

"That's right. Name mean anything to you?"

Strong was thoughtful. "Maybe. And no previous indication she'd do something like this?"

"No, guv. She'd had a few days off at the beginning of the week then just dropped this on her out of the blue. Left her in a bit of a mess, apparently. Felicity was quite popular and had a lot of women booked in."

"Do you have a home address?"

Newell flicked open his notebook. "A flat on College Grove View."

"Right. Get over there and see what you can find out. Be discreet with neighbours if you can."

42

It was early afternoon when Strong and Stainmore walked out to his Mondeo to take the shirt back to Annabel. As they set off, she asked how he and Ormerod had fared with the visit to Brannigan. Strong told her of the conversation with the youth.

"So he's still a person of interest then?" she said.

"It would seem so," Strong replied. "But I'd like to see the car in the flesh first. It's just a pity the quality of the images is so poor. It might be worth trying to have them enhanced but only if we can find something distinctive about it."

They fell silent for a few miles before Stainmore spoke again. "So, how do you plan broaching this one, guv?"

"I thought we'd suck it and see. I just told her I was returning her husband's shirt and we'd be in the area."

"Again?"

"Not beyond the bounds of possibility."

Stainmore merely gave a shrug.

This time the rain was lashing down when they stopped outside the Monk's abode. Mrs Monk spotted them from the living room window, drawing to a halt outside. She opened the door as they walked up the path, inviting them straight in. After making a pot of tea, they all sat down in the front room.

"Was it useful? Did it work for your forensic colleague?" she asked as Strong handed over the garment in a brown bag.

"Perfectly," Strong replied. "That's given him a valuable control sample for a two-year period."

"I'm glad," she said, taking the shirt from the bag and holding it close for a second. "At least something useful has come out of Richard's passing." She placed the shirt on the chair arm and looked across at Strong. She could tell there was something else. "Is everything okay?"

He hesitated then said, "This is a bit difficult, Mrs Monk," he began.

"Oh, Mrs Monk's a bit formal," she said, "I thought I was Annabel to you." The nervous smile evidenced her feeling of unease.

"Well, Annabel," Strong said. "When I asked if I could take Mr Monk's shirt, I wasn't being entirely open with you regarding the reason."

A puzzled expression appeared on her face. "I don't understand."

He took a deep breath before he continued, "As part of Gary's joining process you know he had to agree to us taking fingerprints and DNA samples ...?"

Annabel stiffened. "Go on."

"What that threw up was something I needed to check."

"Which was?"

"Gary's profile provided a familial match to another sample we already had on our database. Do you know what that means?"

Strong could see the turmoil behind her eyes but pressed on. "It means a close relative of your son has had their DNA sampled before."

Annabel said nothing but her eyes became moist.

"However ..." Strong paused for a moment.

The woman wiped the back of her hand across her face and looked away. "I think I know what you're going to say."

Strong remained silent. The atmosphere in the room was almost claustrophobic.

Finally, Annabel looked back at Strong. "Richard wasn't Gary's father, was he?"

"I'm afraid not." Strong looked over to the framed photographs by the side of the fireplace for a second. "I'm thinking that isn't really a surprise to you?"

She stood up. Tears began to trickle down her cheeks. "Excuse me a moment." She covered her face with her hands and walked from the room.

"Christ," Stainmore said softly after the door closed. "Sometimes I hate this job."

"I know Kelly, but we need to find out who Gary's real father is."

"Biological, you mean," she said. "No doubt in Annabel's and Gary's minds that Richard was his proper dad."

Strong nodded. "Quite right," he said.

A couple of minutes later, Annabel returned, eyes red and puffy. She sat down in the armchair, dabbed her eyes with paper tissue, then spoke. "I hoped this day would never come," she said. "I always suspected. In fact, probably, deep down, I knew. When Gary was growing up, I'd look at him … and I knew. Richard never did, I'm sure of that. He could easily have been Richard's."

Strong sat back on the settee where he was sitting alongside Stainmore. They both remained silent, allowing the woman to tell her story in her own time.

Annabel took a deep breath and began to recount. "I was on a night out with some work colleagues. I was working in an accountant's office in Leeds back then. This would have been 1979. A group of us had gone out for the night. I'd just started seeing Richard." She paused, blew out through her mouth and smiled nervously. "We'd … you know, done it the once." She looked to the ceiling. "Sorry," she said. "This is difficult."

"I understand," Stainmore said.

"Really?" Annabel snapped before her expression softened. "No, I'm okay." Another pause. "I suppose it was my own fault. It was a good night and we'd had a lot to drink. I remember getting in this minicab along with two of the others. The driver seemed nice at first. You need to remember this was when the Yorkshire Ripper was still on the loose. Women were frightened to be out alone. Anyway, the way it worked out, I was the last drop." She fiddled with the shirt on the chair arm. "Oh God, it's at times like these I wish I still smoked." A quick nervous smile flashed across her face. "I think I must have been a bit drowsy because the next thing I knew, the car had stopped. A quiet lane near Low Laithes Golf Club, I think. He got into the back seat ... and ..." Annabel could hold it together no longer.

Stainmore got up, knelt down by the woman's chair and placed her hand on her arm. "He raped you?" she asked in a gentle voice.

Annabel nodded then broke down in sobs. "Yes," she said, barely above a whisper. She looked down at Stainmore. "And it was my fault."

"No it wasn't Annabel. You mustn't think that."

"But if I hadn't had so much to drink ..."

Stainmore gently shook her arm. "You didn't give consent and you were attacked against your will."

"But ..."

"So, the taxi driver, Annabel ..." Strong interrupted.

Her attention switched from Stainmore to the DI.

"Can you tell us anything about him?"

She sniffed and wiped her eyes. "I remember he spoke about having been in the army. I think he hadn't long left and had managed to get himself the driving job."

"I don't suppose you remember which taxi firm he was working for?"

She shook her head. "No, but it must have been one based in Leeds."

"I know it's a long time ago but is there anything you can tell us about him? Some sort of description?"

"He was short; shorter than Richard anyway. Stocky, muscular like. It was easy to imagine him having been a soldier. Short hair; brown, I think. A smoker too. His breath was ..."

"That's good," Stainmore said. "Any idea how old he might have been?"

"Perhaps a few years older than me, maybe early thirties?"

"Anything else that might help identify him?" Strong added.

She closed her eyes for a few seconds and shuddered.

"I do know this is difficult," Stainmore said.

Finally, Annabel opened her eyes again. "I think he had a tattoo," she said. "Here." She indicated her left forearm.

"Can you remember what it was?"

"Not exactly, but it looked like some sort of coat of arms."

"That's good. That might be something we can work with."

She wiped her hand across her face and composed herself. "This man," she said, "What's he done? It must be something serious for you to be so interested; to take so much trouble over DNA and suchlike."

"I can't tell you exactly, Annabel," Strong replied. "But as you suspect, it is a serious historical crime we're looking into."

Realisation spread over her face. "So if I'd reported this all those years ago, whatever you're looking into might never have happened?"

"We can't possibly say that." Strong said.

"Oh God, it gets worse." Annabel began to cry once more.

Stainmore stepped in again. "You can't think like that." She looked to Strong then back to Annabel. "What about your friends who were with you that night?"

"I never told them. I was too embarrassed."

"But have you stayed in touch? Could they give a more detailed description of the driver? Remember the cab company even?"

"No, I've not seen any of them since I got married. I can't even remember their second names. We just worked together briefly and had a couple of nights out. I never went out with them again after that. And I don't think the company's still there either."

Strong stood up. "You've done really well, Annabel. We have some solid material we can work with. But please, as Kelly here says, you can't blame yourself for any of this."

She looked up at Strong, a dark expression on her face. "Gary will have to know, won't he?"

"That's not up to me, Annabel, but I can assure you he won't find out from me ... or Kelly."

43

Susan and Sammy walked into The Shepherds Arms at twenty-five past seven to find the pub reasonably full. They'd driven there in Susan's ever reliable Nissan Micra. Various tables had diners sitting enjoying meals. At the bar, Susan ordered a couple of soft drinks for them whilst Sammy grabbed a table for four near the door.

Sammy picked up a menu as she waited for her friend to join her.

"Look at this, Suz," she said, as Susan sat down. "The food seems quite good. We should have eaten here instead of rushing something at home."

"Very professional." Susan said, taking a sip of her J2O. "Sitting here stuffing our faces trying to conduct an interview."

Sammy scanned the customers as best she could. "Anyway, have you any idea what Kenny Green looks like?"

Susan shook her head. "Not a clue. All he said was he'd be in at half seven. I told him I was mid-twenties, dark hair and would be with my blonde-haired colleague."

"Do you know what you hope to gain by this interview," Sammy asked.

"I'd like to hear what he has to say about when they discovered the body and, I suppose, what effect, if any, it might have had on them."

"And don't forget, I wasn't able to track down the other one, Paul Nichols."

Conversation paused while they sampled their drinks.

Sammy looked up as a couple entered the pub. He was about six feet tall with dark curly hair, reminding her of a younger Kevin Keegan but with glasses. The woman clinging to his arm was about four inches shorter with straight shoulder length blonde hair and a fringe.

He glanced round then made eye contact with Sammy. "Susan? Susan Brown?" he asked.

She indicated her companion. "This is Susan," she said. "I'm Sammy Grainger, Susan's colleague."

He smiled nervously. "Of course. Sorry, I forgot, she said you were blonde and she was dark haired."

Susan turned and stood. "Mr Green?"

He nodded. "Kenny, please. And this is my wife, Abigail. I hope you don't mind?"

They shook hands. "Not at all," Susan said, "Can I get you a drink?"

"You're all right," Kenny said. "Are you okay?"

"Fine thanks, just got these."

The man nodded. "I'll just get one for us," he said, making for the bar.

Abigail sat down next to Susan. "Kenny's told me all about that day," she said. "I think it had a huge effect on his life really. So if I think it's getting a bit difficult for him, I'll interrupt."

Susan held up a hand. "I quite understand," she said. "Probably more than you think." Her thoughts momentarily travelled back to the time she found herself trapped and injured in a derelict farmhouse basement eighteen months ago; her strange encounters with Mary and Jennifer, before the truth emerged.

Kenny reappeared with a pint of bitter for himself and a vodka and tonic for Abigail. "You're putting together an article for the twentieth anniversary of Claire's murder, you tell me?" he began.

"That's right," Susan said. "We're looking at two angles. Firstly what effect it's had on her family and those most associated with it. And secondly, we'll be appealing for any new information."

Kenny nodded. "Okay, where do you want me to start?"

Susan flicked open her notebook. "You were with your friend, Paul Nichols that morning, I understand."

Kenny sipped his beer. "That's right. We were best mates then. We were interested in railways, especially anything with a bit of history. We used to meet up and go to the model shop on Dewsbury Road, you know the one near Morrisons?"

Susan nodded. "A bit of a mecca, I believe."

"We'd go there on a Saturday and look at all the models of the old engines and things for sale. Spend hours there." He smiled at the memory. "Anyway, on a Sunday, we used to go to a few places where there was some real old stock, coaches, wagons and that, to see what we could identify. So that day, we went to the old sidings, just the other side of town here." He waved a hand symbolically. "Sundays were good because nobody was ever around so you could wander up and down the tracks and not be bothered." He paused for a second and downed some more of his beer. "I remember I'd just spotted an old LNER Gresley coach ..." he saw that Susan was puzzled. "LNER, London And North Eastern Railway ... anyway, I remember thinking, this thing is older than my dad. We climbed up. It had been used as a crew van but was withdrawn from service, waiting to be scrapped, like most of the stuff there. We poked about a bit then got down and crossed from that siding to another and that's when Paul suddenly stopped. I thought it might have been railway police, but he just stood there looking up the side of this coach. It took me a couple of seconds to register and then ... well." Kenny screwed his face up before carrying on, "At first I thought it was just one of those tailor's dummies dressed in old clothes that someone had dumped." His eyes became moist. "But then I was in no doubt. I stood behind Paul as he took one step then another towards her. I stayed where I was. I could see she was lying on her back. She was wearing jeans ... except they'd been pulled down to her ankles. Her black puffa jacket was open and her T shirt was up." He indicated this with his hands, "The one thing that sticks with me was her white pants. They'd been ripped ... and ..." He stopped. "Sorry," he said.

Abigail put a hand on his arm and gently squeezed, a grim expression on her face.

Susan stopped writing and looked from Abigail to Kenny. "Are you okay, Kenny?" she asked.

He pulled a handkerchief from his pocket and wiped his eyes before continuing, "I'll be fine. It's just I haven't thought about any of this for so long."

After a moment's silence, Sammy joined in. "What happened next?" she asked.

"Er, well, I remember Paul walked closer. I stayed where I was. He approached her, bent down for a second then stood up again. 'We'd best get police,' he said. So we ran back to the road."

"And you both ran for help together?"

"Yes. We got to the road and spotted a phone box, so Paul dialled 999 and that was it. We stayed by the box as they told us to, until the first patrol car came then we led the copper down to where … to where she was."

"Did you know Claire?"

"No. We went to school in Horbury. We found out later she went to one in Wakefield."

Susan paused taking notes and looked directly at the man. "What effect did that day have on you, Kenny? I mean looking back after nearly twenty years."

"Phew." He considered his answer for a few moments. "I had nightmares for a bit. I always worried that whoever did it would come after us. And I never went nosing around the railway after that."

"What about Paul? Did you stay friends?"

"We went on to the same class at school but it was never the same. He changed; started getting into trouble."

"How do you mean?"

"Shoplifting and that. Then he was caught having broken in to some old dear's place and nicking money. I steered clear. I didn't want to follow him down that route. I heard he did some time in the young offenders after that. I've no idea where he is now."

"Sorry Kenny," Sammy said. "Can I take you back to when you found the body – you said Paul bent down next to Claire."

The man dropped his eyes. "That's right."

"Did he touch her?"

He looked up sharply. "God, no. It wasn't like that."

"But there is something else, isn't there," she persisted.

"Look, it isn't important."

"Anything, no matter how insignificant could be important, Kenny."

Abigail squeezed his arm as tears appeared in his eyes once again. Finally, he answered, "It was a button. A tunic button."

"Go on," Susan encouraged.

"I told him he should have given it to the police."

Abigail was open mouthed. "You've never mentioned this to me," she said.

He looked at his wife. "I've never mentioned it to anyone before," he said. Turning back to Susan, he went on, "Paul, apart from his interest in railways, was also interested in the army. He collected things about that too."

"And this tunic button was an army one?"

"Yes. I remember it because it was the same as the name of a Deltic class engine – 55008 was the number, *The Green Howards*."

44
Friday 22nd February 2002

Souter woke with a start as the door crashed open. A sharp pain shot through him as he raised his head.

"Morning, Alison," the domestic called out as she wheeled the catering trolley into the side room.

"Oh God," Souter mumbled, rubbing his neck. He'd spent the night in a chair leant forward onto the bed where Alison had slept.

She looked across and smiled at him. "Excuse my husband," she said, watching the woman in the green uniform put a plate onto the mobile table over the bed, "He's had a rough night."

"You can say that again," he said.

"You been here all night?" the woman asked. "You should have climbed in," she had a broad grin on her face, "A lot of them do. Tea or coffee, Alison?"

"Tea please."

The woman looked at Souter. "Would you like a drink as well?"

"You're a star. Can I have a coffee?"

Once the domestic had left with the breakfast trolley, Alison turned to Souter. "Get yourself back home, Bob, and freshen up. Then get into work."

"But you're in here."

"Being looked after," she insisted. "Best place I can be. It's got to be boring for you."

"But you're on your own."

"That's what they want, so I'm being rested – keep my blood pressure under control."

The door burst open again.

"Hey, how are you?" Sammy asked, leading the way, Susan close behind.

"Have you been here all night, Bob?" Susan followed up.

Souter looked at Alison. "Is it that obvious."

"You look like shit," Sammy quipped.

Alison laughed. "That's just what I was telling him."

Souter surrendered. "Okay, okay, I get the picture." He stood and stretched his legs. "Are you two here for a bit?"

Sammy looked at her watch. "I just called in on my way to the office. About fifteen minutes, maybe."

"I'm in no rush," Susan said.

"Right. I'll go home and have a shower, fresh clothes and be back."

"Look, I'll be fine," Alison protested. "You go back to the Post. I'm sure you've got plenty of work on."

"I'm sure he has," Susan said.

Souter leaned down and kissed his wife. "I'll see you later."

"So, what have they said?" Sammy asked, sitting in the chair Souter had vacated.

As he opened the door to leave, Susan sidled up to him.

"What are we working on then?" she asked.

He paused a minute then walked out into the corridor. "*We* ... are not working on anything at the moment."

Susan dropped her voice. "But there's the Hobson article still being developed. I need to keep working on it for my project."

Souter sighed. "Well I spoke on the phone to Claire's older brother down in London, just before I got the news about Alison. My shorthand notes are in my notepad on my desk. I'll have a read through that. The next thing I was going to do was call the sister, Charlotte. Mrs Hobson had given me numbers for both."

"Listen, don't do that," Susan insisted. "It might be best if I speak to her. There's something you need to know first."

*   *   *

Strong climbed the stairs to the first floor deep in thought. As he passed the CID room, DC Newell came out.

"Ah Trevor, did you manage to speak to that hairdresser yesterday?"

"There was no one home when I called. Luke and I were going to try again this morning," he answered.

Strong automatically glanced at his watch. "And too early to see if she's turned up at the salon?" he said, almost to himself. "What about the electoral roll? See if anyone else is registered at that address."

"On it," he said and returned to his desk.

Before Strong could open his office door, quickening footsteps came up from behind.

"Could I have a word, sir," a young male voice asked.

Strong turned to see an agitated PC Gary Monk standing in the corridor. "You'd best come in, Gary," he said and opened the door.

Monk puffed his way past and stood, waiting for Strong to close the door.

"What's going on?" he asked as soon as the door closed. "Sir," he added quickly.

Strong walked round his desk and sat in his chair. "Take a seat," he said.

Monk stiffened. "I'd rather stand."

"Gary please," Strong went on. "Sit down."

Slowly the young man did as asked.

"What can I do for you?"

"I want to know why you've been round to my house upsetting my mum."

"Your mum misses your dad. I mean, it's been barely two years." Strong leaned forward onto his desk. "As she was talking to me about him, I could see how much she loved him. Just talking about him got her emotional. And I understand that. My own dad misses my mum every day. She died just before he was due to retire. Look, I'm sorry if just speaking about him caused upset but your mother was keen to."

"But the shirt, what was all that about?"

"One of the SOCOs is conducting research into the length of time DNA is present on clothing and when your mother showed me your dad's shirt in the potting shed and how it was his favourite for gardening and it was last worn just before he died, I thought it would help for a two-year test."

Monk shook his head as if he found the answer hard to believe. "And what about conducting the home interview again?"

"That was what we were asked to do ..."

"Look sir," Monk interrupted, "I've spoken to HR and they told me they had all they needed for my recruitment. There was no lost paperwork. I'm sorry, I realise you're a DI but there's something else here, isn't there?"

"HR are not the most efficient department, Gary. I was asked by a senior officer to follow this up. When DS Stainmore and myself had reason to be out your way, I said we'd do it. Now, if they're saying they have the paperwork from your original home interview then they've wasted our time too. But this is news to me. I'll certainly pass it up the line."

Monk didn't look entirely convinced.

Strong leaned back in his chair. "But generally ... how's it going, Gary? Are you enjoying things so far?"

Monk appeared to relax slightly. "It's okay, sir," he answered. "Off to a dramatic start last week with that murder."

Strong nodded. "That was unusual. It won't be like that often. Mostly mundane stuff you'll be frustrated with." He stood up. "But won't someone be missing you?"

Monk also got to his feet. "Er, yes. I'm on refs. I best get back downstairs."

"You take care," Strong said before Monk departed.

He sat back down at his desk and mulled over the conversation. It hadn't taken much for young Gary to work out something didn't add up. It sounded as though his mother hadn't told him about his biological father. How much longer she'd be able to keep that from him, or even if she'd want to, he didn't know. In any event, he'd need to let Flynn know about it.

But he had other matters to deal with. Flipping open his notebook, he thumbed back to notes he'd taken when he spoke to Mark's mother. Yes, there it was – Mrs Thompson's sister Veronica and her daughter by her late husband - Felicity, married to someone by the name of Andy. She never said her married name. But Veronica had been married to George Brannigan for ten years and obviously helped to bring up Felicity. What was it she'd said? 'It was Felicity I felt sorry for.' Exactly what did she mean by that?

*   *   *

"But we can't let on to Charlotte we know about her involvement with Weaver." Susan was insistent.

She was standing by Souter's workstation on the newsroom floor. The area was quiet, no sign of Janey Clarke at the next desk.

"I can see that," Souter agreed. "But it will need careful handling. From what Sammy told you, she was a bit fragile with having to speak to Colin." He thought for a second. "I wonder if he knows she's Claire's sister?"

"He probably does."

"Not necessarily."

"Anyway, I think it's best if I call her. You know, a female voice."

Reluctantly, he picked up his notebook from the desk and flicked over to the page he wanted. He passed the opened book to Susan. "Okay," he said, "but I'm listening in."

A few minutes later, Susan had dialled Charlotte's mobile number on Souter's desk landline.

After three rings, Charlotte gave a guarded answer. *"Hello?"*

"Good morning," Susan began. "Am I speaking to Charlotte Watkins?"

"Who wants to know?"

When Susan explained who she was and her connection to the newspaper, Charlotte almost ended the call. It was only Susan's assurance that she'd been given the number by Charlotte's mother and that it was she who had contacted the paper to draft an article about her sister's murder that persuaded Charlotte to stay on the line. Susan imagined the woman's fear that the call was to probe her involvement with Marcus Weaver. She went on to explain the two main thrusts of the article. "So," she said, "I'd like to talk to you about your sister and the affects it had on you. Would it be better if we met up somewhere?"

"Yes. Yes, that would be better," Charlotte said. *"It's just I'm at work and ..."*

"No, I quite understand."

When Susan replaced the receiver, the two women had arranged to meet after work at a pub in Leeds not far from where Charlotte worked.

*   *   *

Sammy walked down the stairs to the New Claims Section, pausing in the doorway just in time to see Charlotte pressing the button on her mobile phone to end a call, her eyes moist. She watched the woman stare into space for a second or two before standing up and walking towards her.

"Is everything alright?" Sammy asked in a quiet voice.

"Oh, it's you, Sammy," she said, dabbing her eyes with a tissue. "It's just ..." She walked out to the stair lobby and stood looking out over the Leeds cityscape.

Sammy stood behind her. "Not something to do with ... you know, the other day?"

"No. This is something else."

"Alison said you had a good meeting with Colin on Tuesday."

"Yes, he's a nice man." Charlotte turned back to face Sammy. "How is Alison?"

"You know she's in hospital?"

Charlotte nodded. "One of the women from upstairs told me."

"She's got high blood pressure and they've admitted her so they could monitor it."

Charlotte gave a thin smile. "It's quite common. I'm sure she'll be okay."

Sammy put a hand on her arm. "Is there anything else bothering you?"

Charlotte shook her head. "No, it's fine ... just journalists, you know ..."

Sammy cocked her head towards the office door. "Was that the Post?"

Charlotte's mouth fell open.

Sammy cast a glance through the vision panel on the stair doors. The last thing she wanted was for someone else to overhear their conversation. "Look, I know about your sister."

"Oh God." The woman began to pace around the landing.

"It's okay, Charlotte," Sammy said. "Who was it who spoke to you?"

"A woman. Susan Brown, she said her name was."

"Susan's a good friend of mine."

Charlotte put a hand to her mouth.

Sammy tried to reassure her. "I know she's been asked to write an article about what happened to your sister."

Charlotte was dismissive. "We know what happened to her."

"But not who was responsible. And if it jogs memories ..."

"I know, I know." Her shoulders slumped.

"So how has it been left?"

"We've arranged to meet up in the White Swan at half five."

"Look, say if ..." Sammy broke off as one of Charlotte's colleagues came through the doors from the office and out through the double doors to the stairs, a brief smile to the pair.

"If you want me to come with you …"

Charlotte brightened. "You know about all the rest, you may as well hear this," she said.

45

"So, Mr Barrett," Strong began, "We're looking to have a chat with your wife but, unfortunately we haven't been able to catch up with her."

Strong and Ormerod had tracked Andy Barrett down to a site in Rothwell where he was working. A call to June Thompson, Mark's mother, confirmed he had a cousin by the name of Felicity who was married to Andy Barrett who worked for a local construction company. Just routine enquiries, he had told her when she wondered why he was asking about them.

In his office, with the door shut, he leaned against the sloping work surface, a pile of drawings spread out on top. "She's away at the moment," he responded.

"What? On holiday or …"

"She's just having a break."

"Can you tell us where because we do need to speak to her."

Andy turned away and gazed out of the window as another concrete delivery wagon pulled in through the site gates, its barrel slowly revolving. "I don't know where she is."

Strong and Ormerod exchanged glances. "Isn't that a bit unusual? She goes off and you don't know where."

Barrett turned to face the detectives and they could see the anguish on his face. He raised his voice in answer. "Look, she's left me, okay?"

Strong took a breath. "I'm sorry to hear that, Mr Barrett."

He wiped a hand over his face. "She'll be back. I'm just not sure when," he said.

"In which case, we'll have to ask you some questions." Strong looked closely at some of the drawings sellotaped to the office wall. "You're an engineer, is that right?"

"Yes."

"Interesting job." Strong had moved on to a group of photographs on a cork pinboard. "Is this a model of what you're building here?"

Barrett was at his shoulder. "That's right. The architect produced that to help the client get a feel for the project."

Strong faced Barrett. "When exactly did you last see Felicity?"

Barrett walked round his desk and sat in his chair. "We had a short break at the beginning of the week. We went to Whitby. She left on her own on Tuesday. She didn't say where she was going." He nervously juggled a pencil between the fingers of his right hand.

Strong pressed on. "Does she, or indeed did you, know a Mark Thompson?"

Barrett dropped the pencil and bent down to pick it up off the floor. "Yes to both," he said. "He's her cousin."

Strong nodded. "And would you know when she last saw her cousin?"

Hesitation from the man. "I've really no idea."

"Are you sure?"

He shook his head. "I don't know. Why?"

Strong folded his arms. "You do know what's happened to Mark Thompson?"

"It's dreadful," Barrett answered, dropping his head.

"What about you? When did you last see him?"

"I can't really remember. It must have been before Christmas though."

"And your wife, Felicity, does she know about Mr Thompson?"

He looked up at Strong. "Yes. That was one of the reasons she wanted us to go to Whitby. Get a break, a change of air."

Strong turned to Ormerod who'd been taking notes. "I'd have thought she'd have wanted to be around her family at a time like this, wouldn't you Luke?"

"Undoubtedly," Chambers added.

"Was Felicity not close to her aunt, Mr Barrett?" Strong asked.

"Well, yes. I mean they didn't live in each other's pockets but they were in touch."

Strong walked over to the window and watched for a second as the driver of the concrete wagon hosed down the delivery chute. Turning round, he asked, "What about George Brannigan? How well do you know him?"

The question appeared to flummox Barrett. A look of alarm flashed over his face. "He ... he's Felicity's step-dad," he struggled to say.

"We know that. I just wondered how well you knew him?"

He shrugged his shoulders. "Not that well. He came to our wedding, of course."

"Did he pay for it? It is tradition that the bride's father ..."

"No." Barrett jumped in sharply then appeared to think better of it. "Sorry. I mean ... he probably had some input but Veronica, that's Felicity's mum, she wanted to make a big contribution. Felicity didn't want to take anything from him but he put some money behind the bar. Truth be told, he probably did fund a large part of it through Veronica. But we'd saved and paid for most of it."

"So it would be fair to say Felicity didn't get on with her step-dad?"

"She didn't really like him. I think she blamed him for her mother's death."

"How did Veronica die?"

"She had a brain tumour. She'd been diagnosed about five years before she died. I'm just so glad she made it to the wedding. That meant a lot to Felicity. And Veronica, obviously. God knows what she'd say if she knew we've hit problems."

Strong gave a nod to Ormerod. "Okay, Mr Barrett. We might need to speak to you again. In the meantime, if you do hear from Felicity, let me know." Strong handed him a business card.

Barrett took it. "Sure," he said.

At the door, Strong hesitated. "Oh, one other thing, when did you last see George Brannigan?"

The man's mouth opened and closed like a fish before he answered, "Er ... it must have been last year sometime."

"Thanks. We'll be in touch."

*　*　*

Susan walked in to the convenience store on Dewsbury Road and spotted Mavis Skinner behind the tills scanning some groceries for an elderly woman. Keeping an eye on the situation, she walked around the aisles as if browsing for something.

At last, Mavis had packed the woman's shopping for her and loaded the bags into her shopping trolley. She let out a big sigh as the woman left the shop.

Susan approached. "Hello, Mavis. Remember me?" she asked.

"Oh, you're that journalist woman who gave me a lift home with that other man."

"That's right. I just wondered if you could tell me anything about Mark. I gather he lived locally until quite recently."

"He was a nice lad." Mavis became defensive. "I'm not going to say anything that would let you slag him off."

"I'm not expecting you to. I just wanted a bit of background, give him some empathy."

"Big words lady," she retorted. "I'd known Mark all his life. He was a lovely lad, nice family too. He didn't deserve what happened."

"So something like this to happen to someone like Mark is a huge surprise?" Susan saw Mavis's glowering expression. "Look, I do honestly want to put a good gloss on this," she continued. "Anything that gives the public sympathy towards him will help encourage people to come forward to the police with information that could catch whoever did this terrible thing."

Mavis appeared to soften and her eyes glistened. "I can see him now, before he went to school, walking along, holding his mum's hand." She looked straight at Susan. "He was such a lovely looking child; dark curly hair and those big blue eyes."

"What can you tell me about the family?"

Between serving several customers, Mavis gave a potted history of the Thompson family; the father leaving the mother for another woman, her sympathy for the family and how Mark had grown into 'a fine young man' as she put it. She also mentioned his siblings, Becky, about four years younger and Edward, at fourteen, who she reckoned would probably be most affected by the loss of his brother.

"So you couldn't think of any reason why someone would want to harm him?" Susan concluded.

Mavis produced a paper tissue from the sleeve of the cardigan she was wearing beneath her overall. "I know he'd been in a bit of trouble growing up," she said then dabbed her eyes. "But that was when Mr Thompson left. He was a lovely lad. I can't imagine anyone wanting to ..." She left her sentence unfinished.

"I'm sorry," Susan said. "I don't mean to cause upset. Thanks." She leaned over the counter and touched her arm.

Susan left the shop, her thoughts drifting to one of the main reasons she wanted to take up journalism in the first place; the robbery at the petrol station where she'd had a part-time job. The two scumbags who threatened her, one of them jumping the counter, after money and cigarettes. She'd been scared to death and moving out of the way to let them take what they wanted – she didn't get paid enough to be a hero. Fortunately, the CCTV footage was good enough to get useful images and they were soon caught. But that was also her first encounter with the press. The reporting was creative to say the least. But it brought home to Susan that she didn't want to spend a lifetime in dead-end jobs and had thought she could do a much better job of things with accurate reporting, and so she set out on the path she was now following, a degree in Broadcast Journalism.

"Here, are you involved in the investigation?" a voice asked, interrupting her thoughts.

Susan looked down to see a youth of around twelve, sitting astride a bike dressed in an anorak and a baseball cap turned back to front. "You were here on Saturday, weren't you?" she replied.

"You're not police though," the lad said.

"Have you got some information about what happened to Mark?"

"Might have." He sniffed and rubbed the sleeve of his coat under his nose.

Susan smiled at him. "Well if you might have something to say, I might be involved in the investigation."

"He was my friend," the boy said before pedalling away.

"Hey! Wait ..." but he'd disappeared around the corner.

Back inside the store, Mavis was placing cigarette packets on the display behind her. She turned round and looked surprised that Susan had returned. "I thought you'd gone," she said.

"I had, but I was approached by a young kid, maybe twelve years-old, riding a bike too small for him and a baseball cap on back to front."

"That'll be Danny King. Got a lot off and seems to be growing up too quick. What about him?"

"He reckoned he was a friend of Mark."

Mavis raised her eyebrows. "Well he's lived next door to them all his life."

Susan gave that information a moment's thought. "Thanks again," she said and left the store.

46

"You think Monk suspects?" DCS Flynn asked.

"I don't think so, sir," Strong answered, "But he knows something's not right."

The two were seated in Flynn's office, Strong treated to the rare offer of a freshly made coffee from the DCS's coffee machine that stood on the unit in the corner.

Flynn stood up, walked over and gazed out of the window towards the Town Hall on the other side of the street. Light drizzle had fallen for most of the day and he looked down on the people walking past, shoulders hunched, hoods up, no doubt feeling miserable.

Strong sipped his coffee and waited until his boss spoke again.

Finally, Flynn turned and faced him. "He's obviously a bright lad, I'll give him that," he said. "His mother hasn't told him. Do you think she will?"

"I don't think she's much choice. It needs to come from her, and when it does, it's anybody's guess how he'll react," Strong said. "She was devastated when we told her why we'd checked the DNA. Obviously, we didn't tell her what sort of crime we were investigating, but she knows it's serious."

"What about this taxi driver? Anything we can use to try and track him down?"

Strong finished his drink. "Well, he hasn't committed any crime since the introduction of obligatory DNA sampling for convicted criminals in 1994. Who knows, he may even be dead."

Flynn nodded slowly. "Do we need to follow things up with Mrs Monk? Let her know that Gary's been to see you?"

"I'll give it some thought – talk it over with Kelly too."

Flynn was silent for a few seconds then resumed his seat. "What progress to report on the Weaver and Thompson cases, then Colin?"

"I'd have thought the DCI would have kept you up to speed," Strong responded, referring to Hemingford who seemed to have been noticeably absent for the past few days.

"Rupert is becoming more involved with Manchester. Technically, he's only got another week to go before he's officially seconded then transferred at the end of March." Flynn lifted his cup to his lips. "Have you thought about what I said the other day?"

Strong watched him drain his coffee before responding. "Nothing's changed," he said.

Flynn was stony faced. "So where are we with the Weaver case?"

Strong took a breath before telling the DCS that he'd now spoken to the woman who Weaver met that night and, as he suspected, Weaver was conducting an affair with someone from his office.

"And is she a suspect?"

Strong shook his head. "No, not at the moment. She's a witness but she didn't see a lot with the murky conditions. The thing is ..." He hesitated.

"Go on."

"The woman involved links back to what we spoke of earlier."

Flynn looked puzzled.

"She's Charlotte, Claire Hobson's younger sister."

"Good God. Do the rest of the team know?"

"I've only told Kelly. She took Charlotte's official statement."

Flynn nodded and Strong summed up the rest of the progress, or lack of it, on the investigation; the description given of the two men seen approaching the toilets around the time of the attack; the unidentified fingerprints on the disturbed cistern cover in the next cubicle. "But basically, we've stalled, sir," he concluded.

Flynn rubbed his face with both hands. "And the Thompson case?"

Strong outlined where the investigation was on that; the missing cousin, Felicity being the one person they were desperate to speak to. Other than that, no witnesses have come forward and no CCTV footage, apart from the lead they were pursuing to identify the two men who used Thompson's credit card on Sunday.

"Not used since?"

"No. We've got it flagged with the bank but, since then, no other activity."

"And nobody recognises them from the cameras?"

"No. It's not the best quality and they were aware – at least while they were in the shop."

*   *   *

Sammy appeared through the pub door, Charlotte Watkins at her shoulder. There was no hesitation from Sammy as she spotted Souter and Susan sitting at a corner table away from the general hubbub. But Charlotte looked nervously round the gathered throng of after-work drinkers before following her colleague.

Souter saw them, stood and approached the pair. "Thanks for agreeing to this," he said to Charlotte before introducing himself and offering them both a drink.

Settled around the table, Charlotte faced Souter with Susan and Sammy flanking her. "So what do you want to know?" she asked, sipping her tonic water. 'I don't want Steven to smell alcohol on my breath,' she'd told Sammy by way of explanation.

Souter gave a brief outline of what he had learned so far, repeating what Susan had told her of the purpose of their article. They'd both visited her parents and he gave his impressions of how differently he felt her mother and father were dealing with what had happened twenty years before. He also said he'd spoken to her brother, Martin, by phone. When he'd finished Charlotte was silent for a few seconds.

"Your mum said you were close to Claire," Susan began gently. "Perhaps you could tell us about her?"

Charlotte smiled for the first time since she'd arrived. "She was lovely. We were almost like twins. Despite her being nearly two years older than me, she and I got on so well." The smile fell from her face. "I missed her terribly. I still do." She looked to Susan. "I find myself, even now, talking to her about things that have happened ..." She turned to Sammy. "Things I've done; things I shouldn't have. And asking her opinion."

Sammy gave Charlotte's hand a brief squeeze.

When Susan looked to Souter, his expression indicated she should carry on; he was happy the girls were encouraging Charlotte to talk, better than he probably could. He was happy just taking notes.

"And when you realised what had happened to Claire," Susan went on, "how did you feel?"

Tears began to well in Charlotte's eyes. "I cried and cried. It seemed like days, weeks, but ... I was devastated. My best friend as well as my sister ... and I'd never see her again; never talk to her, share laughs, exchange views on who was hot and who was not." She dabbed her eyes with a paper tissue. "She loved Paul Weller. She had posters of The Jam on her wall." She looked down at the table briefly before looking up again. "After ... you know, I used to make a point of watching them whenever they were on Top of the Pops, just for her. Even now, when I hear one of their records on the radio, it nearly brings me to tears, I can't help thinking about her." She broke off and gave a little laugh. "Silly, isn't it?"

"Not at all," Susan said.

The two girls managed to encourage Charlotte to open up about what effects the loss had had on her at the time, especially when she realised what Claire had suffered before she died. They gently led her through how she thinks it has affected her since. Finally, they opened up the conversation, Sammy and Susan revealing a bit about themselves and the obstacles they had had to overcome in their lives. A few laughs were shared along with some concerns.

It was just after six when Charlotte, realising how long she'd been with them, said goodbye and left, hoping her husband wouldn't ask too many questions as to why she would be late home.

"Poor woman," Sammy said. "No wonder she's made some poor choices recently."

Susan looked quizzically at her friend.

"You know, her fling with Marcus Weaver," Sammy explained.

Susan shook her head. "You're not trying to tell me that because she'd been traumatised over her sister's murder twenty years ago, she couldn't see the harm in her, a married woman, having it off with a married man?

"Well ... if you put it like that ..."

"So where are we with pulling all this together, Bob?" Susan asked.

"I think we've spoken to the important people on this, so we have some good responses to work with on the traumatic effects of Claire's murder," Souter responded. "I can work something up about that and follow on with some form of appeal after reminding the public about the case."

"Without upsetting the Hobsons, of course," Susan added.

"Of course." Souter noticed Sammy giving Susan a nudge. "What?" he asked. "What is it?"

Susan looked to Sammy, a sheepish expression on her face.

"What is it you're not telling me?"

"Okay," she said. "The truth is I think we've uncovered some new evidence already."

"Have you been ...?"

"Using our initiative, yes," Susan interrupted then proceeded to tell Souter all about their meeting with Kenny Green.

"So, you're saying this tunic button discovery was never reported at the time?" he said once she'd finished.

"Not according to Kenny. His mate Paul held on to it because he collected army memorabilia," Susan explained.

"And I can't find any trace of a Paul Nichols since he was released from Doncaster Young Offenders in 1990," Sammy added.

Souter was quiet for a second or two. "This could be great," he finally said. "We uncover important information during the course of our enquiries." He looked intently at Sammy. "We'll have to find this Nichols character. We need to get confirmation of this story."

"But I've told you, Bob, I can find no trace of him. It's as though he's dropped off the radar altogether."

"We'll have to take this to Colin," Susan said. "He'll know how to find him — especially with him having a record."

"No, let's not be too hasty with this."

Susan leaned across the table. "You kept things from Colin last year, when it might have made a difference," she said, referring to the tragic events at Lofthouse Colliery which resulted in Kelly Stainmore being shot. He knew Colin still felt he had some responsibility for what happened.

"Susan's right," Sammy joined in.

"Look ..." Souter's mobile interrupted him. He looked at the screen and the Leeds number displayed before answering. "Hello."

The ground felt as it were moving beneath his chair as he listened to the midwife from the hospital relay the message that he should come in as soon as possible. She wouldn't give any details over the phone but Souter knew it wasn't good.

"I'm on my way," he said and ended the call. "Got to go, I'll see you two later."

He was on his feet when Susan asked what he wanted her to do about the Hobson story.

"I don't really care right now," he said, halfway to the door. "Other priorities," he shouted over his shoulder and was gone.

*   *   *

Strong looked around the CID room on his way out of the station. Kelly Stainmore was still at her desk, eyes on her computer screen.

"Nothing better to do, Kelly?" he commented, approaching.

She looked up. "Just thought I'd have another look through this CCTV footage from last Sunday and these jokers who used Mark Thompson's card."

"Nothing from uniform? No one has a clue who they are?"

"Not so far, guv."

Strong sat on the edge of an adjacent desk and watched as she fast-forwarded some images. After a moment, he spoke again. "I had Gary Monk in to see me this afternoon."

Stainmore swung round in her chair. "Does he know?"

"No, it doesn't seem like it, but he is suspicious."

"She needs to tell him."

"I know. I've just been filling the DCS in on it. It's only a matter of time before it all comes crashing down for Gary."

"You seem to have developed a good relationship with Mrs Monk," Stainmore said. "I think it might be an idea to call her and tell her Gary's been in to see you."

Strong nodded.

"She has to speak to him. It'll be far worse if he finds out from someone else."

"You're right. He's a smart lad. He'll work it out for himself eventually."

Stainmore rubbed her eyes with thumb and forefinger.

"Come on Kelly," Strong said. "Leave that for today. Get yourself off home."

She gave the suggestion a second's thought then turned back and powered down her computer. "Okay," she said. "It's been a long day."

* * *

Souter rushed up the stairs to the Maternity Unit, pushed open the door and breathlessly approached the two women who were sitting behind the reception desk engrossed in the contents of a computer monitor.

"Alison Souter," he said. "I got a call ..."

"Yes love," said one of the two who was dressed in a blue gingham uniform. "I'll just fetch Debbie for you. She's our senior midwife who's been looking after Alison." She stood. "If you'd like to follow me, I'll take you through to the office."

Souter sat in a chair opposite a desk in a small office off the corridor that led to the room where he'd last seen Alison. Debbie, or Senior Midwife Berry as her name badge proclaimed, sat down opposite. Souter saw the wedding ring on her finger and wondered if she'd considered what her married name would be beforehand.

"Mr Souter, I thought we should have a little chat before we go in to see your wife," she began.

"What's wrong? It's something serious, isn't it?"

The midwife opened a file in front of her. "You know we admitted Alison because she has a condition called pre-eclampsia, which is quite common but it does need monitoring." She ran a finger down a page from the file. "We're becoming more concerned that the medication isn't as successful in keeping her blood pressure under control as it should be."

Souter's stomach turned over. "What are you saying?"

"I'm saying that the longer we go without bringing her blood pressure under control heightens the risk of fitting and consequently increasing the risk to both mother and baby." She looked directly at Souter. "We might need to intervene at some point. I'm hoping you might reinforce this when you speak to Alison."

Souter was puzzled. "Does she not accept what you're saying?"

"Oh, I think she understands well enough. I just thought, if you were fully aware ..."

Souter nodded. "Can I see her now?"

"Of course." She stood and led Souter down the corridor to the side room where Alison was dozing, wired to monitors that beeped regularly.

He walked in and stopped. She looked different, certainly from this morning, but even from when he called in for half-an-hour this afternoon. Her face looked puffy and swollen and her hands, lying on the covers, looked bloated too. He walked forward and sat down quietly on the chair by her bed. Taking hold of her hand, he kissed it, his eyes moist. As he did so, she opened her eyes and smiled.

"Hello you," she said in a voice just above a whisper. She didn't seem to notice him wiping away a tear.

He stood and kissed her on the lips. "Hey," he said. "What's all this lying around in bed."

She gave a chuckle. "I'm just tired."

He sat back down. "I've just left the girls."

"How are they?"

"Oh, you know, all enthusiastic – especially Susan."

"Is she still helping on your cold case?"

It was Souter's turn to give a little laugh. "You make it sound like *Waking the Dead*," he said referring to the popular TV series.

"She enjoys working with you."

"I know."

"Anyway, how are you feeling?"

"Much the same."

"How's the head?"

"Still throbbing," she responded.

They were quiet for a few minutes before Souter spoke. "You know they're concerned about you," he said, as a statement rather than a question.

"I'll be fine," she said. "We'll be fine, me and the bump." She gently patted her stomach.

Souter kissed her hand again. "You know they may need to help you along?"

"But I'm only 36 weeks. We've got some time to go yet."

"But if something ..."

"I want this to be natural," she said.

"I know you do, love. But if ..."

"It'll be okay," she interrupted and closed her eyes. "I'm really tired."

Souter sat there, studying the woman who'd first entered his life only two years ago. Over that period she'd become his soulmate and just last month, his wife. He thought back to that dreadful day in September when he thought he'd lost her. The same day he'd found out about ... well, the bump, as they both referred to the being growing inside her. And the sheer elation when she'd finally managed to call him five days later. He looked at her now and the thought struck him that, having been through all she had, he couldn't lose her now.

47
Saturday 23rd February 2002

Susan drew her car to a halt outside the brick-built terraced house and switched off. They were on a quiet road just off Southfield Lane. Looking across to Sammy, she asked, "This is the right address?"

"According to what I discovered, this was the last known address of Paul Nichols."

"Okay, but let's go carefully," Susan said, opening the door.

The front door to number 26 was opened by a short elderly lady with white hair and glasses. Susan would put her in her mid-seventies.

"Mrs Nichols?" Sammy said.

The old woman looked confused. "Oh no, love," she said. "The Nichols moved out … oh, let me see … must be five years ago now."

"We're sorry to bother you," Susan responded, "but you wouldn't know where they moved to?"

She adjusted her glasses as she thought for a second. "Just a minute," she said before disappearing inside.

Susan and Sammy looked at each other, eyebrows raised.

"I knew I had something," the woman said as she reappeared at the door with a piece of paper in her hand. "Here we are. They moved to Middlestown." She held out the sheet to Susan.

Susan took the paper and noted down the address in the next conurbation about a mile away. "Did you ever hear of any family they had? A son perhaps?"

"Not that I ever heard of," she said.

Susan thanked the woman, handed the paper back to her and walked to the car with Sammy.

A short time later the pair opened a gate leading to a bungalow in a group that was designed for older people, with various handrails alongside paths and ramps instead of steps. Her knock on the door this time was answered by a tall man with a bald domed-shaped head, dressed in a cardigan and baggy trousers.

"Mr Nichols?" Susan enquired.

"Sorry, love," the man replied. "The Nichols were the previous tenants. I never actually met them but I had a few items of post arrive after we moved in."

"You don't happen to know where they moved to?"

"From talking to the neighbours, I think Mrs Nichols died about a year ago. She were the carer for her husband. I think he'd got dementia and is in a home now. That's if he's still alive, of course."

"You don't happen to know which one?"

The man shook his head. "Sorry," he said.

At that point a grey-haired woman appeared behind him. "Wasn't it that home in Ossett," she said, glancing at the man. "But I think I'd heard that he died not long after he went in."

Susan looked to Sammy, disappointment on her face.

"You don't happen to know if they had any family, do you? A son perhaps?" Sammy asked.

The woman frowned. "I'm sorry but I just don't know." She looked to the man but he shook his head. "Sorry not to be able to help more," the woman added.

"No, that's great. Thanks." Susan felt deflated. "Sorry to have bothered you."

Back in the car, Sammy looked at Susan. "Well that's it then. I don't think it's worth wasting any more time on this. I think we have to speak to Colin now."

"Agreed," said Susan. She paused for a moment, staring off into space.

Sammy looked at her. "Everything okay, Suz?"

She snapped out of her thoughts. "We need to get to the hospital," she said and started the engine.

* * *

The staff midwife listened in to Alison's stomach with the Doppler. This was the regular routine between readings from the CTG machine

"Is everything okay?" Souter struggled to keep the concern from his voice.

"It's fine," she said. "We just want to keep a close watch."

Alison opened her eyes for a moment and looked across at him. "Don't panic, Bob."

Panic? Panic? Souter's mind flicked to the situation he found himself in last September. Sitting in Chandler's office at the Post, he thought he'd lost Alison. And then, to compound matters, he'd discovered she was pregnant.

"I can't help it," he said. "Not after last year."

"It'll be okay." Alison closed her eyes again.

"I'll be back later," the midwife said and walked out of the room.

Souter studied Alison. Despite what the midwife was telling him, he wasn't happy with her appearance. She certainly looked bloated in the face and she'd mentioned the headaches constantly.

The door opened and Susan's face appeared. "Everything alright?" she asked.

Sammy was close behind. "Hi," she greeted. "Susan insisted we come."

Susan turned to her friend. "No, it wasn't like that. I just wanted to see how Alison was."

Souter's unease increased. Susan was trying to hide her concern, he was sure. He knew Susan was prone to 'feelings' that sometimes couldn't be logically explained. She'd once spoken of hearing her mother asking her to keep an eye on her father. Nothing unusual in that, apart from the fact that this was months after her mother had succumbed to cancer. A short time later, Susan became aware of her father displaying symptoms of early dementia. About eighteen months ago, her 'encounters' with two schoolgirls missing for over ten years led to the discovery of their bodies. And most notably, her insistence that Alison was safe when he thought all was lost last September.

He stood and approached Susan. "What is it?" he whispered. "What have you felt?"

"I just wanted to come," she answered.

"We wanted to bring you up to speed with our attempts to track down the other boy who'd discovered Claire Hobson's body," Sammy quickly interrupted.

"You're not still wasting time on that? It's not your article." Souter stopped, aware he'd probably sounded rude. "Sorry, Susan. I know you're working on this for your coursework. It's just not a top priority for me at the moment."

Susan touched his arm. "I know. And that's why we're doing a bit of background work so you'll be able to pick it up when you're ready."

Sammy explained, "We've tracked down his parents' last known addresses but unfortunately, we think they've both passed on and none of the neighbours knew anything about their son. So, the thing is, with what we've discovered, and the fact that this Paul Nichols seems to have disappeared, we think ..." She looked at Susan, as if for reassurance. "We think we should take this information to Colin now."

Alison groaned at that point. "For God's sake Bob, speak to him about it," she said.

Souter turned and looked at her lying in the bed and smiled. "You're right," he said. "As usual."

48
Sunday 24th February 2002

"Hello, ladies. This is an unexpected surprise," Strong welcomed the girls on his doorstep. "Come in, come in."

Susan and Sammy stepped into the hallway out of the steady drizzle that had been falling all morning. The aroma of a joint roasting in the oven wafted out to greet them.

Laura appeared at the door to the kitchen, drying her hands on a towel. "Hello you two. I haven't seen you in ages. No Bob?"

"He's at the hospital," Susan answered.

"Hospital? Is everything okay?" Laura asked. "Here, let me take these." She held out a hand as the girls slipped out of their damp coats. Taking them, she hung them on pegs in the cupboard.

"He's with Alison," Sammy added.

"Bloody Hell, she's in hospital?" Strong exclaimed. "I didn't know that." He looked from Susan to Sammy. "There again, when she brought Charlotte to meet me in Leeds on Tuesday I did wonder if she was coping well. She seemed uncomfortable sitting." He led the way into the living room and indicated for the pair to sit down. "And the last time I saw Bob ... actually, it was the night before, we had a pint together, everything seemed fine."

Laura followed the women into the room, concern evident on her face. "What's actually wrong, do they know?"

Susan sat on the settee. "They're concerned about her blood pressure," she answered.

"Pre-eclampsia apparently," Susan said, sitting beside Sammy.

"When did this happen?" Strong asked.

Susan looked to Sammy. "On Wednesday, wasn't it?"

"That's right," Sammy agreed. "It was her last day at work and she didn't feel well, so I helped her over to the Maternity Unit and they kept her in, there and then."

"I'll give Bob a call when we're done here," Strong said.

"Pre-eclampsia's quite common," Laura added. "Can I get you a drink? Tea, coffee or a glass of wine?"

"A tea would be good, thanks," Susan answered.

"Could I have a coffee, please," Sammy said.

"No problem." Laura looked to her husband. "And you'll stay for some lunch. There's plenty to go round."

"Of course," Strong added with a smile. "No Graham or Amanda to eat us out of house and home this weekend."

"Aw, that's really kind of you," Susan responded, "It smells delicious but we'll need to get back to the hospital and see how Alison's doing."

"Well, the offer's there." Laura repeated.

Strong waited until his wife had left the room. "Now, what was it you wanted to talk about?" Susan had called him earlier and said they had something important to share with him.

Susan leaned forward and hesitated for a second. "You remember when all that business occurred last year?" she began. "Lofthouse?" Strong nodded. "And how you were annoyed that Bob hadn't kept you informed of all he knew quickly enough?"

"You could say that," Strong said with some irony.

"Well, you know Bob's been working on a story about the unsolved murder of Claire Hobson?"

"We spoke about it when we met. He said he was writing an article to focus on the effects of the case as well as appeal for new information." A thought struck Strong. "Are you working on this with him, Susan?"

"I'm using it as part of my course work this term – at least I hope I am."

"Well if I know you two, I'm sure you're very much involved."

This drew a grin from Sammy. "The thing is," she said, "we've uncovered some new information."

"Now why doesn't this surprise me," Strong quipped as he walked over to a unit next to the TV and opened a drawer. He picked out a pen and some paper before returning to an easy chair, readying himself to take notes.

Susan proceeded to tell their story, interrupted on occasion by Sammy, of how they'd spoken to Claire's parents and that Bob had spoken to her brother by phone and they had met Charlotte, her sister. But they'd also been able to track down and make contact with Kenny Green, one of the two boys who'd made the grim discovery.

Strong jotted down the important points.

Laura returned part way through with a tray with some mugs and a packet of biscuits, setting it down on the coffee table in front of the women. "Excuse me a minute, I just need to carry on with preparing lunch," she said and disappeared again.

Susan continued with her narrative, telling him what Kenny had said about what his friend, Paul Nichols, had discovered at the murder scene.

Strong paused and looked up from his notes. "And you say Paul never made this known to the detectives at the time?"

"Kenny says he didn't," Susan replied. "But your records would show that though, wouldn't they?"

"I'll check that." Strong looked from one woman to the other. "But there's something else, I can tell."

Sammy took up the tale. "I was the one who tracked down Kenny's whereabouts and I've been trying to do the same for Paul Nichols." Strong leaned back as she paused for a second. "But there's something strange about that."

"How do you mean?"

"Well, I know he has a criminal record from around the age of about thirteen and he spent some time in Young Offenders Institutions ..."

Strong was surprised at what he was hearing. This could be one of his own team briefing him.

"... but after he was released in 1990 when he was eighteen," Sammy went on, "he just seems to have disappeared. I can find no trace of him."

Strong puffed his cheeks. "Probably moved away. It wouldn't surprise me if he wanted a fresh start."

"But I can't find any trace," Sammy persisted. "No record of anything for him anywhere; no death recorded, nothing."

"We've followed his parents' progress from one address to another, then eventually nursing homes," Susan added. "But no one ever mentions a son."

"He could have moved away, emigrated I suppose?" Susan thought out loud.

Sammy looked to her. "Not with his record," she said.

"Unless he's adopted a false identity."

"Look, I think you might be getting ahead of yourselves here." Strong indicated the notes he'd taken. "I'll look into this and see what I can find out."

Susan glanced at her watch. "We've taken up enough of your Sunday," she said. "I want to see how Alison is."

* * *

"What are we doing here, Suz?" Sammy asked as they turned off Dewsbury Road. "I thought you were in a hurry to get back to the hospital."

"I just need to check something out first." She turned to look at Sammy. "And it's almost on the way."

Susan had pulled up outside a pair of semi-detached houses on the Lupset estate. The nearest one, that on the left, was scruffier than its neighbour. The front door looked as though it could do with repainting and the windows probably hadn't seen a chamois leather all winter. A bicycle leaned against the wall by the door. By contrast, the house to the right looked cared for.

"Is there a reason for this?" Sammy was puzzled.

"Mark Thompson ..." Susan said slowly.

"That bloke who was murdered last week?"

She nodded. "His family live in the house on the right." Susan glanced at Sammy. "He'd only moved out to a flat in town a few weeks ago."

"You're not stalking them, are you?"

"It's the house next door that interests me."

"What way?"

"Hold on." Susan put up a hand as a boy of around twelve emerged and grabbed hold of the bike. They watched as he mounted the machine and began pedalling down the street.

They caught up with him about a hundred yards down the road. Susan wound down her window. "Danny," she hailed.

The lad looked over and wobbled on his bike. "What …? Who …?"

Susan had slowed down. "Can I have a word, Danny?"

The boy braked to a halt. "Who are you? What do you want?" he asked.

"You approached me on Friday," she said. "And you were hanging around when all that police activity was going on the week before."

Danny said nothing, just stood with a foot on a pedal ready to dash off.

"I got the impression you wanted to talk to me."

He sniffed. "Yeah? What about?"

Resisting the temptation to tell Danny to stop pissing about, she responded, "I'm guessing Mark."

"What's it worth?"

Susan studied him for a second. "Depends what you want to tell me."

"Who are you?"

She hesitated. "I'm a journalist. Susan's my name. Susan Brown."

"Who are you with?"

"Freelance – but I work with Bob Souter on the Post."

"Got to go," he said and before Susan could say anymore, he pedalled off.

49

Strong had spent the past twenty minutes searching the Police National Computer for the records of Paul Nichols. He'd read and re-read the list of offences for which he'd been convicted. But as Sammy had said, there were no entries after 1990 when he was released from Doncaster Young Offenders' Institution. Sitting at his desk, he leaned back and rubbed his eyes. After a moment he pulled out the piece of paper from his wallet with the mobile number written on that Sammy had given him for Kenny Green and made the call. Appointment arranged for first thing in the morning, he looked at his watch then stood up.

All through the roast dinner with Laura, his thoughts had strayed to what the girls had told him and what he knew of the Claire Hobson case. It had last been reviewed in 1992, Flynn had told him. Presumably that was when the DNA profiles were obtained from the original evidence, the ones that had now been linked to Gary Monk's biological father, and Charlotte as Claire's sister of course.

He'd also managed to speak to Bob. He didn't like the sound of Alison's condition, Laura had suffered from pre-eclampsia with Amanda but not as severely as Bob was describing. Tomorrow, if he could, he'd call in and see them.

He walked through to the CID room and paused. Kelly Stainmore was the only officer in. She was at her desk studying the computer screen. Silently, he approached.

At the last second, she became aware of him and jumped. "Ah, guv," she said.

"Nothing better to do on this miserable Sunday, Kelly?" he asked.

"Could say the same."

Strong walked over to the display boards for the two murders they were investigating. He studied the photograph of Marcus Weaver and the lines emanating from it. His wife and the written note of two children, aged ten and eight. He scratched his head as he thought of what Weaver had been doing that last fateful night. What drives an apparently happily married family man to engage in some illicit sex? He gave a grunt as he realised how stupid that thought was. How many men, and women for that matter, had thought they could enjoy themselves without causing any harm? What proportion of the population had? Weaver would probably still be indulging in his lust if he hadn't gone to investigate. But investigate what exactly? What had he stumbled across? The displaced cistern lid – was that significant? They had some prints from it, but so far no match to anyone known to them. And what about those two characters seen approaching the toilet block around the same time? Man A and Man B were noted on the board. Man A around fifty, short and stocky and Man B, in his twenties, good looking, according to the witness and nervous as well. Who are those two?

Strong shook his head and switched his attention to the other board. Victim here, Mark Thompson, recently moved from the family home he'd shared with his mother and younger sister and brother. What had he done to be able to give his mother five hundred pounds on the night he died? Why was there a young woman seen visiting his new flat in the days before his death? If the neighbour was reliable, and he didn't doubt it, she was his cousin, Felicity Barratt. How come she's now disappeared, according to her husband, Andy? There was more to be teased out of that thread. And then there was George Brannigan; seeking out Mark Thompson on the night he died. He didn't go for the story Brannigan spun them about looking to do him a favour. Had he been the source of Thompson's previous good fortune, so he was able to give his mother the money? He needed to speak to him again. And then ... he looked over at the other board ... that BMW seen cruising the streets of Lupset not only on the night of the Thompson murder but on the previous evening – that's if it was the same vehicle.

"Guv," Stainmore said, bringing Strong's thoughts away from the display boards.

He turned. "Yes, Kelly."

"Have a look at this," she said, eyes never leaving the computer screen.

"You got something?"

"Maybe. I was just wondering ... these two characters that have been identified as having used Mark Thompson's card ..."

Strong looked from the screen where she had frozen the footage, to Stainmore. "Nothing from uniform?"

She shook her head as she rewound the pictures. "I know these aren't the best quality, but ... look how they walk."

The footage started again, showing the two hooded figures walking along Agbrigg Road towards the camera. As Stainmore had said, the quality wasn't great and the footage was stilted. She then switched to a view of the two of them walking away from the camera.

She looked up at Strong as he studied the screen.

"Play that again," he said once the characters were out of shot. He pulled over a chair from the next desk and sat down. After he'd watched it again, he turned to face her.

"Are you thinking what I'm thinking?" she asked.

"Could that shorter one ..."

"I think so," she said.

"... be a woman?"

"And if so," Stainmore continued, "it would be no good looking for two men – we should be looking for a couple."

"And that prat in the shop should have been able to tell us that." Strong was annoyed.

"Not necessarily, guv. He did say they both had their hoods up and he wasn't paying particular attention."

"We need to get back out there and speak to that little scrot behind the counter again." He rubbed his face with both hands. "We'll do that tomorrow. Get yourself off home now, Kelly. Well done."

"I'll just be ten minutes," she said, "I just want to look at something else."

"Don't overdo it, Kelly," he said.

She watched Strong walk from the room, before turning back to her desk, happy to be on her own once again. She wanted time to gather her thoughts about what Annabel Monk had told them on Friday.

She took out an A4 pad from the drawer and picked up a pencil. She liked to note down and doodle various snippets of information on some of the cases she worked. As well as helping to provide clear thought, she also thought it therapeutic in certain ways which helped her deal with things. She'd only begun to do this after her near-death experience last September.

So it was established that Gary Monk's biological father was not the late Richard Monk. The only possibility, as far as Annabel was concerned, was this taxi-driver. Although Annabel blamed herself for letting herself fall into the situation on that fateful night, Kelly sympathised with her. She could well remember being stupid in her youth, drinking too much and taking risks getting home. But what was Annabel able to tell them? It was a taxi firm working out of Leeds. How many of them were there in 1979? More importantly, how many would still have records of fares from twenty-odd years before? She never mentioned first names but couldn't remember the surnames of her colleagues that were with her that night. And she thought the company she worked for then was long gone too.

But what *did* Annabel remember? This man was short, she'd said, shorter than her husband. From the photos of Richard and Annabel together that she observed on display on the mantelpiece, Kelly reckoned Richard would be around five foot ten inches. That implied the taxi-driver may have been around five six to five nine? Short hair as well, Annabel had said, and probably in his early thirties. That would put him in his early fifties now. He'd told her he'd not long left the army. So someone coming out of the army in late '78 or early '79? A smoker also. In those days, with connections to the services, that was unlikely to narrow things down. But what else? Oh, yes, the tattoo. Left forearm she was sure. A coat of arms of some sort?

Stainmore looked at the clock on the wall; gone five and it was pitch black outside. She looked down at the pad and studied what she'd just been scribbling. The initials AM were central, with RM to the right and a big question mark to the left. Lines linked all three with a line down the page to the initials GM. Below the question mark were all the points of information she'd just been through in her head. And a line leading to another set of initials. In the end, she thought there were just too many unanswered questions; too many lines going nowhere.

She rubbed her eyes and put her pencil down. The DI was right, she shouldn't overdo things; she needed rest. She stood, walked over to the door and picked up her coat from the hooks. Switching off the lights, she left.

50

"What's happening?" Sammy asked as she and Susan ran down the corridor towards Souter.

He was standing outside the room where Alison had been the last time they visited. Running his hand through his hair, he spun around to face them. "I don't really know. They're in with her now."

Susan took in his appearance. He looked grey and drawn; bags under his eyes, at least two days of stubble and crumpled trousers. He probably hadn't changed his shirt for a couple of days either. "Who are 'they'?" she asked.

"A couple of doctors, that midwife who calls everyone 'sweetheart', Debbie, and another one."

Susan led him towards some chairs in the corridor. "So what happened?" she asked as she gently pushed him down onto one.

He slowly shook his head. "I'm not really sure. She was resting and I was talking to her and then … then she started shaking, convulsing like she was having a fit." He looked up to Susan. "I don't want to lose her," he said and turned to Sammy. "I can't lose her."

A tear rolled down his cheek and Susan and Sammy sat down either side and instinctively grabbed a hand each.

"Look at me, Bob," Susan said. When he turned back to her, she continued, "You're not going to lose her … or the little one, trust me."

"I just …"

He was interrupted as the door to Alison's room opened and Senior Midwife Debbie Berry appeared. He instantly stood up. "What's going on?" he asked.

She took hold of his hands and looked at Susan and Sammy. "These your friends, sweetheart?"

"Yes."

"Let's just sit down a minute," she said, easing Souter back down and sitting next to him. Susan and Sammy stood. "We're going to take Alison down to theatre now," she said. "We were concerned with her blood pressure levels, as you know. And what happened earlier ... what you witnessed, was Alison having a fit. Now, we checked baby on the monitor and that showed what we call a pathological trace. That's not good. But we're going to deliver baby as soon as we can."

"Will she be okay?" Bob asked.

"She's in the best possible hands."

Before he could ask anything further, the room door burst open again and Alison on the bed, flanked by a woman and a man in white coats and another woman in a blue midwife's uniform, was whisked out and down the corridor.

Midwife Berry stood up. "You can wait in the room and we'll come and tell you when we know any more."

"But I need to be with her," Souter said, getting to his feet.

"Please, just wait here," she said as she dashed off in hot pursuit of the rest of her colleagues.

Sammy reappeared with three Styrofoam cups with lids on. Susan took one and Sammy offered one to Souter. "Any news?" she asked.

Souter gave no answer but Susan gave a slight shake of the head.

"I can't imagine it would be long," Sammy went on. "I mean, they'd perform a section wouldn't they and get the baby out quickly."

Susan gave her friend a hard stare, as if to tell her to stop gabbling on and causing Bob more worry. Truth be told, he probably wasn't listening to anything anyway; lost in his own little world of worry.

Susan looked at the space where the bed was then back to Souter. "It'll be okay, Bob," she reassured, putting an arm around his shoulder.

Slowly he looked up at her. "Do you really think so?"

Before she could answer, the door opened and Midwife Berry entered.

Immediately Souter stood up, almost spilling his drink. "How are they?" he asked.

"You have a son, Mr Souter," she announced.

Susan and Sammy broke into broad grins and hugged him from either side. He remained tense.

"The paediatricians are checking him over and as he's thirty-six weeks, he'll go into SCBU, I mean our Special Care Baby Unit for a while, until we're happy with his progress."

"But what about Alison?"

"We're stabilising her now before we send her up to HDU, the High Dependency Unit. We'll need to keep a close eye on her blood pressure."

"Can I see them, both of them?" He felt torn apart; delight from learning he once again had a son; fear that he had to have specialist care and terror that he might lose Alison.

"I'll come back and fetch you when we've settled them in. But don't worry, this is all perfectly normal for what Alison and baby have been through. They'll have the best possible care." She gave them a reassuring smile then left.

Souter shuddered. "Oh God," he said.

"Here." Sammy held out the coffee she'd rescued from him. "Drink this and calm down. You heard what she said. You'll be able to see them soon."

He took a deep breath. "I hope you're right," he said then took a gulp of his coffee before making a face. "Aargh! No sugar."

"Sorry," Sammy said, "I've mixed yours and mine up. Here." She held out the other one.

Souter finally laughed and held his arms wide. "I'm so lucky to have you two," he said.

They gave him another hug.

"You're so lucky to have those two upstairs," Susan said. "Now, once you've been to see them, we'll take you home. You need to get yourself a shower, change of clothes and freshen up. You can't let Alison see you like this."

*   *   *

"Your first arrest, then Gary," the desk sergeant said. "Well done, lad."

It was just after midnight at Wood Street and Gary Monk had a broad smile on his face as he saw the pleased expression of the sergeant. "Thanks, sarge."

He and his mentor, a well-seasoned PC were standing in the Custody Suite having handed over a man in his thirties they'd arrested for 'going equipped' to carry out burglary. A known offender, the sergeant decided he'd keep him off the streets for tonight.

"All right, go take your refs now," his colleague offered. "I'll follow this up for you."

Monk began to walk towards the canteen, which although unattended at night, had vending machines from which he could get a drink, a sandwich or some chocolate, and also allowed night staff to sit at tables and chairs. However, another thought crossed his mind and he changed direction and headed for the stairs.

The corridor was quiet, no one around at this time of night. He approached DI Strong's office and tried the handle. No surprise that the door was locked. Walking back down the corridor, he stopped outside the door marked CID Room. He could hear the blood pounding through his ears. If he was spotted up here, his whole career could be at an end before it had really begun.

Glancing quickly up and down the empty corridor, he tried the handle, fully expecting the door to be locked. Surprisingly, it opened. The lights were off but a couple of computer screens gave some light to the room. Light from the corridor also flooded in behind him as well as through some partially open blinds from streetlamps. He stepped forward and took in the array of desks. Also prominent were the display boards. He walked towards them and recognised photos of the scenes from the park where he'd first met DI Strong. Another board had pictures relating to the second murder that was the talk of the canteen – the body found in a skip behind the convenience store on Dewsbury Road.

Interesting as they were, that wasn't why he'd come up here. He wasn't sure what he was looking for, just a clue as to why his mother had been visited recently. If he couldn't have a look at the DI's desk, he would try to look on DS Stainmore's. But which one was hers?

Rather than risk turning lights on, he swung a beam of light from his torch around the room. Over the back of one chair, he spotted what looked like a woman's cardigan. That was his target. There were a couple of files to one side, a photo of an elderly couple, presumably the officer's parents and a desk tidy. In the middle, a few sheets of paper partly covered a pad, a discarded pencil by its side.

Now he was here, he was even more uncertain of what he might find. Casually moving the loose sheets, the doodles and diagrams on Stainmore's pad were revealed. He was about to walk away, thinking there was nothing here for him to learn when it clicked in his brain that he was looking at his initials in the middle of the page. Lines linked them to other sets of initials above. His mother's, AM and his dad's, RM. But what was the significance of the line to the left linking a big question mark with him and his mother? Then the list of features below? And a line down to the initials. CH. What did that mean?

He picked up a pad of post-it notes from the desk and began to copy what he read; Leeds taxi driver, early thirties, five six/five nine, short hair, smoker, tattoo left forearm.

"*Alpha Lima Two Four, where are you Gary?*" His radio suddenly sparking into life made him jump.

Hesitating a second, he pulled the post-it note sheet he'd written on from the pad and folded it together before putting it in his pocket.

"Come on Gary," his colleague's voice spoke again, *"We need to get back out."*

He pressed the button on his radio. "Be right with you," he responded.

Throwing down the post-it pad, he made a hurried exit from the room.

51
Monday 25th February 2002

DCS Flynn approached Strong as soon as he stepped onto the first floor at Wood Street. He seemed to have been searching him out as a matter of urgency.

"Colin," he said, "A word."

Strong flipped through what he'd been up to in recent days to try and work out why Flynn's face was so serious. "Something wrong, sir?"

Flynn said nothing, leading the way to his office.

Strong was still replaying what Kenny Green had told him that morning when he'd spoken to him on the way in. It was confirmation of what Susan and Sammy had told him yesterday.

Once inside his office, door closed, Flynn spoke again. "The Deputy Chief Constable wants to see you," he said.

Strong was mystified.

"Any ideas?" Flynn went on.

Strong shrugged. "Absolutely no idea, sir."

"Right, well …" Flynn frowned. "Best get on up and see him. He asked me to catch you as soon as you came in."

Assistant Chief Constable Roy Mellor's office was on the next floor up, protected by his secretary, a stern-looking woman in her forties. As soon as he walked through the door into her office, she looked up at him. "Ah," she said. "Mr Mellor asked me to let him know as soon as you arrived."

After she lifted the phone and announced his arrival, the office door opened and the man himself beckoned Strong in.

Mellor was a tall man with a straight back and full head of grey hair. Closing the door behind them, he bade

Strong sit in front of the large mahogany desk, walked round the other side and sat in the leather chair behind.

"Detective Inspector Strong," he began, "I've heard some good things."

"Thank you, sir," Strong responded.

Mellor opened a file on his desk and put on a pair of rimless reading glasses. "Now you're probably wondering why I've pulled you in," he said.

Strong remained silent.

"Can you think of anything?"

Strong thought for a second. "Unless you want to speak to me about DCI Hemingford, sir?"

"We might come to that. No, I was thinking about something you've been looking into; conducting a computer search." Mellor lifted a piece of paper from the file. "One Paul Nichols."

It finally dawned on Strong. "Ah, the reason he seems to have dropped off the radar."

"Why have you been trying to locate this man?"

Strong hesitated. "Has DCS Flynn spoken to you about the DNA result from one of our new recruits?"

Mellor took off his glasses. "He has, yes."

"So you'll know he's asked me to investigate discreetly?"

Mellor nodded.

"Well that led directly to the Claire Hobson case from twenty years ago. Paul Nichols was one of the two boys who discovered the body."

Mellor leaned forward. "But all their statements are in the files. Why would you want to contact them again?"

"I understand from Kenneth Green that his friend Paul found something at the scene that he kept and never told anyone about. The only person who knew what he'd done was Green."

"And you think Nichols could confirm what it was?"

"More than that, sir. I think Nichols may still have the object in his possession."

Mellor leaned back. "I see," he said and was quiet for a moment. "Well, as you've probably guessed, Paul

Nichols' file is flagged. He's actually in a witness protection scheme. He's not living under that name. He's not even in West Yorkshire anymore either. At the moment, I can't divulge any further information. I've been contacted by the liaison officer from the force responsible. All I can do is request an interview for you. But if they refuse because they don't deem it safe for you to meet, or Nichols himself refuses to cooperate, there's not a lot more we can do."

Strong exhaled loudly. "I understand, sir. But it would be important to the Hobson case if we could recover some new evidence. Even if the object is no longer in his possession, I'm sure he could give a pretty useful description."

"As a matter of interest, what object are we talking about?"

"It was an army tunic button."

"Okay, Colin, leave that with me." This was the first time Mellor had used Strong's Christian name. "But before you go," he continued. "Have you given serious thought to what might happen when DCI Hemingford goes over the Pennines?"

"I can't see how that will concern me, sir."

"Come on now ..."

"After last time," Strong interrupted.

"The timing might be different now."

"'Might be'?"

"Just don't do or say anything to close doors, that's all I'm saying."

Strong stood. "Thank you, sir," he said.

Mellor also got to his feet and held out a hand. "I mean it, Colin," he said.

* * *

Susan and Sammy joined a grinning Souter looking through the observation window to the Special Care Baby Unit. In an incubator next to the glass a pink, healthy-looking baby with an identification band on his little wrist was wriggling.

"Isn't he the best thing you've ever seen," Souter said.

"Well he's bald and wrinkly, just like ..." Sammy's quip was cut short by a nudge from Souter's elbow.

"How is he?" Susan enquired.

"Great. He's doing well, despite being four weeks prem. The nurses reckon he can come out of the incubator tomorrow."

"And Alison?"

"We'll go up and see her next. She's likely to be in HDU for a few days yet." Souter's demeanour grew serious. "She had a post-partum haemorrhage after he was born."

Susan tried to lighten the mood. "Get you, talking like a medic now."

"It's been serious, especially with her pre-eclampsia. At one point in the night I thought ..."

"Well don't. She'll be fine," Susan interrupted.

He stood a moment and looked at the pair. "Listen," he said, "thanks for taking care of me yesterday."

"Come on, you big pudding," Sammy said, leading the way to the door. "I want to see my friend."

The three approached the nurse station at the doors to HDU. Souter recognised the white-coated doctor with her stethoscope dangling around her neck that seemed to be the badge of honour all the medics wore. She was huddled over a file and writing some notes into it. Her name badge on a lanyard was turned wrong way round but he knew she was Dr Moore.

"How's Alison this morning? Mrs Souter," he added quickly.

She looked up and smiled. "She's still tired. All that effort yesterday, plus the scare she put us through during the night, but she seems stable." She looked at the two women with him. "Three might be a bit much just yet," she continued. "Perhaps five minutes only, two at a time maybe?"

"Sure, doctor." Souter looked round at his friends. "Who wants to come in first?"

"You go, Sammy," Susan said. "With staying with Alison last year and helping to get your job and all, you're probably closer."

Sammy smiled. "I won't be long."

Souter led the way into the room where Alison lay on a bed coupled up to an array of monitors, cannulas in both hands. Her eyes were closed.

"Hey," Souter said softly. "How are you this morning?"

Her eyelids fluttered.

"I've got someone to see you."

"Hi, Alison," Sammy said. "You've done really well."

A thin smile appeared on Alison's face. "Hello you," she said. "I hope you're looking after this big lummox."

"This big one here has been going all soft," Sammy replied. "We've just been down to see the little one and he looks gorgeous."

"I hope they can let me see him again soon."

"Have you settled on a name yet?"

Souter's face broke into a broad grin. "We have, haven't we," he said.

"We're going to call him David," Alison said.

"After my dad," Souter added.

"Aw, that's lovely." Sammy reached over and squeezed Alison's hand. "How are you feeling though?"

"Tired. Ripped apart. Other than that ... you know."

"Susan's outside. I'll just let her come in for a minute." Sammy said. "I'll come back and see you later. Get some rest."

52

Deep in thought, Strong made his way down from the ACC's office to the CID room. It all made sense now, Nichols disappearing off the face of the earth, or so it seemed. He wondered what he'd been involved with that made him so valuable they'd placed him in Witness Protection. He might never find out. More to the point, he might never be able to establish whether there was a piece of missing evidence from the crime scene at Horbury railway sidings.

About to turn into the CID room, he came across Stainmore and Ormerod on their way out.

"Ah, there you are, guv," Stainmore said. "I was looking for you earlier."

"I got waylaid on my way in, Kelly. Where are you two off to?"

"I thought we'd follow up on that CCTV footage we looked at yesterday and pay our friendly off-licence manager a visit."

"Give me a minute and I'll come with you," he said.

Weak sun had appeared as the trio left the pool car Ormerod had parked on a side street off Agbrigg Road. They walked around the corner and opened the shop door. Brian, the same assistant Strong and Stainmore had spoken to nearly a week earlier, was serving an elderly woman with cigarettes and some cans of soft drinks. Two schoolboys were browsing the lager section but made a hasty exit when they saw the detectives.

The woman placed the cans in a carrier bag and the cigarettes in her coat pocket before holding out a hand for change. As Brian placed the coins in her hand, he spotted Strong, Stainmore at his shoulder.

"Oh, it's you again," the shop assistant said.

"Indeed it is, Brian," Strong replied.

The woman gave them a stare as she shuffled past and headed for the door.

"I think you might be able to help us a bit more than the last time," Strong said.

"I told you all I know."

"I don't think that's strictly true."

Further conversation was disrupted by sudden activity at the shop door. The woman customer stumbled into a display of cans on a shelf as two figures bundled past her and made a hurried exit.

Ormerod, who'd wandered towards the other side of the shop rushed over to help her up. Stainmore dashed towards him. "I'll look after this lady," she said, "You get after those two."

Strong watched, surprised for a second, before dashing for the door.

Outside, there was no sign of the two fugitives but he just caught sight of Ormerod racing up the road on the opposite side and disappearing down a side street. He quickly followed but, by the time he made it to the corner, all was quiet.

Ormerod had been suspicious of the two characters towards the corner of the shop behind the blanked-out window since he spotted them furtively looking at the display of white wine. It was as he turned to watch what progress his colleagues were making by the cash till that the two sprinted for the door, knocking over the elderly woman who had just been served. He rushed to help but then set off in hot pursuit once he saw Stainmore was assisting the woman.

It surprised him how agile they were. By the time he made it outside, one had already crossed the road and was sprinting up the other side, the second narrowly missed being knocked over by a taxi, rolling over the bonnet and back onto their feet before following their companion.

Traffic had momentarily stopped and Ormerod took advantage to sprint across the road and hurtle after them. By the time he reached the corner where they had turned, the lead individual had disappeared but he was gaining on the second. After about a hundred yards, the character turned sharp left and into a ginnel. A few yards later, he was close enough to grab the collar of their anorak and haul them to the ground. A barrage of muffled expletives and insults were thrown at him as he pulled their arms behind them and put the cuffs on. It was only as he turned his prisoner over that he realised the twisted face before him, still hurling insults and spittle, was a woman.

"Calm down," he told her. "We need to talk to you."

"Bastard!" she yelled, "Get your ..."

But Ormerod blanked her out, hauling her to her feet and marching her down the street and back to the shop.

Stainmore had helped the woman to her feet by the time Strong returned. With assurances she was fine, the woman just wanted to be on her way.

"Have you seen those two before?" Stainmore asked her.

"Not sure," she responded. "Hoods up, they all look the same."

"Are you sure about that, Mrs er ...?" Strong joined in.

Her body language and expression told him she would have nothing to say but he always had hope in situations like these.

"Like I said, they all look alike. Now, can I go? I need to get home, the grandkids are coming round after school."

"Okay, but we may need to speak to you again," Strong said resignedly.

The woman left the shop reluctantly giving a name and address to Stainmore.

Strong focussed his attention on Brian who was standing behind the counter having watched all the action. "You know what I'm going to ask you?" he said.

Brian nodded. "The CCTV tape, yes."

Before anything further, Ormerod bundled the young woman back into the shop.

"Get your fucking hands off me," she was saying, although with less enthusiasm than she had out on the street.

She looked from Stainmore to Strong. "Are you his boss?"

"And you are?"

"Never mind that," she said looking to Stainmore now, "I want to make a complaint. He was havin' a feel of my tits, dirty bastard."

"Before we get onto that," Strong said, "Can you tell us why you shot off out the door in such a hurry? Causing injury to that other customer, by the way."

She looked round. "Where? I don't see anybody. We never hurt anyone."

"That's the other thing we want to speak to you about. Who's 'we'?"

"Did I say that? Never seen them before."

Strong smiled. "So why did you leg it?"

"Remembered I had to be somewhere."

Strong had had enough of the prevarication. "Can you take this ... lady to the car, Kelly. We'll continue this 'discussion' at Wood Street."

The woman began to protest again. "You can't do that, I've done nothing wrong."

"In which case we can clear this up fairly quickly."

As Stainmore bundled the woman from the shop, Strong turned back to Brian. "Now," he began, "can we have a sensible conversation from you. Those two ... who are they?"

"I'm not too sure. I think they call her Trace – I assume that's Tracey."

"So you have seen them around?"

"A couple of times, yeah."

"So what about the other one – the bloke?"

Brian had coloured. "Si. I think I've heard her call him Si."

"So where do they live, Brian? Obviously nearby?"

He shrugged. "I've no idea – honest."

Strong looked over at Ormerod who'd been standing silently by the door. "I don't think Brian here could be honest to save his life."

"But I don't," Brian protested. "I see them come in here and I see them leave. I've no idea where they go."

"But they come in regularly?"

"Not that regular."

"But they were in the Sunday before last." Strong leaned over the counter towards the man. "The Sunday when they came in and used the stolen card."

Brian looked down and slowly nodded his head then looked up. "But I only realised that long afterwards."

"Well, thanks for calling us to say that."

A shrug.

"Okay, we'll have the CCTV from today. DC Ormerod will give you a receipt."

53

Later that morning, Sammy went back to work, no doubt to face a barrage of questions about Alison's condition, the new baby and when the rest of her colleagues could visit. At the same time, Souter, accompanied by Susan, walked down to the Post's offices. The pair went up to see John Chandler, the Deputy Editor, to let him know what was happening with Alison.

Chandler was all smiles. "What a different atmosphere in this office to the last time all three of us were here," he said, referring to when they watched events from New York unfold on the television last September, not knowing Alison's fate.

He opened a drawer in the filing cabinet behind his desk and drew out an opened bottle of single malt whisky and three glasses. "Just a small one to wet little David's head."

Toast made, and reassurances given to Souter about taking time off, he finally asked about progress on the story Souter had been asked to work on regarding the Claire Hobson murder.

"You know Susan is assisting on this? Souter replied. "Part of her university coursework."

Chandler nodded. "How is the course faring up?" he asked her.

"Great," she said, "Really enjoying it."

"Well, you know I have no problems with you continuing to help Bob on this. Your work last summer was very promising."

Susan looked suitably embarrassed. "Thanks."

Souter then outlined what work they'd done on the story telling Chandler about Susan's conversation with one of the boys who'd discovered the body and the possible new evidence uncovered.

Chandler raised his brows. "Good stuff. And you think this may be significant?"

"We're not sure yet," Souter said, "but I told Susan to speak to my contact at Wakefield CID who I know is looking into the case. Probably a cold case review, although he's already got his hands full with those two murders."

"Ah, yes, the man in the park toilets and that other young lad."

"I need to speak to him again and see if this tunic button we learnt about is significant."

"But don't be afraid to use this one's talents, Bob," Chandler said, thumbing towards Susan. "Stay on it and stay in touch, but don't forget your main priorities at the moment."

"I'll make sure he doesn't," Susan joined in.

After being shown where Souter's notes on the Hobson article were in his desk, Susan left him to return a few calls and answer some emails and walked back down to reception.

About to leave through the main doors, one of the women who manned the desk called her over. "You're Susan, aren't you?" she asked.

"Susan Brown, yes." She walked to the desk.

The receptionist held out a piece of paper. "Sounded quite young when he rang up this morning."

Susan read it.

'Danny King. I'll be at the shop at 5.'

"Thanks," she said and left.

*   *   *

The wipers swept over the front screen of the black BMW. The car was parked in a bay of the supermarket car park facing the road. On the other side of the street was a hairdressing salon. This was Timperley on the southern outskirts of Manchester. The drizzle had started about ten minutes ago, always threatened by the leaden sky.

The salon was well-lit and he watched the tall, pretty girl with the long dark hair busying herself around a chair on the left hand side, half way down the length of the shop. Patrick was as reliable as ever. He'd been able to trace Felicity to this quiet district on the other side of the Pennines.

Brannigan thought back to the television programme he'd watched the night before. Some man had fallen out with all his family some twenty years before he died. And when it happened, there were no members who had wanted anything to do with him. Until, that was, they discovered he was worth a small fortune. Then, they'd challenged the will. But the man had left all his wealth to charities. And all this after his funeral where no one, apart from the undertakers had turned up.

He wondered if that could happen to him? With all that had happened in recent years, with Veronica's passing and the stroke that Felicity had pulled. He was surprised at how it had affected him.

He mulled over what he was going to do next. If truth be told, he wasn't sure. It was vital he found his step-daughter, but he wasn't concerned about the money anymore. God knows she would probably be left that and more when he passed on. Despite not being a blood relative, she was the only family he had. But he was incensed that she had found it necessary to do what she did.

It had been over two years now since her mother, his beloved Veronica, had died. It was time to try and make peace with Felicity and try and convince her of the truth. He had loved Veronica deeply, but she made him promise to keep her brain tumour between themselves for as long as possible. That was difficult for him. There were times when he felt he needed to explain that to Felicity. Behaviour Felicity witnessed that was ambiguous gave her completely the wrong impression. Finally, two months before she died, Veronica sat Felicity down and broke the news. Felicity was angry, annoyed, then sad. She felt she had missed the opportunity to enjoy as much of her time with her mother as possible. Had she known the full picture, she would have made more of an effort to ensure they could have spent more time together. For that, she also blamed Brannigan. He should never have kept that secret from her. Felicity wouldn't listen to reason that it was her mother's wish that she wasn't told.

And now, with what she had engineered, it didn't look as if she would accept anything different. But he had to try. A glance to his watch. It would probably be some time yet before she left work. And where was she staying? Was there another man involved? He honestly hoped not.

He pulled his mobile from his pocket and dialled the yard number. A young lad answered on the fourth ring.

"Anything to report," he asked.

The lad mentioned a couple of people who'd called in; one looking for a door from a Mark 1 Ford Mondeo, and somebody trying to find a front wing for a Renault Clio.

"He'll be lucky," Brannigan said. "Any further visits from the plod?"

"Nothing," the youth answered.

Brannigan ended the call and dialled another number.

"What do you want?" Andy's sharp tone answered.

"Hey, calm down. Don't get stroppy," Brannigan said. "I just wondered if you'd heard anything from Felicity?"

"Not a peep. You?"

"She's hardly likely to call me now, is she?"

"I suppose not." There was a pause before Andy continued, *"I had a visit from the police on Friday. A DI Strong and another one called Ormerod."*

"What was that to do with?"

"Mark's murder. They were asking about Felicity, seeing as she was his cousin. And then they asked if I knew you and when I'd last seen you."

"So what did you say?"

"Couldn't really remember, but before Christmas."

Brannigan thought for a moment. "Would you want her back?"

"Felicity? Of course. I love her but she doesn't make it easy."

Brannigan gave a small chuckle. "All right Andy, but you tell me if she does get in touch."

54

"So where are you living, Tracey?" Stainmore asked, as she sat opposite the woman they'd brought in from Agbrigg Road. Strong was alongside.

She wriggled in her seat. "What about my complaint?"

"We can deal with that once we've established a few facts."

"Sweep it under the carpet you mean."

Stainmore ignored the comment. "Are you and Si an item?"

There was a slight reaction before Tracey put on the act. "Si? Who's Si?"

"Short for Simon. The man you were with, in the off-licence. The man you were following when you both ran from the shop."

"Never met him before. I just legged it because I thought there was going to be trouble, especially when he knocked that old girl over."

Strong had had enough. "Okay, Tracey," he said, "here's the deal. We have you and your boyfriend on CCTV using a stolen credit card in the same off-licence the Sunday before last ..."

She shook her head and interrupted. "No, it wasn't me. Those cameras are not good enough. Besides, I always have my hood up."

Strong leaned forward and stared hard at the woman. "But the really important thing to bear in mind, Tracey, for all your smart-arse attitude and answers, is that this particular card belonged to a man who was murdered just hours before."

She paled and looked down. "Well I don't know nothing about that."

Stainmore took up the questioning again. "So you can see how it looks, Tracey. At the moment, we have a direct connection with you – and Simon – to our murder victim within hours of the incident." She paused for effect. "Now stealing his wallet and credit cards, that would be a pretty good motive for murder."

"We didn't touch no wallet." Almost as soon as she said it, she seemed to realise the mistake she'd made. "That's if it was us."

Strong and Stainmore exchanged looks.

In a calm tone, Strong said, "We'd like to help you Tracey. But to do that, you need to help us. So … where are you and Simon living? I'm assuming you are living together. And probably some bedsit just off Agbrigg Road."

"Look, I had nothing to do with that card."

"Oh I know," Strong responded. "It was Si who used it in the shop. We can see that. But …"

"I never touched the card. He got it."

"Simon?"

Tracey slowly nodded.

"So where is Simon? Where would he go?"

"Probably back at the room."

"Which is?"

She reeled off an address near where Simon was last seen. Strong stopped the interview as Stainmore took Tracey to a holding cell. Despite initial protest, she quickly realised she would be at the station for a while.

*　　*　　*

Susan parked her Micra by the entrance to the service yard of the corner shop where Mark Thompson's body had been found, and waited. A check of the watch; five to five. The radio was on and she was looking forward to the five o'clock news bulletin when she spotted him, pedalling up the road towards her. He passed by and looked in, making sure who she was. Then he turned round, gave a little wave and pedalled off back the way he came.

She started the car and followed him. He turned left and then left again into a dirt track leading to some garages. She followed slowly, not sure what he might be leading her to. Her car's headlights swung round to reveal an empty road. The boy was nowhere to be seen. She paused and waited again. From between two garages a head appeared and then a hand, beckoning her forward. Slowly she did and came to a stop by the first structure. But she had the car in reverse gear in case she had to make a quick exit.

Danny looked up and down then approached the passenger door. He opened it and climbed inside.

"What's with all this cloak and dagger stuff?" Susan asked.

"Kill the lights," Danny said. "I don't want to be seen talking to anyone."

Susan did, then turned to the lad. "What's scaring you, Danny?"

"Me? Nothing." His head swivelled, looking all round.

Susan paused a moment. "So, what do you want to tell me?"

Danny's breathing quickened. "I'm not even sure this is a good idea."

"Look, Danny, it feels to me like you need to talk to someone, share something. I can listen. And I promise you, I can keep secrets too."

He took a deep breath.

"You liked Mark, didn't you?" she pressed on. In the dull light she could see his eyes begin to glisten. "He was your friend, you told me."

Then, his shoulders began to heave up and down.

"Do you know what happened to him?"

The floodgates opened and he burst into tears, barely able to breathe before turning to her and burying his head in her chest. Awkwardly, she put her arm around his shoulder.

After a few minutes, his anguish subsided and he pulled away. "Sorry," he said.

"In your own time," she encouraged.

55

It was gone six o'clock when the lights began to go out in the salon opposite. Felicity emerged a minute or two later alongside another, shorter woman of around the same age. The rain had become heavy and, after the other woman had locked the door, the two of them raised umbrellas and set off up the road.

Brannigan started his car, backed out from the space he'd occupied for hours, and headed off in pursuit.

As he waited at the lights, he watched Felicity and her colleague walk to a bus stop on the opposite side of the main road. Seconds later, a car horn bipped behind him, telling him the lights had changed.

He set off, turning right, before pulling in to a space on the left-hand side of the street behind a delivery van. Despite the weather and the gloom, he could see the double yellow lines at the kerb but trusted there were no traffic wardens around at this time of day. He adjusted the interior mirror so he could observe the queue at the bus stop without turning around in his seat.

After about five minutes, a bus pulled in and he watched as the dark figures boarded, including Felicity and her friend. Waiting until it had passed, he pulled out, several vehicles in between.

Several stops later, he'd pulled in behind the bus at another stop and saw half a dozen passengers, including Felicity and her friend, get off. Fortunately, they began to walk up the road, away from him. He was suspicious she might recognise his car.

As the bus pulled off, he could see them hurrying away, heads down, umbrellas shielding them. They crossed the road and turned right into a side road.

As he followed and managed to squeeze between a gap in the traffic, he just caught sight of the pair disappearing through the door of a terraced house on the left.

"I'll get it," came the familiar voice from within in answer to his ring on the bell. "It's probably that stuff you ordered from the ..." Felicity stopped as she opened the door and saw who was standing outside.

She went to close it again quickly but Brannigan had his foot on the threshold.

"I just want to talk to you," he said, trying to sound calm.

She'd turned ashen. "How did you find me? Does Andy know?"

Footsteps came from a room at the back of the house before approaching along the hallway. "Is everything okay, Felicity?"

Brannigan shook his head in answer to Felicity's question. "No, but interesting you ask." A slight pause before he continued, "Look, I don't want any trouble, I just think we need to talk."

The young woman from the salon had appeared at Felicity's shoulder. "Is this ...?"

"My step-father, yes."

The woman stiffened. "Do you want me to call the police?"

"No, it's fine," Felicity responded, turning to her friend. "Do you mind if we use your front room?" She looked back to Brannigan. "We won't be long."

The woman frowned, looking suspicious. "If you're sure."

"It'll be okay," Felicity reassured her.

Her friend took a step back. "You've got ten minutes, and then I'll call the police."

Brannigan couldn't help a slight smile form on his face. Had Felicity told her friend everything surrounding the events of a fortnight ago? He doubted it, otherwise she would understand why Felicity wouldn't want any police involvement either.

Felicity stepped back and led the way through a door to the left and into a room with a dining table in the middle, cutlery set out for four places. The curtains were open and a gas fire was unlit in the Victorian fireplace.

As the other woman closed the front door, he shut the room door behind him. He could imagine her hanging around outside, hoping to hear whatever conversation he and Felicity were about to have.

His step-daughter sat on a chair at the far side of the dining table and folded her arms. "So how did you find me?" she asked belligerently.

He took the chair opposite. "It doesn't matter. I haven't told Andy but I think you should consider him."

Her features softened slightly but her arms remained folded.

"You'll probably think I'm angry with you, Felicity," he went on.

She raised an eyebrow.

"I was, initially. In fact I was fuming. But I've had a chance to think about things."

She said nothing but the colour had begun to come back to her cheeks.

"What I can't understand is why. Why did you feel the need to do what you did?"

She snorted. "I wanted to hurt you," she finally said. "Just like you hurt Mum."

Brannigan shook his head. "At the end of the day, it would all come to you anyway. You know I've got no one else."

"Right," she said disbelievingly.

"It's true. Who else have I got?" He held his arms wide. "There's only you ... and Andy."

"And look what you got him involved with."

Brannigan gave a grim smile. "I think you did that."

Felicity slumped in the chair, her hands in her lap now.

"Look, I've tried to tell you how things were but you just closed me out. I know you resented me – coming into your lives. You wanted to have your mum to yourself after what happened to your real dad. I get that." Brannigan paused a moment and leaned forward onto the dining table, slightly adjusting the positions of the cutlery in front of him. He looked up at Felicity.

"I know you're still hurting about your mum," he continued. "I wanted Veronica to tell you about the tumour. We had arguments about that. I didn't think it was fair that she was depriving you of knowing ... of enjoying what little time you two had left. But it was what she wanted."

He watched her face as tears began to run down her cheeks. "Finally, I persuaded her to tell you – when it became obvious that something wasn't right."

Through tears and spittle, Felicity finally spoke. "But I saw you. I saw what you were doing."

Brannigan responded calmly, "Sometimes when you saw me holding her arms, it was because I was restraining her. She used to have these attacks ... I don't know ... fits sometimes, and I would hold on to her to stop her from hurting herself. You saw what you wanted to see. You saw me hurting her, but that wasn't the case."

She was shaking her head. "I don't know. I just don't know."

"Look, I'm not interested in what's happened recently. But I think you need to contact Andy. He's a good lad and it's not fair the way you've treated him." He stood. "I'll go now. I just had to speak to you. I don't want you to destroy what you and Andy have. He loves you, I'm absolutely convinced of that." He walked to the door, turning to face her. "Think about it eh?"

*   *   *

Strong and Ormerod approached the scruffy terraced property where Tracey had told them they rented a room. It was on the first floor at the front. The detectives were on the other side of the street.

"No lights on, guv," Ormerod said quietly to his boss.

"I'm not so sure, Luke. Is there a low glow behind those ... what are they, sheets up at the window?"

Ormerod squinted. "Could be. Candlelight maybe?"

Strong crossed the road, took hold of the house door handle and turned. As he thought, it opened. He glanced at Ormerod then stepped inside. The hallway was in darkness, only the street-lighting providing illumination. Two doors led off to right and one to the left, the staircase coming back towards them on the left-hand side at the far end. A TV was on behind the first door and music was coming from the second. A smell of cabbage cooking mingled with stale curry as the pair made their way quietly to the stairs.

Strong led the way cautiously, one careful step at a time. He paused when he could see through the banisters onto the floor at first level and picked out the door to the room at the front. Looking to Ormerod, he indicated a dim wavering glow below the bottom of the door; definitely a candle. Ormerod nodded and took another step up. A loud creak from the wooden tread startled them. With that, the glow under the door disappeared.

That made up their minds. They rushed for the door. Ormerod turned the handle. Locked. Inside, they could hear scuffling. Ormerod put his shoulder to the door and crashed in. Halfway out the window, a young man looked back startled. Strong dashed past a stumbling Ormerod and grabbed the man's legs. He struggled and almost broke free before Ormerod lent his efforts and the man was dragged back in and onto the floor.

"You're not making this easy," Strong said.

"Who ... who are you?" the man squeaked.

Strong flipped open his warrant card as Ormerod held the man. "Police," he said. "And you are?"

The man struggled before replying indignantly, "Nobody."

"Well, Mr Nobody," Strong said. "We believe you can help us with our enquiries into the murder of Mark Thompson and we'd like you to accompany us to Wood Street Police Station."

With identities established as Simon Glover, originally from Wakefield, and Tracey Morris, originally from Mirfield, Strong decided the pair should be held overnight in the custody cells, to give them time to think about the position they were in. It had been a long day and it would be best to question them fresh tomorrow.

Ormerod had gone home and the Incident Room was quiet. A glance at his watch and he headed for his office. Time to catch up with Bob before he went home.

A number of messages had been left on his desk. He sat down and flicked through them. The one that stood out was a sealed envelope marked Private & Confidential. He opened it and read; it was from the ACC.

'Contact Det CH Supt. Gilfoyle from Staffordshire re our friend.'

A mobile number was written below.

He felt more positive. He didn't think he'd have a number to ring if there was no possibility of talking to Nichols. Unless, of course, it was to tell him there was no chance. In any event, he'd make that call in the morning. In the meantime, he'd give some thought to the two they were holding in connection with Mark Thompson's murder.

But now, something more uplifting. He pulled his mobile from his pocket and dialled Bob's number.

* * *

Susan closed the front door to the flat and leant back against it. She was exhausted; and shocked. Danny had told her everything he saw that night. And he told her where the killer hung out. The lad was scared, no doubt about that. He maintained he wouldn't tell his story to the police. But that placed the strain on her. She'd have to talk to Bob. He'd know what to do. Somehow, Susan thought she was the first in tonight. But suddenly, the living room door opened and Sammy appeared.

Sammy looked at her, a confused expression on her face. "I thought I heard you come in," she said. "Is everything alright? You look as though you've seen a ghost. Oh, God you haven't had a premonition have you?"

Susan shook her head. "No." She pushed herself off the door and walked towards her friend. "Have we got any wine in? I think I need a large one."

Sammy watched her walk past into the kitchen. "I think there's half a bottle left in the fridge from Saturday night."

"You want one?" Susan asked over her shoulder.

"Might as well. Sounds like I might need it once you tell me what's got into you."

When they'd sat down on the sofa, a glass of wine each in front of them, Sammy began the conversation she knew they'd have to have. "So, what's upset you, Suz?"

Susan looked to the ceiling, drew a deep breath and responded. "You remember we spoke to that lad, Danny?"

"The lad on the bike – next door neighbour to the murder victim?"

Susan nodded. "He contacted me today, asked me to meet him. That's where I've been."

Sammy swivelled on the settee to face her friend. "Well whatever he's said, he's upset you."

"He saw it."

"Saw what?"

"The murder."

"He needs to go to the police – to Colin."

"He's scared. The guy's not right in the head; addled by drugs."

"He knows who it is?"

Susan gave a nod.

"Well you need to speak to Colin. I'll come with you."

"Not yet. I was going to speak to Bob first.

"And what's he going to tell you? The same as me."

Susan paused a moment, a grim expression on her face. "Danny told me where he hangs out. I thought I'd check it out first."

Sammy looked incredulous. "You mean you plan to walk up to his front door and confront him? I can think of a few good reasons why that's not a good idea."

"It's not as straightforward as that. I thought I might check it out tomorrow; lunchtime maybe. Will you come with me?"

Sammy picked up her wine glass. "Well I'm certainly not letting you go on your own."

56
Tuesday 26th February 2002

"So what's the strategy, guv?" Ormerod was standing in the doorway to Strong's office.

Strong looked up from his desk. "I think you and John take Simon Glover and Kelly and myself will handle Tracey Morris. Get them up into the interview rooms and we'll coordinate the questioning at …" he checked his watch, "nine-thirty. Give them time to sweat a bit longer."

The DC grinned. "Will do."

"Can you just close the door a minute, Luke."

Ormerod did as asked and left.

Strong waited until he'd gone before lifting the receiver and dialling the number from the bottom of the ACC's note. It was answered on the fourth ring.

"Is that Detective Chief Superintendent Gilfoyle?" Strong asked.

"Who wants to know," came the guarded reply.

"I'm Detective Inspector Colin Strong from Wood Street CID in Wakefield. Our ACC Mellor has given me your number."

"You're in your office now?"

"At my desk, yes."

"I'll call you back."

The line went dead. Strong put the phone down. No more than he expected. He could have been anyone ringing that number and claiming to be a detective.

Three minutes later his landline rang.

"DI Strong," he answered.

"Colin, right? It's Joe Gilfoyle." The voice had the slightest hint of an Irish accent. *"I understand you've been making enquiries about a certain Paul Nichols?"*

"That's correct, sir," Strong responded. "I've been tasked with reviewing an unsolved murder case here in West Yorkshire from twenty years ago. Paul was one of two boys at the time who discovered the body."

"But you have the original statements?" Gilfoyle queried. *"Why would you want to speak to him again?"*

"I have new evidence which I believe he could help me with." Strong then proceeded to make the case for having Nichols confirm what Kenny Green had told him about the tunic button found at the murder scene but never reported to the enquiry at the time.

"And you think he might still be in possession of this button?" Gilfoyle asked.

"I'm not sure about that. If he has, that would be useful, but if he could at least confirm that he picked it up and what it actually was would be great. According to his friend, he collected them as a hobby and would be able to identify which regiment it would have come from."

The line was quiet for a second or two. *"Okay, let me talk to him. I can't tell you why he has a new identity but we have to be careful here. If he doesn't want to talk to you, I can't force him."*

"I understand. But this seems to be an interesting piece of new evidence we didn't know about before."

"Leave it with me, Colin, I'll be in touch." Gilfoyle hung up.

Strong replaced the receiver and pushed his chair back from the desk. What had Nichols become involved with that made his identity so sensitive? He'd probably never find out but he only hoped that Gilfoyle could persuade him to at least talk to him on the phone; face to face would be better, but he couldn't raise his hopes. In the meantime, he had a couple of interviews to conduct.

*　　*　　*

"Are you sure this is a good idea, Suz?" Sammy was flicking her eyelashes with a brush in front of the mirror in the living room.

"I need to check it out," Susan responded. "I know what you said last night about taking it to Colin – and I will. But I'd like to make sure Danny hasn't given me some duff info."

Sammy put her eyeliner back in its case and closed up her make-up bag. "You never told me exactly what this Danny said to you," she said as she faced her friend.

Susan shrugged into her coat. "No. It's best you don't. The fewer people who know the details might help give credence later, if what he told me is true."

"Have you spoken to Bob?" Sammy grabbed her bag and coat and headed for the door.

"No. I thought I'd see if he was in this morning. You know they're letting me use his desk part-time for this piece we're writing on Claire Hobson?"

They closed the front door behind them and Susan led the way outside to her car.

"You dropped on lucky there," Sammy said.

"Right, I'll drop you off first then head to the Post. And I'll pick you up at twelve?"

Sammy climbed into the passenger seat. "I'll text you once I've confirmed I can have a longer lunch break. I'll have to make it up tonight though."

Susan started the engine and set off into the rush-hour Leeds traffic.

* * *

"What can you tell us about the card you and Simon Glover used in Agbrigg Road off-licence on Sunday 17th February this year, Tracey?" Stainmore was once again leading the interview with Tracey Morris in Interview Room 3. Next door, Ormerod and Darby were conducting a similar one with Simon Glover.

Strong leaned back in the chair waiting for Tracey to respond.

"It weren't my idea," the young woman finally replied. She glanced at the duty solicitor on her left, the only other person in the room.

"But you were with Mr Glover when that fraud took place. And I don't need to remind you that we are investigating a murder here."

Her head dropped for a second. "I know." She took a drink from the styrofoam cup of coffee brought in for her, then continued, "Simon told me someone he knew had found a wallet with some cash and cards in it. This friend had kept the cash, obviously, but thought Simon might be able to use the card."

"This friend, has he got a name?"

"I only heard Simon refer to him as Billy the Fish."

Stainmore couldn't hide the brief smirk that appeared on her face. "Billy the Fish?"

Tracey glared at Stainmore. "I'm not taking the piss."

"And you don't know this character's real name?"

"No. Apparently, he went to school with Simon."

Stainmore scribbled some notes. "And he claims this 'Billy the Fish' found the wallet containing this card?"

"Yes."

"And where is the card now?"

"I think Simon destroyed it after he heard you were looking for it."

Stainmore turned to Strong. "Our ever-helpful shop assistant, Brian," she said.

"I think we'll pause the interview for now," Strong said, rising to his feet.

Strong knocked on the door and entered the other interview room. Ormerod made the necessary announcement that, for the benefit of the tape, he had come in.

"How are we doing here?" Strong asked.

"Our Mr Glover doesn't seem to know anything about anything," Ormerod answered.

Strong glanced a moment at the duty solicitor drafted in for Glover's benefit, a young lad in a shiny suit with gelled hair, before turning to Glover himself. "You do realise the seriousness of your situation Mr Glover," he said.

Glover shrugged.

"Well let me remind you that this is a murder enquiry and our evidence shows that you used the deceased's credit card just hours after he was killed."

"Got no evidence for that," Glover retorted.

"Oh but that's where you're wrong."

"Can't rely on CCTV."

"Is that what your mate, Brian told you?" Strong leaned onto the table and spoke closely to the man. "You see, Simon – if you don't mind me calling you Simon, we have witnesses who saw you use that card. Now as you were the last one to use it … well, you can see how it looks from our side of the table." Strong stood back up and walked to the back of the room.

Glover leaned in towards the solicitor and mumbled a few words.

"If I could have a few minutes with my client?" the brief said.

"Okay," Strong agreed. "We have plenty of time. Just you consider your position, Simon."

Outside in the corridor, Strong updated Ormerod and Darby on what Tracey had told them in her interview.

"You think he's scared of this character, Billy the Fish?" Ormerod was unable to keep his face straight as he asked the question.

"I know it sounds a bit far-fetched," Strong admitted, "but let's just give him another ten minutes to think about things. I'd rather he told me about this character than mention the name to him, but we'll see."

The trio were about to walk back to the CID room when Glover's solicitor opened the door. "My client is ready to tell you what he knows," he said.

With the interview resumed, Ormerod, sitting opposite, kicked proceedings off. "I understand you have new information for us, Mr Glover," he said.

John Darby had taken up his seat alongside Ormerod as before and Strong leaned against the wall next to the door.

"I didn't steal the card," Glover began. "An old school friend gave it to me. He said he'd found the wallet the night before."

Ormerod flicked through his notes. "That would be Saturday 16th February?"

Glover nodded. "Yea, the day before we used the card."

"Did he say where he'd found the wallet?"

"No. Just that he'd had the cash from it and he thought he'd do me a favour and give the card to me. He thought I could use it if I was quick."

"So who is this school friend of yours?"

Glover looked down and hesitated.

"You will need to tell us," Strong confirmed.

Glover looked to the solicitor who gave a slight nod. "He was in my class. Billy Pollock, but since we discovered what a Pollock is, we all called him Billy the Fish."

Ormerod gave a slight reaction when he heard this. "And where can we find this ... Mr Pollock."

Glover let out a deep breath. "His dad died when we were in primary school and his mother when he was thirteen. He went to stay with his grandparents after that."

"So where do they live?"

"Well his grandma died three years ago, so it's only been him and his grandad, but he's been going doo-lally. When he was younger, Billy used to help on his grandad's allotment but he got into drugs a while back. Since his grandad's not been so great, the allotment's been left alone. Except ..."

"Except what, Simon?" Ormerod prompted.

"Billy tends to go there to smoke a bit of weed and that. There's this shed."

"On the allotment?"

"Yeah."

"We'll need some details here – his grandad's address, and this allotment's location."

Glover told them what they wanted to know and the interview was terminated.

57

Strong and Ormerod pulled up in one car outside the council house address that Glover had provided for Pollock's grandfather. Stainmore and Darby were close behind in another vehicle.

Strong stepped out of the Mondeo, Ormerod close by, and approached the front door, Stainmore and Darby covering the rear. The front garden was overgrown and the windows looked dirty.

Strong's knock on the door received no answer at first. After a moment or two, he tried again. This time they could hear some movement inside.

"Who are you?" an elderly male voice sounded behind the door.

Strong bent down to the letterbox. "We're police officers," he said. "We'd like to speak to your grandson, if he's in."

"Who?"

"Your grandson, Billy."

"Billy? There's no Billy here."

"If you could just open the door, Mr Wood. We'd just like to make sure you're okay."

"Who did you say you were?"

"Police, sir." Strong held his warrant card up to the glazed part of the door.

Another car drew to a halt behind Strong's Mondeo, Ormerod turning to look.

Eventually, bolts were slid and the door opened, on a safety chain.

Strong presented his card again. "Good to see you acting so safely, Mr Wood. Now, can you tell me when you last saw your grandson?"

"That would be William," the old man answered. He shook his head. "I haven't seen William for years."

A woman in a district nurse's uniform walked up the path. "Everything alright?" she asked. The expression on her face told Strong she wouldn't suffer fools lightly.

He held out his identity again. "Police," he said. We're looking to speak to William Pollock who we understand is Mr Wood's grandson and lives here."

"Mr Wood has dementia," she responded. "I visit regularly but I haven't seen that waste of space for a few days now."

"Mr Wood seems confused. I just wondered if you could check the house for us?"

She studied Strong for a moment.

"Are you my daughter?" the old man asked. He'd been ignored on the doorstep.

"I'm Lizzie," the nurse said, stepping forward and gently taking hold of the man's arm. "You remember me? I've come to change your dressings."

She led the man back inside, giving a slight nod of acknowledgement to Strong as she passed.

A minute later. she reappeared. "No sign of Billy," she said. "I don't think he's been here since I last visited yesterday morning."

"Thanks," Strong said.

As they walked back down the path, Ormerod said, "The allotments?"

"The allotments," Strong confirmed.

*   *   *

Susan picked Sammy up from her office on the stroke of midday. Bright sunlight dazzled her on the drive south to Wakefield. A frosty start had given way to a crisp winter's day.

"So where exactly are we going, Suz?"

"Dewsbury Road, near St Michael's."

"The church?"

"Near there."

"Don't give anything away, then."

They were silent for a while as Susan drove along the M1. Eventually, Sammy spoke again. "So did you see Bob, or have you spoken to him?"

"He wasn't in." Susan wasn't in the mood for much conversation.

Finally they drove down Dewsbury Road, past the shop where Mark Thompson's body was found. Just past a big Morrison's supermarket, Susan turned in to a side road on the left and parked up.

Sammy looked up and down the street full of red brick terraced houses. "Does he live in one of these?" she asked.

"No."

"Good, because I was going to suggest we turn the car round for a quick getaway." Sammy's attempt to lighten the mood failed.

"Come on," Susan said, already out of the car.

Sammy quickly followed and the car was locked. They walked back to the main road and Susan made to cross.

"Where exactly are we going?" Sammy struggled to keep up.

On the other side of the road, Susan walked to a gate in the picket fence that bounded allotment land.

"Oh," Sammy said, "Are we cutting through? Because you could have parked on the road on the other side."

Suddenly Susan stopped. "Look Sammy, this is it. This is where I need to check out. Now I don't get a good feeling about this but please ... do me a favour and stop talking."

Sammy was taken aback. She held up her hands and mouthed, 'Okay.'

The allotments were deserted apart from one old man on a plot near the road lifting some leeks. He paid the two no attention as Susan led the way down a path towards the middle of site. They passed by various greenhouses, sheds and water butts, heading towards an overgrown plot near the far side. A timber shed with a felt roof stood at one side of it.

As they neared, Susan saw a man and a woman working on an allotment near to the road at the top end. Again, they were oblivious to the two women. Susan paused. "This is where Danny told me I'd find him," she said in hushed tones.

Sammy looked surprised. "In an old shed?" she whispered.

Susan put her finger to her lips and approached the door to the shed. The padlock was unlocked. "Hello?" she called. "Are you in there? I'd like to talk to you."

There was no answer.

"Hello?" she repeated and took a step forward.

* * *

Strong drove the few minutes from Mr Wood's house to the allotments where the old man had a plot. He'd coordinated with Stainmore and Darby to park on Dewsbury Road and make their way in from the opposite side. According to Glover, Pollock's grandfather's allotment was about one third of the way down the site, more or less central.

He pulled the car off the street and on to the track that ran down the middle of the allotments, Ormerod sitting alongside. They came to a halt and got out. A man and a woman looked up from a nearby plot where they were harvesting some cabbages.

"You can't leave it there," the man said.

Strong held up a hand. 'Police,' he mouthed and showed his card.

The gardeners paused in their work, now more interested in the police presence on their field than the brassicas.

Strong led the way down the path towards an overgrown plot he thought was the one described. He could see Stainmore and Darby enter through the gate off Dewsbury Road, and walk towards them. About fifty yards away from his target, he stopped. Two women were by the old shed to one side of the allotment, one dark-haired, the other, blonde and shorter. They appeared to be in their twenties. He looked hard at their profiles. No, it can't be?

Just then, the woman with the dark hair pulled the shed door open. There was a gap of a few seconds before she stumbled backwards, her hands covering her mouth. Her companion moved past her to look inside the shed then looked back to her friend.

By their body language, Strong knew instantly something was wrong. "Susan! Sammy!" he shouted. "Step away from the shed!"

They looked towards him, surprised expressions taking over from the shocked ones of a second earlier.

"It's ...," Susan hesitated.

Sammy grabbed her friend's arm and pulled her back to the path as Stainmore and Darby broke into sprints.

Strong reached the shed first. "Just stay there," he said to Susan and Sammy, holding up a hand.

He turned by the side of the building. The door was still ajar and bright sunlight streamed in. He took a step forward and opened the door further.

Immediately in front and to the side there was a collection of old tools and plant pots, netting and other garden paraphernalia, all draped in a lace of spiders' webs. Towards the rear of the shed, a space had been cleared for a chair, some blankets and a cushion. On top of the blankets lay the prone body of a man.

He was in no doubt the man was dead. A sleeve had been rolled up and a needle was sticking out from the crook of the elbow. The flesh was white.

Ormerod peered around him. "What a waste," he said.

Strong turned and glared over the DC's shoulder at Susan and Sammy who appeared distraught. "But how the Hell did those two know to come here?" he said quietly to Ormerod.

Stainmore and Darby arrived. "Don't go in there," he said to them. "Call it in and get Forensics down here."

Ormerod had already walked a few paces away, mobile phone to his ear.

"In the meantime ..." Strong approached the two women, "I'd like you two to go back to the station and make a statement."

Stainmore stood by her boss's side.

"But before you do," Strong went on, "What in God's name were you doing here?"

"I ... I need to get back," Sammy stuttered.

"Look," Susan said, calmer now, "Sammy only came with me so I wasn't on my own. She didn't know what I'd come to do. She didn't even know where we were going until we got here."

"That's true." Sammy looked pleadingly.

"What had you come here to do?" Strong persisted.

"I would have come to you but I wanted to check this out, to make sure it was genuine," Susan replied.

Strong shook his head. "I'm sorry Sammy, but the two of you are going to have to go to Wood Street. You'll need to be formally interviewed."

Susan pointed back to Dewsbury Road. "But my car's parked over there."

"DC Darby can drive you to Wood Street. You do need to make that statement."

In the distance, sirens could be heard. The couple with the cabbages had left their plot and come nearer.

"Luke," Strong addressed Ormerod who'd re-joined them, "Have a word with those two. See what they can tell you about this plot and our friend in there. And then get them out of here. When uniform arrive, we're going to have to close these allotments off for the rest of the day."

Sammy had recovered some composure. "I'll need to call the office," she said. "I can't just disappear for lunch and not come back."

"All right," Strong agreed. "But tell them you're unwell or something."

58

It was mid-afternoon by the time Strong and Stainmore took their seats in the interview room where Susan had been waiting since she'd arrived a couple of hours earlier.

Strong had left the allotments a hive of activity; SOCOs in white coveralls investigating the old shed, uniforms at both entrances keeping nosy gardeners from entering. The black ambulance had arrived just before he left, waiting patiently for the order to collect the body.

Before Strong returned to Wood Street, Ormerod had briefed him about his conversation with the couple on the nearby allotment. They'd confirmed the plot where the body was found was indeed that of George Woods. He'd worked it for decades. But the association were looking to re-allocate it because of his failing health and inability to look after it properly. A year or two back his grandson, Bill Pollock had helped out but he'd lost interest. They had seen him use the shed from time to time but gave him a wide berth. "Didn't want to get involved," Ormerod had quoted.

Strong raised his brows. "I can believe that," he said sarcastically.

Ormerod remained at the allotments to liaise with Forensics and speak to any of the holders they could identify.

In the interview room, Strong flipped open a pad ready to note what he was about to be told.

"Okay Susan," he began, "In your own words, how did you come to be at that allotment this afternoon?"

She leaned forward on the table that separated them. "This is going to sound strange but you remember when Bob and I came across you the other week when you'd just found the body of Mark Thompson?"

"Right."

"Do you remember a kid on a bike? About twelve with a baseball cap on back to front?"

"I do, as it happens. Bike too small for him."

"That's him. Well, you know I'm helping Bob on his story to mark the twentieth anniversary of the Claire Hobson case – I'm doing it as part of my coursework."

Strong nodded and jotted a few notes down.

"As well as that, I thought I'd help Bob out again and get a bit more background on Mark Thompson." She paused a second. "So I went back to the shop to speak to the woman who found the body and when I came out of the shop this kid approached me."

"The lad on the bike?"

"Yes." Susan then told him what the boy eventually told her and how the man he thought responsible for Thompson's murder used the shed to do drugs.

Strong finished writing and exhaled loudly.

"So rather than bring this information to me, you thought you'd go investigating on your own?" he said.

"It wasn't like that, I told you ..."

"After all that happened last year."

She straightened up and looked straight at him. "You can't compare this with last year. I told you, I wanted to see if this added up, then I was going to tell you."

"And what if he'd been alive in that shed? Drug-addled with a knife. God knows, there would have been any number of gardening tools he could have attacked you with. And the only people around would have been an old man, probably deaf as a post, about a hundred yards away down near the road, or an elderly couple in the opposite direction. Christ, Susan ..."

"Okay, okay, I know."

There was an awkward silence for a moment before Strong broke it. "I'm sorry," he said. "I shouldn't have gone off like that."

"No, you were right. It was stupid."

Strong looked at her for a second then said, "So tell me about this kid?"

59

Gary Monk couldn't help brooding on what he'd seen scribbled on Stainmore's pad. He couldn't make sense of it. Then there was the change in his mum. He studied her closely; she had become quieter, more insular since Strong and Stainmore had visited that second time, supposedly to bring his father's shirt back. All that story about SOCO research didn't ring true to him. He'd asked several of his colleagues about it and they'd never heard anything.

And then there was the repeat of the home interview. Nobody had ever been asked to do that but, there again, none of them had a good word to say about HR either.

But what about those doodles? Why was there another character noted only by a question mark on that chart? Stainmore obviously thought they were linked somehow. He'd have to choose his time, but he needed to delve a little into what had changed with his mum as well.

That opportunity presented itself several days after his unofficial visit to the CID Room. He woke around two in the afternoon following the last of his current batch of night shifts. At first he thought he was dreaming. The gentle sobbing seemed to be part of some dark vision behind his eyelids. But no, as he opened his eyes, the sound was definitely a reality. It was coming from his mother's bedroom through the wall from his own. He listened for a short while then got up and padded his way to her bedroom door.

He gave a gentle knock. "Mum? Is everything alright?"

There were sniffling sounds before she replied in stuttering words, "I'm fine, love. Honestly."

"You don't sound it."

"Make me some tea," she said, "I'll be down in a minute."

He walked downstairs and switched on the kettle. A few minutes later, his mother appeared, eyes puffy and red.

"Is it Dad?" he asked. "Because I miss him too."

She shook her head. "I know."

He squeezed the tea bag out of the mugs and added milk for the pair of them and handed one to her. He looked at her for a moment then decided he had to ask. "Is it to do with the detectives' visits?"

She looked sharply at him "Why do you say that?"

"Mum, I know you. Something's not been right since that second visit. The one when they brought Dad's shirt back."

She put her mug down and stood by the window looking out over the back garden. "You know he really loved you, don't you?"

Gary was puzzled. "Dad? Of course I know." He stood behind her with his hands on her shoulders. "Mum, what is it? What's really the matter? You can tell me."

She bowed her head then turned to face him. "Sit down, Gary."

"Mum?"

"Please, Son."

Slowly Gary lowered himself into a kitchen chair.

"This isn't easy for me to say."

"Just tell me."

"Your Dad …" Tears welled in her eyes. "He wasn't your biological father."

Gary felt a burning sensation in his throat. He was unable to speak for a second. "How? I mean, when …? What?" he eventually managed.

Tears ran down Annabel's cheeks. "I only just found that out … when they brought back your father's … your Dad's shirt."

He'd suspected something serious and somewhere at the back of his mind, he probably had considered this possibility. But now, having heard it spoken out loud … and by his mother … it was … he couldn't take it in.

He stood up and shook his head, pacing the small kitchen. "No, no, no! This can't be." He stopped and faced her, anger in his eyes.

"I'm sorry," was all she could manage.

"Sorry?" Gary waved his arms around. "But, who…? You must have known."

"I didn't. I honestly thought your father …"

"No. No, you must have had a clue." He was shaking his head. "I mean, who else did you sleep with?"

That remark sparked an incensed reaction. "I **did not sleep** with anyone," she said slowly and deliberately. "I loved your father."

"So what am I? An immaculate conception?"

She looked down, unable to face her son. "I was attacked," she finally said in a quiet voice.

"What?"

She looked up into Gary's face, inner strength coming from somewhere. "I was attacked," she repeated.

The enormity of what he'd just heard threatened to overwhelm him. Gary had to find somewhere quiet, away from all the noise. Not just the traffic noise but the noise in his head.

He was sitting in his car in a field entrance on a country road high up on the moors. The wind was whistling around the car, but apart from that, all was peaceful. No other vehicles had passed by. He looked out over the wild desolate landscape. Heavy clouds threatened from the west. His vision blurred as tears welled in his eyes. How could he make sense of this? He was the product of a rape. There was no pre-programmed emotion to tell you how to cope with that. And the only reason he'd found out; in fact the only reason his mother found out was because of his joining the police. Ironic really, he joins the force to uphold law and order and immediately discovers an unlawful past. That, after all, can be the only reason all this has come to light.

So what prompted the CID officers to delve into his past? Who was his real father? What was he saying? His real father was dead. This ... this imposter ... This character who was being called his 'biological' father ... he wasn't his 'real' Dad. But who was this mysterious taxi driver? He'd managed to avoid telling his mum he knew something about this man. What she told him only added weight to Stainmore's scribblings. But if that bore out, who was HC?

The sky was growing dark, not just because of the impending storm; daylight would have gone, even if it had been a sunny afternoon. Gary struggled to gather his thoughts again. Was there anything significant about the timing of this? Did something come to light during the current CID investigations? What was on those whiteboards he'd seen up there? The two murders – the man in the park toilets and the body discovered behind the convenience store on Dewsbury Road. Was there a connection in those investigations linking to the mysterious taxi driver? He'd have to get back in there again to look.

60

"I can't believe you've let her walk out of here with no more than a promise to persuade this kid to come and talk to us, guv." Stainmore was drumming her fingers on the steering wheel.

"Sometimes you just need to have a little faith, Kelly." Strong was calmly seated beside her, looking over the notes he'd taken during the interview they'd had with Susan. Sammy hadn't been able to add anything to Susan's story and had left the station about half an hour before.

After Susan had told them about Danny, they'd driven down to where the boy went to school and parked on a nearby street. Susan had got out, hoping to meet up with him.

"What if she doesn't?"

"Relax. We know where he lives."

Any further discussion was cut short as Strong's mobile rang. After a brief conversation, he ended the call. "That was Luke," he said.

"What news from the scene?" Stainmore asked.

"They found Thompson's wallet in Pollock's jacket."

She nodded. "That could be good, although he may just have found it."

"But then they also discovered a sock with chunks of red brick inside which they're testing now. Looked like traces of blood on the material but they're running tests."

Stainmore nodded, took a deep breath and exhaled. "She'd better come back," she said.

*   *   *

Susan stood at the school gates, hunched into her coat, hands thrust deep into the pockets, keeping a watchful eye on the children as they emerged from the building. Just as she was wondering if she might have the wrong school, she saw him come out with a couple of other lads. Eventually, he looked up and made eye contact.

A slight move of her head and she strolled off down the road. He would follow, she was sure. She wondered if news of the grim discovery in the allotments had broken.

A few minutes later, Danny had caught up with her. She slowed. "Have you heard?" she asked.

He was also walking with his hands in his pockets. "No, what?"

"Billy the Fish."

"What about him?"

"He won't be a danger for you Danny. He was found dead this afternoon."

Danny stopped. "How? I mean, are you sure?"

"Fairly sure. It was me who found him."

The boy looked stunned. "Are the police involved?"

"They turned up the same time as me."

"You told them?"

"They were already looking for him. They must have had a lead." She watched his face as he took this in. "What are you doing now, Danny?"

"Me? I've got to go and check on Mum." He started walking again.

"The police need to talk to you."

He stopped, turned and looked at her. "No way. I'm not grassing on anyone."

"Nobody's asking you to do that. But, like I said, Billy can't hurt you now. And you need to tell them what you told me, what you saw that night. Mark was your friend, right?"

Danny nodded his head.

"Well you need to do that for him. For his mum and his family. I'll come with you, if you like?"

"Would you?"

"Of course. Now the officer that needs to talk to you is a nice guy. He helped me last year, and he's helped a good friend of mine too. He'll look after you."

"Do I need to go to the police station?"

"Not yet. He's waiting in a car round the corner. I'll take you there and stay with you." She watched him as he processed this information.

"Okay," he finally said.

*   *   *

"There you are, Kelly," Strong said looking through the windscreen and indicating the two figures walking towards them. "Told you to have some faith."

Susan opened the rear nearside door and Danny slid in, shuffling across so she could join him.

"Danny, this is DI Strong," she said. "And DS Stainmore. I've said you wanted to speak to him after what happened this afternoon."

Strong half turned in his seat to face the boy. "This is really helpful, Danny," he said. "I understand you may have seen something on the night Mark Thompson died."

"Is it true?" the boy asked.

"Is what true?"

"That Billy is dead?"

"We believe so. You knew him?"

Danny nodded. "Weirdo. Got into drugs and all sorts."

"Did you see him on that night?"

Another vigorous nod before he looked up at Strong, tears in his eyes. "He did it, you know. He attacked Mark."

Strong threw Stainmore a brief glance. "Now this is important, Danny. Can you tell us exactly what you saw?"

The boy swept a sleeve under his nose and wiped his eyes. "I was on my bike, going home, heading down Dewsbury Road – not the main road, the small one that runs in front of the houses."

"I know it."

"I was about to bounce up onto the pavement and cut the corner on the grass when I saw Billy creeping around the back of the chippy near the corner of Townley Road. So I quickly swerved and went to go round the other side of the building. But before I got to the road I heard some shouting... from the other side of the chippy like."

"Go on, Danny," Strong encouraged. "You're doing well."

"I stopped at the corner – the chippy was closed. I didn't want to be seen by Billy. That's when I saw Mark walking up the road. And it was him that Billy was shouting at. Mark was trying to ignore him. I don't know, maybe Billy'd been smoking something but he was getting more irate. Mark was about to walk past him and asked him what his problem was. The next thing, Billy swung his arm round and something from his hand hit Mark on the head. Mark staggered to his knees. I heard Mark say something like, "You daft bastard." Then Billy swung again and hit him a second time and shouted, "Give me what you've got.""

This time, Danny folded, huge sobs coming from his shaking frame. Susan put an arm around him and tried to offer him a handkerchief but he just buried his head in her shoulder.

Strong let out a big sigh and looked to Stainmore.

"We'll need to get a proper statement," she said quietly.

Strong turned back to the boy. "I realise how difficult this is for you, Danny," he said. "But can you tell us what happened next ... when you're ready."

Susan rubbed his shoulder and gently eased his head back from her arm. "It's okay, Danny," she said. "You're doing really well."

Through sobs, he went on to tell how he had been frightened that Billy would spot him so he went back the way he'd come on his bike and made it home by another route. He just thought Billy had mugged Mark. He didn't realise how serious it was until all the police activity by the convenience store the following afternoon. Even then, he didn't realise it was Mark they'd found. It was only later he heard. But he was scared Billy would find out he'd seen him.

Later that evening, Danny made a formal statement at Wood Street, Susan acting as appropriate adult. He didn't want his mother involved. She was ill and he and his older brother cared for her.

After Susan had left to take him home, Strong was about to do the same when DCS Flynn collared him in the corridor.

"So, is this character you discovered this afternoon the murderer of Mark Thompson, Colin?" he asked.

"It's looking that way, sir. Forensics have confirmed the trace material found on the sock with bits of brick in it is human blood. We're waiting to see if the DNA's a match for Thompson. His empty wallet was found in the shed along with the body of William Pollock."

"And Mark Thompson was just in the wrong place at the wrong time?"

"It would seem so from what the lad has just told us. Obviously, we'll be investigating Pollock's background and the results of the PM will tell us more."

"Well done."

"It was good policing from the team. Kelly's persistence with the CCTV and pursuing the off-licence manager, Luke's arrest of the female and altogether the processing of the information that came to light."

"Have you given any thought to what we discussed earlier?" Flynn obviously referring to the soon to be vacant DCI position.

"No, sir."

Flynn gave him a look. "And now all we need to get to the bottom of is the Weaver case," he went on.

"And don't forget the review of the Claire Hobson murder. I'm waiting for Gilfoyle to come back to me once he's spoken with Paul Nichols, or however he calls himself now."

"Well keep me informed of that, Colin. I mean it's not a full-blown re-investigation of the case at the moment but ... if this is a significant find ..."

Strong watched Flynn walk off then made his way out of the building.

*   *   *

"You did really well there, Danny." Susan was driving him home after they'd left Wood Street.

The boy didn't answer. He still seemed traumatised by the effort of reliving the events of a week and a half ago. Eventually, he mumbled something.

"Sorry, what was that?" Susan asked.

"I said I hoped he wasn't into any drug deals."

"Who?"

"Mark. He said he wasn't. But with Billy approaching him and telling him to give him what he'd got."

"Have you ever known Mark to be involved with drugs?"

Danny shook his head.

"So what makes you think he might have been?"

A shrug then, "I dunno. It was just when he asked me to ... It doesn't matter now."

Susan swung the car off the main road and onto an estate road before pulling to a halt. She looked over at Danny. "If there's something else, you can tell me, you know."

"He wouldn't tell me what he was up to but it involved a lot of money."

"How do you mean?"

Danny put his head down for a second before telling Susan all he could remember about Mark contacting him and asking him to take delivery of a bag and how he had to wait at the back of a hedge for it to be pushed through. Danny had scooped it up then the man had made to grab it back but he'd been too quick for him and he'd made off with it. Later he met up with Mark and handed it over, receiving a £20 note for his trouble. "But the bloke had driven round for ages afterwards," Danny said. "Looking for me ... but I was too fly. I know this estate inside out."

Susan smiled. "I'll bet you do. So you got the impression this bag contained money?"

"Yeah. I asked him if it was to do with drugs but he said not."

"And did you believe him?"

"I think so. But then, what else was the cash for?"

"Indeed."

"He just said it was about teaching someone a lesson."

"So was there anything else about this man you can remember?"

"He was driving a Beamer," he said. "A big one."

"Anything else?"

"Not really, he was old. Well, not a pensioner but he wasn't young."

Susan smiled at an eleven-year-old's perception of age.

"And then ..." he went on. "He had a tattoo on his arm. Here." Danny indicated his left forearm.

"And what was it?"

"Dunno, some sort of crest I think."

Susan pulled away from the kerb. "Okay Danny, let's get you home."

61
Wednesday 27th February 2002

*TWENTY-YEAR-OLD MURDER STILL
UNSOLVED*

*On a cold damp Sunday morning almost
twenty years ago the body of 14-year-old
Claire Hobson was discovered by two
young boys in railway sidings in Horbury
just outside Wakefield. She had been
raped and strangled, having disappeared
on her way home from a friend's house the
Friday before.*
*So far, no-one has ever been charged in
connection with these offences.*
*As the anniversary of this shocking crime
approaches, the Yorkshire Post will be
reporting on the traumatic effects this has
had on Claire's family and friends, as well
as appealing for fresh information which
may lead to a breakthrough.*

Strong folded up his copy of that morning's Yorkshire
Post and stood up from his desk. Souter and Susan had
both been credited with the article. Souter had told him in
the pub a few weeks back that he'd been asked to write a
human-interest story combined with a fresh appeal. No
doubt Flynn would have been contacted and get a
mention. He made a mental note to ask him. In the
meantime, he had a briefing to conduct.

"Okay, listen up everybody," Strong announced as he
stood in front of the whiteboards in the CID Room. "It
looks likely we can close down the Thompson enquiry

285

now, thanks to some good work by you lot." He looked over towards Ormerod. "Luke, can you tell us what we know about William Pollock?"

The DC reported on the findings of the post-mortem, cause of death by an overdose of heroin, extra pure by all accounts. The wallet found in Pollock's jacket pocket was confirmed as belonging to Thompson and analysis of material found on the sock containing broken brick was also confirmed as being the blood and DNA of Mark Thompson.

"So with Danny King's statement we think we know what happened that night, plus the statement of Simon Glover increases the circumstantial evidence we have," Strong summarised.

A few murmurings were heard from the assembled officers.

"Now, Marcus Weaver." Strong turned his attention to the first whiteboard they'd set up in the Incident Room nearly two weeks previously. "Let's focus on this." He tapped a photo of the victim then faced the room. "What do we know?"

Ormerod took up the hint. "Arranged to meet Charlotte Watkins, a work colleague in his car in the park's car park at seven-thirty on Wednesday 13th February. She was late – turned up around seven-fifty. They were disturbed by some activity near the toilet block about eight o'clock which Weaver went to investigate. Some ten minutes later, Charlotte gets a call from her husband and when Weaver hasn't returned, she takes off."

"And the body is discovered by the dog walker at ...?" Strong prompted.

"Around eight-twenty."

"What about our witness? The one who approached those two characters, also seen by the dog walker."

Ormerod referred to his notes and related descriptions of two men outlined by Timothy Pearson who had been lurking around the toilets that night.

"So, two men, one in his fifties, short, stocky, around five six and a younger man, early to mid-twenties, taller, around five ten," Strong repeated, drawing two boxes for the descriptions with a marker pen. "Any other witness statements referring to these two?"

"Ties in with what the dog walker told us, guv," Ormerod confirmed, "but other than that, nothing."

Strong tapped the marker against the palm of his hand as he thought for a second. "What about this car seen on CCTV, Sam?" he asked Kirkland. "Are we definitely connecting it to this incident?"

The DC was leaning on the front of his desk. "Haven't been able to get any better images," he said. "We don't know if there is any connection but we saw a similar one on the night Thompson was killed, as well as the previous evening. But, if we now know it was this character Pollock who attacked him, there's no real connection."

Strong looked over to Ormerod again. "Have you managed to speak to Brannigan again, Luke?"

"Not yet. I can get over there after this briefing, if you want."

"Do that." Strong was quiet for a second, studying the board. "We've got to be missing something here." He turned round to face the group. "No matches for those prints found on that disturbed cistern cover?"

"Nothing, guv," Stainmore said, "Might not have anything to do with it."

"I know, but we need to explore every avenue."

Stainmore waved a pen in the air. "Just a thought," she said. "With this article in this morning's Post, do you think it would be worth an appeal for witnesses to this in the park? You know, anonymity guaranteed etcetera. Anyone who was there for a ... clandestine reason might not be too keen unless we persuade them?"

"Nothing to lose, I suppose," Strong considered. "You lot put the word out before to your connections on the street and we got next to nothing. Okay, Kelly, get in touch with the Post and see if they'll run something."

Strong had only just rested his backside in the chair in his office when the desk phone rang.

"Yes," he said.

"DI Strong?"

"Yes."

"It's DCS Gilfoyle, Joe," the familiar voice responded.

"Morning sir, what news?"

"I've spoken to our mutual friend and he's agreed to talk to you, face to face. How long would it take for you to get over to Stoke?"

He studied his watch and thought for a moment. "I suppose I could get over there by, say three this afternoon?"

"Perfect. This is the address of a garden centre on the A500 about two miles from the centre of town. Give me a call on my mobile when you get there." Gilfoyle related a postcode.

Strong made a note of it before thanking him and ending the call. No mention of a name for Nichols, but that didn't surprise him.

He was studying his AA Road Map when ACC Mellor appeared at his door. He was surprised. It was unusual for officers of his rank to come to the likes of Strong's door, unless it meant trouble.

"Sir," Strong greeted.

Mellor waved a dismissive hand. "Relax, Colin," he said. "Has Joe Gilfoyle been in contact?"

"Just ten minutes ago."

"So you're going to see Nichols?"

"We've arranged to meet this afternoon. Well, I say 'we', DCS Gilfoyle has given me a garden centre address near Stoke and said to call him again from there, so I assume we'll be meeting Nichols nearby."

Mellor nodded. "That's good. Hopefully you'll get what you've been looking for."

There was an awkward silence for a moment. "Was there something else, sir?"

"You know we'll be a senior officer down from Friday ... officially, I mean?" Mellor was referring once again to DCI Hemingford.

"I'm aware of that."

"Applications are open," he said.

"I'm aware of that too, sir."

"Good," was all Mellor said before opening the door and disappearing down the corridor.

62

For the third time in ten days, Ormerod pulled up by the gates of George Brannigan Scrap Metal Merchant Ltd's yard and stepped out of the car. At least, this time, it looked as though the man himself would be about. Parked in front of the green portakabin office was a dark blue BMW 5 series. He made a point of walking all round the vehicle. There was nothing he could see that might give him help in matching it to the one seen in the CCTV shots.

Suddenly, the crane at the far end of the yard dropped a scrap van into the crusher. The noise startled him. Looking down from the cab was the recognisable face of George Brannigan. Ormerod was in no doubt he'd been seen entering the yard but there was no indication that Brannigan intended to break off from what he was doing. The machine began to squeeze its sides together and crush the van that had been dropped in.

Ormerod approached the crane and waved his arms.

Finally, Brannigan stopped the engine and swivelled out of the cab. "You again," he said. "Not brought your mate with you? What do you want now?"

"Can we talk? In the office?" Ormerod said.

Brannigan gave a nod and picked up a rag and began to wipe his hands as he walked towards the office.

Ormerod followed Brannigan through the door. "Thought we'd let you know," he said. "We think we've found Mark's murderer."

"Made an arrest, have you?" Brannigan threw the rag into a bin by the desk.

"Not exactly. The suspect was discovered dead yesterday."

"Can't very well deny it then, can they?" The man relaxed. "Sorry, it was just ... with your previous visits, I wondered if you considered me a suspect."

"Until we can rule people out Mr Brannigan ..." Ormerod let the sentence hang.

Brannigan smiled and folded his arms. "But you didn't really come all the way out here to break the news."

"Nice car," Ormerod remarked indicating the office door and the vehicle that lay beyond.

"I like it."

Ormerod pulled an envelope from inside his coat then a couple of photos from it. "This was you on the Friday night Mark was murdered, wasn't it?" He showed the CCTV still images to him.

Brannigan took them and gave them a cursory glance. "Probably, yeah. Times would be about right."

"So what about these?" Ormerod took more images from the envelope and passed them across.

Brannigan paid more attention to these ones. Finally, after flicking through them, he passed them back. "No, not me," he said. "Dates are wrong. These were from the night before."

"And that wouldn't be you in that area then?"

"I said so, didn't I?"

"So where were you on Thursday 14th February when these images were recorded?"

Brannigan furrowed his brows as if to give the question some thought. "I'd have been here, watching telly probably or listening to some music."

"Can anyone confirm that?"

"Would they need to?"

"Just asking."

"Well I'm just telling you I was here, at home, alone."

"Okay." Ormerod slowly and deliberately pulled some final images from the envelope. "And this wouldn't be you driving down Horbury Road the night before that, with someone in the car with you?"

Brannigan's expression hardened as he took hold of the next two pictures. Another cursory glance. "Nope.

Why do you think that might be me? What happened that night?"

"Just routine enquiries. It does look like your vehicle, Mr Brannigan."

"I suppose it could. But there must be quite a few dark BMWs on the road in West Yorkshire, not to mention further afield." He gave the photos back to Ormerod. "Sorry I can't help you."

Ormerod slowly nodded his head. "Well, thanks for your time," he said.

*   *   *

Around the corner, he watched as the detective drove away. He was becoming concerned. George was attracting too much attention. It had been easy to track down his step-daughter. Surely he should have had his money back by now? But George had gone quiet on him. A little seed of doubt was beginning to grow in the part of his brain that looked after his own preservation. He'd owed George. Back in Ulster on that day in 1978, he was a dead man. Until George appeared from nowhere and shot them. It had never been reported, kept quiet by the Army, and never mentioned by the IRA. But he'd repaid George since; debt wiped out. And he certainly didn't want anyone else to make the connection between them.

Patrick Davidson stepped out of the car, dropped his cigarette on the ground and trod on it before walking through the scrapyard gates.

Brannigan appeared from the office when Davidson was about ten yards away.

"Patrick," Brannigan said, a surprised look on his face. "I didn't expect to see you."

"I thought I'd just come and see how you were."

Brannigan held his arms apart and gave an awkward smile. "I'm well, as you can see."

"A nice mug of tea would be good," Davidson said, indicating the office.

"Sure." Brannigan turned and led the way inside.

As Brannigan fussed around the kettle, putting tea bags in mugs, he was aware of Davidson looking around the walls of the office, eyes flitting from the glamour calendar to a notice board with registration numbers written on.

"Did you speak to Felicity?" Davidson asked.

"Yes. Yes, I did, thanks for that. No idea how you tracked her down so quickly."

"Training, George." The man finally settled onto a chair. "So did you get your money back?"

The kettle clicked off and Brannigan poured water into the mugs. "No." he answered. Facing his ex-colleague, he continued, "I changed my mind."

Davidson looked at Brannigan for a moment and smiled. When he replied, it was in quiet, measured tones. "You should have involved me sooner."

When he spoke like that, it always unnerved Brannigan. In the army, when Davidson had dropped into those quiet tones, he knew there was a storm coming. Although he'd saved him that day, he had always wondered how Patrick had found himself in that situation in the first place; on a remote farm on a quiet country road near Armagh. Purely by chance on a clandestine patrol, he'd come across the situation. Two men dead and a dash for the barracks followed. And shortly after, Patrick Davidson was back in Yorkshire, out of the game, as he put it. And nothing more was ever said about the incident.

Brannigan brought the drinks over to the desk where Davidson was sitting.

"What did he want?" Davidson asked, gently stirring his tea.

"Who?"

"That detective."

"Oh, him. Did he see you?"

Davidson's expression told him that was a stupid question.

"He came to tell me they thought they'd found who was responsible for Mark's death."

Davidson sipped his tea. "Anyone you know?"

"He didn't say and I didn't ask. But whoever it was, they're dead."

"Convenient."

"You didn't have anything to do with it, did you?"

"George," Davidson said disdainfully. "What do you take me for?"

"You can't blame me for wondering." Brannigan put his mug to his lips.

"Anyway, why've you not recovered your money?"

Brannigan put his mug back down on the table. "I've done a lot of thinking over the past couple of weeks. Suddenly, it doesn't seem so important. Other things rank higher."

"Such as?"

"Family."

"But she's only your step-daughter, not a blood relative. And she tried to tuck you up."

"Maybe so. And maybe I had some part in how she viewed things," Brannigan said before looking away. "Anyway, I did manage to speak to her and told her what I thought. The rest is down to her." He looked back at Davidson. "But I'd like to see her reconcile with Andy."

"Ah, the youthful Andy." Davidson appeared thoughtful. "You do know he's the weak link?"

"How so?"

"He was with you in that grubby toilet block. He witnessed what you did."

"He didn't actually see anything."

"A moot point. The fact is, he can place you at the scene of a death. A death the police are classing as murder."

"Andy'll be fine. He won't say anything. Especially if Felicity patches things up."

Davidson raised his eyebrows. "That's a lot of ifs and reliance on others. Have you forgotten our training? You can't necessarily rely on anyone else outside of the 'team'."

"I hope you're not suggesting anything?"

"Merely pointing out the facts, George. But bear in mind, nothing links you and I."

"Nothing does."

"Good." Davidson stood. "Thanks for the tea," he said and left.

63

Gary Monk was sitting in the patrol car with his mentor colleague PC Dennis Tate. It had been Dennis who had called in the discovery of Mark Thompson's body. They were having a quiet ten minutes, Tate reading that morning's Yorkshire Post.

"What's so interesting, Dennis?" Monk asked.

"Just remembering this," he responded. "But you won't remember, it's twenty years ago now." He looked up into nowhere. "Bloody Hell, twenty years." He turned to the young PC. "It seems like yesterday."

Monk looked across. "What does?"

"This murder case." Tate prodded the paper with his finger. "Never got anyone for it."

Monk closed his eyes. "Must be loads of unsolved cases," he said. "Especially from that long ago."

"This was in Horbury. The young lass was off the Lupset estate. Claire Hobson," Tate said quietly. "I remember it well. I was about eighteen then. I suppose, thinking about it, that might have been one of the things that made me want to become a policeman."

Monk opened his eyes. "Sorry, who did you say?"

"I said it might have been one of the things ..."

"No, the name?"

"The girl? Claire Hobson. Why? You didn't know the family, did you?"

"No, I'm from Denby Dale." Monk could feel himself flush and his heart rate quicken. CH, he thought. "Here, let me see that Dennis," he said.

"Didn't think you were interested." Tate passed the paper across.

Monk began reading but before he'd read more than a few lines, their radio sparked into life and relayed a message about a burglary in progress near where they were parked. Tate fired the engine into life and they set off with blue lights flashing.

*   *   *

"That's great news, Bob," Sammy said. She and Susan had called in at the house in Ossett.

"What time are you collecting them?"

"About ten."

"I bet you can't wait," Susan said, as she came in from the kitchen with mugs of coffee.

A broad grin spread over Souter's face. "What do *you* think?" He took a mug from her and put it on the low table in front of him.

Sammy was in a comfortable chair, legs tucked beneath her. "So you're up and running with the articles then?" she asked.

"Chandler seems pleased," Souter responded.

"Are you still going ahead mentioning the new piece of evidence?"

"That's in Friday's article." Susan sipped her drink as she sat on the sofa next to Souter. "But we had Wood Street contact us this afternoon when you'd gone," she looked over at Souter. "We're doing a fresh appeal for witnesses to the Weaver murder in the park. Janey was working something up when I left."

"They must be struggling then," Souter suggested.

"Probably. Has anyone spoken to Wakefield CID about what we're running?"

"I called DCS Flynn on Monday and said we were running this series of articles," Souter offered. "I asked him if they were actually conducting a cold case review but he dodged that one."

"We'll take that as a 'no', then," Susan quipped.

"Anyway, you two, I still haven't had a proper explanation as to how you stumbled on a body on the allotments."

"Ah, that was Danny."

Souter took a drink. "Who's Danny?"

"The lad on the bike who was hanging around the shop when we stumbled over the Mark Thompson murder." Susan put her mug on the coffee table.

"I didn't know you'd been in contact."

"That time we went to see Mr Chandler ... on my way out, I got a message from him."

"Why didn't you tell me about it?"

"To be honest, Bob, you had other things on your mind."

"So when did you see him?"

"That evening."

"On your own?" Souter's eyes narrowed.

"I was careful."

"Like when you went to the farm, you mean?" Souter was referring to the incident, nearly eighteen months ago now, that had been the catalyst for their meeting in the first place. "Sorry," he said, thinking better of it. "I know you'd be careful."

Susan glared at him for a second. "It was obvious he wanted to tell somebody what he'd seen the night Thompson was attacked," she said. "But he was scared. We were going to tell you ... and Colin, but I just wanted to check the facts of what he'd told me first before I took it to him. Christ, I didn't know they were on the same track. You could have knocked us over with a feather when he and his team turned up just as I opened the shed door."

"I can just imagine Colin's reaction when he saw you two."

"Not sure who was more surprised," Sammy said, "him or us. But he let me phone in sick to the office."

"He's alright with you now?" Souter looked from one to the other.

"I helped persuade Danny to come in and make a statement," Susan said. "That seemed to tie things up for him."

"I'll bet the young lad was relieved."

Susan paused.

"Is there something else?"

"Well ..."

"Go on."

Susan then related what Danny had told her of his involvement with Mark and the man dropping the bag through the hedge and how the man had spent a fair bit of time trying to track him down afterwards.

"And it wasn't this character found dead in the shed?"

Susan shook her head. "No, this man was a lot older, fifties maybe."

"So the lad's still on edge about this?"

"I suppose so."

* * *

"We've done as much as we can for tonight, Gary," Denis Tate said. "SOCOs will test what they can and CID will take it over." He looked at his watch. "By the time we get back to the station and write up our reports, it'll be time to knock off."

Monk was only half listening.

"I said, it'll be time to knock off."

"Yeah, right."

The pair were on their way back to Wood Street having attended a break-in at a building site where the offices had been ransacked and expensive tools and equipment stolen.

Monk left Tate finalising his report on the burglary and managed to slip upstairs and onto the CID corridor. Once again outside the Incident Room he paused. Trying the door handle, it was unlocked. His heart was hammering against his chest wall. If he was caught up here, it would certainly be a disciplinary.

Some light came in through the windows from the streetlights, enough for him to get his bearings. Carefully, he closed the door behind him. Nothing would be more suspicious than an open door on the corridor. He approached the whiteboards he'd seen before. Taking out his torch, he scanned the first board, the one concerning the murder of Mark Thompson. This had new lines drawn indicating links to someone named as William Pollock with the nickname below given as 'Billy the Fish'. That must have been the character discovered in the allotment shed yesterday, he thought.

Switching off the torch for a moment, he listened. All seemed quiet. Moving along to the Weaver murder boards, he began to study more closely. The lines and links to Weaver showed someone called Charlotte Watkins with a note that caused him to take a step back before bending forward and following the line from Charlotte to a box with the initials CH.

Christ, he thought, this can't be a coincidence. What had he heard during his training? There's no such thing as coincidence. So what is this woman, Charlotte Watkins' relationship with Claire Hobson? The more he studied the lines and brief notes, the more he felt the answer to his real father's identity was here. But where? Surely not that the victim, Marcus Weaver was his father? No, he'd be too young. Was there some DNA evidence found at the scene of this crime which matched his? Come on Gary, think. But it couldn't be, the timing was wrong. Whatever it was had to have been discovered before this case, otherwise it wouldn't have had time to make it onto the DNA Database.

Some shouting from out in the street disturbed his concentration. Torch switched off, he studied his watch, angling the face towards the windows so he could see. He'd been here too long.

At the door he paused, opened it and slipped out into the corridor. Just about to put his foot on the bottom step, a voice called out.

"Now then, young Monk," Sgt Sidebotham said. "What are you doing up there?"

"Oh, er …I was just putting something underneath the Inspector's door," he flustered.

The sergeant looked to his watch. "Your shift's finished isn't it? Get yourself off home."

"Yes sarge." Monk walked away but could feel Sidebotham's eyes boring into his back. He only hoped he wouldn't repeat the lie he'd just told him to Strong.

64
Thursday 28th February 2002

*EFFECTS STILL FELT FROM
UNSOLVED MURDER*

*Today, in the second of our features on the
unsolved murder of 14-year-old Claire
Hobson nearly twenty years ago, we focus
on the devastating effects still felt by
Claire's family and friends.*

*NEW APPEAL FOR WITNESSES TO
PARK MURDER*
*Police are launching a fresh appeal for
anyone in the vicinity of Wakefield Park on
the evening of Wednesday 13th February
and saw any suspicious behaviour near
the toilet block to come forward and speak
to them. Any information given will be
treated in the strictest confidence.*

Souter led Alison gently down the corridor towards the
lifts. He was carrying baby David snug in a blanket, she
was wrapped up in a warm coat. Behind, Sammy carried
a small case containing Alison's clothes and all the new-
born paraphernalia they would need for the first week or
so at home.

"You didn't need to take any more time off work,"
Alison had said.

"But you've just had an operation and you'll need an
extra pair of hands today – just to get you home," Sammy
had responded.

Alison had relented. "Well, only just today."

Souter drew the car to a halt by the entrance and came to help Alison outside. The cold air was a shock after the past few days being inside a building with stifling temperatures, and she drew her coat tighter around her neck. A couple of smokers dressed in pyjamas and dressing gowns were huddled nearby. Sammy looked at them and shook her head.

With David asleep in his new car seat strapped in the back, Alison alongside him and Sammy in the front, Souter checked all round and slowly set off for Ossett.

"Are you going in to the office today?" Sammy asked as they drove past the Post building.

"Not when my new family are coming home," he said.

"But you've got some work to do, Bob," Alison said from behind them. "And Susan said she was going in at lunchtime to tweak some of the articles you've been working on together."

"Anybody would think you wanted to get rid of me," he replied.

Sammy looked across at Souter and caught Alison's grin from the seat behind him.

* * *

Ormerod knocked on Strong's office door and was beckoned inside. "Guv, might be something and nothing …"

"Go on, Luke."

"I've just been speaking with Trevor and he's dealing with a break-in on a building site in Morley last night. Uniform attended and called it in. Some expensive kit was lifted."

"What sort of 'expensive kit'?"

"Surveying instruments – laser levels, that sort of thing."

"A site in Morley, you say?"

"Yep. And it's as you think – the same one where Andy Barrett is based."

"Is Trevor there now?"

"About to head out there."

"Good. Get yourself along with him, Luke, and have another chat with Barrett. You can tell him about Pollock, if he doesn't already know. I've got something else to attend to here."

"Will do."

"Is Kelly in?"

"Yes, guv." Ormerod left and closed the door.

Strong produced an item from the plastic bag he'd brought in with him that morning and studied it. He switched on his desk lamp, held it beneath and inspected it more closely.

After a few seconds, he put it back in the bag, stood and made his way to the CID Room. He searched out Kelly Stainmore and, with a discreet nod of the head, encouraged her to leave the room and follow him.

"Something up, guv?" she asked once out in the corridor.

"We're going to see the Super," he said. "I need to tell him about my visit to Stoke yesterday and I want you to be in on it."

"Stoke?" Stainmore queried as she followed her boss up the stair to the Flynn's office. "I wondered where you were."

"I went to see Paul Nichols, not that he lives by that name anymore. I can't really tell you anything else, but it was a productive afternoon."

He'd seen Flynn briefly earlier that morning and told him he needed a word.

"Come in and sit down," DCS Flynn greeted the pair.

Sitting opposite, Strong began to recount his visit to the garden centre in Stoke the previous afternoon. DCS Joe Gilfoyle had met him in the car park and explained as much about the nature of Nichols new identity as he felt he could. He was working in the garden centre and, after a brief phone call from Gilfoyle to Nichols, Strong was asked to meet the man in the cafeteria on his own.

"I wasn't told what had led to Nichols' entry into the Witness Protection Scheme, only that he'd agreed to speak to me provided I wasn't told about it or even his new identity."

"So what was he able to tell you?" Flynn asked.

He reached into his pocket and brought out the evidence bag and produced the tunic button. "He found this by the body of Claire Hobson."

Flynn picked it up and examined it. "Are you sure this is genuine?"

"I'm checking it with the MOD, but I'm fairly sure."

Flynn passed the button to Stainmore. "Can we get some images of this regiment's coat of arms, do you think?" she asked Strong.

"There's got to be something available, Kelly."

"What are you thinking?" Flynn asked.

"The tattoo on Mrs Monk's attacker's arm could be this coat of arms. In which case we would need to speak to her again to see if it prompts anything she could remember."

"Good idea."

"But then ..." Strong thought, "do we release information on this lead to the press? You know the Post is featuring the case, focussing on the family and an appeal for new information. Have they spoken to you about this series of articles they're running?"

"I had that Souter fellow call me a few days ago," Flynn responded. "Cheeky beggar asked me if we're conducting a cold-case review. I left my answer fairly non-committal." At that, he stood, walked to the window and looked out.

Strong and Stainmore exchanged looks and waited for Flynn to continue.

"Let's just see what Mrs Monk says first," he finally said turning back to face them. "If she thinks it could be connected, then we might make an appeal on what we know."

"But there's Gary, sir," Strong said. "How do you suggest we handle that?"

"He doesn't know anything about the connection with the Claire Hobson case though, does he?"

"Not from us. And we haven't said anything to his mother either."

Flynn was silent for a few seconds then said, "Okay, get some image of the Green Howards crest, check when PC Monk is on duty and visit his mother then. If she confirms, I'll think about briefing the papers. Meantime, I'll speak with ACC Mellor and put him in the picture."

*   *   *

The site offices were a hive of SOC activities. The thieves had used bolt cutters on the gates and broken into the offices with relative ease. Unfortunately, there was no CCTV coverage. The site manager was trying to keep progress on the construction works flowing as best he could.

Ormerod was back in Andy Barrett's office, leaning against the sloping drawing desk. "So most of these instruments were what your department used, Mr Barrett?"

"That's right. I've had to send out for hire replacements."

An officer was dusting the smashed door frame to the equipment cupboard at the rear of the office for prints.

"So who would know these instruments were stored there?"

"Could be anybody who's worked on the site."

"But who would normally have access to them?"

"Me and young Michael, the chain lad, normally."

Ormerod thought for a moment and caught the eye of the Scenes of Crime Officer who indicated he'd found something to work with. "Would you object if we took some fingerprints ... for elimination purposes? You and Michael for a start. What about the site manager, would he have access?"

"Of course he would."

"Okay, I'll organise that. If you say a lot of those who worked on site knew you kept them in there, then you never know, they may show up."

Barrett shrugged and seemed distracted. "Whatever," he said. "I just need to get on. We're ten days behind already with this freezing weather, but we're trying to catch up."

Ormerod pushed himself off the desk, casually walked to the window and looked out at the activity on site. "Last time I was here," he said, in a matter of fact fashion, "we asked you about your wife, Felicity ..." He turned and faced Barrett. "Have you heard from her since?"

"What? Well, yes actually. She texted the other day to say she just needed some space for a while."

"Do you know where she is?"

Barrett hesitated. "No. it was from a withheld number."

Ormerod raised his eyebrow in surprise. "Really? You know we think we know who murdered her cousin, Mark Thompson?"

Barrett looked up from the drawing he was studying. "I didn't, no. Who was it?"

"Well, tests are still being carried out but we think the perpetrator is dead."

A fearful expression came over Barrett's face before he seemed to relax. "Was it anyone Mark knew?"

"We're still looking at connections, but probably."

"And how did ...?"

"We can't really divulge any more details at the moment. But if Mrs Barrett gets in touch again, perhaps you could ask her to give me a call?"

A questioning look came over the man's face.

"I just need to tidy up a few details, that's all." Ormerod walked over to the SOCO. "If you could take Mr Barrett's prints, this lad, Michael's and the site manager's when you're done," he said to him.

Before he left the office, Ormerod turned back to Barrett. "You can tell her the news about Mr Thompson's attacker too," he said.

*   *   *

Alison had convinced Souter that she and baby David would be absolutely fine with Sammy in the house alongside them. "After all, she'd already taken the day off to help," Alison argued. "And you can't be away from your stories for too long."

Reluctantly, he drove back to Leeds and in the early afternoon, climbed the stairs to the newsroom floor and his desk. Susan was sitting in his chair looking through some notes she'd made. Janey Clarke's desk at the next work station was empty.

"Kicked you out then?" Susan quipped when she saw him approach.

"Anybody would think I was a nuisance," he said.

"Not like you were driving Alison nuts by fussing around?"

"Is that what she thinks?"

Susan just grinned and indicated Janey's chair. "She's gone out," she said.

"Do you know if there's been any response to the Weaver murder witness appeal?"

"Not that I've heard, but I've been thinking …"

"Go on."

"What do we know about the case?"

Souter began to relate his conversation with the dog walker who'd found the body, the position and how it was presented. "But we now know Weaver was definitely there for a bit of physical exercise with Charlotte," he went on. "Which makes it seem that he was positioned in an attempt to make it look like he was there for slightly different reasons. And fair play to Colin's team, they've never mentioned that."

"But was it to disguise the fact that Weaver had stumbled into something else? Not any homosexual activity but …" Susan thought out loud, "… oh, I don't know."

"And the dog walker also spoke of the three men he'd seen, one on his own and two more approaching the toilets when he was walking away from the direction of the building. He also mentioned the car driving off when he was heading back, which we now know belongs to Charlotte.

"So was he able to expand on any description of these men?" Susan asked.

Souter puffed out his cheeks. "I did press him, but how accurate this was, I can't say, but talking about the two men approaching the toilets, he thought one was quite young, twenties maybe, with the other man middle-aged, shorter, stockier. But, like I say, that probably wouldn't stand up to any degree of close scrutiny."

"So the older one ... could be in his fifties ... oh, I don't know."

"What are you thinking, Susan?"

She stared into the middle distance for several seconds. "I was just wondering if there was a connection with the Weaver incident and Danny's grabbing a bag full of money the next night for Thompson?"

"Bit of a leap, isn't it?"

"What if the exchange should have taken place at the toilets but something went wrong? Weaver walks in on something he shouldn't have. The operation is pulled and rearranged for the following evening, but by different means. Hence Danny gets a call that day to do Mark a favour."

"But you said that Mark had told Danny it wasn't drugs. So what else could have been so important?"

"Blackmail?" Susan suggested.

"It's possible I suppose, bearing in mind the time of night and dubious location ... but we've nothing to suggest that. I think it's all speculation at the moment. We need more information."

*   *   *

About an hour after his briefing with Flynn, Strong received the email attaching an image of the Green Howards crest. It certainly matched the button.

Gathering Kelly Stainmore from the CID room, they set off for Denby Dale to visit Mrs Monk.

"Does she know we're coming?" Stainmore asked once they'd set off.

"I spoke to her before I came to see you," he responded. "And Gary's on duty, I believe."

"It'll be interesting to see if she's told him the truth."

"Hmm," was all Strong said. The rest of the journey passed in silence.

For what seemed like the umpteenth time in recent weeks, Strong and Stainmore walked up the path to the Monk residence. Again, the front door opened before they reached it.

Mrs Monk led them into the front room. "So what do you want to show me?" she asked.

"Before I do, Mrs Monk ... Annabel," Strong began. "We wondered if you'd had a conversation with Gary about the situation?"

She bowed her head and Strong knew what the answer would be. She looked up at him defiant and related the exchange she had had with her son a few days before. "But, like me, he doesn't have any clue as to why you're so interested in this man – his biological father."

Strong sighed before producing a sheet of paper from the briefcase he'd brought with him. He held it out towards her but she didn't take it. Instead she turned away and closed her eyes.

"I understand if this is too painful for you, Annabel," Strong said, turning the image from her. "But ..."

She held up a hand. "Give me a second," she said. "I'm just trying to recall something. I've been trying to think about this ever since Gary and I had the conversation." She waved in the direction of the sheet of paper. "If that's what I think it is ..."

Slowly, she opened her eyes and stared at Strong. "I remember some figures," she said. "*X / X*. And a date, *'1875'.*"

Strong looked to Stainmore then back to the woman. "And what was that from?"

"The tattoo ... on his arm. I told you it seemed to be some form of crest. And God knows, I looked at it for some time that night."

Again, Strong held out the sheet of paper. Finally, she took it and looked at the image before closing her eyes again, forcing the tears from them. She wiped her cheeks with the backs of her hands and gave the paper back to Strong. "That's what I remember," she said. "That was the tattoo on the man's arm."

"And I think you told me last time, but can you tell me again, which arm?"

"Left."

"Thank you, Annabel."

As they stood to leave, Strong handed her his card. "You've been a great help," he said. "But if you think of anything else, no matter how small, give me a call."

65
Friday 1st March 2002

APPEAL FOR NEW INFORMATION IN TWENTY-YEAR-OLD UNSOLVED MURDER

Today, we focus on what is known about 14-year-old Claire Hobson's murder. Her body was discovered by two young boys in railway sidings in Horbury just outside Wakefield twenty years ago on 7th March 1982. It is believed she had been raped and strangled two nights earlier, shortly after she went missing on Friday 5th March 1982.
We also understand from our own enquiries that a major new piece of evidence has been uncovered. Its significance is being investigated by West Yorkshire Police.

Strong was back in his office after conducting the morning briefing on the Weaver case. There had been no further progress and, so far, no significant response to the newspaper appeal for witnesses.

He had his copy of that morning's Post open on the desk in front of him. The mention of a new piece of evidence in connection with the Claire Hobson case puzzled him. Had Flynn authorised release of some limited information on this, or had Bob acted on his own with what Susan and Sammy must have told him?

The answer came with the door bursting open and a furious DCS Flynn entering, a copy of the newspaper in his hand. The door closed and he stood in front of Strong's desk. "What the Hell's the meaning of this?" he asked.

"I've only just seen it myself, sir."

"I told you yesterday I'd give it some thought, but only after Mrs Monk had confirmed her memory about that crest. Has she?"

"She did."

"And you go and tell them about this."

"I did not," Strong said firmly.

Flynn paced the small area of the office. "The ACC will go mad. He wanted to be informed about this before we went public."

Strong leaned back, calmly reviewing the situation. "But remember where we got this information from in the first place. They even claim subtly that it was them who discovered it. Susan Brown and Sammy Grainger came to me with it last Sunday. In fact my checking the details brought to light the fact that Paul Nichols is in Witness Protection. They've published this off their own backs. We never told them to keep it confidential." He leaned forward and prodded the newspaper on the desk. "But when you read the article, they haven't actually said what this new piece of evidence is. I don't think there's a lot of harm done."

Flynn seemed to calm. "I'm going to have to say something to Mellor though."

"Tell him the truth. The reporters were the source of this in the first place. And at the end of the day, they've been tasked with running a series of articles with the joint aim of some public interest and appealing for new information."

"I suppose you're right."

*   *   *

The phone sounded insistent. When he answered, Strong heard the familiar tones of Sgt Bill Sidebotham. *"Colin, there's a fellow down here says he needs to speak to you about the Weaver case."*

"Is Luke not around?"

"He wants to speak to you. He's that man who spoke to you before, if you remember, a couple of weeks ago. He says he's remembered something else and wants to follow things up with you."

"What's his name?"

"Pearson, Timothy Pearson."

"Oh, yes. Thanks, Bill, I'll be down."

On his way past the CID office, he collected Ormerod and the pair headed downstairs.

Sidebotham came out from behind the front desk when he saw the CID officers approach. "I've put him in the front interview room," he told them.

Timothy Pearson was sitting nervously behind the desk in the middle of the room. Dressed in a smart suit, his tie was loosened at the neck and he had a briefcase at his feet.

"Mr Pearson," Strong greeted. "I understand you have some new information for us?" Strong and Ormerod took their seats opposite the man.

Pearson quickly pulled the case up onto the table and clicked the locks. Before he opened the lid, he spoke. "I saw the fresh appeal in yesterday's paper and I've been thinking a lot about what I saw that night." He paused a second as if considering what he was going to say next. "You probably don't know, but one of my hobbies is drawing. I've been having some scary recalls of those events. One of the positives from that has been that I managed to see clearly the faces of the two men who approached me."

Strong looked to Ormerod then back to Pearson. "Go on," he said.

Pearson slowly opened his case and took out a sheet of A4. He turned it round and carefully placed it in front of Strong and Ormerod.

Both officers stared at the two images that the man had drawn in pencil before looking at one another.

"Can we keep this, Mr Pearson?" Strong finally asked.

"Of course."

"That looks ..." Ormerod began to say before Strong cut him off.

"And this is how you remembered these men?" Strong asked.

"The older one wore a black woollen hat and the younger one had an anorak hood up, that's why I've drawn them as they are. They've given me nightmares since their faces come back to me. But after I'd sketched them out yesterday I had my first good night's sleep in ages."

"I really appreciate you coming in Mr Pearson. Now, if we need a further statement from you, you would be okay with that? We would be as discreet as we could."

Pearson looked down at the table, closing up the briefcase. He nodded slightly. "If you must," he said.

Strong stood and held out a hand. "Thank you, Mr Pearson, this is most useful. But could I just ask you to keep this confidential too?"

"Of course." Pearson seemed satisfied with the response.

Ormerod led the man out then re-joined Strong at the bottom of the stairs.

"It is, isn't it?" Ormerod said indicating the sheet of paper Strong held in his hand.

"Uncanny," Strong agreed.

*   *   *

"What now?" Andy Barrett whined as Strong and Ormerod entered his site office.

"I think we need another word, Mr Barrett..." Strong looked pointedly at the young lad who was writing something on a drawing from his notebook, "...in private."

"You can do that a bit later, Michael," Barrett said to his colleague.

The youth was bemused but took up some papers and left the office.

Barrett leaned back at his desk. "So what can I do for you now?"

"Well, you can start by telling us the truth."

Barrett coloured. "I don't know what you mean. Is this to do with the break-in?" He looked to Ormerod. "You already told me you've discovered who murdered Mark."

Strong flicked open a notebook. "For the record, Mr Barrett, can you tell me where you were on the evening of Wednesday 13th February between the hours of seven-thirty and eight-thirty?"

The man flustered, shuffling letters and papers around on his desk. "Why do you want to know about then?" Strong didn't answer. "I was at home, in the flat."

"And can anyone vouch for that?"

"Well, yes, I suppose Felicity can."

"Have you heard from her again since we spoke yesterday?" Ormerod asked.

Barrett dropped his head. "No. No, I haven't."

"So," Ormerod continued, "she's not available to confirm your whereabouts and we can't even speak to her about the sightings of someone matching her description at Mark Thompson's flat around this same time?"

"What? No, I haven't been able to speak to her. As I told you yesterday, I've only had a text."

"When was the last time you saw George Brannigan?" Strong took up the questioning again.

Barrett's head swivelled towards the DI, alarmed at the change of tack. "George? I ... I don't know. It's been a while."

Strong flicked through his notebook. "Last year sometime, you said when we last spoke."

"Er, yes. Yes that's right. It must have been."

"So you weren't with him on the evening of Wednesday 13th February, Mr Barrett?" Strong persisted.

"No. Look, what's all this about?"

"Would it surprise you to know that we have a witness who's described you and Mr Brannigan in a location we're interested in in connection with another enquiry?"

"What enquiry?"

"I'll ask you again, Mr Barrett, where were you on the evening of 13th February? In the company of Mr Brannigan?"

"I've told you, I was at home."

"So you weren't in the vicinity of the park in Wakefield?"

"No. No, of course not. What are you implying?"

Strong shrugged. "I'm implying nothing, merely asking questions."

"Do you know what type of car Mr Brannigan drives?" Ormerod asked.

"Er, a BMW, I think."

Strong kept up the pressure. "When was the last time you were in that vehicle?"

"The car? I can't think I've ever been in it."

"Sure."

"I've told you."

Strong nodded to Ormerod who produced a still from the CCTV images that Sam Kirkland identified on the night of Weaver's death.

"So this wouldn't be you?" Ormerod asked as he placed the photo on Barrett's desk. "In the passenger seat."

The man picked it up and looked at it for a few seconds. "This could be anybody," he finally said. "You can't possibly tell who this is with this quality."

"We could get it enhanced," Ormerod responded.

Barrett seemed to grow in confidence. "If you could you would have done that already and shown me that."

Strong unfolded a photocopy sheet of the sketches Timothy Pearson had given them. "What about these images, Mr Barrett? Surprisingly like you and Mr Brannigan."

"Could be any two men," Barrett said dismissively.

Strong studied the man for a second. "I'll give you one last chance to tell the truth, Mr Barrett. Were you in the location of the park in Wakefield on Wednesday 13th February between the hours of seven-thirty and eight-thirty in the evening?"

Barrett looked defiant. "No," he said.

Strong looked to Ormerod. "He's had his opportunity, DC Ormerod," he said. "Let's go."

Outside, as they got into the car, Ormerod sighed, "I don't believe a word of that. No way those sketches weren't him and Brannigan."

Strong settled in the driver's seat. "We need something concrete to place them at the scene, Luke. Pearson's eye-witness statement probably wouldn't be enough. We'd need some forensics." As he turned and pulled his seatbelt into position, he could see Barrett through the office window on the phone. "I wonder who he's speaking to now?" he wondered.

"Brannigan?"

"Let's see what he has to say, Luke."

Strong started the engine and they pulled off the site.

*   *   *

"They've both denied they were anywhere near the park on the night, let alone the toilet block," Strong said. "To be honest, unless we uncover more evidence, there's not a lot else we can do."

In DCS Flynn's office, the man himself rubbed his face with both hands. "And we really have nothing else?"

"Nothing much, sir."

"What about forensics Let's get them to look again at the samples. There must be something on Weaver's clothes? His skin? Something?" Flynn began to sound desperate.

"I've asked the lab to run more tests."

"What about your investigations into Claire Hobson's murder? The press have been badgering again, especially the Post. They're pressing me to confirm if we're actually conducting a cold-case review."

"What have you told them?"

"Nothing yet. But I suppose we'll need to make some sort of official announcement."

"Do we use them to ask for help on this? Especially as they're running a campaign off their own back."

"I'll speak to Mellor."

"About that, sir," Strong said. "Do you think it's time to open out the re-investigation? Bring other members of the team onto it?"

"Not just yet, Colin. I don't want to draw their attentions away from the Weaver case. God knows we need some progress on that." Flynn relaxed slightly. "Anyway, how are you and Stainmore getting on?"

"As I told you this morning, we saw Annabel Monk yesterday and I'm convinced the taxi-driver who attacked her and is Gary's biological father was a member of the Green Howards until sometime around 1978 or 1979."

"And are you trying to track down likely suspects?"

"I've been in contact with the MOD to get what information they have about who left that year. I did tell them it was urgent, but we're in their hands at the moment."

"Here," Flynn said, handing over a slip of paper. "ACC Mellor thought you might need some help unlocking information from those buggers at the MOD. This is a good friend of his who should be able to help you. If he can't or won't, let me know."

Strong took the proffered sheet and folded it up into his wallet.

"No need to tell you that's strictly confidential."

"Sir," Strong acknowledged.

Back in his own office, he took out the piece of paper Flynn had just given him. There was no question, to get better information, Strong definitely needed an 'in' at the MOD.

Picking up the phone, he dialled the number.

"Hello," a male voice answered.

"Good afternoon, my name is Strong, Detective Inspector Colin Strong from Wakefield CID. I understand you may know our ACC, Roy Mellor?" he asked.

"Are you in your office now?" the man responded.

"Yes."

"I'll call you back."

The line went dead and Strong stared at the handset for a moment before replacing it. A pattern is emerging here, he thought. That's the second time the authenticity of his identity was being checked.

A minute later, his phone rang.

"Colin," Bill Sidebotham said, *"I've a call for you. Wouldn't give his name but said you were just speaking to him and got cut off."*

"Thanks, Bill, put him through."

The same voice he'd just spoken to came through the handset. *"Colin, what can I do for you?"*

Strong outlined the information he had and what he hoped to find out from official records. He gave the man dates and hoped he could hear sooner rather than later.

"Is this the best number to get you, or would you prefer me to call on your mobile?" the man asked as the call was winding up.

Strong related his mobile number.

"I'll be back to you as soon as I can," the man said. *"By the way,"* he concluded, *"old Roy must trust you."*

Strong was left with a dialling tone buzzing in his ear. Only when he replaced the handset did he realise the man hadn't given his name.

66
Monday 4th March 2002

RE-INVESTIGATION INTO THE
TWENTY-YEAR-OLD UNSOLVED
MURDER OF CLAIRE HOBSON

Tomorrow marks the twentieth anniversary of the rape and murder of 14-year-old Claire Hobson. She was last seen leaving her friend's house on Friday 5th March 1982 Her body was discovered on railway sidings in Horbury just outside Wakefield two days later on Sunday, 7th March 1982. We understand that officers from West Yorkshire Police based at Wood Street in Wakefield are conducting a fresh review of this case, following the discovery of a major new piece of evidence, uncovered by our own investigations.

"It's official then, guv," Stainmore said. "It must be if it's in the papers." She had a wan smile on her face. "We're conducting a review of the case."

Strong was reading the front page of that morning's Post. He'd been amused that Susan had managed to get joint credit for the article alongside Bob Souter. "Flynn okayed the request for information based on the taxi driver, recently ex-army, in his thirties with a tattoo," he replied.

"That'll narrow it down," she said with irony. "Most squaddies will have tattoos."

"He didn't want to give too much away at this stage. If we get some common names to allow us to conduct interviews, we might be able to narrow things down even more. I asked him if I could get the others involved in this, but he said they had to concentrate their efforts on the Weaver case." He folded up the paper and put it to one side. "I suppose it's too early to gauge any response from Joe Public?"

"Nothing when I left the CID Room just now, although the team has been wondering where this has all come from."

"Not surprised their curiosity's piqued." Strong settled back in his chair. "I suppose it may take a little while, it's only just hit this morning's paper."

"Anyway, how was the rest of your weekend?" Stainmore asked.

"Went to see my mate's new baby."

"Is that your journalist friend?"

"That's him. He's asked Laura and me to be Godparents."

"That's fantastic."

"Yep, us and Susan and Sammy."

"Are they his wife's friends?" Stainmore wondered.

"Friends of both of them really. You remember Susan? She's had a hand in writing those articles." Strong indicated the newspaper. "She was the one who fell through the farmhouse floor last year."

"Right. She's working at the Post now then, is she?"

"Partly, when she's not studying at Uni. And Sammy was the girl whose friend had gone missing and was found …"

"Oh God, yeah, I remember from the same time."

Suddenly, the door burst open and Luke Ormerod shot forward. "Sorry guv, sarge."

Stainmore turned round. "You don't normally call me 'sarge'," she said. "It must be something big."

The broad smile on Ormerod's face told them that was the case. "That breakthrough? I think we've got it."

Strong and Stainmore said nothing, waiting for Ormerod to tell them.

"The fingerprints on the cistern casing ..."

"I thought they'd been run through the system and there was no match," Strong said.

Ormerod held up a finger. "That was before the break-in at Andy Barrett's site. I persuaded some of those who usually had access to the store to give their prints."

"And you're going to tell me it was a match for Barrett himself," Strong guessed.

"Absolutely."

Strong got to his feet. "Brilliant. Now we bring him in, under caution if necessary."

*   *   *

Davidson stormed into Brannigan's office in the scrapyard. "What the fuck have you been doing?"

The young lad Brannigan gave some work to looked up, alarmed. Brannigan looked to him. "Take a break, Stevie," he said. "Take your time."

The youth scuttled past Davidson and disappeared out the door.

"What's got into you, Patrick?" Brannigan asked, trying to sound calm.

Davidson slapped a newspaper on the counter. "This. Have you seen it?"

Brannigan picked it up and began to read the main story. *'Police investigating the rape and murder of 14-year-old Claire Hobson are keen to speak to an ex-army soldier who was driving for a Leeds taxi firm at the time and is likely to be in his mid-fifties now,'* he read. Putting the paper down, he looked up at his former colleague. "Don't look at me, I had nothing to do with what happened to that girl," he said.

"Description fits you to a tee."

Realisation dawned on Brannigan. "And you, Patrick."

"Don't give me that shite! That's you and that incident in the park toilets. That's what's brought this on. And I tell you, when they come knocking on your door … and they will, you'd better not make any connections to me. After what happened in 1978, there are some seriously heavy people would love to get hold of me."

"Was it you, Patrick?"

Davidson stabbed a finger at Brannigan. "Don't you dare get any ideas, George. You don't know me," he said, spun on his heel and left.

"I think I do, Patrick," Brannigan said quietly. "I think I do."

*   *   *

Andy Barrett was sitting in Interview Room Two on the second floor of Wood Street Police Station, biting the skin to the side of his nails. Strong and Ormerod had visited the site in Morley and told him he was required to accompany them. He had gone pale when the officers had arrived for the third time to speak to him. They were waiting for a duty solicitor to turn up before they conducted a formal interview. In the meantime, the man nervously fidgeted in his seat.

Finally, the solicitor arrived and after allowing them a few minutes together, Strong and Ormerod entered the room. After the formalities for the tape, Strong took up the questioning. "Mr Barrett, I had hoped things wouldn't come to this," he said. "We have given you every opportunity to tell us the truth when we'd spoken to you before." He looked to Ormerod who gave a reaction confirming what Strong had just said.

"I don't understand," Barrett said. "Why am I here?"

Strong opened a manila folder he'd brought with him. "We are investigating the murder of Marcus Weaver. Previously," he continued, "we'd asked you for your whereabouts for the evening of Wednesday 13th February last, specifically between the hours of seven-thirty and eight-thirty. You claim that you were at home with your wife, Felicity."

"That's right," Barrett responded.

"And this is Felicity who seems to have disappeared and is uncontactable. So there is no corroboration to this statement."

"But it's true," he persisted.

"The last time we spoke, we showed you sketches of two men who had been seen in the vicinity of the toilet block in Wakefield park at the time in question." Strong produced the sketches from the file. "This man here," he pointed to the younger of the two images. "He bears a striking resemblance to yourself, does he not?"

Barrett shrugged. "A lot of people my age look like that."

Strong paused a beat. "Do you know what VIPER is, Mr Barrett?"

The man looked to the solicitor, puzzled, then back to Strong. "A snake, why?"

"VIPER stands for Video Identification Parade Electronic Recording," Strong stated. "It's a system that's being developed here in Wakefield which will mean the old style of identity parades can be carried out in front of a computer screen." He looked to Ormerod. "Much more cost effective and convenient."

"I've heard some talk of that," Ormerod confirmed.

"Unfortunately, I don't think it'll be ready until next year. A pity really, because it would have saved us some money. But now we'll just have to organise a traditional identity parade here at the station." Strong looked across at his DC. "Do you think we'll have any trouble selecting some men who look like Mr Barrett for the parade, DC Ormerod?"

"No, I don't think so, guv. After all, as Mr Barrett has told us, quite a lot of young men look like him."

The solicitor spoke for the first time. "Inspector, this is all very interesting but, as I understand it, you have put these matters to my client before and he's told you on previous occasions exactly what he's told you today."

"And we also showed you these stills, obtained from CCTV footage of a vehicle in the vicinity of the park on the night in question." Strong placed photographs on the table in front of them. "We think the passenger in that car looks a lot like you."

The solicitor picked up one of the photos. "Not very good quality," he commented. "I doubt very much that any identification would be possible from these. And the car … a dark BMW? There are thousands like these on the roads."

Strong leaned back on his chair and paused a moment. Eventually, he pushed himself forward and spoke again. "Mr Barrett, you remember that when DC Ormerod visited your office on Thursday last, he asked if you, along with some other work colleagues, would be prepared to give your fingerprints, to eliminate them from any we might find on the door to the store which had been forced to facilitate the theft?"

Barrett slowly nodded.

"Would it surprise you to know that we found a match for some of the prints taken?"

"You mean somebody working in the site offices has a record?"

"No, Mr Barrett, not exactly. You see, your prints were a match for those found on a disturbed cistern lid in the toilets where we found Mr Weaver's body." The solicitor was about to interrupt when Strong held up a finger. "We can also confirm that the operatives from Wakefield District Council who clean those toilets had done so earlier that day and all covers were in position."

The colour drained from Barrett's cheeks and he stared at Strong like a rabbit caught in headlights.

The solicitor leaned forward. "Inspector, I think I need to consult with my client," he said. "In private,"

"Of course," Strong said, making the announcement for the tape and switching off the recording. Both he and Ormerod stood and left the room.

Within fifteen minutes, the interview had recommenced.

"So, Mr Barrett, what have you got to tell us?" Strong asked.

Barrett looked down to the floor. "I have nothing further to add," he said.

"You can't seriously tell me that the evidence we have which puts you at the scene of a murder at the time that murder was carried out doesn't warrant a meaningful response from you?" Strong was shocked. He had at the very least suspected that the man would explain more about the incident. "Are you telling us that you were acting alone in this?" he went on.

"No comment."

"Was Mr Brannigan involved?"

"No comment."

Strong paused a moment and glanced at the solicitor who seemed embarrassed by the turn of events. "Are you frightened of Mr Brannigan in some way?" he asked.

A pause, then, "No comment."

Strong let out a breath. "You do realise that we will have no alternative but to charge you with the murder of Mr Weaver?"

This time Barrett remained silent.

Strong looked at his watch. "Well we do have time, but for now we'll be keeping you in custody pending further questioning."

Barrett seemed resigned as Strong ended the recording and arranged for him to be taken down to the cells.

"What do you reckon to that?" Strong asked Ormerod once they were on their way up to the CID Office.

"I think he's scared of Brannigan, assuming he was the other man spotted by our sketcher."

67
Tuesday 5th March 2002

"There's a young lady down here to see you, Colin," Bill Sidebotham announced.

"Intriguing, Bill. Did she say what it's about?" Strong was reviewing some paperwork in his office when his desk phone rang.

"She's the missus of that guy you have in custody, Andy Barrett."

"Felicity?"

"If you say so."

"Be right down."

On his way past, Strong looked in to the CID Office and searched out Luke Ormerod.

"Looking for me, guv?" he asked.

"Yes, Luke. Guess who's turned up downstairs? The elusive Felicity Barrett."

Ormerod got to his feet. "So he didn't do away with her as well then?"

"Apparently not."

Felicity Barrett was sitting on a hard plastic chair in reception. She stood as Strong approached. Flicking a hand through long dark hair, she appeared a confident young woman, neatly dressed in an unbuttoned coat revealing a figure-flattering red dress to the knee with matching red court shoes.

"Mrs Barrett, is it?" Strong asked, holding out a hand.

She shook it lightly. "Yes. I understand you have my husband here."

"Come through," he said. "By the way, this is my colleague DC Luke Ormerod."

Strong led them to the 'soft interview' room, set aside for difficult sexual assault cases and interviewing children.

He thought it would be a better environment for their questioning.

Declining the offer of a drink, Felicity was keen to talk. "This is all my fault," she began, as she sat awkwardly on the edge of one of the sofas.

Strong and Ormerod were each sitting in one of the armchairs either side.

"First of all, Mrs Barrett," Strong began, "I understand from your husband that you had ... how can we put it, taken a break from your marriage. Would that be correct?"

She looked down and nodded.

"We were trying to contact you but Andy said he didn't know where you were."

"I didn't tell him. It's been a difficult time."

"Of course, with your cousin, Mark. I'm sorry, you have my sympathy."

She looked up. "I understand you've found who was responsible?"

Strong nodded. "Apparently somebody who was in the same class as Andy at secondary school."

"Who was that?"

"We believe it was a man by the name of William Pollock."

A faint quiver of the lip. "That weirdo. They called him Billy the Fish."

"Yes we know. He was found dead a week ago. Drug overdose, we suspect."

"Doesn't surprise me."

Strong eased back in his chair, an arm draped over the back of it. "But we're investigating the murder of Marcus Weaver in the park toilets on 13th February, which is why we are holding your husband."

Her eyes filled with tears. "Oh God."

Ormerod leaned over and handed her some tissues from the box on the low table in front of them.

"We were asking Mr Barrett to confirm his whereabouts on that evening and he repeated that he was at home with you, Mrs Barrett. However, we couldn't contact you to corroborate that. But since then, we have discovered evidence which links your husband to the murder scene on that evening. So far, he's refused to explain that or give an account of where he actually was."

Felicity finished dabbing her eyes then spoke. "As I said, this is all my fault."

"Can you explain that statement?" Strong asked.

Felicity outlined her plan to extort money from her step-father, George Brannigan under the pretext that she'd been kidnapped and that it was supposed to be some sort of ransom payment.

"And your husband knew nothing of this?"

"Not until after."

Ormerod took up the questioning. "But you roped in your cousin, Mark Thompson to help you, didn't you?"

Again tears appeared. "I didn't know what would happen to him. But that was nothing to do with what we did. That was just some nutter he went to school with. Wasn't it?"

"So that's why you were seen coming and going from Mark's flat in town?" Ormerod persisted.

"I suppose so. I stayed there to keep a low profile. Just until George paid the money."

"But something went wrong, didn't it?" Strong took up the questioning again.

She nodded. "The first I knew was when Mark came in to say something had gone down in the park. Then the papers next day."

"So what happened next?"

"Mark said he'd try Plan B."

"Which was?"

"He had some little mate who could help him with the money transfer."

"Little mate?"

"Yes, his next-door neighbour. Little Danny, he called him."

Strong looked surprised. "Danny King, you mean? He was involved?"

"Mark never told me the details but Danny ended up with the money and delivered it to him."

"So the successful transfer happened the day after Weaver died in the toilets?"

"Yes."

"What happened then?"

"Mark called Andy and he came and picked me up where I'd been dropped off."

"But didn't Andy recognise Mark's voice?"

"He disguised it."

"So when did Andy know the truth?"

"I told him when we got to Whitby, the day after I found out about Mark."

"What was his reaction?"

"He said we had to give it back. The money was tainted. George had already been round several times and then Aunty June said he'd been round her house on the Friday looking for Mark. He was obviously on to us. I actually thought he'd ... but from what you've said, he hadn't."

"Did Andy tell you what had gone on in the toilets?"

"He didn't actually see what happened. He was standing on the toilet in one of the cubicles. They were supposed to leave the money in one of the cisterns."

"But he told you another man had appeared?"

"Yes."

"Did he tell you how they left him?"

"No. Only that George said it was an accident and they left him so he could be found."

Strong and Ormerod exchanged glances.

"And after Whitby?" Strong continued.

Felicity went on to tell how she decided to take off and stay with a friend in Manchester.

"So Mr Brannigan was still searching for you?"

"Yes"

"When was the last time you saw him?"

"He came to see me last week."

"He tracked you down?"

"I don't suppose it was too difficult, he'd been in the army you know? Probably used his mate, Patrick."

"Patrick?"

"Davidson, yes. Creep. They'd served in Ulster together. Some sort of bond they had, he reckoned."

"Do you know where this Mr Davidson lives?"

She shook her head. "No. I only ever saw him a couple of times when Mum and I were with George. She always felt uncomfortable when he showed up."

68

Strong's mobile rang as he walked along the corridor towards his office.

"Strong," he answered.

"DI Strong, I have some information for you." It was the same familiar voice of ACC Mellor's contact at the MOD he'd spoken to on Friday.

"Just let me close the door," Strong responded as he entered his office. Settled in his chair, he was ready to speak. "So what have you got for me?"

Strong noted down all he was told. One name didn't surprise him but the background to a second name did. Both had left the Green Howards in 1979, one in April and the other in June and both had similar distinguishing marks – the regimental crest tattooed on their left forearms. One other item of note related to the second man. The caller also outlined what linked these two men and some brief background to an incident in their careers the year before. That information, he was told, was in strictest confidence.

When the man finished, Strong thanked him and pressed the red button on his phone. He sat there stunned. A deep breath as he re-read the notes he'd just taken.

About to search out Luke Ormerod, his desk phone rang.

"Yes," he said.

"A woman for you, Colin," the desk sergeant announced.

"DI Strong," he announced once the call had been put through.

"Mr Strong, it's Mrs Monk here, Annabel."

"Yes Annabel, what can I do for you?"

"I'm worried ..."

"What about?"

"It's Gary. He's gone out and I'm afraid he'll do something stupid."

"What makes you say that?"

"It's all this business with that shirt and what's been in the papers. It's obvious the man you're after killed that poor girl."

Strong stayed silent.

"Gary thinks he knows who it is and he's gone off to find them."

Now alarmed, Strong responded, "Who? Who does he think it is?"

She sniffed and there was a pause as if she was wiping her nose. *"Some bloke who runs a scrap business in Huddersfield, that's all he told me."*

"And how long ago did he leave?"

"Just before I rang you. I tried to reason with him, told him to leave it to your people, but he wouldn't listen. He was very wound up."

"Okay, thanks Annabel. I'll get people over there now."

"There is one other thing ..."

"Yes."

"I've remembered something else about my ... attacker."

"Anything you can tell us would be helpful."

A loud intake of breath down the phone line. *"He had a piece of his ear missing. His left one, near the lobe."*

Strong's heart rate increased and he could feel the tension build in his body. "A missing ear lobe?"

"Well, near there."

"Thanks Annabel. I'll be in touch."

"But please ..." she added, before Strong could end the call, *"... look after Gary."*

"I'll do my very best."

Strong grabbed his coat as he left the office and hurried down to the CID Room. Sweeping those officers present, he called out. "Luke, John, Kelly ... with me please."

DS Stainmore, DC's Ormerod and Darby exchanged glances then grabbed their coats and followed their boss out of the room and down the stairs.

* * *

There it was; the premises of the bastard. *George Brannigan Scrap Metal Merchant Ltd.* It was time. Gary Monk pulled the car in through the gates and drew to a halt by the unmanned crane. Stepping from the car, he felt the comforting shape of his truncheon through his zipped-up leather jacket and strode over the muddy yard to the Portakabin office. He opened the door.

"Be with you in a minute," came a voice from the man dressed in oily overalls bending down to the bottom drawer of a filing cabinet. Before he could straighten up fully, a sharp pain shot through his lower legs and he collapsed to the floor.

Monk, truncheon in hand, stood over the grimacing huddle that was George Brannigan. "That's just the start for what you did to my mum," he said.

"I've no idea what you're ..." Brannigan wheezed, before another blow from the weapon caught him sideways across the face.

"Don't you give me that load of old bollocks!" Monk exclaimed.

Brannigan looked stunned for a second then put his hand to the side of his face. A trickle of blood ran down towards his chin. Recovering slightly, he tried to speak again. "Who are you? What is all this about?"

This time, Monk let him complete his sentences. "You drove taxis out of Leeds in 1979," he said.

A confused expression pushed the pained one from Brannigan's face. "Well, yeah ... and so did a lot of other people."

Monk brought the truncheon down on the man's shoulder this time. "Ex-army too."

Brannigan yelped, the collar bone snapped. "Wait. Wait," he pleaded. "I think you have the wrong man." He strained to sit himself upright, leaning against the filing cabinet he'd just been looking in.

"You're George Brannigan, right?" Monk slapped the truncheon into the palm of his hand as he spoke.

"Yeah, but I'm not who you want."

Anger swept over Monk as he swung the baton from left to right this time, catching the man on the floor on the right side of his face. "Don't treat me like an idiot. I know it was you."

The man struggled to keep his eyes open. Before they lost focus, they flicked to one side. If Monk had been trained properly, he would have realised the meaning of that movement.

Before Monk could do or say anything else, a sharp pain shot through the right side of his head as something heavy struck him, and he lost consciousness.

*   *   *

Strong explained the predicament to his officers as he drove to the scrapyard in Huddersfield. Various calls to the control room ensured they would be met by a number of marked cars and uniformed officers.

"But I don't understand, guv," Stainmore said, sitting in the front passenger seat. "How did Gary Monk know about Brannigan?"

"He was obviously suspicious when we went to speak to his mum. She told me he had a big argument with her a week or so back and she ended up telling him about his biological father." Strong paused to change gear and negotiate a roundabout. "And I think he's been sneaking into the Incident Room and looking at the boards with the information on," he resumed. "Bill Sidebotham tells me he'd seen him coming down the stairs one night. Gave him a story about leaving a note under my door."

"That makes sense of what I felt then," she continued.

"How do you mean?"

"Remember I mentioned it when we were in on Saturday? When I got back to my desk the other week, I thought the paperwork had been disturbed, as though someone had been rifling through it. It wasn't as I'd left it."

"I remember you saying that. Do you think it was him?"

"Could well have been."

"And that would have given him the link to Claire Hobson, or CH as you'd noted."

"He'd have drawn that conclusion from these newspaper articles too."

"Have you two been working on reviewing that case?" Ormerod asked from the rear.

"I asked Flynn to involve the rest of the team but he only wanted me and Kelly to know."

"Christ," Ormerod said. "And this young PC's real dad is Claire Hobson's killer?"

"Could be." Stainmore said.

"So what did you find out about her attacker?" Darby joined in the discussion.

Stainmore related the facts as they saw them; taxi-driver, short, stocky mid-fifties, ex-Green Howards and tattoo of the regimental crest on the left forearm.

"Brannigan has a tattoo like that," Ormerod said.

"But I don't remember part of his left ear missing just above the lobe," Strong said.

"No, he doesn't," Ormerod agreed.

"Where did that come from?" Stainmore puzzled.

Strong ignored the question. "Nearly there," he announced. "Let's be careful."

*   *   *

The explosion of shattering glass and crunching metal roused Gary. Slowly his senses returned - hearing first, the growl of a diesel engine under load; then the perception of movement. He felt as though he was being hoisted into the air and had a swaying sensation. Finally his blurred vision began to clear and he saw Brannigan slumped in the passenger seat beside him. Both men were strapped in by the seatbelts. He looked out of the space where the window had been. Below, a man, not dissimilar in appearance to Brannigan, was in the cab at the controls of the grab crane, a determined expression on his face.

He watched as the car he'd just picked up rose into the air. He could see the policeman inside looking round, trying to make sense of his situation. The collapsed figure of his ex-army colleague sitting alongside him was clearly visible. The movements became more frantic as the young lad realised his predicament. A few more actions of the controls and the car swung over the yawning jaws of the crusher. He paused the crane and dropped the engine back to idle speed.

"Let me out! Get me down from here!" the young policeman yelled.

He hadn't been aware of anything for the past few minutes but now sirens could be heard above the engine noise. Flashing blue lights attracted his attention and he looked round to see the yard filling up with vehicles, mostly marked with 'Police'.

A Mondeo drew to a halt in front. Three men and a woman got out.

*   *   *

Strong drove his Mondeo into the yard and was stunned to see Gary Monk's car dangling about twenty feet in mid-air, the grab arms through the doors and roof. He could see the agitated figure of the young constable in the driving seat. Another stockier figure was motionless in the passenger seat alongside. Brannigan.

He slowly stepped from the car and switched his focus to the crane cab. Ormerod, Stainmore and Darby got out too. Uniformed officers stood behind.

Monk was yelling from the car.

"Stay still, Gary!" Strong called as he took a few steps towards the crane.

"That's far enough," the man in the cab shouted.

Suddenly, Strong saw what he had in his hand. He turned his head slightly to Ormerod who was on his shoulder. "That's a gun, Luke," he said quietly. "Get onto control and tell them we need Armed Response here as soon as."

"On it," Ormerod said, taking his mobile phone from a pocket.

"And tell Kelly to stay back. We don't need a repeat …" He left the sentence unfinished.

Ormerod turned away to make the call and gestured for Stainmore and Darby to step back.

Strong held his arms out and edged forward again.

"I said …" the man yelled.

"Okay, okay," Strong said. "I only want to talk to you, Mr Davidson. It is Mr Davidson isn't it? Patrick Davidson?"

"Seem to have all the answers, don't you?"

Behind him, he could hear Ormerod requesting firearms officers.

"It's over Patrick. Why don't you bring them down?" Strong glanced at the swaying car.

"It was all his fault, stupid bastard."

"Who?"

"George." Davidson looked from the car back to Strong. "I know I owed him big time after what happened."

"You're talking about Armagh, seventy-eight."

"You have done your homework."

"He saved your life, I heard."

"That's right."

"But what he's never understood is how you came to get yourself in that predicament in the first place," Strong said.

"What do you know?" Davidson sneered. "I'll bet you've never been to Northern Ireland."

Strong shrugged. "True," he said. "But I did hear about it." The figure of John Darby creeping around the rear of the portakabin caught Strong's eye for a split second. Fortunately, Davidson's attention was focussed on the crusher in front of the crane. He didn't notice the slight eye movement.

"You have been busy." Davidson turned to look at Strong again. "Did they tell you everything? I'm assuming it was some faceless bastard from the MOD you've been talking to."

Strong's periphery vision clocked Darby slinking from the rear of the offices to the cover of the back of the shed that stored recovered electrical equipment. "But was it true?" he asked.

"Depends what you mean."

"The double agent bit." Davidson gave a short laugh as Strong continued, "They were going to kill you, weren't they? Only George here stumbles across it. Did he ever know?"

"Official secrets." Davidson chuckled. "Can't find out now." He increased the revs on the crane's engine and the car swayed again.

"Whoah! Wait!" Strong called. "You don't want to do this."

"Don't I? Why not?" Davidson shouted. "What have I got left?"

"Can I tell you something?"

"Is this a ruse?"

"Please, you need to hear this, but I don't want to have to shout it."

Davidson aimed the gun at Strong. "Two steps only."

Strong slowly took one step, then a second as he spotted Darby sneak towards a van that was only ten yards from the other side of the crane's cab.

"The young lad," Strong said. "There's something you need to know."

"What? What do I need to know?"

"He's your son, Patrick."

A puzzled expression softened Davidson's face. "What sort of joke is this? This is a wind up."

"No joke."

"How can he be? I've never seen him before in my life."

"That's true, you haven't. But he is yours. DNA can prove it."

Davidson shook his head. "No, he couldn't be."

"One night in 1979. You drove a group of women from Leeds to various addresses in the Wakefield area. Only you stopped near Low Laithes with the last woman." Strong could see the expression change on Davidson's face.

"Him?" Gary Monk exclaimed from the car. "But I thought he was the man." Monk indicated the still figure of George Brannigan.

Strong looked up at the vehicle. "But your mother was lucky that night, Gary," he said. "On two counts, I'd say. She was lucky to escape with her life, having encountered this man." He pointed at the crane cab. "But, if you ask her, really talk to her, she'd tell you she escaped with your life too. And she is so glad you've been part of her life. And if you could ask him, I'd bet your dad would agree – I mean your real Dad. Richard."

"I've heard enough of this sentimental old bollocks," Davidson shouted from the crane. The engine revved and the car began to swing towards the crusher.

Darby could wait no longer and jumped up onto the steps of the cab on the other side and made a grab for the gun in Davidson's hand. The man was surprised at the attack but quickly recovered and the pair tussled.

Strong dashed forward and grabbed the man from his side.

Monk screamed from the car. "No! No! Don't let him do this!"

Suddenly, the gun went off and the struggle in the cab stilled.

There seemed to be a collective intake of breath from the assembled police officers and a second of inaction before Ormerod and Stainmore rushed towards the crane.

Davidson slumped forward and the car shot down towards the crusher. Strong pulled the man from the cab towards him as Darby pushed from his side. Just as the car disappeared into the jaws of the crusher, Darby pulled a lever back and the load slowly lifted clear. More movements on the controls and the car swung round and was slowly brought back to the ground. Finally, the grab arms were released.

Strong held Davidson on the ground but there was no fight in him. "Ambulances!" he shouted back to Stainmore and Ormerod.

They were already on their phones.

Davidson was bleeding heavily and Strong pressed tight on the stomach wound. Stainmore joined in the effort and a look passed between them.

Darby and Ormerod rushed to the car and started pulling at the tangled metal to open the doors and free the two men. Uniformed officers joined in. One knelt down by Strong. "I used to be a paramedic," he said, feeling for Davidson's carotid artery.

Strong caught the look on his face.

"Keep pressing on the wound," the officer advised.

A couple of minutes later, three ambulance crews were in attendance and Strong and Stainmore could stand back.

By the car, they'd managed to release Gary Monk who was being attended to by one of the paramedics. Brannigan's condition looked worse. He was being worked on by two of the green-clad ambulance crew.

69
Wednesday 6th March 2002

SUSPECT ARRESTED FOR CLAIRE HOBSON MURDER

In dramatic scenes yesterday, a man of 55 was shot in Huddersfield and taken to hospital under armed guard, arrested on suspicion of the rape and murder of 14-year-old Claire Hobson twenty years ago to the day. He is also believed to be facing charges of the attempted murder of a police officer. Another man of 52 was arrested in connection with the death of Marcus Weaver from Horsforth, whose body was found in a park in Wakefield on 13th February. More details are expected to emerge later today.

As readers will know, this newspaper has been reporting on Claire's case all this week, focusing on the traumatic effects on her family and friends as well as appealing for new information. It is not known at this stage, whether this paper's actions contributed in some way to yesterday's arrest.

Strong folded up the copy of the Yorkshire Post he'd bought on the way in to work that morning. A good scoop for Bob, he thought; and Susan, because she had become involved too.

His mobile rang and he took it out of his shirt pocket and saw Souter's name.

343

"Hey," Strong answered. "How's that little Godson of mine?"

"Aw, just lovely. I only wanted to make sure you were okay after what happened yesterday," his friend said.

"I must admit it did remind me of something similar. You know, when that gun went off, there was a split second when I was waiting for the pain to hit. After that I just grabbed him out of the way."

"And DS Stainmore was there too, I gather?"

"I made sure she kept back, yes."

"You sure it was him? Claire Hobson's killer, I mean?"

"We're just awaiting DNA results, but I think it's fairly certain. But listen, don't print that until we say so."

"Of course not. What about Claire's family?"

"Officers are visiting them this morning."

"And the other one, Brannigan – he was responsible for what happened to Marcus Weaver?"

"You know that though, don't you?"

"That little lad, Danny. He told Susan Mark Thompson involved him in the money exchange on the Thursday night. Took us a while but two and two ..."

"She never mentioned that to me." The line was silent for a second before Strong resumed, "Thank those two for me, will you?" he said. "If Susan and Sammy hadn't pursued that lead with the two lads, we wouldn't have had the tunic button. It made all the difference."

"No problem, Col."

"Hey, why don't you all come over to ours on Sunday? I mean you, Alison, little David and Susan and Sammy. Laura would love to see you all again. Sunday roast?"

"It's a deal. We'll bring some bubbly to celebrate Laura's new job. See you Col."

DCS Flynn had gathered Strong, Stainmore, Ormerod and Darby in his office. "Well, I have to say well done to you all. The ACC is really proud of you, as am I."

Strong was seated at the desk opposite his boss. "Just a pity we lost Davidson, sir. Robbed of our day in court."

"On the other hand, it could have been you or John or any one of you on that slab."

The mood was solemn as they all considered what might have been.

"Brannigan was kept in Pinderfields overnight," Strong reported. "Apparently, his condition is comfortable. We've got uniform covering him."

"What about young PC Monk?"

"Minor cuts and bruises, nothing broken but they also kept him in overnight for observation, suspecting concussion. He's due to be discharged later today."

"Have we got evidence now that Davidson murdered Claire Hobson?

"We've taken samples and they're being rushed through. Hope to hear shortly."

"Let me know as soon as you hear," Flynn requested.

"Of course. But," Strong added, "I'd just like to put on record that we have John Darby to thank for their rescue. If he hadn't acted when he did, that car would have gone into the crusher."

"I hear you played a part too, Colin."

"I rushed it from the other side. When that gun went off … you know there was a split second when … well, I just hoped to God it wasn't John. Bad enough last year …"

Flynn nodded and looked at Stainmore. "I know," he said.

"But it wasn't over then," Strong continued. "John got into the cab and lifted the car clear."

"Where did you learn those skills?" Flynn asked Darby.

"I used to work with my uncle on his building sites before I joined up."

Strong's mobile rang. He checked the screen. "The lab, sir," he said.

Flynn nodded.

Strong took the call, listened asked if the caller was sure, thanked him, then ended the call. "Davidson is a match for the samples recovered from Claire Hobson's body," he announced.

"That's good," Flynn responded. "Now I'm sure you all have plenty of paperwork to deal with to wrap all this up, so I'll let you get on," he said in dismissal.

Strong was last to exit.

"Oh, just a minute, Colin," he said. Standing up and walking round his desk. "Just close the door for a second, would you."

Strong did as asked and turned to face the DCS.

"I just thought I'd tell you, Mellor is extremely pleased."

"I'll bet he is."

"No, with you, Colin ... and the team."

"That's good, I'll tell them."

"You know Hemingford has gone permanently now and we need an experienced DCI."

Strong gave a slight nod.

"Mellor wants you in post," Flynn said.

Strong knew something like this was coming but was still smarting from last year's events. "And then, after a year or so in an Acting role, you bring someone else in like last time," he retorted.

"This wouldn't be an Acting position. This would be permanent." Flynn leaned in closer. "So, come on, Colin, what do you say?"

THE END

346

Enjoy TAINTED?

Then please review on Amazon, Goodreads etc.

Have you read more in the series?

See the next few pages ...

Book 1   TROPHIES

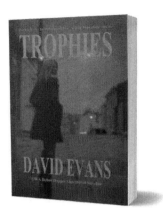

By the turn of the millennium, memories had dulled. But the discovery of a trophy case at the scene of a murder leads to the realisation that a series of attacks on women over the previous twenty years had gone unconnected. DI Colin Strong is convinced there is also a link with one other notorious unsolved crime. His best friend from schooldays, journalist Bob Souter, has returned to Yorkshire and begins to probe. Working separately and together in an awkward alliance, they seek the answers.

Available through Amazon:

Getbook.at/Trophies

Book 2   TORMENT

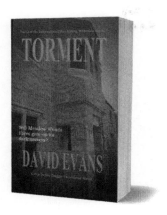

A message left in error on a young woman's answerphone is the catalyst for uncovering some dark deeds. Three young women are missing; luxury cars are being stolen; and just what did happen to two young schoolgirls, missing since the 1980's?

DI Colin Strong and journalist Bob Souter are drawn into murky and dangerous worlds

Available through Amazon:

Getbook.at/Torment

Book 3   TALISMAN

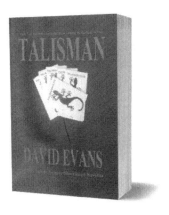

A man's body found naked and shackled to a frame in a house fire; a body lying undiscovered in a bath for over a year; massive European funding for a controversial construction project. Is there a link between the bodies and the business deal? And what exactly is the Talisman Club?

In the third instalment of the Wakefield series, DI Colin Strong and best friend, journalist Bob Souter must work together to bring the guilty to justice before time runs out.

Available through Amazon:

Getbook.at/Talisman